Saving Rebecca

Alex Amit

To Galia
Who told me her childhood story, and allowed me to weave it throughout this book

Contents

Chapter One

Paris

Paris Police Headquarters at Place Louis Lépine, August 1941. The city had been occupied by the Germans for about a year.

"And you are Sarah Bloch?" The police inspector reads from the paper while sitting on the other side of the wooden office desk.

"Yes, sir."

"And how can I help you, Mrs.?" He raises his eyes from the paper, puts down the fountain pen in his hand, looks at me, intertwines his fingers, and leans back comfortably.

"Please, sir, I need a pass," I say, sitting upright on the hard wooden chair in front of him.

"To the Free Zone?" He examines me, his eyes lingering on my lips even though they're unpainted. I don't want to draw any attention to myself. His black eyes look like tiny beads that stand out against his light skin.

"Yes, sir." I look at his ironed blue uniform. Although his shoulders bare no officer rank insignia, shiny gold-colored buttons adorn them as precious coins that emphasize his high status. His black mustache is also neatly trimmed, as if it were part of his uniform.

"Besides this paper you gave me, can I please see your certificates?" His beady eyes continue to scan me while he hides under a blue peaked cap that proudly presents the Vichy police insignia. The same government that acts on behalf of the Nazis who occupied the city.

"There you go." I place the two temporary residence permits on the mahogany table, keeping them closed. Maybe he won't look at what is written in them.

"Mrs., why do you need a permit to cross to the Free France Zone?" He holds the upper cardboard certificate with his manicured fingers, opens and checks it. For a moment, he looks up and examines me, comparing my face to the photo attached to the certificate with two pins before he lowers his eyes again, and his finger gently runs over the black and white photo as if trying to see if I didn't try to fake it and exchange a photo with another woman who had this certificate.

"Please, sir," I look at the copper plate placed on the dark table bearing his name, "Please, Inspector Plessis," I slowly read his name and put my hand on the smooth table as if begging. My black and white photo in the yellowish certificate looks at me with a serious look. I haven't smiled for months now, and it seems that even if I try, I won't succeed.

"And you are Sarah," he reads my name from the certificate and smiles at me politely.

"Yes, Sarah Bloch," I answer him again and look at my black and white picture. How much have I changed since I took that photo in Berlin? My dark brown, almost black, hair is still pulled back in the same low chignon style, but my deep, brown eyes now carry a worried look that wasn't there before. The confident gaze I had as I sat in the studio chair, facing the photographer, has vanished, replaced by a haunting uncertainty. My fair skin and high cheekbones remain unchanged, but my pale face has grown slightly skinnier over the past year. The gentle curves of my small waist have also disappeared with the rationing of food, and my once medium-sized breasts have shrunk. I used to love my body more, appreciated its graceful lines.

"And where is Rebecca?" He opens the second certificate and carefully reads it before looking back at me. His black eyes scan my neck and my simple green dress. Its buttons are closed all the way to my neck, but his gaze lingers on them as if trying to get them open.

"This is my daughter," I hold my child's hand, who is standing next to me. I bring her closer to me, wanting her to be a barrier between me and his eyes scanning my breast through my dress's fabric. But I don't think it's necessary. The prominent yellow badge embroidered on my dress ensures the distance between us. Also, the ugly red stamp "Jew" stamped on our temporary residence certificate, which he holds in his hand, and my foreign accent. They all create a wall of distance and hatred every time I open my mouth and speak or show someone the certificate.

Inspector Plessis looks down at Rebecca, who stands next to me, and gives her a little smile. Her head reaches the height of the large wooden table. She looks back at him and does not smile back but moves in an almost invisible motion as she clings to me while I keep sitting on the simple wooden chair. She doesn't trust him either. I can feel her body heat through the fabric of her burgundy dress. I made sure to dress her this morning in her festive dress, although it also has a prominent yellow badge.

"And there's no Mr. Bloch?" Inspector Plessis asks me. I look around the large reception hall at the police station. All around, there are soft voices of conversations and typewriters ticking like crickets on a hot summer night.

"He's waiting for us, Erwin Bloch. He left Paris a year ago. We're married," I bend down to my bag while feeling Rebecca's small hand holding me tightly. "Here, I have those," I take a piece of paper out of the bag and place it on the table between us.

"What are these?" The inspector holds it, scans it, and starts reading.

"It's a letter he sent us from Madrid, Spain, a month ago. He's waiting for us there."

"Don't you have an official document?" He places the paper on the table and pushes it back at me.

"No sir, please, you must help us."

"And I understand that you are not French citizens, that you are guests here in Paris with temporary residence permits," he gives me a small, polite smile.

"Yes, sir, we do not have French citizenship."

4

"And what about Mr. Bloch, who chooses to stay in neutral Spain?"

"My husband is a businessman, sir. He left for Spain for his business before they arrived. We will join him as soon as we get permission to leave Paris for the Free France Zone." I'm holding Rebecca's hand. She clings to me with the fear of little girls.

"You mean he left Paris before our German partners got here?" He's no longer smiling.

"Yes, sir," I look at him and smile as much as I can. I must be nice to him. He's the only one who can help us.

"And is he a French citizen? Has he evaded his duties as a citizen?"

"No, sir, he does not have French citizenship," I take mine and Rebecca's cardboard passports out of the bag and place them on the table next to our residence permits, "We all came from Berlin. Mr. Bloch also has German citizenship. He is thirty years old, two years older than me. Of course, he has his passport with him." I smile at him.

"And when did you arrive in Paris?" He holds my passport and opens it. It has a large round seal of an eagle holding a swastika.

"We arrived in March 1940, and Mr. Bloch left a month later," I whisper and hold back from crying, remembering our last moment together at the Gare du Nord train station. He wore a thick woolen coat while hugging me and assuring me that he would arrive in Madrid, get organized, and send us tickets to join him. Then he bent down to Rebecca and pinched her cheek lightly before turning and entering the train car. But a month later, the Germans invaded France,

ALEX AMIT

and in one moment, everything changed. Train traffic was stopped, and the wails of sirens against airplanes filled the city's air. A few days later, the Germans marched here, filling the Champs-Élysées with the sound of their hobnailed boots. Why didn't I insist on joining him then at the train station?

"Mrs. Bloch?" I hear a voice and look up at Inspector Plessis, who is still holding my passport.

"Sorry, sir," I wipe a tear from my eye.

"It's okay, Mrs. Your situation is clear," he answers and stands up, still holding our passports and residence permits. "I'll see what I can do," he walks away from the table and disappears into the corridor at the back of the hall.

"Where is he going?" Rebecca asks me in German.

"He'll help us, honey, and please speak French," I stroke her black hair and adjust the beret on her head. "He'll take our papers and replace them with better ones," I smile at her.

"And after that, we'll leave and go to Dad by train?" She continues to speak in German.

"Yes, sweetie, we will travel by train like last year and meet Dad. Do you remember how we traveled together last year and arrived in Paris?" I adjust her dress and fight back tears again, remembering our last trip together as a family back then, when we left Berlin. "But only if you are quiet," I say to her. "You must be quiet when the policeman returns, do you promise?" I don't want Inspector Plessis to hear her speaking German.

"Yes, Mommy," she smiles at me, "did you see that our flag is hanging on the wall next to a striped flag in blue, white, red with something in the middle, and a picture of that man in the middle?" She asks.

"Yes, honey," I look up at the wall at the end of the hall. There are two flags side by side above the large windows. The French flag of the Vichy regime with the ax in the center, and on the side, the red Nazi flag with a white circle in the center and a black swastika. There's a large picture of the Führer between the flags overlooking the hall.

"There are many people here in blue uniforms and funny hats," she adds.

"Yes, sweetie, everyone will help us, and now be quiet," I look around. Other police officers are sitting at tables just like the one we're sitting next to, as they inspect documents or write down reports. On the side of the hall, several secretaries are typing away on their typewriters. "Remember what you promised me? That you would be quiet," I hold Rebecca's hand in mine when I notice Inspector Plessis approaching our table while carrying a large binder. I straighten up in my chair and smile at him.

"How old are you?" Inspector Plessis places his hand on Rebecca's nape; his fingers touch her black hair cascading over her shoulder, and I shudder.

"Five years old, sir," she looks up and answers him in French, but her German accent is still prominent.

"You're a cute girl," he pinches her cheek and smiles. Rebecca keeps silent but I feel her hand searching for mine.

"Thank you, sir," I smile at him.

"Well, Mrs. Bloch," he sits back in his chair. "I understand you came here from Berlin a year ago," he places our passports on the table and opens the thick cardboard notebook.

"Yes, a year and four months ago, sir."

"A year and four months ago," he repeats and starts to write something down in the large binder. I can tell it's already full of names. Will he give us the papers allowing us to go south from Paris to the Vichy area, the Free Zone, and from there to neutral Spain? I tighten my grip around Rebecca's hand.

"Mommy," she whispers to me, "you're hurting me."

"Sorry, sweetie," I release my grip and stroke her hair again. In a few days, this year will be behind us.

"Mrs. Bloch, where are you staying here in Paris?" I hear Inspector Plessis and look up.

"We stayed at a hotel in the third arrondissement."

"What is the name of the hotel?" He continues writing in the large binder without looking up.

"We've been in it since we arrived in Paris a year ago," I answer, feeling my stomach and trying to buy time.

"And what is the name of the hotel?" He stops writing and looks at me, his black mustache shaking as he speaks.

"The New Republic Hotel," I reply after a moment, wondering if I'm doing the right thing, seeing how he writes it down.

"Mrs. Bloch," he finally looks up and puts the pen down, "and Rebecca," he turns his look to my daughter and smiles.

"Yes, sir," she answers back and smiles at him.

"Well," he looks at me again, "I checked your issue. Since you are both German citizens of the Third Reich, unfortunately, it is not within my authority to help you."

"But sir," I lean in and whisper to him, "we escaped from there, you know why," I refrain from pointing with my hand to the red Jewish stamp stamped on our passports and the temporary residence certificate, "they don't want us there."

"Madam, you are guests here, and it is not within our authority to help you. For any assistance with your citizenship or a request for permission to move, you must contact the German Ministry of the Interior. According to the law, you are German citizens." He continues to speak without smiling. I notice his brown leather belt holding a shiny oiled pouch and inside a gun. "You must report any change of address to me immediately." As he speaks, his black mustache constantly keeps moving, and I look up at the large picture of the Führer at the end of the hall. He seems to be looking down at me.

"Mrs. Bloch," I hear Inspector Plessis say. I turn my gaze to him; he stands up and extends his hand in greeting.

"Please, sir," I stand up and shake his hand tightly. "We must leave Paris and meet my husband."

"The representative of the German Ministry of the Interior in Paris will be happy to help you," he releases his grip. "Now, if you'll excuse me, I have other people waiting for my help." He politely smiles at me and Rebecca.

"Good day to you, sir, thank you very much," I collect the documents from the table, take Rebecca's hand and hurry to leave. On the way out we walk among the other tables and police officers in the hall. I avert my gaze as we pass under the picture of the Führer, who examines us from his place on the wall.

"Now, can we go to Dad's?" Rebecca asks as we exit the police station and head to the street, passing across the sentries at the entrance.

"No honey, we can't go to Dad's yet." I pull a handkerchief out of my purse as we start walking towards the Notre Dame bridge.

"Why can't we go to Dad?"

"Because he's not as good a man as I thought."

"That man with the mustache doesn't like us?"

"No, honey, it's not because he doesn't like us."

"Is it because of the yellow badge you sewed on to my new dress? Is that why he doesn't like us? Like the saleswoman at the grocery store who always tells us to wait at the end of the line until there's no food left?"

"No, my beautiful girl," I stop and lean in, look into her dark brown eyes, and caress her black hair. I start searching for an answer and fight the tears that threaten to burst. "This Star of David protects us," I caress with my fingers the yellow badge embroidered on her dress. "It is like a star that lights and guides our way," I say to her after a moment. "Do you remember when we walked in the dark and all the streetlights were off?" Since the war, there have been blackouts at night, and the streets are dark.

"Yes, and I almost fell, and you held my hand," Rebecca nods.

"And do you remember that the moon and the stars helped us see the way in the dark street?" I say, as I keep stroking her hair.

"Yes," Rebecca nods again.

"So the yellow badge on your dress is your private star that helps you find your way in the dark. Like the stars and the moon." I smile at her.

"Okay, Mommy," she smiles back at me.

"Remember that the yellow badge on your dress always protects you." I stand up, take her hand, and we continue walking toward the bridge. I wish my husband Erwin were here to protect me right now.

Before the Pont Notre-Dame, I slow down and tighten my grip on Rebecca's hand. There's a German guard post and anti-aircraft cannon on the other end of the wide bridge, protected by a wall of sandbags. The cannon's barrels are pointed at the sky as if they were waiting to hunt birds of prey should they come and attack. A German soldier stands outside the post and indifferently watches the people crossing the bridge while smoking a cigarette. Will he say something or stop me? Like that German soldier who stopped me a few months ago on the street and forced me to stand for hours wet in the rain while standing under the shelter with his friends and laughing?

I have no choice; I have to cross the barrier. I wait for a moment until two women pass me by, and then I take a deep breath, and start following them. I hold Rebecca's hand tightly, and she is forced to run as we cross the bridge. I want to stay close to them. My shoes are bothering me; they are already torn, but I don't slow down. There is no way to buy new shoes these days. The Germans take all the leather for their military shoes.

Across the bridge there's a wire fence with a narrow passage for vehicles and people. To pass, I have to get close to the German soldier who is smoking his cigarette. I don't look at him but look ahead at the back of one of the women walking in front of me. I focus on her dark blond hair and brown hat. I can hear my own footsteps on the cobblestones and smell the tobacco coming from the German soldier's cigarette. It feels like the yellow badge is burning a hole through the dress. *Please don't stop us, please don't stop us.* A step and another step, and we cross the barrier and move away from the bridge. I slowly start breathing again. Despite my hand starting to sweat around Rebecca's, I refuse to let it go.

"Mommy, there are flags everywhere," she says, pointing at the large swastika flags in the streets and at the city hall.

"Yes, it's just like back at home, in Berlin," I reply, and feel a lump in my throat. The Nazi flag is the only one she knows. The Nazis were already in power when she was born. I hate and fear this flag so much.

"Mommy, this says 'Paris'," Rebecca reads the white, wooden road sign on the street corner. Its arrows are written in German, for the benefit of all the German soldiers coming to the city. 'Paris City Headquarters,' 'Officer's Club,' and 'Military Hospital' all point in different directions. Many German soldiers take their vacations here, carry cameras, and sit in the cafés next to the Champs-Elysées. I'm afraid to go to this area. I wish she would forget how to speak German and speak only French, so we stop standing out.

Only when we cross the main Rivoli street, which is full of German soldiers searching for souvenirs, do I walk down one of the smaller streets and bring two fingers to my lips, kiss them lightly, and brush over the yellow badge on my dress. I call it 'The Star of Life and Death.' It is in charge of my life, watching over me. If they catch me on the street without it and find out that I'm Jewish, I'll be sentenced to death. It said so on the posters that were hung on the bulletin boards a few weeks after the Germans occupied Paris last year. I saw what they did to the girl they caught on the street a few months ago. They pinned her to the wall. I quickly turned and retraced my steps, as I tried not to scream when I heard the shot. "This star keeps me alive," I whisper to myself, even though most of the time, it feels like this star will lead to my death.

"Mommy, what are you whispering?"

"I remembered I forgot to buy something," I answer her.

"Mommy, I'm hungry. We haven't had breakfast yet."

"Soon, we'll get to the hotel, and I'll give you something to eat," I say, as we pass a grocery store that has a long line of women waiting outside. 'We have butter today,' is handwritten in white chalk on the black wooden board outside the shop. I don't have any butter. I walk past the line of women and look at the last three, all of whom have yellow badges on their dresses. It's the law: Jews must always stand at the end of the line to buy groceries. Usually, there's nothing left when our turn comes, and only sometimes do the sellers take pity on us and bring out some goods they put aside.

"Mommy, look, it's a bear," Rebecca takes her hand out of mine and stops next to a bookstore in the narrow alley. She presses her nose to the glass. "Mommy, what's the bear's name?" She shades her eyes from the sun, and peers into the store.

ALEX AMIT

I look to the sides to see if there are any policemen or German soldiers on the street. It's all clear. All I see is an elderly peddler pushing a wooden cart loaded with fabrics. I approach the shop window and look at the colorful books on display. They look back at me as if were a group of people engaging in an argument. "Sylvie, the bear's name is Sylvie," I smile as I notice the red book with the brown bear.

"He looks like he's a man walking on the street," Rebecca says in German and laughs. I notice at the end of the street two French policemen walking in our direction. They stand out with their blue uniforms.

"Come in," I hold her hand and walk into the store. It's best if we stay away from them.

"Good afternoon," the saleswoman in the shop greets us as she approaches. "How may I help you?" she asks. I notice her gaze fixed on the yellow badge on my dress.

"Mommy, look," Rebecca approaches the children's bookshelf. "There are more bears here," she points to other books.

"How much is this book?" I point to a book titled 'Sylvie in Paris.' I need to make sure she learns French. She can't stand out so much.

"Seventeen francs," the saleswoman hands me the book, as she looks up at the street outside. I turn my head and see the two French policemen standing next to the store outside. What will the saleswoman do? Will she kick me out with some excuse? I look at Rebecca who's standing next to a bookshelf. She caresses the cartoon bear on the cover. She hasn't asked for anything in a year; she knows I have no money. I reach into my handbag and touch our temporary residence permits,

14

ensuring they're there. I might have to present them to the police officers.

"Thank you," I put the book back. I don't have enough money to pay for it.

"Madam," the seller turns to me, "would you like to come with me and bring your daughter? I have a used copy. One of the customers returned it," she starts walking across the bookshelves. I take Rebecca's hand and follow the woman to the back of the store. "Come with me, look here," she says and leans in. I lean in beside her as she takes out a copy of 'Sylvie the Bear' and hands it to Rebecca. "Take it," she smiles at her.

Rebecca takes the book and puts it in her lap.

"Say thank you," I tell her.

"Thank you."

"Wait here and take time to think if you want that book. It's used. It costs seven francs," she said, touches my hand and stands up. I follow her with my gaze as she walks to the front of the store and looks outside.

"Mommy, can we buy Sylvie?"

"Give me the book," I stroke her hair and open the first page. I read the dedication written in round handwriting:

'Dear Claire
I hope you enjoy this book. It was made just for you.
Love
Mom'

"May I?" She looks at me with her dark brown eyes, and I think of those seven francs that I'll need.

"You can stand up. So, are you interested in the book?" The saleswoman returns.

"Yes, we will buy it," I hand it to her. "Thank you," I quickly take the coins out of my wallet and hand them to her before I change my mind. Rebecca is going to learn French; she has to. "Thank you for everything," I say to her as I place the money in the palm of her hand and look out the shop window. The officers are gone.

"Five francs; that's enough. I've had this book for a long time," she gives me back two coins. "Go to the left. They turned right." She says goodbye as we stand at the store's door a few minutes after she wrapped the book in flowery paper and handed it to Rebecca. I want to hug her, but it's not proper.

"Thank you for everything," I smile at her awkwardly, grab Rebecca's hand, and we walk into the alley.

On the street, among the passers-by, I make sure to keep Rebecca close by until I see our apartment hotel. We've been living there alone since I said goodbye to my husband Erwin at the train station. From a distance, it looks like a safe haven in a forest full of hounds with metal collars engraved with swastikas around their necks.

"Eins, zwei, drei, vier, fünf," Rebecca counts aloud while she jumps up the five wide steps at the hotel entrance.

"And now in French," I say to her.

"Must I? It's a strange language."

"Yes, you must."

"Un, deux, trois, quatre, cinq," we count together aloud and enter the hotel hand in hand.

"Good afternoon," Angelina, the owner of the small apartment hotel greets us when we enter the reception room and close the door behind us.

"Good afternoon," I reply and smile at her as we approach the desk. She is about my age, twenty-eight or a little older. She turns and takes our key out of the dark mahogany mailbox behind her on the wall. I look at her slender figure and black hair styled in a chic updo. Despite the war and the rationing imposed on all supplies, from food and fuel to fabrics and shoe leather, Angelina always dresses in style and wears makeup. However, tights are no longer available. So she uses an eyeliner to draw seam-like line on the back of her legs to make it look like tights.

"Your key," she places the large metal key on the counter.

"No mail?" I ask her and look at the cabinet behind her.

"I'm sorry," she says. "What did you get?" She turns to Rebecca and smiles.

"A book."

"What is the book about?"

"About a bear," Rebecca answers, saying the word 'bear' in German as she presses to her chest the book wrapped in flowery paper.

"I need her to learn to speak French," I say to Angelina quietly, "she hasn't met other children in a year."

"She will be alright, you will get all the necessary approvals, and everything will be fine. Meanwhile, maybe Rebecca can go to school here," she whispers to me while we look at Rebecca caressing her book.

"I hope so. She stands out on the street anyway, and her speaking German doesn't help," I answer. Even though I speak French, my accent is still pretty prominent.

"You'll be fine," she touches my arm, "Rebecca," she calls her.

"Yes?" Rebecca looks up.

"Every guest in my hotel leaves something behind…" Angelina reaches out and takes something small wrapped in a piece of parchment paper out of the drawer in the counter. "Take it," she reaches out to Rebecca.

"What is it?" Rebecca asks her.

"It's a chocolate cube that one of our guests forgot at the hotel." She tells her and whispers to me, "May I?"

"Yes," I nod, knowing no guest would forget chocolate at her hotel.

"Mommy, can I?" Rebecca turns her gaze to me.

"Yes, sweetie."

With a gentle movement of her small fingers, Rebecca peels off the paper and reveals the brown cocoa cube. She puts it in her mouth and smiles when she feels the sweetness.

"It's not real chocolate. It's just a substitute for chocolate," Angelina whispers to me.

"Thank you, thank you for everything," I say to her. I have no idea where she managed to get chocolate. Such supplies are no longer available in stores, or even with ration coupons. Getting chocolate in the city is impossible except on the black market or from the German soldiers. "Rebecca, did you say thank you to Mrs. Angelina?" I bend over to Rebecca, who is slowly chewing the sweet chocolate.

"Thank you, Mrs. Angelina," she smiles at her.

"Thank you, Mrs. Angelina," I say too, and take Rebecca's hand as we head for the stairs. She doesn't have any children. I never asked why.

"Sarah," Angelina calls out to me before we leave.

"Yes?"

"Do you remember the monthly payment?"

"Yes, I remember. I'll come down later and pay you." I smile at her awkwardly. I was really hoping she would wait a few days with the payment. I don't know what I'll do next month if we don't get the necessary documents.

"Mommy, come on," Rebecca holds the banister and jumps up the stairs that shake.

"Rebecca, be quiet," I rush after her. "If you quietly go up the stairs without disturbing the guests, I'll read to you from the new book."

"Remember what you promised me: not to talk until we enter the room," I whisper to Rebecca as we approach our room at the end of the corridor on the fourth and last floor. Despite the sun outside, the corridor is almost dark and lit only by a single electric light bulb attached to a wall covered in dark green wallpaper with delicate flowers. I notice that the wallpaper is torn in several areas. The broad room's brown carpet is also ripped in multiple places that reveal the parquet floor underneath.

"Mommy, come on," Rebecca whispers to me as she impatiently waits next to our door.

I stroke her wavy hair and open the door, locking it behind me. In the room, I approach the single window facing the inner courtyard and pull back the yellowish curtain, letting in the afternoon light.

The room is small and cramped, but it feels safe, as if protecting us from the outside world. Its walls are covered with floral green wallpaper. My bed is in one corner of the room, and Rebecca's is on the opposite wall. When we arrived here a year ago from Berlin, after escaping the Nazis, Erwin was with us for a few days, and for a moment, we were like a free family. But a few days after we arrived, he traveled to Madrid, and promised to send us tickets so we can join him. But then the Nazis invaded France and declared war on England. We are no longer together, and all the streets in Paris are full of swastika flags, just like Berlin.

I approach the dark wooden dresser, pour some water from the enamel jug into an enamel bowl, and wash my face, enjoying the cool water. Then I slice a thick piece of bread from the loaf I made two days ago and serve it to Rebecca. I watch in silence as she slowly eats it. I'll eat later.

A warm summer breeze blows in from the open window, slightly swaying the curtain. I take my dress off and have nothing but my camisole on. Although I'm almost naked, I feel less exposed without the Yellow Star of Life and Death stitched onto my dress.

Rebecca finishes eating the slice of bread and sits on her bed. She gently unties the thin rope around the book, removes the floral paper, and holds the book in her hand. "Mommy," she whispers even though we're in our room and we don't need to whisper anymore. I want to stand by the window, look out, and let the summer breeze caress my skin, but instead, I go over and sit beside her. I take the book and open it. Promises need to be kept.

"Sylvie in Paris," I begin to read.

"Mommy, what is it? Why did you skip it?" Rebecca stops me and points to the handwritten dedication.

"It's a dedication."

"What's dedication?"

"When someone gives another person a gift and writes nice words so that they remember who gave it to them."

"Did the lady at the shop write the dedication for me?" Rebecca looks at me smiling as her eyes sparkle.

"Yes," I reply, not wanting to disappoint her.

"What did she write?"

"Dear Claire, I hope you like this book. It was written especially for you."

"But my name isn't Claire," Rebecca looks at me awkwardly.

"Maybe she got confused and mistakenly thought your name was Claire."

"Okay," Rebecca says and turns the page to the drawing of the bear. "What does it say here?"

I start reading to her the story about a bear in the forest, whose mother was shot by hunters one day.

"Mommy, why did the hunters shoot his mom?"

"I don't know, honey," I take a deep breath and look out the open window. On the horizon, I can see a Nazi flag on one of the rooftop. It looks like a black dot in a drop of blood.

"Did the hunters have guns like the soldiers we saw on the street back then?" Rebecca looks at me and doesn't smile, her dark eyes wide open.

"No, these are other guns," I quickly answer. The hot summer wind blowing in through the window makes me sweat despite my thin camisole. What should I say to her? "The soldiers on the street have good guns. They don't shoot mothers," I add. Why did I buy her a book with hunters and guns?

"Maybe the hunters didn't mean to," Rebecca suggests, looking at the drawing in the book. Her finger covers the guns.

"I think I was confused," I stroke her hair. I have to change the story. "Sylvie the bear grew up in the middle of the Tiergarten in Berlin. Do you remember the big park we'd go to in the summer?" I try to distract her.

"With the big trees and statues, and the lake with the boats, where you'd buy me ice cream?"

"Yes, exactly. That's where Sylvie the bear grew up. He had fun in that cozy park." I remember the last time we went there when we still could.

"Then why did he go to Paris? Because of the hunters who shot his mother?"

"They didn't really shoot his mother. They just wanted to scare her."

"Why did they want to scare her?"

"So he'd run away to Paris, like we did by train. I got confused when I read it," I try to smile at her.

"Like the bookstore lady who got my name mixed up?"

"Yes," I reply. "Now you keep looking at the pictures, and I'll look out the window for a bit, okay?"

Rebecca nods, and I go to the water bowl again, dip my hands, and wet my face. Then I stand in front of the windowsill and let the wind cool my face. How will I protect her from the world? What good did it do when we fled from Berlin to Paris if the Nazis chased us all the way here?

Two boys and a girl are playing in the inner court between the buildings. They're throwing stones at an empty glass bottle they put in the center of the yard. Their laughter spirals like an evergreen climber plant, entwining the building's walls until it reaches the window bars. I won't allow Rebecca to go outside and play with them. It's too dangerous. A police patrol might enter the court, and I don't know these children or their parents. How would they treat a girl with a yellow badge, who speaks German and wants to play with them and laugh?

I turn around and look at her. She sits on the carpet in the center of the room, which is our safe place but also our prison.

"Mommy, I fixed it," Rebecca smiles at me. She has a pencil in her hand and proudly waves the book. I can see that she erased the name 'Claire' with a bold line and wrote 'Rebeca' over it with a spelling mistake. "He's not a boy bear either; he's Sylvie, a girl bear, I gave her a ribbon," she shows me a doodle she drew on the bear's head.

"Now, this book is really yours," I say, caressing her head. It'll soon be evening time, and after Rebecca falls asleep, I'll go downstairs and have a talk with Angelina. I'll also pay her for this room that keeps us safe.

23

The cool night breeze blows through the open window, and I lean against the windowsill and look outside. The blackout shrouds the city with darkness. All the streetlights are off. People are also required to close the blinds and curtains to dim the light. The moon has not yet risen, and I cannot see the distant rooftops. I'm afraid of the darkness outside. I miss Berlin and the days when Erwin and I were young and would walk hand in hand in the Unter den Linden boulevard on summer nights. It was lit with hundreds of lanterns, which seemed like little stars forming a path, and showing us the way. But this was before the Nazis came to power, and we had to flee. And now we're trying to escape again. Only this time, I'm the one in charge.

Rebecca is sleeping in her little bed. I close the window and the dark curtain, and feel my way to the dresser to light a candle.

All evening, we sat together and read the book, and now she's embracing it in her sleep. Her black wavy hair is spread on the white pillow. I watch her for a moment, observe her calm breaths and caress her forehead, making sure not to wake her up. Angelina is waiting for me downstairs.

I turn to my bed, bend over, pull out the suitcase from under the bed and open it. My fingers search through the suitcase's hidden compartment until I find the velvet bag and breathe in relief. Each time I look for the velvet bag in the suitcase, I have a horrible fear that it will disappear and, with it, our last chance to get out of this city.

In the candlelight, I open the velvet bag and spread its contents on the bed. A year ago, when we arrived from Berlin, it was heavy and full of gold coins, bills, and our family jewels. Now, all that I have left are a few gold coins and some of the jewels. This is what Rebecca and I have been living off here, without work and without certificates that would prove we are entitled to receive the food rations that the city's residents receive in paper coupons.

Which of the remaining jewels should I choose? I touch the wedding ring on my finger. I will never give it up. It reminds me that someone is watching over me even if we're not together right now. I look at the gold bracelet Erwin bought me for Rebecca's birthday. Should I give it up? Or should I use another heirloom we took with us when we left? I've already exchanged most of them for money and food. My fingers tremble, and finally, I choose a pair of gold earrings with pearls. I gently kiss them before I tuck them into my pocket and return the bag to the suitcase. They were my mother's, but I mustn't think about that. She will rest for eternity in Berlin's cemetery. She would want me to use them if necessary. I linger a few moments to wipe my tears away before I kiss Rebecca on the forehead and leave the room. I close the door behind me and go down the stairs.

Although it's still early, the corridor is quiet; I can't hear people talking in their rooms. All the guests are locked up in their rooms. I go down the wooden stairs as quietly as I can, not wanting to make any noise, even though we're safe here in the hotel.

I see a faint light at the bottom of the stairs, and I walk towards it as if it were a streetlight calling me to come and bask in its light.

"Good evening," I say to Angelina, who is sitting in the corner of the room reading a book by candlelight.

"Good evening," she smiles at me and puts the book aside. She invites me to sit in the chair beside her.

"I brought you these," I take my mother's earrings out of my pocket and place them in her outstretched palm. I feel the warmth of her fingers as they close around my hand, and she takes the earrings from me.

"Thanks," she says, "I'll see how much I can get for them."

"Make sure to haggle for them; these are gold earrings studded with Tahitian pearls. They're considered especially valuable because of their size and color."

"You know I always haggle, but it isn't easy these days." She examines them by candlelight before tucking them into her dress pocket.

"Yes, I know," I look at the locked hotel door. It's covered with a dark curtain in order to keep the blackout instructions.

"Like we agreed, food stamps and fifty-fifty on the black market?"

"Yes, fifty-fifty," I reply, knowing I have no other option. She is doing me a favor by exchanging my jewelry on the black market. Although she isn't Jewish like us, she's also risking her life. There's an image of a noose on the posters that the government hung all over the city; a clear warning for those who trade on the black market.

"I'll go tomorrow, and we'll see how much we can get on them," she smiles at me, "there's a trader who I think would be interested in them. It seems to me that he's not buying the jewelry for himself but for a senior German officer who wants to indulge his mistress."

"His mistress will surely enjoy them," I say bitterly, so glad that mother has passed away and won't know where her jewels will end up. For a moment, I imagine the German officer in his black uniform taking my earrings out of his pocket and giving them to a young woman in a transparent camisole. I'm revolted.

"Sarah, are you okay? Shall I get you a glass of water?"

"It's okay, I'm fine," I try to smile at her, wondering if she got the chocolate she gave Rebecca earlier from the same dealer. But it doesn't matter if Rebecca ate Nazi chocolate. At least she ate *something*. She has lost weight these past few months.

"How did it go at the police station?"

"I hope the inspector will be kind and help us," I reply, not wanting to tell her that he refused and sent us back to seek help from the Nazi's claws at the Ministry of the Interior. What if she thinks we won't have any money left or that it's risky to have us and banish us from her hotel? What will we do then? Who will offer us a place to stay? "He also asked us to provide him with our address here at the hotel," I add. "Maybe this is a good sign; perhaps he wants to let us know when he issues our permits for the Free Zone."

"I hope so. This must be a good sign," she smiles a little. "Are there any other places you can try?" she adds a moment later. She too doesn't trust the French policemen roaming the city with the German soldiers.

"Where can I go? I was at the British embassy a year ago and applied for documents, but then the Germans invaded France and occupied Paris and the English closed their embassy and ran away," I place my head on my hand. "Angelina, what will I do if the Nazis enter the embassy, find our immigration applications and come looking for us? I feel like they're chasing me."

"They're not chasing you, Sarah, and that happened a year ago. They probably didn't find anything there." She puts her hand on mine. "And there are other embassies. Spain has an embassy in Paris; they're neutral, and you want to arrive in Spain."

"He told me to be careful; that things are complicated, and that I should be patient."

"Who? Erwin, your husband?"

"Yes, in the letter he sent me," I look at her. "I'm waiting for another letter from him. He'll surely find a solution."

"How many letters have you sent him since he left?"

"Ten, but I have no idea if he received them," I say. I write to him almost every month and tell him what we're going through. Although it's difficult, I only give him hints about our situation. I don't want him to worry too much. This is what he expects of me.

"When did you last get a letter from him?" she looks at me.

"Eight months ago, but you know how it is today with the post office during the war. He's in Madrid, and the letter had to come all the way from Spain. It's not easy for him without us either."

"Yes, it isn't easy for anyone," Angelina sighs and leans back.

"What about your husband? Have you heard anything from him?"

"No," she shakes her head, "nothing."

"He's fine, I'm sure."

"I'm not sure of anything anymore," Angelina says after a moment. "There's almost no food left, and it seems like the war will never end. The Nazis invaded Russia and are defeating the Russians. You must escape, you and Rebecca, while you still can."

"As soon as we get our travel permits, we'll leave. We won't wait."

"You know," she leans in and whispers, "have you heard of the Appelbaum family? They live here on the second floor. They..." She waits a moment before saying, as if hesitating, "they're also Jewish."

"Yes, I know them," I whisper back. I met them several times in the corridor and exchanged polite greetings. They're a couple, about ten years older than me, without any children. They're refugees like us, only from Belgium.

"They're planning to cross the roadblocks into the Free Zone without permits," Angelina continues to whisper and looks at the closed door, as if afraid that any minute now, it will open and the Nazis will rush in from the darkness. "I think you and Rebecca should join them."

"It's dangerous. You know what the Nazis do to people who try to cross into the Free Zone without permits," I look into her brown eyes.

"You should leave," she stares back.

"I'll go to the Spanish embassy tomorrow," I reply and stand up. It's late.

"Sarah, promise me you'll think about it," she holds my hand.

"I promise," I give her a bitter smile, "I'll think about it."

"Wait," Angelina goes to the counter and pulls out of her purse several paper coupons for the food rations. "Take them," she hands them to me. "And here's another piece of chocolate for Rebecca," she smiles at me as she places in my hand the chocolate wrapped in parchment paper.

"Thank you for everything," I hug her and climb up the stairs to the fourth floor. Should I consider her idea to escape? Why isn't Erwin here to make decisions for us as he always did, being the head of the family?

In our room, I open the last letter he sent me yet again, wondering who he had asked to give it to me and how many hands had touched it until it reached me here at the hotel. The thin paper is wrinkled and slightly torn from all the times I opened and read it. By now, I know it by heart. But still, I reread it, delving into the words, looking for hidden meaning in them. '...Sarah, promise me that you'll be careful and trust me, I'll take care of you and Rebecca...' he wrote to me then. I'm his wife. I have to listen to him.

After I put out the candle, I open the window and look at the black sky. Why haven't you sent me a letter telling me what to do?

In the city's silence, I hear the footsteps of a German patrol, their hobnailed boots hitting the cobblestones, and I hurry to close the window and get into bed. But the softness of the mattress doesn't comfort me, on the contrary. I feel like I'm being sucked into a swamp, and my husband isn't here to help me.

Chapter Two

Sucked into the Swamp

"Mommy, can we play too?" Rebecca asks me the next morning as we walk down the main avenue and stumble across a playground.

"No, we don't have time," I hold her hand and continue walking past the white wooden sign with big black letters, 'Jews and dogs are not allowed.'

"Can we go later?" She stops and watches the children swinging and running in the park.

"Hands up. I'll shoot," shouts one of the boys at a girl in a cream-colored dress as he points a wooden stick at her.

"I'm not afraid of you," she shouts back and throws at him a bunch of leaves she picks up from the ground.

"Yes, later we can go to the playground if it won't be too late," I answer Rebecca, knowing I'll surely take a detour on our way back and tell her I'm sorry because I took a wrong turn.

"Good," Rebecca says as we continue walking, but she still looks back at the children playing in the park.

"Rebecca, watch where you're going," I scold her as she stumbles over a small rock. What will happen at the Spanish embassy? Will they agree to give us a temporary passport or visa allowing us to go south of Paris?

Rebecca doesn't reply. She gets up and continues walking, but after a few steps, I notice she scraped her knee and starts tearing up. I stop and open my purse, take out a handkerchief and wipe her eyes and then her bruised knee. I shouldn't have been angry at her. She's just a little girl.

"I promise we'll play in the playground," I hug her and whisper to her, knowing I'd break my promise.

We sweat in the August morning sun, and after we finish walking around the Place de la Concorde, I stop to rest. Rebecca is just a child, and we've already walked quite a lot. I look at the big square from a distance.

Barricades of barbed wire wrapped around diagonal wooden poles are spread across the square. Along the passages in the barricades, German soldiers stand behind sandbags, holding their weapons and carefully examining passersby. This is the Nazis' headquarters area, and huge red flags with swastikas wave along Rivoli Street.

At the newspaper stand on the side of the square, I notice the black newspaper headlines stating that the German army in Russia has captured Smolensk and that nothing will stop the Germans. What should we do? How do we get out of their clutches?

A German army car passes us by and drives along the wide Champs-Élysées. The vehicle resembles a black beetle moving away towards the Arc de Triomphe among the French citizens. Some are walking on the empty road and move aside when they hear its engine approaching. There has been no gas for months, and people are walking or cycling everywhere. I watch from afar the German cars parked outside the Nazi headquarters building on the other side of the square. Only the Nazis have fuel, food, and flags that wave proudly.

"Mommy, look," Rebecca points to a band of German soldiers crossing the square while playing music. At the head of the orchestra walks an officer holding a conductor's baton. They march behind him in straight lines while playing German folk songs. The band's march serpentines between the military checkpoints and barbed wire fences in the square until they pass us and begin marching up the Champs-Élysées in the center of the avenue. I hold Rebecca's hand and take a few steps back. We stand in the shade of a large tree as the sounds of the trombone and drums echo through the quiet street.

"...a little flower, and that means Erika..." Rebecca sings in German when she recognizes the song.

"Traitors," whispers a French woman passing by on the street and hears Rebecca. She looks at me angrily and spits on the sidewalk at our feet, and I cringe. How can I teach Rebecca what is allowed and what is not? She is only a five-year-old girl. How could she know?

"Mommy, did you hear how I sang the song? Why did the woman spit? You told me that spitting is not allowed."

"Rebecca," I kneel, pointing to the white signs in German in the square, directing the German soldiers. "Do you know what these signs say?" I ask her, grateful she can't read.

"What?" She looks at me with her big brown eyes.

"They say that since we're in France, all the people should speak only French."

"Do the soldiers also have to speak only French?"

"No, soldiers are allowed to speak German, but only soldiers."

"So when I grow up, I'll be a soldier. I don't like speaking French."

"When you grow up, I promise you that you'll love speaking French," I kiss her. "We have to keep walking. We're late and remember, at the Spanish embassy, you should be quiet and not speak French or German."

"Like yesterday at the police station?"

"Yes, just like yesterday."

"And you'll buy me another book on the way back?"

"No, but I promised you that you could play in the playground," I tell her, regretting it. It's so hard for me to be with her all the time. "Remember, we're getting close to the embassy. Now, you need to be quiet."

"Okay." She answers and runs beside me, trying to match her steps to mine as we approach the embassy.

There's a line of people patiently waiting outside the Spanish embassy, which is surrounded by a black metal fence. Two French policemen guard the gate on both sides, and a man in a suit stands at the entrance, questioning the people waiting in line. I notice two more men in brown suits standing on the side of the street in front of a parked black car, watching us. Who are they? Are they Germans from the Gestapo? Just thinking about them gives me chills. I take a step closer to the man standing in front of us in line, trying to hide the yellow badge on my dress. "Sweetie, move to my other side. You'll be more comfortable," I move Rebecca and try to hide her with my body. I don't want them to see her.

"Mommy, I'm hungry," she whispers to me.

"I have something for you," I take out of my pocket a small apple that I had brought especially for her. While waiting, I notice how quiet the avenue is. This silence is strange without the noise of the cars driving down the road. All I can hear are people whispering around me and Rebecca munching her apple. More and more people join the line behind me, and I lower my gaze and look at my shoes. I fight the urge to stand at the end of the line like Jews are required to do at the grocery store. I make sure to move forward behind the man in front of me. I hope the policeman won't order us to go back. Just a few years ago, I was a proud young woman married to a wealthy businessman in Berlin. We had some shops and a lovely apartment. What happened to my honor? How did they manage to terrify me?

I try not to look at the two men standing next to the black car, but I feel like the yellow badge on my chest is shining like a target duck in an amusement park booth. Will they pull us out of the line? I keep my eyes on the ground.

"Madame," the man at the gate calls me, and we advance towards him. I smile politely. My heart pounds in my chest as he checks our documents.

"What do you need?" He asks while comparing my face to the passport photo in his hands.

"The consular section."

"Second floor, on the left," he hands me back the passport.

"Let's go," I say quietly to Rebecca. "What about the apple? Have you finished it?"

"Yes."

"Where's the core?"

"I ate it," she answers as we climb the stairs to the second floor.

"Good girl," I stroke her hair, feeling sorry she didn't leave some of it for me.

"How can I help you?" the clerk asks us when we sit down in front of him. Even though he's wearing a suit and not a uniform, when he looks at my passport with the word 'Jew' printed on it, he reminds me of the police officer from yesterday. This word is engraved like a mark of Cain on my clothes and every document I carry.

"We're requesting a visa to visit Spain," I politely smile at him. If he grants us a visa, we can ask again for permission to move to the free zone and leave Paris.

"Madame," he smiles at me politely, "I understand you're a German citizen."

"Yes sir, we left Germany for France."

"And thanks to the Führer, the Third Reich rules all of Europe," he smiles at me, and I cringe.

"We would love to visit Spain, my daughter and I," I answer him quietly.

"Why do you want to leave the territories of the Third Reich?" He scrutinizes me. What should I tell him? I'm afraid to reveal that I long to reach my husband and never return to the territories of the Third Reich. I'm afraid to admit that I'm terrified of the Nazis. I'm afraid to say that I'm weary of fearing so much for my daughter and myself.

"We want to visit Spain for a short trip, and that's why we're applying for a visa," I reply, almost whispering.

"Madame, you are a citizen of the Third Reich. You should return to Germany, not go to Spain."

"Please," I take all the bills out of my wallet, reach forward, and place them in his hand, "We're requesting a visa to Spain."

The clerk remains silent for a few seconds, and I put my hand back on my lap. What if he sends me away because I tried to bribe him or calls the police outside? I feel imprisoned by the German Reich.

"Wait a minute, I'll see what I can do," he finally says, getting up and leaving the office. What would I do without the money I gave him? I'll have to eat less next month.

Rebecca and I sit silently, with only the sound of her shoes hitting the chair as she swings her legs being heard in the room.

"He'll be back soon," I tell her, "and then we'll return to the hotel."

"And go to the playground, you promised."

"And got to the playground," I smile at her. My stomach grumbles; I'm hungry.

"Madame," the clerk reenters his office after a few moments, escorted by another man in a suit. Is this one of those people who stood outside the embassy watching us? I can't remember.

"Yes, sir," I reply quietly. Was it a mistake to come here?

"Unfortunately, your request is currently impossible," he says, "but if you come back next month, we'll try to review your request again."

"Thank you," I smile at him and exhale. Who is the other man in the suit? Why is he whispering something to the clerk?

"But if you leave us your details," the clerk continues, "and your address, we can contact you if we can resolve your problem sooner." He smiles at me politely and sits down. I look at the other man, who nods and leaves the room, closing the door behind him. What should I do? Can I trust him?

"Thank you," I get up from the chair, and take my passport from the table. "We'll be back in a month. Thank you very much," I take Rebecca's hand, and we both leave his office without even shaking his hand.

"Mommy, you're hurting me," Rebecca says as we descend the stairs leading to the first floor and leave the embassy.

"Sorry," I respond and loosen my grip slightly. We must escape. What if the other man was a Gestapo agent? I feel like I'm sinking deeper into a swamp and can't escape. I need a lifeline. What if they stop me in a month when I try to return?

Leaving the embassy, I avert my gaze from the men standing next to the black car and hurry away in the opposite direction. I'm tense and afraid they will call out to stop me. Only when we're far from the building do I slow down my pace, but the sound of a car makes me alert again, and I watch the green truck full of soldiers speeding by on the boulevard. I turn my back to the vehicle and wait quietly. The Star of Life and Death on my dress is prominent. Only after the German truck drives away and the street is quiet again, do I take out a handkerchief and wipe my eyes. I have to decide what to do next.

"How was your visit to the Spanish embassy?" Angelina asks me in the afternoon when we return to the hotel. We're both hungry and tired after walking around the Nazi headquarters in Concord Square on the way back.

"We tried to avoid the German army checkpoints, all day" I whisper to her. "The Spanish embassy won't help us. I'll go up with her to rest for a while."

"We saw an orchestra playing, and I'm not allowed to speak German because I'm not a soldier, and Mommy lost her way and couldn't find the playground," Rebecca summarizes for Angelina.

The rays of the afternoon sun penetrate through the curtain and shine on my face. I feel their warmth and keep my eyes closed, wanting a few minutes to myself. I need to banish the scary thoughts and let my mind rest a little.

The room is quiet. Rebecca must have fallen asleep as well or is reading from Sylvie the bear's book, which she decided is a girl bear. I'll try to sleep a little more, but then I hear a faint metallic screeching noise. What is this noise? I open my eyes and look around.

Rebecca is sitting with her back to me, wearing nothing but underwear and a tank top. She is concentrating on something, and the metallic noise continues.

"Rebecca, what are you doing?" I sit up.

"I fixed the yellow badge," she turns to me with a smile. She has scissors in one hand and the yellow badge she cut out of her dress in the other.

"Rebecca, what did you do?" I get up quickly and take her dress, looking in horror at the hole where the yellow badge was sewn.

"I don't want it," she hands it to me.

"You can't do that," I raise my voice and hit her hand with force, taking the scissors from her and watching her burst into tears. "You're not allowed to take mommy's things without permission," I shout at her. What did she do? How will I fix her dress?

"I don't want it watching over me. I hate it," she cries and throws the yellow badge on the floor.

"You have to. You must never be without your yellow badge," I slap her. Her crying intensifies, and she looks at me in shock as tears roll down her cheeks. What have I done? I've never hit her before. I cover my face with my hands and start to cry. This room feels like a trap closing in on us. This city looks at us as if we were trapped animals on display.

"Rebecca," I hold her shoulders, "look at me."

"What, Mommy?" She raises her eyes and continues to cry.

"Promise me that you will never take off the yellow badge again. Do you remember I told you that the yellow star protects you?"

"Yes," she nods.

"Then you mustn't take it off, ever," I take out a handkerchief and wipe her eyes. "Promise me you'll never take it off."

"Okay, Mommy," she nods and hiccups.

"Now I'll sew it back onto the dress, and it will be as good as new," I smile at her, even though I want to sit in the corner of the room and burst into tears. I hate the Star of Life and Death.

"Okay, Mommy," she sniffles and goes to sit on the bed with the book. I open the suitcase and take out a thread and a needle.

My fingers are shaking as I silently sew the hole and the patch back. From time to time, I hear Rebecca sniffle, but she doesn't say anything, and only the rustling of the pages disturbs the silence. In another world, I would have appreciated this silence. But I want to scream and cry at the same time.

Later, after Rebecca falls asleep, I leave the room and quietly close the door behind me. I have to do something. The hotel is quiet, and I follow the light at the bottom of the stairs to find Angelina. She is sitting, as she does every night, in her armchair at the entrance, reading a book by candlelight.

"Good evening, Sarah," she looks up at me. "Come, join me. Is everything alright?"

"I want to talk to the Appelbaums," I whisper to her. "I want to join them when they leave Paris for the Free Zone."

A few days later, a warm summer night breeze enters the room from the open window as I gaze into the dark night. The city outside is quiet. I look at my watch, close the curtain, sit on the floor, and light a candle. There's still some time before we have to go. Although I try to relax, my whole body is tense. Rebecca is sleeping in her bed. I'll wake her up soon. I breathe slowly and try to calm myself down. Our suitcase is packed and ready. Everything is ready; we are ready.

On the spur of the moment, I open my suitcase and take out my small makeup bag, the one I haven't used in a year. I take out a thread and a needle, and start working. Every once in a while, I look at the watch on my wrist, checking the time.

"Rebecca, sweetie, time to get up," I gently nudge her when I finish.

"Mommy, no..." she speaks in her sleep, but I touch her again. We have to hurry. I return the thread and needle to the makeup bag and close the suitcase. "What did you do?" She asks me as she sits up in bed, yawning and rubbing her eyes.

"I fixed the dress; it was torn. Come on, I'll help you get dressed. Put your arms up," I take her dress from the chair and help her get dressed and tie her shoelaces. She still can't do it on her own, even though I tried to teach her.

I hear the German patrol hobnailed boots through the open window, marching down the street. I look at my watch. It's 11:40. That's our sign to come down.

"Let's leave quietly," I whisper to her as I hold the candle in one hand and the suitcase in the other. I put it down on the floor in order to open the door and let Rebecca step outside first. I linger and look back at the small hotel room that had been our home for a year and four months before I close the door for the last time. "Come down the stairs quietly. Don't make any noise. All the guests are asleep," I whisper to her.

Angelina and the Appelbaums are already waiting for us at the entrance. Mr. Appelbaum, Walter, has a fancy long, thin, brown summer coat and a fedora hat that hides his face in the dim candlelight. He's standing next to his wife, Fosette, as if protecting her. He's taller than her and me. Fosette also has a luxurious long coat, and her black hair is tied up. They're holding their suitcases and looking at Rebecca and me as we descend the stairs.

"Are you ready?" Angelina asks me in a hushed voice.

"Yes, we're ready," I place the candle I held on the counter and take Rebecca's hand.

"She's a little girl. She'll get in the way," Fosette whispers to Angelina while looking at Rebecca. I feel Rebecca clinging to me and holding my hand tightly, even though Mrs. Appelbaum speaks French, and I'm not sure Rebecca understands everything she is saying.

"She's not a little girl; she's five years old, and she's quiet," I reply.

"Fosette, it's fine, they're like us. We agreed they'll join," Mr. Appelbaum puts his hand on her shoulder, approaches, and whispers something to her. I can't hear what he's saying to her.

"You agreed, I didn't," she turns to him.

"We both agreed, you too, we need them," he continues speaking softly.

Fosette brushes Mr. Appelbaum's hand off her shoulder and turns to Angelina. "Did she bring what we agreed upon?"

"Yes," Angelina answers and turns to me.

I take out of my handbag the gold bracelet I prepared earlier; the very same Ervin had given me for Rebecca's birth. "It's yours," I place it in Mrs. Appelbaum's outstretched hand, watching it sparkle for another moment before her brown leather gloved fingers close over it.

"Then everything is fine," Mr. Appelbaum says softly, "as agreed."

"Goodbye, God bless you," Angelina shakes the Appelbaums' hands.

"Goodbye, Rebecca, promise you'll be quiet," she bends down and hugs Rebecca.

"Goodbye, Mrs. Angelina," Rebecca answers and smiles.

"Goodbye, Sarah, may God protect you," she hugs me tightly. "Every guest leaves something at my hotel. Someone forgot this," she hands me a block of hard cheese wrapped in parchment paper. "Take it for the road."

"I can't take it, it's yours."

"I don't need it, and you have a little girl," she whispers to me. "Take it. You'll need it."

"Thank you for everything you did for me. Your husband will be back soon, I'm sure," I hug her back. Why is she so kind to me?

"We must hurry. We have to leave before the next patrol," Mr. Appelbaum says softly.

"Leave, leave," Angelina breaks away from me, approaches the counter and blows out the candle. After a moment in the darkness, I hear the key turning in the hotel door and feel the wind coming in from the street.

"Let's go," Mr. Appelbaum whispers, and we all walk out into the dark street. I hold Rebecca's hand tightly.

Behind me, I hear the front door close and the metallic click of the lock.

The dark city houses loom threateningly as we walk down the dimly lit street. There is no moon in the sky, and black clouds obscure the stars. In the distance, I can hear the growl of a car; it must be a German army vehicle. I feel sweat on my back despite the night wind.

Mr. Appelbaum leads us down the street, followed by his wife and me holding Rebecca's hand behind them. Rebecca is forced to run, and I hear her shoes hitting the pavement. We have no choice but to keep up; we can't slow down and risk losing them. I don't know where the smuggler is waiting to take us to the Free Zone and from there to Spain.

"Shhh..." Mr. Appelbaum stops at a street corner and whispers to us. We remain silent as he checks for German patrols nearby. I hear Rebecca gasp and I place a hand on the back of her head. She, too, is sweating. We're close to Les Halles, the city's central market. Although I don't recognize the streets, the smell of rotting vegetables and occasional squeal of a rat are unmistakable.

We continue walking, and after a while, Mr. Appelbaum stops. I hear him passing the closed metal store doors and counting softly. "One, two, three, four..." When he reaches the fourth door, he stands and knocks on it several times.

After a moment, the door creaks open. Mrs. Appelbaum rushes in, followed by Mr. Appelbaum, but when I try to enter, a man stops me and blocks my way.

"Who are you?" he asks. I can hardly make out his face; the street is completely dark, and there is only a faint light inside the store behind him. He is a big man, and his clothes smell of sweat. I notice the scent of Pastis liquor on his breath as he speaks to me.

"I'm with them. I also need to get out of Paris," I whisper to him, hurrying to wedge my shoe in the doorway so he can't close it and leave us in the deserted street.

"Does she have money?" He turns to Mr. Appelbaum, his large hand still holding the door almost closed, "We agreed on two. Why did you bring her?"

"I have a way to pay you," I reply. I need him to let us in. I can hear a vehicle in the distance.

The stranger at the door opens it a little wider after a moment. "Come in," he whispers. I push in, holding my suitcase tightly and pulling Rebecca after me.

"Who's this?" He stands in front of me and points at Rebecca.

"She's with me," I reply. In the dim candlelight in the room, I notice we're in a butcher's shop, although now the shelves are empty. Only the knives hanging around serve as a reminder of its former use. The man blocking our path is wearing a beret and a dirty white shirt.

"You can come, but she can't. Get out of here," he tries to move past me to the closed door.

"I told you she couldn't come," Mrs. Appelbaum says quietly to her husband as she watches me. They stand together in the corner of the shop. I have to think of something.

"She's with me. She's my daughter, please," I lean back against the door so he can't open it.

"You're healthy and young, but she's small and weak. She can't climb mountains. She doesn't have the strength," he says, his face close to mine. The smell of Pastis and sweat is overpowering.

"I'll carry her on my back," I whisper to him.

"You don't seem strong enough to me," he reaches out and grips my arm forcefully. "You won't be able to carry her in the mountains. She's a burden." His hand tightens around my arm, making me flinch. The cold metal door rivets hurt my back.

Where is my husband to protect us like Mr. Appelbaum watches over his wife? Why am I alone?

"We'll manage. We won't be a burden on you, you'll see." I answer. I need him, his cooperation.

"Really?" He comes even closer. "What if she makes a noise when we cross a German roadblock and we all get caught? We have to hide in the truck and be quiet as mice, not making a sound. What if she starts crying? Girl," he turns to Rebecca and grabs her hand, "Do you want to be killed by a German bullet?"

Rebecca doesn't respond but tries to free herself from his grip, kicking him with her little leg.

"She'll be fine," I lean down and pull his hand away from Rebecca. "I told you she's a strong girl, trust me." I keep talking to him, hoping Rebecca doesn't understand what he's asking. From the corner of my eye, I see Mr. and Mrs. Appelbaum watching us, as if observing a play. "I have a way to pay you," I add. I have no one else to trust but him.

"You do?" He releases Rebecca and stands up. I feel her clinging to me, her small hand hugging my legs under my dress.

"Yes, I do," I take out a pearl necklace from my handbag. It's the last piece of jewelry I have left. I show it to him but hold it tightly, so he won't snatch it. I don't trust him, but I have no other choice.

"Come with me for a moment," he looks into my eyes and smiles. "This journey is dangerous. I want to examine the necklace closely, in the light." He breaks away from me and walks into the back room, turning on a dim electric lamp. "Are you coming?"

"Rebecca, stay here with Mrs. Appelbaum," I instruct quietly and follow him, clutching the necklace in my hand. Under the weak light of the lamp, I notice a scar on his neck and a half-broken tooth.

"It's a dangerous journey. Your payment is sufficient for one person. Choose: either you or the girl," he approaches me again.

"I can't pay you more, please. We need to leave," I whisper to him. I mustn't tell him about the gold coins I've sewn into the hidden pocket of the dress. I need them for the rest of the journey in Spain – if he doesn't betray us on the way. "I'll pay you when we get to Spain. My husband is waiting for us there." I try to smile, even though my entire body tenses in his presence.

"I think you're lying. I don't think anyone is waiting for you in Spain," he reaches out and grabs the pearl necklace. "I'll take this for you," he whispers, "and this for the girl." He reaches out his other hand and grabs my breast, squeezing it over my dress. "It seems fair."

My body freezes with shock and tension. His touch disgusts me. *What should I do?* I'm afraid to scare Rebecca and I need him to take us. "I'm a married woman. I can't do that. I have a wedding ring," I manage to say after a moment.

"I don't see a husband who cares for you. I'll take care of you," he continues to squeeze my breasts forcefully and tries to kiss me, his mouth reeking of alcohol.

"Enough, no," I come to my senses and whisper, pushing him off. In the midst of the struggle, I feel the pearl necklace break, and I hear the pearls scattering across the small room like raindrops. What have I done?

"Now you only have one payment left to make," he whispers angrily. "You can start paying now or take the little girl and go outside into the night, where ravenous German wolves wait to hunt her." He grins and grabs my hand, trying to pull it between his legs. What choice do I have? I feel tears filling my eyes.

"Mommy?" I hear Rebecca call from the other room.

"It's okay, honey," I answer. "I'll be right back." I see him smiling with satisfaction. But then I push him away with all my might. I can't do what he wants. I'm a married woman. A feeling of suffocation and nausea rises in my throat.

"Mr. Appelbaum," I call out, and that stops him for a moment. I manage to free myself from his grasp and rush back into the store. I feel the crunch of the pearls scattered on the floor under my shoes, but I know I lost them. "Rebecca, let's go," I take her hand and pick up my suitcase.

"Get out of here," he calls from the back room, straightening his shirt, tucking it into his pants. He goes to the store door, cracks it open and whispers, "The Germans are waiting for you," as I pass him and exit the store into the dark night.

"I told you that we shouldn't trust her," I hear Mrs. Appelbaum say to her husband before the door slams behind us, leaving us alone in the dark street.

"Are you okay?" I ask Rebecca as we hide behind a pile of empty vegetable boxes.

"He hurt me," she whispers.

"When he held your hand?" I gently caress her hand.

"Yes," she nods. "He's not a nice man."

"He didn't mean to hurt you," I say as I hug her. I look around, trying to get a sense of where we are. I'm scared. How will we get back to the hotel? How will we avoid the German patrols?

"What did he ask me?" Rebecca whispers.

"He didn't mean to scare you," I try to think of some answer. "He asked you if you knew any hunters," I tell her after a moment. How can I protect her from getting scared?

"Hunters like in Sylvie's book?"

"Yes, like in Sylvie's book," I smile at her in the darkness.

"And they shot at us?" She asks, and I shudder.

"No, these are different hunters. They're good hunters."

"But he said they shot at us," she says.

"He got confused. He didn't read Sylvie's book," I continue to hug her. "Now we'll go back to Angelina's hotel and go to sleep. Do you want to sleep?"

"Yes," she answers and leans on me.

"So now we'll quietly go to the hotel. We'll take off our shoes so the hunters won't hear us," I whisper to her.

In the distance, I hear a car driving and I cringe, protecting Rebecca with my body amid the empty wooden crates.

"Mommy, you're crushing me," she whispers.

"Let's go, and if we hear hunters, we'll hide like we're hiding now," I say once the car noise fades. I take off our shoes, put them in the suitcase and we both start walking down the dark alley.

At first, I try to remember the way we came, but all the streets look similar, and after a while, I realize we are lost.

"Mommy, the hunters are coming," Rebecca whispers to me, and I freeze, listening. The sound of a patrol's hobnailed boots comes from a nearby street. I search for somewhere to hide. What will I do if we get caught? Maybe I should have given the smuggler what he wanted? I shake with fear, fatigue, and stress.

"Let's go," I hold her hand, and we turn and run in the dark to the other direction of the street and hide in an alley. I hug her and breathe in the darkness, hoping the patrol wouldn't find us in this street.

Only after dawn arrives and people begin to appear in the streets do I put on Rebecca's shoes and mine. We leave the alley, walk the main street, and head toward the hotel.

"What happened? Are you okay? Come in," Angelina opens the hotel door when she hears my knock.

"Thanks," I say as I walk in, gasping. I hold Rebecca in my arms while she sleeps on my shoulder, and with my other hand, I carry our suitcase. I am so tired from this night.

"What happened? Where are the Appelbaums?" She asks. "Come, sit," she takes the suitcase from my hand and leads me to the small armchair in the reception.

"They went with the smuggler," I say as I sit carefully in the armchair, supporting the sleeping Rebecca. My legs hurt so much.

"And why didn't you leave with him?"

"It didn't work out," is all I can say. I can still feel my breast aching from his unwelcome touch. All I want is to sleep. I didn't close my eyes all night while we hid in the alley.

"Are you fine?" She asks, touching my arm.

"Yes," I give her a tired smile, "I just need to breathe and relax a little."

Angelina says nothing; she goes to the back room and returns after a moment, holding a small glass of whiskey, "Drink it. It's what you need now."

I sip the drink in one gulp, feeling its burn in my throat, and tears fill my eyes. "He wanted a payment from me that I couldn't make," I tell her after a while, sighing. Rebecca continues to sleep peacefully on my shoulder.

"You can continue to use the same room. Go upstairs to rest," she takes the empty glass of whiskey from my hand.

I thank her and climb the stairs slowly with my sleeping child in my arms. I can't tell Angelina that I forgot to retrieve the gold bracelet from Mr. Appelbaum and that I lost my pearl necklace. I am left without jewelry. I have only the gold coins hidden in my dress and my wristwatch. What will I do the next time I have to pay her? And what about a month from now?

A few days later, I find myself standing at the end of the line at the grocery store on Rue des Gravilliers. Another Jewish woman is ahead of me, waiting patiently. My legs ache from standing for so long. I've been here since morning, consistently moving to the back of the line each time customers without yellow badges arrive. That's the law; Jews must always go to the end of the line. At least we're close to the store entrance now.

"We've run out of groceries for today. Come back tomorrow, I'm sorry," the shopkeeper announces, coming out the store and waving his hands helplessly. "Try the grocery store on Rue Meslay. Maybe there's something left there," he adds before he puts away the wooden sign announcing today's oil and flour.

"I'm going home. My children are waiting for me. I'll try tomorrow," the Jewish woman ahead of me says. "I've lost enough weight today standing in line," she adds with a bitter smile and walks away.

I turn around and begin walking toward Meslay Street. I'm out of flour, so I have to find a grocery store that might have some leftovers for the Jews at the end of the day. Rebecca stayed in the hotel room. She is too young to stand in line for so many hours.

The small streets are quiet at noon; only a few people walk around. Suddenly, I notice several elderly people with yellow badges attached to their clothes coming out of one of the buildings on the street.

The building's facade is different from the others around it; there is a large black door with an arched top.

"God bless you, my dear," one of the old men says to me as I stop walking and stand in front of the big door. "Do you want to come in?" He smiles at me. He has a long white beard, blue eyes, and wears a black suit.

"Yes, thank you," I reply. The men step aside as he slowly opens the heavy wooden door and kisses the mezuzah with his fingers.

I kiss the mezuzah as he did, feeling the cold metal on my fingertips, and enter the synagogue. Since leaving Berlin, I haven't been to a synagogue.

Step by step, I walk into the empty, large hall. There's nothing but dark wooden benches in straight rows in front of the Torah Ark at the end of the aisle. I lift my eyes to the women's gallery and the color-stained glass windows at the ceiling that cast a bluish tint.

"You're welcome to go up to the women's gallery," the old man points to the stairs, "but you can also stay down here and pray. So few people come here these days. To God, it doesn't matter where we pray." He smiles.

"Thank you," I smile back and head up the stairs to the women's gallery. It feels too strange for me to sit and pray where the men usually sit.

My hand brushes against the varnished wooden railing as I ascend to the second floor and the women's gallery. It's also empty. The wooden benches wait for women to accompany their praying husbands, looking on with pride.

I sit on one of the benches, taking out my husband's letter and holding it tightly.

"God," I whisper, "please help Rebecca and me get to my husband. Please make us a family again. Please give me a sign that I did the right thing with the smuggler who wanted to take advantage of me," I continue to whisper, still feeling my aching breasts. "God, please give me a sign for the right path, because I lost it." I nearly crush the letter between my fingers.

Then, I straighten the letter, kiss it, and tuck it back into my handbag before getting up and heading back down the stairs.

"I'm sure God listened to you, my dear," the old man says quietly as he escorts me back to the heavy black wooden door leading to the street.

"Thank you, Rabbi," I answer and walk away further down the street toward the grocery store. Only after a while do I realize that I forgot to ask his name, but when I turn and look for him, he's no longer there, and the narrow street is empty.

Later, when I return to the hotel with some flour and oil that I managed to get at the grocery store, Angelina informs me that a police officer arrived at the hotel at noon and requested that Rebecca and I come to the station.

"This is the sign," I whisper to myself as I put down the package of flour and the bottle of oil and hold the letter asking Rebecca and me to come the next day to the police station in the city center.

"What sign?" Angelina asks.

"We have permits. They summoned us to the police station because we have permits."

"Don't go, please, I don't trust the police," she says, placing her hand in mine.

"But it's the police; they know what they're doing," I look at her. "This is our chance to get out of Paris."

"I don't trust them. They work with the Nazis; since the Nazis occupied Paris, the police have collaborated with them. I don't trust the government anymore."

"But what can they do to us? There must be a reason they invited us to the police station after we asked for transit permits. There must be a reason they asked for our address," I hold the sheet of paper with the Paris police insignia printed on top. The swastika symbol embedded next to it makes me feel sick, but I should be used to it. Even in Berlin, swastikas appeared everywhere after the Nazis came to power.

"Sarah, please don't go. I can't explain it, but I have a bad feeling," she looks into my eyes.

"We have to," I look back at her. "The police will come looking for us here."

"We'll find another smuggler, or you can move to another hotel. You know I love Rebecca and you, but move to another hotel. I'll tell them you ran away. Please, don't go."

"I have to. I promised Erwin that I wouldn't act hastily," I still can't tell her what happened with the smuggler a few days ago and what he asked me to do.

"But he's not here, only you are."

"But he's my husband. Even if he's not here, you know how it works. We, women, must always listen to them. Even when they're not around."

"Maybe that's the problem," Angelina responds quietly. "That we always listen to our husbands. Do you know why I don't have children?" she asks after a moment. "No, I say, embarrassed," I always saw her treat Rebecca so nicely, I was ashamed to ask her about it.

"Because I listened to him, my husband," she says quietly. "A few years ago, we inherited this hotel, and we worked hard and didn't have much money. When I got pregnant, he said it would be a problem to raise the child," she sighs. "So I did what women know how to do, and I went to one of these doctors, because I listened to him," she continues, and I see her eyes watering. "And then we were no longer able to get pregnant, even though we tried. No doctor can say why," she pauses and takes a breath.

"Angelina, I'm so sorry," I put my hand on her and want to hug her.

"Then the war started," she continues, "and he volunteered to join the army, even though he didn't have to, but he convinced me that it was a patriotic act to fight for France, and I agreed. And look what happened to me?" She pauses for a moment. "He's probably a prisoner in Germany, and I haven't heard from him in a year. I have no idea what happened to him. Sarah, what's the point of listening to what men say?" She looks at me with tears in her eyes.

"You know we have to. You know we have no other option," I hug her. "You'll see that everything will be fine. You'll see that your husband will come back, and you'll have a baby, and you'll see that they prepared papers for Rebecca and me to cross to the Free Zone. They don't call us for nothing, you'll see." I continue to hug her.

Chapter Three

Into the Trap

A pleasant morning sun illuminates the Pont Notre-Dame as Rebecca and I cross the bridge on our way to the police station on Île de la Cité. A line of several people stands in front of the barrier spread across the bridge, while a soldier guards the checkpoint. He inspects each person who walks between the barricades and barbed wire fences that create a narrow passage on the bridge.

The soldier stands indifferently, his rifle resting on his shoulder as he smokes a cigarette. As we get closer, I can smell the cheap tobacco. Despite having passed through many such checkpoints in the past year, I still feel tense as the line of people moves towards the soldier. At least we are close to the police station and our transport permits. With these permits, the next barriers we face will be on our way to the Free Zone and Spain. In the distance, I can see the towers of Notre Dame Cathedral.

"Stop," the soldier yells as I try to pass in front of him. "Certificates," he continues, the cigarette still tucked in his mouth.

I take out my passport and hand it to him. Why today? Why when we're so close to leaving this city forever?

"Are you German?" He asks in German when he opens the brown passport and compares my face to the photo. A large red letter "J" is stamped next to an eagle holding a swastika.

"Yes," I reply.

"So why are you here and not in your homeland? We're at war," he looks into my eyes. Smoke rises from the cigarette tucked in his mouth, swirling in the morning sky. He gives me a penetrating look; his blue eyes almost disappear under the green helmet that covers his short, fair hair. What can I tell him to avoid being detained and missing our appointment at the police station?

"I'm on my way to the Institut Pasteur," I answer in German. "I'm a pharmacist, researching medicines for our army." I hope he doesn't know that Jews are not allowed to practice pharmacy in Germany since the Nazis came to power. Jews are prohibited from many professions. Fortunately, we had our shops until we had to close them and flee.

He continues to scrutinize me. Will he believe me? I smile politely, even though I can feel the sweat on my nape.

"You can go," he says finally, throwing my passport on the pavement. He continues to watch me with a smirk, the cigarette still in his mouth.

"Thank you," I respond as I bend down, clutching Rebecca's hand tightly. My brown passport lies next to his hobnailed boots. Will he kick me in the face? I close my eyes and become tense as I expect pain. But then I hear footsteps behind me.

"Madame, you dropped your passport," someone says, touching my shoulder. I open my eyes and stand up, looking at the hand of a stranger who's handing me the passport.

"Thank you," I take the passport. There are several men and women standing behind him, watching the soldier in silence with angry expressions.

"Keep moving forward," the German soldier says, turning his back to me.

"Rebecca, let's go," I breathe a sigh of relief as we continue walking. I search for the man who helped me just a moment ago, but I can't recognize him among the men in brown suits ahead of us on the bridge. Soon, I will once again have a husband who cares for me, and not a stranger. We will receive our documents shortly.

When we arrive in Spain, I swear to myself, I will never have to bow to anyone again.

"Mommy, who is Mr. Pasteur?" Rebecca asks when we reach the middle of the bridge.

"Why are you asking?"

"Because you told the soldier we were going there."

"There is a man at the police named Mr. Pasteur," I reply.

"We'll meet him, and then he'll let us go to Dad?"

"No, we're going to meet the policeman we met last time, before I bought you Mr. Sylvie the Bear's book. His name is Mr. Plessis. Do you remember that you need to be quiet during the meeting?"

"Sylvie is a girl. Will we then go to the bookstore with the woman who wrapped the book for me?"

"No, then we'll go to the hotel, and I'll read to you from the book. We'll pack up, and then we'll go meet Dad. But only if you stay quiet during the meeting with Mr. Plessis at the police station."

"I promise, I miss Daddy."

"Me too," I smile at her as we approach the entrance to the police station. Finally, after a year, we're going to leave this city. I miss Ervin so much. I want us to be a family again.

"Names, please?" Police Inspector Plessis leans over the thick notebook while holding a fountain pen.

"Sarah and Rebecca Bloch, we were here a few weeks ago, and yesterday we received a summons to report to the police station," I place our passports on his mahogany desk.

"Yes, of course. We were expecting you," he looks up and smiles at me briefly before leaning back over the binder full of names. Some of the names are crossed out with black lines. Are those names of people who have already received transit permits to leave Paris?

Mr. Plessis continues searching the binder, and when he finds our names, he crosses them out. "Please come with me," he rises from his chair and smiles at me. "What a cute girl," he bends down to Rebecca and tries to pinch her cheek, but she pulls away and clings to me.

"Follow me, please," he says, turning and walking down the hall.

"Mommy, he's not a nice man," Rebecca whispers to me in German as we walk down the hall. The police officers around us are either seated at their desks, or have lively discussions.

"Remember you promised to be quiet?" I scold her. "If you stay quiet, I'll read Sylvie to you when we get back to the hotel."

"Promise?"

"Yes, I promise," I hasten my pace to keep up with Mr. Plessis as he descends the stairs and heads toward the backyard. Where is he taking us? What about the transit papers we need to get to the free zone?

There's a large group of men and women in their forties in the courtyard. Some of them are holding suitcases. I notice that they all have a yellow badge on their clothes. What is going on here? Several police cars are parked on the other side of the parking lot, and in the center, there are two green buses with the Paris municipality symbol on the front. A policeman stands next to each of them.

"Please join the group. Mrs. Bloch, have a good voyage," Mr. Plessis smiles at me. "Have a good voyage, Rebecca," he turns to her but doesn't try to pinch her cheek again. I follow him with my gaze until he disappears at the entrance to the station.

"Ladies and gentlemen," I hear a voice and turn around to see another policeman standing in front of the group. He has a rifle slung over his shoulder. "Please board one of the two buses in the yard. Please do not push; there are seats for everyone."

Where are they taking us?

"Something is wrong," I whisper to myself as I turn around and start walking away from the people boarding the buses. I want to speak to Mr. Plessis. I didn't have time to pack or say goodbye to Angelina. Where are they taking us?

"Madame, please get on the bus with the girl," another policeman standing at the corner calls out to me. Only now do I notice that we're all surrounded by armed policemen.

"Sir, there's a mistake," I say as I pick up Rebecca and approach him. "We haven't prepared for the trip."

"Madame, it's all been taken care of," he blocks my way. "Please get on the bus now."

"You don't understand," I tell him. "I must return to the hotel and pack my luggage. Angelina is waiting for me."

But the policeman steps forward and forces me back towards the people boarding the buses. All around, there is chatter, but I don't listen.

"Madame, board the bus. Don't worry, everything is taken care of," he continues to slowly push me toward the other people. Rebecca clings tightly to me. What can I do? What choice do I have? There must be a misunderstanding. I need to explain this to someone.

"I need to talk to the inspector. Mr. Plessis. He knows me."

"They will speak to you later. Now, get on the bus. Do you need help with the girl?" He reaches out and tries to take Rebecca from me.

"Mommy," Rebecca shouts in German. But her voice is hardly audible amidst the noise of the crowd boarding the buses.

"She's my child; don't take her from me," I hold her tightly, feeling the policeman's rough uniform and his hands trying to take her.

"Get on the bus now and stop making trouble, you stinking German Jewess."

"I'll go; just don't touch my girl," I hold back the tears. Where is my husband when I need him most?

The policeman steps back and continues to watch me. I turn my back to him and hold Rebecca tightly as we huddle between the people climbing onto one of the buses. It will be fine. I mustn't worry; I'll find someone to talk to about this.

"Sweetie, sit by the window so you can see the road." I place Rebecca on the hard leather seat, but she refuses to sit alone, so I keep her on my lap and hold her close.

"Sweetie, everything is fine. We're going on a trip. That policeman was just not nice," I whisper to her and stroke her hair. "That's why he didn't get on the bus and won't join us on the trip."

"Where are we going to?" She keeps hugging me.

"It's a surprise," I whisper to her. "But riding the bus is fun."

"Where are they taking us?" Asks an older woman behind us. She's wearing a beige dress, and her black hair is neatly pulled up.

"They're deporting us," another fair-haired woman in a brown dress answers her.

"They can't deport us. We're French. They probably just want to register us at another police station," says a man in his fifties wearing a suit and sitting next to his wife. The yellow badge stands out on his tailored suit.

"I heard they're moving the Jews to the Free Zone to keep us safe," says the woman sitting behind me.

"I don't trust them," growled a young man in brown pants and a white shirt sitting across the aisle. He placed his suitcase next to him. "You saw what they did to the Jews in Germany on Kristallnacht."

"Mommy, what is a Kristallnacht?" Rebecca asks me.

"A crystal is a beautiful, sparkly glass," I explain and cover her ears with my palms, so she won't hear the conversation on the bus, "Now don't ask any more questions. Look around the bus; it's beautiful. Can you count how many seats there are on the bus?" I try to distract her.

"One, two, three, four..." Rebecca starts counting while pointing around, and I look at the people around me. Who should I believe? The woman who trusts them or the young man who mentioned Kristallnacht? I still remember that horrible night in Berlin when the Nazis marched through the streets. All our family's shop windows were shattered, and we had to hide because they beat every Jew they found outside.

The driver boards the bus and starts it, and a French policeman armed with a rifle boards with him. Another second passes, and the driver pulls the handle to close the door at the front of the bus. The bus begins to move slowly, its engine rumbling. Where are they taking us?

At the Pont Notre-Dame, the bus stops in front of the checkpoint, and the driver opens the door while the policeman shows the German sentry a piece of paper. He is the same soldier I passed through at the checkpoint just an hour ago.

The soldier reads the paper and nods. I look down and shield Rebecca with my hand, afraid he will board the bus and recognize us. But after a moment, I hear the bus door close, and when I look up and out of the window, I see the soldier open the wooden barrier and the barbed wire, allowing the bus to continue its journey.

After the bridge, the driver turns left and drives on the nearly empty streets.

"He's leaving Paris," one of the women says. "I told you they're taking us to the Free Zone."

"Mommy, what about Sylvie?" Rebecca asks. What should I tell her? I look at the people around me. Most of them have luggage. Why didn't I bring our suitcase? Why didn't I think they would immediately get us out of Paris? What will I do?

"Sylvie the bear is waiting for us at the hotel. Angelina is looking after her for us," I tell her after a moment. I look out the window as the bus passes through the city's suburbs. Are we saying goodbye to Paris? Has our year here come to an end? The boulevard becomes a road, and the surrounding houses become lower, with gardens in between. Some people walk along the side of the road, watching the bus with curiosity.

"But Mummy, I want to read the book. You promised."

"Rebecca, quiet now," I reply impatiently as I continue to look outside. I try again to make her sit on the seat next to me, but she refuses and hugs me tightly. A German army commander vehicle with an open roof passes us. I look at the officer sitting in the back seat. Next to him is a young woman with golden hair and a blue dress. He leans towards her while she holds a fashionable summer hat to her head.

"Finally, we're getting out of Paris, finally away from the Nazis," sighs the woman behind me. I slip my hand into my handbag, feeling our passports. I so want to believe her.

"It's a scam. They're going to do something to us," growls the young man in a white shirt sitting on the other side of the aisle. "We're heading north to the German border," he points to the sun. Which should I believe? I'm trying to calm myself and not frighten Rebecca, but I want to scream. What about our suitcase? How will we manage?

The bus suddenly stops, and I must hold Rebecca so she doesn't fall. Why did we stop? I look ahead. The policeman who guarded us also turns his gaze outside the bus.

Two cows are walking on the road, herded by a local farmer, blocking the road in front of the bus. Some people stand inside the bus and look out curiously.

"They won't take me back to Germany," I hear a whisper, and suddenly, I see the young man in the white shirt moving to the front of the bus. In one quick movement, he opens the bus door and escapes, running along the fence surrounding one of the houses.

"Stop!" the French policeman shouts at him, "Stop immediately!" He takes the weapon off his shoulder.

All the people on the bus are talking excitedly, and I can't understand who's saying what. "Mommy, why is that man running away?" I think I hear Rebecca asking me, but I don't answer her because I'm watching as the policeman aims his weapon and shoots.

The people on the bus around me shout, and I cringe and close my eyes while I hug Rebecca and cover her eyes. Another shot is heard, and there is screaming and shouting, and then silence.

"Sit down, everyone, be quiet," I open my eyes and see the policeman getting back on the bus, still holding his rifle in his hand and panting. "Let no one move," he continues, looking at us. "You," he turns to the driver, "start driving."

The bus continues to drive slowly, and I avert my gaze. I can't see if the young man in the white shirt was hit. Why did he run away? Why didn't he stay on the bus? Despite the warm sun, my whole body is shaking, and it's hard for me to breathe.

"Mommy, why did the man shoot him?" Rebecca asks me. Why didn't anyone prepare me for such questions? I take a deep breath and look at the policeman who is standing next to the driver, still holding his rifle.

"Because he was a bad man."

"Is that policeman a hunter too?"

"Yes, he's also a hunter, but a good hunter. He protects us." I answer and feel sick.

"Mommy, the bad guy forgot his suitcase," Rebecca points to the young man's suitcase, which was left on the bench.

"The hunters will give it to him, just like they'll bring us the suitcase from Mrs. Angelina's hotel," I stroke her hair and continue to hug her tightly. The people on the bus are quiet now under the policeman's angry gaze. *Where are they taking us?*

'Drancy' is written in black on the white sign on the side of the road between the houses, and after a few more minutes of driving, the bus turns and stops in front of a huge building.

"Everybody, get off and line up outside the bus, and no one try to escape," the policeman instructs us and gets off the bus.

The people get up and start getting off the bus. I take Rebecca in my arms and, with a moment's decision, take the young man's suitcase with me. If he's not hurt and they catch him and bring him here, at least he'll have his suitcase.

"You, Jews, don't push. We don't hand out money here," the driver says to the people getting off the bus before me. I want to kiss the Star of Life and Death on my dress, but my hands are busy. What is this place?

"Mommy, there are a lot of hunters here too," Rebecca says as we step off the bus with the other people.

"It's okay, honey, these are good hunters," I tell her, looking at the barbed wire fences surrounding a complex with many guards around.

Chapter Four

Drancy

"Everyone, line up," announces a policeman holding a gray metal megaphone to his mouth. His voice sounds strange coming from the metal tube that looks like an ice cream cone. "Madame, put the girl down," he turns to me. "Everyone lines up."

"Get down, the man wants you to get down," I say to Rebecca, but she holds me tightly and refuses to do so. I have no choice, so I put the suitcase on the ground and force her down. Where are we? I look around.

We're standing in front of a large four-story gray concrete building in the shape of the letter **n**, each side about 200-feet long. It was built in a modern style, with square lines and large windows. But it looks as if it has not yet been finished. The concrete is exposed, and the windows are just gaping holes without glass. In many of them, people are standing and watching us.

A high barbed wire fence and guard towers surround the large concrete building, and outside the fence stand two wooden huts. Policemen and German soldiers are standing next to them and watching us. What is this place? Will they send us to the border from here?

"Everyone, follow me," the policeman with the megaphone announces, and all the people who got off the buses begin to follow him through a gate in the fence, and into the yard at the center of the building. People are standing in the yard and watching us. Is everyone here Jewish? Most of them have a yellow badge on their clothes. My body is tense as we walk inside. While walking, I look back and see two policemen slamming the wire gate behind us. I've never been locked up like this. I feel pressure in my chest while walking among everyone in our group, looking around and trying to understand where we are.

The two buses that brought us here are moving away back towards the city with a monotonous rattle as if they want to escape this place. Driving slowly, they leave behind a cloud of bluish smoke and a stinking smell of gasoline that disappears into the air. For a moment, I envy the young man in the white shirt who ran away from the bus.

"It'll be fine, don't worry," I lean in and tell Rebecca, even though she walks by my side in silence as we follow one of the men who got off the bus. He wears a tattered blue suit, beret, and a backpack over his shoulder. Step by step, we move toward one of the entrances. There is a sign labeled 'Office' above the door.

"Name and certificates," a woman in a brown dress asks me once my turn arrives. She is sitting behind a simple table in the empty room. Only one simple lamp hanging from the ceiling illuminates her hands holding an open notebook.

"There was a mistake. My daughter and I need to get permits to cross into the Free Zone. We're both German, not French," I tell her while standing in front of the desk. I purposely let everyone pass before me in line so I could talk to the person in charge and explain our situation.

"Name and certificates," she repeats. "I'm sorry, I can't help you," she adds and reaches for our passports.

"Who can help us?"

"The French police, but are you sure you want their help?" She looks at me for a moment before lowering her gaze and writing our names in her notebook. I look at the yellow badge on her simple brown dress.

"What shall I do?" I ask her when she returns our passports.

"Find a place to sleep in one of the rooms in the building. The daily food distribution will arrive soon; don't miss it," she closes the notebook. "I'm sorry you arrived at this place," she adds. "We're all sorry we arrived at this place."

"Thank you," I tell her and walk away, leaving the room in tears. I shouldn't have come here.

"Let's go, Rebecca, let's find us a place to sleep," I pick her up, and we enter one of the entrances of the big building and start climbing the stairs.

"Mommy, when do we leave this place?" Rebecca asks later when I put her to sleep in one of the rooms we found. It is already dark outside, and a cool night wind penetrates through the missing window in the wall.

"Are you comfortable?" I stroke her hair. She's lying on a piece of cardboard and some straw I spread on the floor. A woman on the other side of the room gave it to us.

"My back hurts," she answers.

"I'll try to arrange something better for us," I try to open the suitcase of the man who ran from the bus, even though it's not mine. Maybe it has something to keep us warm, but it's locked, and I can't open it. "Tomorrow, I'll try to get us something softer to sleep on," I tell her and place the suitcase between us and a group of women sleeping on the other side, trying to give us some privacy. At least we ate something today. Earlier, we all received the daily meal of bread and soup.

"When are we going back to Angelina?"

"Try to sleep," I stroke her hair. Everything is dark outside; even the city of Paris is dark. Occasionally, I notice the beam of light from the searchlight placed on the guard tower outside the camp, scanning the barbed wire fences repeatedly.

"I want us to go to Dad."

"Me too," I whisper to her. I long to write him a letter so he'll come and get us, but I don't even have paper or a pen.

"I don't like this place."

"Tomorrow will be a better day, I promise. I'll go to the policeman, and he'll get us out of here," I whisper to her. I will go to one of the police officers and ask to meet with the commander. We are German citizens. We arrived here by mistake.

"The policeman of the good hunters, not the bad ones?" Rebecca asks in a sleepy voice.

"Yes, one of the good hunters."

73

"Where is my watch? Where did it go? I caress my bare arm. I get up in a panic and rub my eyes, looking around.

The morning sun penetrates through the window, and Rebecca is still sleeping on the floor. I search for my watch on the floor, maybe it fell during the night. With quick movements, I pick up the cardboard, move the straw, and search in every corner, but no, it's gone. I can't find it under the stranger's suitcase either. I keep stroking my arm, where the watch should be. What would I do without my gold watch? How will we survive without it? I feel my whole body tense with fear.

"Rebecca, wake up," I shake her.

"What?" She answers sleepily.

"Wake up, wake up," I pull her to her feet, checking where she slept and her dress. Maybe the watch fell when I hugged her at night, but it's not there. And where is the bread portion I saved for the morning? Where did it go? Did they take it from us too? How could I have been so careless?

I look at the French women sitting on the other side of the room. They're talking quietly to each other. Could it be that they stole my watch and bread?

"Excuse me, did you see if anyone walked around here at night?" I ask them.

"No," one of them shakes her head. "Did they take anything from you? You have to be careful here. There are thieves hanging around this place," she adds, turning her back to me. How does she know my things were stolen?

"Thank you," I reply and sit down, put my head in my hands, and start to cry. What will I do? Why didn't I hide the watch? How will I survive like this?

"Mommy," Rebecca starts to cry too. Why is this happening to me?

"Don't cry, sweetie," I hug her. "Mommy was just sad for a moment; everything is fine," I comfort her.

"No crying here. This is not a place for tears," I hear one of the French women say. "And if you want to keep food for yourself for the morning, sleep on it," she adds from the other side of the room. I don't respond and continue to hug Rebecca. We must get out of here. We won't survive like this. What about the gold coins I sewed into the hidden pocket of my dress before we went to the smuggler? I reach for them and sigh with relief when I feel their hard touch through my dress's fabric. At least I have these left. I have to do something. I'll get us out of here.

"Enough, Rebecca, no more crying," I wipe her eyes. "Let's go wash our faces, and Mommy will get us out of here."

"And we'll go to Dad like you promised?"

"Yes, we'll go to Dad as I promised." I hold her hand, take the stranger's suitcase, and we go down the stairs, leaving behind us only the piece of cardboard we slept on at night. I'll get us out of here. I'm a German citizen. We don't belong here.

We walk among all the people strolling in the courtyard at the center of the building, enjoying the morning sun. Some men play pétanque with small stones.

"Rebecca," I stop and bend down. "Do you see the girls over there?" I point to a group of girls standing in the center of the yard. "Go play with them for a few minutes while Mommy goes to talk to the policeman."

"I want to come with you," she clings to my legs.

75

"Sweetie, stay with them for a few minutes. They are lovely girls, and you can be friends." I walk with her towards the girls. Four girls in simple brown and gray dresses are standing and arranging wooden sticks on the ground, preparing to play a game.

"I don't want to play with them," she says in German.

"You have to," I gently remove her little hands clinging to me. "It's only for a few minutes, and if you behave well, I'll read to you about Sylvie the lady bear later."

"But the book is at Angelina's hotel."

"They'll bring it to us, I promise," I tell her, even though I'm no longer sure of anything. She must learn to be with girls her age, and I must get us out of here, back to Paris, and escape to Spain.

Rebecca doesn't answer, but walks and takes hesitant steps toward the girls. I watch her get close to them, take my passport out of my handbag, and head toward the entrance gate to the complex. I'll demand to speak to the commander. I'll explain everything to him.

I walk towards the barbed wire gate, noticing some people in the yard watching me. Am I acting right? I've been under Nazi rule for several years now, and I already know how to fear them, but I don't see the swastika flag anywhere.

As I approach the gate, I feel that maybe I'm making a mistake and I need to turn around and go back. Keep walking, keep walking. I've already turned around once when you could have tried to escape from Paris. I keep walking even though as I get closer to the gate and the two policemen guarding it, my steps become slower and slower. They're standing on either side of the gate, looking at me while their guns are resting on their shoulders. They have French police uniforms.

"What do you want?" One of the guards asks me when I stand before him. He is a big man with a thin black mustache. Now, it's too late to regret and turn back.

"I'm a German citizen. I shouldn't be here," I hand him my passport.

"You were brought here, so you should be here," he replies, handing me back the passport.

I take a deep breath. "I want to talk to someone in charge." I have to do everything I can to get us out of here.

"No problem," the policeman smiles and opens the gate for me. I look at him in disbelief. "Go, you can talk to him," he points to a German officer standing in the distance near a barracks. The officer is wearing a black uniform and talking to two German soldiers standing upright in front of him.

Is he serious? Is he setting a trap for me? I look at him in disbelief but start to walk past the barbed wire gate. This is our chance; maybe they'll let us out of here and take us back to Paris.

"Please, go," he continues to smile at me, making no move to stop or grab the rifle hanging over his shoulder.

"What are you doing?" I feel a strong hand grab my arm, pulling me back. I turn around and almost stumble. The suitcase in my hand falls to the ground. This is the other policeman. He's a little taller than me and thinner than his friend, who let me pass. He has brown hair and wears Windsor glasses with golden metal frames.

"Mathéo, let her through," the other policeman tells him. "She's German."

"Get out of here," Mathéo pushes me back into the yard, still holding my arm tightly. "Get out of here, and don't try to talk to the Germans," he releases me, turns around, and takes a few steps back.

I gasp and look at him as he picks up the suitcase and walks towards me, taking my hand and closing my fingers around the hard handle. "Don't do that again," he whispers to me and walks back to the gate.

I look at him for another moment, debating whether to argue with him. Is this policeman for me or against me?

"Get out of here, you dirty German," he yells at me, and I turn around and start walking down the yard, looking for Rebecca. She's playing with the other girls. What should I do?

"Go away, you're German, you're not French," I hear one of the girls shouting at Rebecca as she pulls one of them by the hair. I watch the girl scream in pain and start crying.

"Hit her," shouts another girl and pushes Rebecca, trying to pull her by the hair, but Rebecca escapes by running in the yard in a big circle. Her hair is wild and her brown dress swirls while the other girls chase her.

"Stop," I shout at them and start to approach them, but Rebecca doesn't notice me and runs to the group of men playing pétanque, bends to the ground, picks up some stones, and starts throwing them at the girls chasing her.

"Stop," I run towards them and see several other adults intervene and stop the girls from hitting each other.

"She's a dirty German, like all Germans," cries one of the girls, her face covered in tears.

"She said something mean," Rebecca runs to me, tearful and sobbing in German.

"We don't want Germans here," some women and men surround us. One woman hugs the crying girl.

"I'm sorry," I say to the girl's mother. "She doesn't speak French.

"Not only did you come here and conquer our country. Now your daughter is throwing stones at my daughter?" She yells at me. "Get out of here, go to a camp in Germany, not here."

"I can't go," I yell back at her as I start to cry. "Trust me, I want to."

"Transfer her to the Germans' camp," several women shout and approach me. A broad-bodied woman in a dirty beige dress snatches the suitcase from my hand.

"Give me back the suitcase," I yell at her and follow her while holding my sobbing Rebecca. I have no idea why I try so hard to guard the suitcase that isn't even mine. The people push us, and I feel their rough hands on my back.

"German woman, don't worry, no one wants your things. We have our own beautiful country," the woman answers, continuing to walk toward the building. I walk behind her, and several women follow me.

"This is your place," she throws the suitcase into one of the entrances. "Not in our area. There's a German woman like you," she adds. "And keep your misbehaved girl away from our children."

"Stay in your area," the other women mutter and walk away, leaving us in front of the empty stairs.

"I didn't do anything. They chased me, and I just pulled her hair, and she hit me," Rebecca continues to whine in German as I hug her, wiping away my tears.

"It's okay. You'll be friends in the end," I whisper to her and try to arrange her hair with my fingers. "Let's go upstairs. We'll find a room. Food will arrive soon."

We climb to the third floor, looking for a free room until we enter one of the rooms occupied by a woman who's slightly younger than me. She's twenty-four or twenty-five, has shoulder-length chestnut hair, and is leaning over a garment while holding a thread and needle.

"Excuse me, is there room here?" I ask her.

"Yes, of course," she answers in French with a German accent as she looks up at me.

"Nice to meet you, Sarah Bloch," I approach her and hold out my hand. "This is my daughter Rebecca."

"Nice to meet you, Charlotte Salomon," she puts down the garment and shakes my hand. "Is there a Mr. Bloch?" She looks at the empty door.

"No, there isn't," I answer, not wanting to tell her where he is.

"You are welcome in my humble place," she gestures with her hand, "a haven for German women without husbands who will protect them and give them a feeling of security."

I shiver in my sleep from the cold air and feel someone touch my hand. Is it Rebecca? I reach out to hug her, but it's not Rebecca. Who is it? I hold the hand tightly. Is someone trying to rob me again?

"It's okay, wake up," someone tells me. It's a woman.

"It's not okay," I shout at her and sit up while holding her hand. I won't let them steal from me again.

"Sarah, it's okay," she tries to reassure me. In the morning twilight, I notice her disheveled hair and the silhouette of her face. I reach out and pull her hair hard, hearing her scream.

"You won't steal from me. Enough! No more! Get out of here," I continue to pull her hair.

"Mommy!" Rebecca wakes up and shouts in tears. "What is she doing to you?"

"Sarah!" the woman shouts in pain. "It's me, Charlotte, your roommate. You're hurting me!"

"I don't care that you're my roommate. You won't steal from me," I release her hair and push her away. "Stay away from me!" I keep shouting, standing up and ignoring Rebecca's cries. Rebecca clings to the wall and watches us.

"Sarah, I woke you up so we could go together and get buckets of water. I'm not a thief!" Charlotte yells back at me.

"What is going on here?" Several women enter the room and ask in French. "Are you having problems with the German woman?" One of them asks me.

"Did you try to steal again?" Someone else asks.

"She tried to take something from me," I answer them, panting and pointing at Charlotte. "But I woke up." I carefully grope the fabric of my dress to make sure she didn't discover my hidden coins. Why is Rebecca crying so much?

"Once a thief, always a thief," says one of the women, thin and tall with curly hair.

"Come to me, Rebecca," I bend and hold her, trying to calm her down. No one will steal from me again. "And you, stay away from me," I tell Charlotte, feeling braver in the company of the other women standing at the door.

"I didn't steal from you. I tried to wake you up to go get water before the men took all the buckets and there wasn't any left," Charlotte takes a step back and shouts.

"Maybe we'll check her pockets to ensure she didn't steal anything. Show us your hands," says a large woman in a dark dress, approaching Charlotte.

"Get away from me," Charlotte screams and backs away, clinging to the wall, her voice sounding like a wounded animal. "Will you always hate me because I'm a stranger?"

"No, because you're a thief," the tall, curly-haired woman answers.

"Let's go, leave them alone; she's already learned her lesson," the big woman moves away from Charlotte. "And you," she turns to me, "don't be afraid of her. If she tries to take something from you, call us. We're on the other side of the corridor."

"Thank you," I say quietly and continue to caress Rebecca's back, taking her in my arms. "Shh... It's okay. Everything is okay. You can stop crying. Mommy is here protecting you."

"I won't wake you up again in the morning," Charlotte fixes her hair and dress and leaves the room. I hear her going down the stairs. Could it be that she wasn't trying to steal from me, and I blamed her for nothing? But the other women said she stole from them.

I put Rebecca down and look out the window. In the morning twilight, I see Charlotte standing among several men in the yard, holding a wooden bucket while waiting in line for the water tap.

"You can use the water," Charlotte later places the bucket of water in the center of the room. "Don't worry, I won't come near you. I'll stay in my corner," she says and sits down against the wall.

"Good," I respond, placing the stranger's suitcase between us to create a clear border. Why are they so angry with her?

"Why do they hate you?" I ask after a while. I mustn't trust her.

"Because everyone has to hate someone, and it's convenient for them to hate me." She looks up at the ceiling, and I think she has tears in her eyes.

"Did you steal from them?" I don't hold back and ask.

"It's none of your business." She wipes her eyes and looks away.

Two days later, the cold night's wind causes the raindrops to enter through the missing window. I hug Rebecca in the dark, trying to keep her warm. Her peaceful breathing calms me. Occasionally, the wind blows raindrops that hit me. Finally, I take the suitcase that stands as a borderline between me and Charlotte, place it between me and the window, and bend down as much as possible. I'll try to sleep.

"Don't you have something warmer in the suitcase?" Charlotte's voice comes out of the darkness. She lies on the other side of the room, next to the inner wall.

"The suitcase isn't mine," I reply.

"Whose is it then? Did you take it from someone?"

"It belonged to a young man on the bus that brought us here."

"And where is the young man?"

"He ran away when the bus stopped briefly and left the suitcase behind," I answer her. "When everyone got off, I saw it was left and took it. I didn't steal it," I add.

Charlotte says nothing, and I listen to the wind whistling outside. She must think I should have left it there, especially after I called her a thief two days ago. From the window, I can see the searchlight beam from the guard's tower traveling in the darkness, reflecting the raindrops as if they were stars of gold. "I didn't see what happened to him; maybe he managed to escape," I say. "So I took his suitcase; in case they catch him and bring him here, he'll have something."

"I think you can open his suitcase. He won't come back."

"I know," I reply. I hope he managed to escape to the Free Zone. Still, I can't bring myself to open the suitcase and rummage through his personal belongings.

"A makeup brush and an eye pencil," Charlotte says quietly after a few minutes.

"What?"

"That's what I stole from them. A makeup brush and an eye pencil," she continues. "I needed them, and they didn't, but they found out, and they've hated me ever since."

"Why did you need them? You don't wear makeup."

"Never mind, you wouldn't understand," she says into the darkness.

"And they didn't forgive you?" I ask her after a while. I want her to tell me so I can understand.

"The fact that I'm German didn't help. Nobody likes foreigners. I think it didn't help you either," she says. "Where did they bring you from?"

"From the Paris police station. I thought they would give us permits to pass into the Free Zone."

"I was in the Free Zone," she laughs bitterly. "I thought I had managed to escape them when I arrived from Germany to Nice three years ago."

"And what happened?"

"It turned out that even in the Free Zone, there are policemen who hunt Jews, put them on buses, and send them to Drancy."

"Have you been here long?"

"Long enough to know how things work in this place."

"Do you think we'll be here much longer?"

"You're cold, aren't you? You're getting wet," she ignores my question.

"We're fine, thanks," I feel a wave of raindrops hit me.

"Come by my side; the rain doesn't get in here."

"We get along fine here," I answer her, even though the rain is wetting us. I don't trust her.

"You need to take care of your child, so she doesn't get sick. There are no doctors or medicine here to treat her."

"Thank you," I say after a while. She is right.

I pick up my sleeping Rebecca, feel my way through the dark, and sit close to Charlotte.

"That way, it will be more comfortable for you. You won't get wet," she whispers to me. "And I think you should open this man's suitcase; pretend it's yours. Maybe there's a coat in there."

"I'll open it," I tell her, but I know I won't. I can't. I continue to hug Rebecca and get a little closer to Charlotte until I feel her body warmth. I'll try to close my eyes and sleep. The women in the other room will help me if she tries anything.

"Everyone, get to the square," I hear the announcer the following morning. I sit on the floor, hugging Rebecca and looking at Charlotte. What's going on outside?

"Captain Carl Becker," Charlotte says as she gets up. The stairwell is filled with the sound of people going down the steps. "Let's go," she approaches the entrance, "we have to hurry."

"Who is Captain Carl Becker?" I ask her as I lift Rebecca in my arms, and we join the people going down. A feeling of apprehension runs through my back.

From all the entrances, people come out to the yard, dotted with puddles of water from last night's rain. Everyone hurries to the yard's center until we all look like a dark mass. I walk through the crowd with Rebecca in my arms. The mud seeps into my old shoes, and I am careful not to slip.

"Pull back," Charlotte says and pulls my hand, trying to drag us back as we make our way. But more and more people arrive and fill the place, and I am pushed by other people until I have to let go of Charlotte's hand. The crowd is too big and pushes me forward. All I can do is hold Rebecca tightly in my arms and keep her from being crushed by the people. I feel like a log moving in a river of people, uncontrollable by the current. Where is Charlotte? I look around for her. She's the only one I know. But I can't see her, and I turn my gaze forward. Rebecca and I are almost at the front of the crowd.

"Put her down. She stands out," I hear a whisper, and a hand touches my shoulder. I turn my gaze, and it's Charlotte. "Do it now," she whispers, and I rush to lower Rebecca into the mud.

"Rebecca, sweetie," I whisper to her, "now stand up and don't talk. We all must be quiet, do you understand?" It seems to me that she is so frightened that there is no way she will speak. She looks at me with big eyes, and I am afraid she will burst into tears. I have to calm her down. "Everything is fine," I bend down and say to her while caressing her hair. "You will stand behind me and hold my leg tightly, and as soon as the policeman is done talking, we will go back to the room with Charlotte. Do you agree?"

Rebecca nods, and I get up and look forward, feeling her hands holding my dress from behind.

Several policemen stand before the crowd, their guns on their shoulders. I can distinguish between them the two I talked to at the gate that day, the big one with the thin black mustache and the slimmer one with the Windsor glasses. It seems to me that he surveys the crowd, and his gaze stops when he recognizes me. I cringe. I must be wrong. There are so many people here.

Suddenly, the audience falls silent.

I look to the sides and see that everyone is looking towards the entrance gate to the complex. The two policemen by the gate open it and salute a German officer in a black uniform who passes through it. He briefly salutes them back and enters the yard. Is he Captain Carl Becker? I look at Charlotte. She says nothing but points her finger at me to signal me to stay quiet and look ahead. The Nazi officer is tall and thin, his hair a dark wheat color, almost brown, and his chin is sharp and narrow. I can't see his eyes, which are almost hidden under his black visor hat.

One of the policemen, who is holding a megaphone in his hand, turns to the German officer, stands tall, and salutes while the Nazi officer walks slowly, his eyes scanning us. I shudder as he stands up, salutes back to the policeman, and motions to him with a slight movement of his hand covered in a black leather glove.

"Recently," the policeman picks up the megaphone and begins to speak, "new people have arrived here. These individuals do not fit and no longer deserve to be free citizens in the French National Socialist society that we established in cooperation with the Third Reich," he pauses and moves along the crowd, examining us. "We have decided that this is the right place for people like you..." He continues with the camp regulations, "... and by the grace of the Third Reich, you will receive one meal a day. You should appreciate the German people, who are at war against the English and Russian enemies, and are still ready to provide you with food." He finishes, taking the megaphone away from his mouth, and returns to the yard's center, careful not to step in a large puddle with his boots.

"How long will we be here?" Someone asks from the crowd, and murmurs are heard from every direction.

"Don't say a word," I hear Charlotte whisper as her hand holds mine behind my back.

"Come, come out, don't be shy about the question; it's an important one," the policeman calls out. After a moment, a woman emerges from the crowd and walks toward him hesitantly. She is about forty years old and wears a long blue dress. "Repeat the question," he addresses her.

"How long will we be here?" She asks quietly, her feet stepping in the puddle.

The French policeman looks at the Nazi officer, and he signals him with a slight, almost imperceptible movement of his head.

"Go to him. He will answer your question," he tells the woman, turning his head toward the Nazi officer.

In the silence, I hear the gusts of wind and the sounds of her steps in the mud as she walks slowly towards the Nazi. We all watch her.

A slight cough is heard as she stands before him and looks down. What will he do to her? How foolish was I a few days ago to try to talk to him? I can feel Rebecca's hands holding my legs tightly and Charlotte's holding my hand.

The Nazi officer waits a second, then raises his hand and strikes the woman with a small whip he holds. She screams and falls into the mud. Everyone around me is silent, and no one moves.

"Does anyone have any more questions?" The policeman raises the megaphone to his mouth and asks us. Only the sound of the wind answers him with a soft whimper.

"In this camp, you are guests of the Third Reich, and only he will decide how long you will be here," he speaks into the megaphone and then turns and salutes the Nazi officer, who salutes him back and walks towards the exit gate, passing the guards on his way out.

Only after he disappears into the wooden shack outside the fences does the policeman turn around and leave the gate, and the people slowly start to disperse. I pick up Rebecca and hug her, ignoring the mud from her shoes that stains my dress. My feet are frozen from standing in the puddle for so long.

"Let's go back to the room," Charlotte tells me quietly, and I nod. But before we start walking, I turn and look towards the gate. Most of the policemen had already left the yard. Only the policeman with the round glasses who shouted at me at the gate remained standing. It seems to me that he's watching me, but I'm not sure. There are so many people around me. Why did he protect me that day?

Chapter Five

Autumn

"Mommy, when will my beautiful dress arrive from Paris? And my book, too?" Rebecca asks me a few days later while we stand by the fence and look at the houses in the distance.

"In a few days," I reply quietly as I place my hand on the barbed wire fence, feeling the coolness of the metal. I notice a few people walking between the houses. I long to trade places with them and not be confined to this cage.

"But you said that a few days ago," Rebecca continues to ask.

"Yes, and it hasn't been a few days yet," I continue watching a woman in a dark dress walking and pulling a cow tied with a rope behind her. She leads her cow leisurely until they both disappear into one of the yards. I imagine the taste of fresh milk on my lips.

"But you promised," Rebecca insists, "and you always say that promises should be kept."

"That's right, the suitcase with Sylvie's book will arrive," I stroke her hair. Since we got here, I haven't been able to shower her, and her hair is disheveled and messy. "Promises must be kept," I look back at the houses outside and the road leading to Paris. "You also promised to take care of us," I whisper. "You promised we would follow you to Madrid."

"What?" Rebecca asks me.

"Nothing," I notice a rumbling bus coming from the road toward the camp. In front of it is a black police pickup truck leading the way. A few policemen come out of the barracks and watch its arrival. I think I can spot the policeman with the glasses among them. I think his name is Mathéo. That's what his friend called him. "Sweetie, let's go back," I say to Rebecca. I don't want to be at the gates when the people get off the bus and walk in, not knowing they have arrived at a prison.

"Can we stay a little longer? Please?" She looks up at me.

"Only for a few minutes."

"I promise," she says and grabs the wire fence, her little fingers wrapping around the metal wire.

The bus stops in the parking lot with its engine still running for a few moments, filling the air with the pungent smell of burnt gasoline. I breathe it eagerly; I miss the smell of the city so much.

"Mommy, he opened the door," Rebecca points, placing her hand over the fence. I glance sideways at the guard, worried he might do something to her, but his attention is on the bus parked outside the gate.

The policemen who emerged from the barracks surround the bus; their rifles slung carelessly over their shoulders. But I don't think they need their rifles. No one can escape now; it's too late.

"One, two, three..." Rebecca counts the people who get off the bus, holding their suitcases and looking around.

"This way," one of the policemen shows them the open gate waiting for them, and another policeman shouts at them to start walking inside. I look at the policeman with the glasses. He stands motionless and watches the people walking into the camp, not rushing them in like his colleagues but also not helping the elderly woman with her long coat, to which her yellow badge is sewn. She's struggling to walk from the bus to the gate. What kind of man is he? Why did he choose to work here?

"Everyone got off," Rebecca whispers, and I hear disappointment in her voice.

"That's right," I reply when the bus driver starts again and closes the door. "Let's go back."

"And no one brought my suitcase. Can I stay a little longer?" She asks sadly.

"No, it's late. The sun will set soon."

"But maybe another bus will arrive."

"There won't be another bus today," I tell her. "They drive in together."

"Maybe there will be another bus," she insists, "and with it our suitcase." Her grip tightens around the barbed wire.

"Buses are not allowed to travel at night, and it's almost dark. Maybe tomorrow the bus will bring the suitcase," I pick her up. I don't want to tell her that our suitcase will never arrive. "Let's go; it's time to keep promises," I tell her, although it's not her promise I'm referring to.

"Charlotte, do you have any paper and pencil?" I ask her when I enter the room. She is facing away from me and quickly tried to hide something under the cardboard she sleeps on. "What are you doing?" I ask her.

"Nothing," she says, turning to smile at me. "I think I have some. Why do you need it?"

"I want to write a letter. I know there's no mail, but I have to write one," I say as I take Rebecca off my hands and look at Charlotte's piece of cardboard. *What is she hiding from me?*

"This is all I have," she says apologetically, taking a small, crumpled piece of paper and a pencil from her bag and handing them to me. "Who are you writing to?"

"I want to write to my husband to come help us. He must do something," I say, looking at the clouds outside as they cover the last rays of sun.

"What exactly will he do?" She asks, somewhat mockingly.

"I don't know," I hesitate before answering, "but he will find a solution. He always does. He is a respectable businessman."

"A respectable businessman who left you in Paris?"

"He went to Madrid a month before the Germans started the war. He didn't intend to leave us behind. The plan was for us to join him and then continue to America," I explain as I place the paper on the floor and begin writing.

"He's your husband, and you know him better than I do, so I probably shouldn't interfere," she says. "But he won't come here to help you."

"He must. He told me to trust him, so I must trust him," I respond, trying to focus on writing the first words.

"No one will come from Madrid back to Nazi Germany to save you, even if you write him thirty letters."

"Mommy, are you writing Dad a letter?" Rebecca interrupts our conversation.

"Rebecca, what did I tell you about interrupting adults' conversations?" I turn to her, my tone stern.

"Sorry," she steps back and leans against the wall, her fingers fiddling with the simple ribbon tying her hair. I think she's about to cry.

"I'll finish talking to Ms. Charlotte, and then you can join the conversation," I tell her. Why is all this happening to me while my husband escaped? "He's going to do something; he has to," I whisper to Charlotte, trying to keep Rebecca from overhearing.

"You need to understand that the only ones who can do anything here are you and the police who guard us," Charlotte whispers back. "They can organize and arrange things if you have a way to pay them."

"They're police officers; I don't trust them."

"There's also Mr. Charpak," she adds.

"Who's Mr. Charpak?"

"I haven't met him, but I've heard of him. He's stuck in here with us. He was a trader in Paris, in markets you and I wouldn't go to, if you know what I mean," she smiles slyly. "Now he's a trader here. There's always a demand for traders, even inside a detention camp."

"And how do they get paid?" I ask her, feeling my stomach churning. I think I know the answer.

"French francs, German money, cigarettes, he and the officers accept everything, even that kind of payment," she points at her breasts.

"Mommy, what's 'payment'?" Rebecca asks.

"Never mind," I reply. For a long time now, she has been hearing more than she needs to hear. "Mr. Charpak can send a letter for me?"

"I think he can do anything, if you're willing to pay the price," she approaches me and whispers, so Rebecca won't hear. "But it's a waste of your money; no husband will come to save you. It's time you start trusting yourself."

"Where can I find him?" I ask her as I bend down, continuing to write on the floor.

"People like him are like stray cats; when you look for them, you find them."

"Can you watch over Rebecca for a few minutes?" I ask her when I finish writing. I'm not like Charlotte. I have a husband. I have someone to trust. I also have a way to pay him.

⸎

"Excuse me, where can I find Mr. Charpak?" I ask as I walk down to the yard in the center of the building. I turn to a man wearing a Homburg hat and a brown suit, which is covered with mud stains.

"I don't know," he answers, but he seems to be lying.

I turn to the group of men playing pétanque in the center of the yard, but they also don't know, so I continue to walk around the yard asking people.

"Why do you need him?" A woman asks me. She is about my age and leans indifferently against the wall near one of the entrances.

"He's a trader, isn't he?" I ask her.

"Yes, he's a trader, if you have something to trade," she replies, scanning my body, her gaze lingering on my chest.

"I need something from him," I say, crossing my arms to hide my hands.

"Entry three, second floor, you'll find him there."

"Thank you."

"You're welcome," she replies as she lights a cigarette. "What are we women here for if not to help each other?"

I thank her again and walk away. I have another way to pay him. If the rumors are true, he can send my letter to my husband.

The stairs leading up to the second floor are similar to the ones in our entry, but here, blankets and fabric cover the apartment entrances, offering privacy.

"Who are you looking for?" Asks a young man leaning against the wall in the stairwell on the second floor. He's smoking a cigarette and wears a light button-up shirt, suspenders, and a beret.

"I'm looking for Mr. Charpak," I answer, trying to get used to the cigarette smoke that fills the stairwell.

"What do you want from him?"

"I need something from him," I say, standing before the young man and feeling tense. He also scans my body, his eyes examining my face and then moving down to my chest and hips.

"Mr. Charpak, someone is looking for you," he calls into the room, moving aside the floral sheet covering the doorway.

"Let her in," someone replies from inside, and the young man signals me to enter.

Inside the smoke-filled room, an upside-down wooden crate serves as a makeshift table. Several men sit on upside-down wooden buckets, playing cards around it.

"What do you want?" One of the men asks, turning to me. He wears a wrinkled blue jacket and has a cigarette in his mouth.

"I'm looking for Mr. Charpak," I answer, feeling embarrassed as all the men stare at me.

"What do you want from him?" Asks the man in the blue jacket. Is he Mr. Charpak?

"I need something," I say, raising my chin.

"I'm out," a big man, almost bald and about fifty years old, says to his friends. He puts his cards on the table, then stands up from the improvised table and approaches me. He wears a blue workman's shirt and plain blue trousers secured with a brown belt. "What do you want?" He holds my arm and guides me to a side room. In the room, he stands uncomfortably close to me, and his breath reeks of cigarettes.

"I was told you could arrange things," I say, looking up at him.

"People need things. We are Jews, and we help each other. It's a mitzvah," he says with a smile I don't trust. It makes him seem like a fat cat eyeing its prey.

"I need to send a letter to my husband in Madrid," I show him the paper I'm holding. Saying the words 'my husband' gives me courage.

"How much are you willing to pay for the delivery?" He touches the folded paper in my hand.

"I have this," I take out the remaining money in my wallet and the food coupons. They hold little value here.

"I'm a merchant, not a beggar," he laughs, revealing yellow teeth in the weak light. "Do you know how many hands this letter must pass through to reach Madrid? And each of them will want their share."

"So what do you want as payment?" I try to distance myself from him in the small room. The rough concrete wall rubs against my back. I consider my hidden gold coins. Should I use them to pay for the letter?

"You can give me what women know how to give," he steps even closer. His hand reaches out and touches my waist. I struggle to breathe, and my body tenses.

"I'm a married woman. You know I'm not allowed to do such a thing," I whisper.

"I don't see that God is watching over us here," Mr. Charpak looks up at the ceiling. "But if it doesn't suit you," he steps back from me, "bring me some clothes. Winter is coming, and people will pay a lot for warm clothes. You can decide," he chuckles, "a letter in exchange for a few minutes of warmth with a man who isn't your husband, or giving up clothes for the winter. That's how it is in Judaism; God has always presented us with difficult choices."

"I'll think about it," I say, feeling my face flush. "I'll be back," I turn and hurry out of the small room into the larger space where the men continue their game. I'll get him his clothes. I'll find a way to pay him. But on my way down the stairs, I feel the cool breeze and think about the approaching winter.

"Charlotte, do you have a knife?" I ask as I walk back into our room. I need to hurry; soon the curfew will begin, and it will be forbidden to be outside.

"Why do you need a knife? Did you send the letter?"

"No, I didn't send it. I wasn't willing to pay what he wanted. I want to open this." I hold the stranger's suitcase. "He won't arrive."

"And what about our suitcase? It won't arrive either?" Rebecca stands beside me. What should I say to her?

"Sweetie, they decided to switch, and we received this suitcase instead of ours," I tell her as I take the knife Charlotte handed me and try to break the lock.

"What about my green dress and my book?"

"Maybe there's a dress and a book in here too," I say, giving her a quick glance before returning to the lock. "Perhaps it's a better suitcase with surprises," I tell her.

"Okay," Rebecca nods and approaches the suitcase. She watches my hand, holding the knife, as I struggle to open the lock. "Maybe there's a Sylvie teddy bear and chocolate inside," she suggests.

"Maybe, we'll see," I whisper to myself, hoping she won't be disappointed when she discovers there isn't a Sylvie teddy bear and chocolate. I hope I won't be disappointed to find there are no warm winter clothes.

"Try using a stone," Charlotte suggests.

"Rebecca, go down to the yard and get me a stone," I tell her without turning around. I hear her running as she descends the stairs.

"Is it okay that you sent her all by herself?" Charlotte asks after a moment.

"I can't watch her all the time," I reply, but then I go to the window and look out into the yard. Rebecca runs across the yard, picks up one of the stones used by the pétanque players from the empty yard, and hurries back.

"I brought it," she says, entering the room after a moment, panting. She hands me the stone and stands beside the suitcase, waiting for her surprise. I hold the knife close to the lock, and Charlotte strikes it with the stone until the lock breaks, making a metallic sound.

"Let's see what's inside," Charlotte whispers as I open the suitcase.

"A jacket," I say, pulling out a men's blue jacket.

"And two pairs of pants," Charlotte lays them out on the floor.

"And underwear."

"Is there a green dress?" Rebecca asks, hopeful.

"And good leather shoes," I take them out of the suitcase. "I need shoes; mine are falling apart."

"They'll be too big for you," Charlotte points out.

"It's better than worn-out shoes."

"Mommy, is there a green dress, a book, and chocolate?" Rebecca bends down and takes out the remaining clothes from the suitcase, searching under them.

"No, there isn't a green dress, a book, or chocolate," I say to her in a disappointed tone. "Again, they got the suitcases mixed up." What else should I tell her?

"They keep mixing them up," she whispers, and I see she's about to cry.

"You need to tell her the truth," Charlotte whispers to me in French. "She needs to grow up."

"She's five and a half years old," I whisper back. "She hasn't played with other children for a year. In Berlin and Paris, she was a Jew who wasn't allowed to enter playgrounds, and here, she's bullied because she's German. She has very little child-hood left to hold on to."

"So, what will you tell her?"

"You know what?" I hug Rebecca and stroke her hair. "To-morrow, we will go back to wait for the bus. I will talk to the person in charge of the buses to see what happened to our suitcase."

"Are you crazy?" Charlotte whispers to me.

"I'm a mother."

"And what will you do?"

"I'll be fine. Is there anything you need here?" I gather the stranger's clothes from the suitcase and set the shoes aside. They are more valuable.

"These," she takes two tank tops.

"I'll be right back." I collect all the other clothes and shoes. "Charlotte, can you watch Rebecca for a few minutes?"

"Would you give up all these clothes to send a letter?" She asks me.

"Please, it's important. Just stay with her for a few minutes," I answer and leave the room, holding the clothes in my hands. I have to do this; I won't regret it.

"Is this what you're offering for the letter?" Mr. Charpak approaches me a few minutes later in the side room. He feels the fabric of the stranger's pants and shoes in his hands. "I thought you'd changed your mind. Where did you get them? They're men's clothes." In the other room, I hear the men playing cards and raising the stakes.

"They are my husband's," I reply quietly and try to stand tall. He mustn't sense my fear.

"The one you're sending the letter to?" He laughs mockingly. "Okay, give me the letter. I'll see what I can do."

"No," I reply, taking a deep breath. "I want something else."

"What?" He watched me closely.

"A coat for a girl and a pair of women's shoes for myself."

"You're giving up the letter?"

"The letter will wait," I push the clothes into his arms. "I want a warm coat for the winter for a girl, and a fabric to seal a window against the rain."

"As you wish," he takes the clothes and steps back. "You must know that the Germans have been advancing in Russia for months. At this rate, they'll rule the world, and we will have to get used to it. I can't promise I'll be able to send the letter in the future."

"A warm coat for the girl, shoes for myself, and fabric for the window," I respond, hoping I made the right decision.

"Let's go back. It's late," I say to Rebecca a few days later. The sky is cloudy, and it will rain soon.

"But Mommy, the bus hasn't arrived yet," she continues to stand there, holding the barbed wire fence with her small hands.

"Maybe it won't come today. Maybe it went to a different camp today."

I look at her. She's lost weight in the last months, but at least she has a coat to keep her warm. I shiver slightly in the autumn

103

breeze, and I reach out to touch the hidden gold coins in the dress. Soon I'll have to decide – a coat for me or food for her.

"Will the bus give our suitcase to someone else?" She turns and looks at me with a concerned expression.

"No, of course not," I say, placing my hand on her cold palm that clutches the wire fence. "Your suitcase belongs only to you. We'll wait a few more minutes; if the bus doesn't come, we'll go back and return tomorrow."

"And if the bus doesn't come tomorrow?"

"If it doesn't come tomorrow, then we'll ask the hunters when it will arrive," I answer without thinking. I hope the bus won't come soon or at all, as the camp grows more crowded each day. Queues for food distribution and the water tap grow longer, as do the arguments and quarrels among the people who have nothing to do but gossip and fight.

One of the policemen standing near their barrack begins to approach us, and I instinctively step back. But then I see another policeman approach him and whisper something, prompting the first one to turn back while the other walks toward us.

"Let's go, Rebecca. We need to leave," I say, picking her up in my arms. The approaching policeman makes me nervous, even though they are French and not Nazis. I can't forget what happened during the muster in front of the Nazi officer.

"But, Mommy, you promised a few more minutes."

"Those minutes have passed," I tell her. The policeman reaching us is the one with the Windsor glasses, and he signals us to stop. What should I do? I feel the urge to turn and blend into the crowd behind us. But I have to stand still. These are the rules here.

"Do you need anything?" He asks, standing on the other side of the fence.

"No," I respond, keeping my eyes on him. I can see his brown-green eyes through his round glasses.

"Then why are you standing by the fence and looking outside?"

"We're looking at freedom," I reply, regretting my words as soon as they leave my mouth. What was I thinking being so rude to a policeman who could punish me? I have to thank him for saving my life when I wanted to speak with the Nazi commander.

He remains silent, his eyes fixed on me. I slowly lower my gaze, observing his perfectly ironed uniform, the embroidered ranks on his arm, the rifle strap hanging over his shoulder, the leather belt around his waist, and the pistol placed in a shiny, oiled leather holster. I must apologize; I have a child to care for.

"I apologize, and thank you," I whisper to him, standing with a humble look. I know how to stand like this since the word 'Jew' became a curse, and we were forced to embroider the yellow Stars of Life and Death on our clothes.

"Join the others. It will rain soon," he says after a moment.

"Yes, sir," I respond and turn around, walking away slowly, my entire body tense. Will he do anything to me once I turn my back?

"Mommy, what did you say to him?" Rebecca asks me in German.

"I asked him when the bus would come," I reply, continuing to walk slowly, feeling my back painfully exposed.

"And what did he say?"

"That the bus will not come today," I near the group of people standing in the yard and allow myself to turn around and relax. He is still there, watching me, his hands at his sides and his gun resting on his shoulder. After a moment, he turns and rejoins his friends sitting on a wooden bench outside the barrack, observing us.

"Mommy, is he a good hunter or a bad hunter?" Rebecca asks, and I feel her arms wrap around me.

"I don't know, sweetie," I keep my eyes on him, "I don't know."

It's night and dark outside as Charlotte and I lie in our room. Rebecca is already asleep, and the people in the surrounding apartments have finally fallen silent.

The searchlight from the watchtower occasionally passes over the walls of the building, its strong beam illuminating the room for a moment before being replaced by the blackout darkness. I can hear a woman and a man faintly talking outside at one of the entrances, but they also fall silent, and peace reigns in the camp again.

"There will always be women willing to sell," Charlotte says quietly.

"Themselves?" I whisper to her. "Who will buy? Everyone's money is running out."

"There are always those who have money," I hear her from the darkness. "They say the French police also come to visit at night," she says ironically. "In the morning, they point a weapon at you, and at night, they point another weapon at you."

"They delight in taking the hardest payment from us."

"Especially when we're alone; we're easy prey."

"It's hard to be alone again, especially after I got used to trusting him," I say to her, debating whether to tell her about the offer I received from the smuggler just because I was alone with a girl and my husband wasn't there. I'm sure she faced such suggestions during the years she was without a man to protect her. "What about Mr. Salomon?" I ask after a while, even though it may not be appropriate. "Wasn't there someone?"

"Men don't want to marry women like me," she whispers.

"What does that mean?"

"Scatterbrains, women who want to be independent, to create," she says. "Those who love their freedom."

"There must also be men who love their freedom, don't you think?" I try to understand what she means. I like having a man who watches over me, even if he isn't here now.

"The Nazis came to power in 1933. They've been persecuting me for eight years," she pauses for a moment before continuing. "I wanted to be free from them, so I fled to the south of France, to Nice. The men I knew in Berlin at that time didn't think freedom was so important and stayed. But it didn't change anything. The Nazis had other plans, and they also came to France and caught me."

"And you came here alone? Didn't you meet anyone there?"

"Do you see anyone else in this room with me besides you and your girl?"

"Sorry, I didn't mean to offend you," I say quietly.

"I left my family in Berlin. I had grandparents in Nice, and I stayed with them," she says after a while.

"And what happened to your family?"

"They had different notions about freedom, like committing suicide instead of living under the Nazis regime, except for one of them who tried to touch me. Apparently, the desire for women to pay with sex doesn't go away with age. Nor does it disappear within the family. As you can imagine, after that, I wasn't into men."

"I'm sorry that happened to you," I say, wanting to hug her, but unsure how she'll react or if it's appropriate.

"It's okay. I've always had my world that allows me to escape into my freedom."

"What worlds?" I ask as I caress Rebecca's head, who is sleeping next to me.

"You're also alone now, without a husband," she changes the subject.

"Yes, I'm on my own, and with a girl I have to care of."

"There is a classroom here for all the children. She should go there. The people here took one of the apartments and turned it into a school, so the children don't wander around all day doing nothing and fighting with each other like the adults."

"She doesn't know how to get along with other children. She has already met them in the yard, and they started fighting. She barely speaks French, and they make fun of her."

"They say there's a strict teacher there, Mr. Gaston. He'll take care of her."

"I'm worried about her. How will she manage with the other children?"

"She has to learn to get along."

"Did you have a strict teacher at school? I don't think you knew how to get along with him," I whisper.

"No, I didn't know," she answers me, and I think she's laughing, "but I could run away to Nice in the south of France. She has nowhere to run, so she'll learn."

"Tomorrow, I will try to send her to the classroom," I continue stroking Rebecca's hair.

"You have to, so that she grows up like you and not like me."

"I just want us to get through this war and get out of here."

"Then send her tomorrow so she can learn French, at least."

"Good night, Charlotte," I say to her after a while.

"Good night, Sarah," she answers, and I close my eyes. It's good to have someone here to talk to at night, not just a five-and-a-half-year-old girl.

"Do I have to go to school?" Rebecca asks me the following morning.

"Yes, you must," I give her two slices of bread I saved for her from yesterday.

"And what if the bus arrives?"

"It will come after you finish studying and playing with the other children," I bend down and tie her shoelaces. "The rabbit runs and jumps into the burrow, and there are his ears," I tell her as my fingers tie the loops, and she laughs. She needs to learn to tie her shoes. She also needs to laugh more.

"Do you think the hunters will hunt the rabbit?"

"No, the rabbit will run away quickly, they won't catch it. Now we're going to class."

"What if the other kids hit me?"

"You need to learn to manage alone," I hold her hand as we leave the room.

"Bye, Ms. Charlotte," she says.

"Bye, Rebecca, behave yourself," Charlotte says, and we go down the stairwell between the neighbors' apartments and down to the yard.

A line of people is already waiting by the single faucet to fill buckets with water. I notice two policemen walking in the yard, patrolling the area. In the last few weeks, the fights and conflicts have increased as the camp becomes more crowded. Luckily, no one else has come to our room yet.

"Mommy, my stomach hurts," Rebecca whispers as we approach the class. On the concrete wall is a small sign that reads 'School.'

"You'll have fun and meet new kids," I promise her, even though I don't believe my own promise. She needs the company of other children.

Slowly and quietly, I open the classroom door, and we both go inside.

The small room is full of children of different ages sitting on wooden chairs beside simple tables. At the front, the teacher stands next to a wooden board, writing words in French with chalk. Everyone turns their gaze toward us as we stand in the doorway.

"Yes, please?" The teacher stops writing on the board and asks me in a sharp voice. He has a large, narrow nose and is nearly bald, his baldness glistening in the sunlight coming through the window.

"I brought my daughter, Rebecca, to study," I say to him and smile awkwardly.

"Sit there," he points with a large wooden ruler he holds, indicating an empty chair at the end of the room. I lead Rebecca to the corner of the room and sit her in the empty chair. The girl sitting next to Rebecca is much older.

"Mommy, I don't feel well," she whispers in German as she tries to hold my hand tightly and refuses to let go. I hear the children around laughing.

"Quiet," the teacher thunders in his voice and hits the wooden ruler on his table, and everyone falls silent.

"Bye, Rebecca," I let go of her hand and stand next to her for another moment, looking around at the students. Most children are older than her, and they all look at us, scrutinizing Rebecca and me.

"Madame, may we continue our lesson?" The teacher turns to me with a scolding tone, and for a moment, I feel like a six-year-old girl who wants to run away from the classroom in the face of his angry look and the wooden ruler in his hand.

"Sorry," I say and rush out of the classroom in front of all the children's eyes and close the door behind me.

"Girl, get up and say your name," I hear the teacher say behind the closed door, and after a moment, the children laugh. What are they laughing at?

"Quiet," I hear him thunder again, and then the strike of the ruler. Although I want to go back in and take her with me, I turn my back and leave the building. She must learn to get along with the other children.

Later, shortly before the children finish school, I stand at the window and look out. I wait here for her, watching to see how she manages on her own. Many people walk around the large yard between the fences, enjoying the rays of the winter sun. They escape from the crowded rooms where there is only boredom, laundry hanging on ropes, and the smell of sweat. Anything is better than being idle and quarreling with each other.

The guards near the gate also come out of their guard post and stroll along the fence. In the distance, on the road that emerges between the houses and leads to the camp, I notice a German commander's army vehicle. I'm startled, even though there is no reason to be. They've already imprisoned us here. What else can they do to us?

"What did you say?" Charlotte asks and approaches the window beside me.

"I muttered something about being locked up here," I continue looking at the vehicle painted in gray-green camouflage colors as it slowly drives and stops in front of the German commander's barrack. A soldier gets out of the car and opens the back door. A woman in a gray coat and two girls in yellow dresses and brown coats emerge. The woman bends down and speaks to the girls, who nod their heads and start running in the grass in front of the hut while she stays to watch them. From a distance, they look a little older than Rebecca.

Suddenly, the door opens, and the Nazi officer emerges in his black uniform. He politely kisses his wife on the cheek and walks toward the girls, leaning down and spreading his arms toward them. They run to him for a hug. How can such an evil man be such a good father and hug his daughters like that? I look down and search for Rebecca in the large yard, but she hasn't left the study room yet.

"Captain Carl Backer. His wife and daughters come to visit him now and then and play out here," Charlotte says bitterly. "Like every good German family, they come to visit dad at work."

"We Jews are their job," I say and look at them again. I think he takes a candy out of his pocket, and they clap their hands excitedly. "Sometimes I think they just want to wipe us from the earth."

"Then they won't have any more work to do," Charlotte chuckles. "Sarah, the children are out of school," she points with her head at the yard, and I stop looking at the commander's daughters who are playing outside the fence and search for Rebecca inside our prison.

She is playing tag with the other children. They chase each other in the yard among all the adults, and I smile. Maybe she will manage after all. I can try to imagine that everything here is almost normal. Without the wire fences surrounding us and without the Nazis who hate us. Without the French police who guard the gates, the watchtowers, and without the constant nagging hunger in my stomach. I look again at the commander's daughters. One day, Rebecca will also be free like them.

Shouting voices from below make me move my eyes and look for Rebecca. To my horror, I see her pull another girl's hair while the girl screams in pain and tries to hit her. Why did she get involved again? I have to go down to separate them.

"Let her fend for herself," Charlotte says to me.

"But that girl is hitting her."

"If she doesn't learn to fight back, they will always beat her," she says quietly, and I remain standing, watching as several other children surround them and beat Rebecca, who struggles with them like a wounded animal.

"I have to go down and help her," I feel the tears well up in my eyes.

"She's doing fine. Look, that's how kids are," Charlotte points with her head. Rebecca manages to free herself from them and runs away toward the fence surrounding the complex. The children chase her at first, but as they get close to the fence, they leave her and return to their game of tag as she watches them from a safe distance. I hope she didn't rip her dress. I've already had to sew it twice.

I look at her. She's so alone there, standing by the barbed wire fence. But Charlotte is right. I can't protect her. I must let her learn how to manage on her own. She turns and looks at the camp commander's daughters, who are playing outside the Germans' barracks, and then she starts walking and approaches the gate. What is she doing? Does she want to join them?

"Rebecca," I shout to her even though she is far away and can't hear me, "Rebecca," I scream again, step away from the window, leave our room, and run down the stairs to the yard. Why is she going to the gate? She knows it's not allowed. Why didn't I go downstairs when she started fighting with the kids? Run, run, don't stop. I pass two women and a man slowly climbing up the stairs, pushing myself between them without apologizing and keep running. What will the police do to her if she approaches them?

From the building's exit, I continue to run toward the gate. I see her standing with her back to me and talking to one of the gate policemen at the gate. I approach and pick her up.

"Sorry, officer, she's just a little girl," I tell him as I hold her tightly while panting, "Rebecca, you mustn't talk to the policeman like that," I say and take a few steps back from him, so he won't punish us.

"Then why did she ask me?" He asks me, and I turn my eyes away from Rebecca and see that it is Mathéo, the policeman with the round glasses.

"Sorry, I apologize," I say, still panting. "What did she ask you? Rebecca, did you want to go outside?" I look at her again.

"She asked me if I was a good hunter."

"She's sorry," I say. "She's just a little girl. She confuses reality with stories she hears," I look into his eyes. Does he have kind eyes? He doesn't smile at me, and the other policeman at the gate, who is not far away, listens to us. "Rebecca, apologize to the policeman," I tell her firmly. Why did she do that?

"I didn't mean to," she begins to cry.

"Tell her I can't protect her from the other kids." The policeman says.

"Sorry, it won't happen again, I promise," I start slowly walking back, away from him, while holding her tightly. I want to scream at him, and tell him to speak to her directly. I also want to yell at her father that I need his help.

"You can go now," he tells me quietly and nods. Still panting, I turn my back to him and start walking to the building. I'll have to figure out how to discipline her.

"You're not allowed to talk to the police," I raise my voice at her when we reach our room. "Now turn around and face the wall." I lose control of myself and spank her, ignoring her cries. "You need to behave," I hit her again while she whimpers in pain. Around me, I notice some neighbors from the surrounding apartments have come to see what the noise is about, but I ignore them. I feel a surge of anger until I want to scream. "You need to learn to get along with the other kids," I continue yelling at her.

"Great, it's time to teach the little German a lesson," I think I hear one of the neighbors say, but I don't respond.

"She causes trouble for everyone. It's good her mother realized it was time to discipline her," says another neighbor.

"Enough, enough, she's learned her lesson," Charlotte puts her hand on my arm.

"She needs to learn," I respond to Charlotte and turn back to Rebecca. "I'd rather you cry now than later," I shout at her while she screams. "Now go to the corner and calm down." I release her and walk past the onlookers who have entered the apartment to witness the scene. I head to the stairwell. It's so difficult to care for her all the time in this wretched place.

Only in the stairwell do I sit down and let my tears flow, not bothering to wipe them away. Why isn't he here to discipline her? It's the father's job.

Later that night, when it's already dark, and Rebecca has fallen asleep, I stroke her hair. I couldn't bring myself to hit her with a belt or a shoe as others did.

"She'll be fine," Charlotte whispers to me.

"Yes," I reply, trying to wipe away the tears that pour down my cheeks every time I think about what I did to her. Life here is so hard.

"She has to grow up. There's no other option."

"She's a five-and-a-half-year-old girl, not yet six. She doesn't even know how to tie her shoes yet. How grown up does she have to be?"

"I don't know anymore," Charlotte says. "What will happen if you won't be here to protect her?"

Chapter Six

Day by Day

"Behave yourself in class," I bend down and say goodbye to Rebecca at the beginning of another day. After she enters the classroom, I will take the wooden bucket and head to join the never-ending line at the water tap, followed by the line for food.

"But he disciplines me," she replies in German.

"What language have we decided we speak?" I remind her.

"French," she answers reluctantly.

"Then say it in French."

"Bye, Mommy," she turns and runs into the classroom, and I get up and sigh. When will she grow up and realize she has to change? When will he stop disciplining her?

I look at my fingers, remembering all the times in which my teacher, Mr. Werner, used to hit me with his ruler when I was a child. She must grow up and understand, like I did. I clutch the empty wooden bucket and walk to the line of men, positioning myself between them, and ignore their looks. I don't have a husband to help me in carrying the heavy water bucket. At least today's line is shorter, so I won't have to wait long.

"You're early," Charlotte remarks when she notices me standing in the room's doorway and hastily turns her back to me. I think she's trying to hide something. What is she up to? I put the bucket of water down and step inside. Did she take something from my belongings? Was I wrong to trust her?

Inside, I spot another man in the room. He's about thirty years old, dressed in a light, plain button-up shirt, and dark trousers, and seated on an upside-down wooden bucket. His brown jacket had been discarded on the floor. What's going on here? What's he doing here?

"Who is he?" I inquire, approaching Charlotte. What is she hiding from me? The unfamiliar man smiles awkwardly at me and stands up. What is she doing with him?

"Sarah, I need you to leave here for an hour," Charlotte approaches me and whispers as she grabs my arm and attempts to lead me toward the door.

"Why? What's going on here? What are you doing?" I ask, angrily. Despite her previous help, I still don't trust her.

"I apologize," the man interjects, turning to put on his jacket, "I didn't know you lived here too."

"Who are you?" I ask him, raising my voice. Why did she let him into the room in which Rebecca and I were sleeping at night? "That's why the other women hate you?" Did she lie to me before?

"Shh...please, Sarah, I'm begging," Charlotte continues to whisper urgently, "they hear everything here, please, it's not what you think. And you, don't go, wait a minute, please, everything's fine," she rushes to grab the stranger's arm, removes his jacket and guides him back to the upside-down wooden bucket. "Please, Sarah," she pleads with me, "I'll explain everything to you in an hour. I swear I'm not lying to you," she leads me to the apartment entrance.

"Are you doing this with him here, in the middle of the day?" I whisper. What will happen if Rebecca hears about it?

"No, I swear. An hour, come back in an hour, I'll explain everything," she implores while looking into my eyes.

"Okay," I finally concede and turn to the stairwell, debating whether to express my disbelief to her, but finally stop myself and slowly go down the stairs, out into the large yard. I'll give her one hour. Not a minute longer.

In the yard, I walk among the people standing and talking to each other or strolling around in the sun. Do they feel like I do in this place? I move away and approach the fence until I place my hands on the barbed wire and look out at the distant houses. They look so peaceful. Near the closed entrance I notice Mathéo, the policeman that Rebecca spoke to without permission a few days ago. He looks at me and smiles, but I don't smile back at him. I don't trust him either, even though he saved me and behaved nicely toward Rebecca. I can't trust anyone here, certainly not a French policeman. I feel he's looking at me, but I ignore him and watch the distant houses, searching for free people around them. What about Charlotte? She is probably lying to me. I will soon know.

Laughter makes me look toward the German commander's barracks, and I notice Captain Becker's two daughters sitting on the wooden porch, holding a book, and laughing. It had been so long since Rebecca had laughed. If only I could make Rebecca laugh like that.

The barrack door opens, Captain Becker emerges, stands on the balcony, and looks around. I tense up and hurry to release my hands from the fence, slowly turning around and walking away. I shouldn't have gotten so close to their area. Few people dare to stand near the fence in this area. Only when I get close to a group of women standing and talking among themselves do I feel that the tension in my body has dissipated. It must've been an hour already. It's time to go back.

I enter our room and look around. The man who was here before is gone, and the upside-down wooden bucket is placed in the corner of the room, next to the water bucket I brought earlier.

"Take it, it's yours, thanks," Charlotte approaches and hands me a cigarette from her dress pocket.

"I don't smoke," I stand in front of her and refuse to take it while looking around. She owes me an explanation.

"Me neither," she says, continuing to hold the cigarette she offered me. "It's not for you to smoke."

"Then why are you giving it to me?"

"You know it's the best currency in this place. Camp replacement for the German Reichsmarks or the French Francs."

"You owe me an explanation. You won't buy me with cigarettes," I stand before her and examine her brown eyes.

"As you wish," she tucks the cigarette into her dress pocket, but after a moment takes it out, this time with a box of matches. She lights it up, and inhales the smoke with pleasure, while closing her eyes.

"I thought you didn't smoke."

"I haven't smoked in a very long time. I can't afford it," she gives me with an embarrassed smile while holding the cigarette, "but every now and then I have to." She walks over to the window, looks outside, and after a moment looks back at me, "It's not what you think, I didn't steal anything from you, nor did I do anything immoral with him; I didn't sleep with him. I think we're old enough to say that word," she awkwardly smiles at me.

"So, what did you do with him?"

"I did this," she takes a small pencil out of her dress pocket and holds it up, showing it to me.

"It's a pencil, I don't understand," I remain standing at a distance from her, alert.

"I draw," she says after a moment and inhales from the cigarette she's holding. "I draw people, I sketch them down with the pencil, they come here, and I sketch down their portrait. And they pay me in cigarettes," she lifts the cigarette she's been holding a bit higher.

"Why are they coming to you to paint them? I don't understand."

"For the same reason that people go to a photographer to take their pictures, so they have a memory to be proud of."

"But we're in a detention camp. There's nothing to be proud of here."

"No one here has a camera, and people want to be remembered as they are, even here," she says quietly.

"And why are you hiding it?"

"Because this camp is a dangerous place. The people here are unemployed and are willing to tell the Nazis about you in exchange for a handful of cigarettes; everyone has enemies here, and if you don't have one yet, you will in the future," she replies while carefully stubbing out the half-smoked cigarette on the sole of her shoe and tucking the remaining half back into her dress. "I'll save the rest for next time I need it," she smiles at me awkwardly.

"And why did you want to pay me with a cigarette?" I slowly walk into the room, pointing to her dress pocket, feeling safer to go inside.

"For not shouting and bringing all the nosy neighbors into the room. They might've informed me to the Nazis. They don't like us anyway."

"Do you think the Nazis will do something if they know?"

"You and I already know how the Nazis are. They don't need a reason to do something."

"And that's why you stole the makeup brush from them?"

"Not to draw people. A simple pencil is enough for me to do that."

"Why then?"

"To paint, I paint, I've always painted. I studied at an art school in Berlin before I ran away. I paint people, situations, and feelings, and I want to paint this horrible place."

"Why would you want to draw this place? Everything here is so terrible."

"Because when I paint, I'm alive, and also to leave something behind me, for them to know," she replies. "To know that once was a young woman named Charlotte Salomon, to know that this woman lived in this terrible place."

"And did you paint?" I sit down next to her. I'm not mad at her anymore.

"Very little," she replies and raises the cardboard she sleeps on. Underneath it are several paintings of the camp, the policemen, fences, and people queuing for water. Some characters are drawn flying in the air, like birds escaping this place.

"These are great paintings," I run my finger gently over one of them.

"Thanks, but I can't paint anymore. I ran out of colors and couldn't get more. Eventually, that other woman hated me for nothing," she sits on the floor and leans against the wall. "At least I have some kind of job in this place, sketching people with a pencil. Something to do in exchange for cigarettes. Cigarettes are worth an extra soup portion, and in this place a soup portion is equivalent to not losing weight and coming down with an illness."

A few days later, the children run out of the classroom, and I look at them as they pass me by while talking and laughing. Where is Rebecca? She is not with them. Could the teacher have left her in the classroom?

Through the open door, I can see him standing with his back to me, erasing the blackboard. I go in and look around. The classroom is empty. *Where is my daughter?*

"Excuse me, Mr..." I address him.

"The name is Mr. Gaston," he turns and looks at me as if noticing me for the first time. "Can I help you?" He asks as he bends down and picks up his leather bag from the chair next to the board.

"My daughter, Rebecca, where is she? I brought her to class this morning."

"The German girl?" He asks me while picking up his coat and hat hanging on a hanger next to the board. He acts as if we were in a normal school and not in a Nazi detention camp.

"Rebecca, my daughter, and yes, we're from Berlin," I reply. I want to add that we did not come here of our own free will, just like any of the thousands of people in this camp, but I remain silent.

"Your daughter is uneducated. She is rebellious," he watches me, his eagle nose pointed in my direction.

"She's a little child, she needs to study."

"She needs a parent to educate her."

"Where is she?" I ask him, what did he do to her?

"She deserves to be disciplined, but she ran away from class," he approaches me on his way out, "Mrs...."

"Mrs. Bloch," I cringe at his brown eyes as they size me up.

"Mrs. Bloch, make sure that Mr. Bloch educates your daughter. Even if students laugh at you because you got the question wrong, you do not snatch their notebook away. And if the teacher calls you to come forward and be disciplined, you don't run away from class."

"Yes, Mr. Gaston," I quietly reply, feeling smaller by the moment under his inquisitive eyes.

"I look forward to seeing your daughter in my class tomorrow," he says.

"Yes, Mr. Gaston," I take a step back.

"Good day, Mrs. Bloch," he puts on his hat and tugs on it, gesturing goodbye before leaving the classroom, leaving me to look at the empty desks and chairs. Where is Rebecca? She didn't come to our room. Where could she have gone?

I walk through the yard full of people, searching for her, but she's nowhere to be found, not even near the water tap or the line of people waiting to use it. Where can she be? She is also not with the men playing pétanque or with some girls playing catch in the yard. I'll discipline her for running away from Mr. Gaston's class. She will be a well-behaved girl, like all the other kids in his class. I scan the yard again. Where can she be? But then, as I approach the fence and gate, I happen to look out and find myself filled with dread. Rebecca is on the other side of the fence, playing with the camp commander's daughters outside the wooden barrack.

How did she get there? How did she manage to get past the barbed wire fence? Rebecca is running in front of his two daughters. They wear pink, flowery dresses, and their light, curly hair tied with colorful ribbons. They both stand and laugh as they throw stones on the grass, and Rebecca chases them. She runs nonstop, her plain, brown dress fluttering and her untied, dark hair waves around like a wild foal's mane. The ribbon I tied in her hair that morning is gone.

I cling to the barbed wire fence and hold it tight, feeling the metal spikes hurting me through my dress. Shall I try calling out to her? Isn't it dangerous and will attract attention to her? What should I do? My entire body freezes as I see a German soldier getting out of the barracks. What will he do to her? I'm shaking.

One policeman is sitting on the bench outside the French police officers' barracks. Why isn't he doing anything? Why doesn't he bring her back in? I try to shout at him while watching the German soldier, but I can only let out a stifled shout.

As if in slow motion, I see the soldier descending the two stairs leading out of the hut and approaching the girls. One of the commander's daughters ignores him and throws another stone, and Rebecca runs to bring it. How did she get past the fence? Step by step, the German soldier approaches her. As he draws nearer to her, he keeps walking and passes her by, toward a nearby military vehicle. I bend down and throw up, holding on to the wire fence so as not to fall on the hard ground.

Breathe, breathe. I take a deep breath and open my eyes. The sour taste is still in my mouth. I have to do something. I have to bring her back; someone will eventually catch her. I walk toward the gate, my hand occasionally gripping on to the barbed wire fence for support. I'll ask the policeman at the gate to bring her back.

"Wait, where do you think you're going?" He stands in front of me.

"I have to go outside just for a moment," I tell him, panting. I'm even afraid to explain to him what had happened, fearing they'd discipline her.

"Go back," he points his gun at me, "stay away from the gate. Are you new here?" He bursts out laughing, his big belly shaking.

"No," I breathe, "just for a moment. I won't run away," I shift my gaze from the three girls outside to his gun pointed at me. There's a bayonet attached to the end of his rifle, and the long blade is pointed at my stomach.

"You Jews should be inside. It's your place," he shouts at me. "Go back. These are the rules, you know that." He pushes his rifle forward a little, until the blade of the bayonet almost touches my belly.

"Please," I beg him, "I have to, just for a moment." My eyes look at the policeman sitting outside the barracks. Maybe he'll help me? It is Mathéo. Why doesn't he bring her in?

"Back!" The guard shouts at me, and I step back and stand next to the fence. What will happen to her?

Rebecca continues to run between the two girls, ignoring everything around her. Please look in my direction, notice me, and come back inside. I try to signal to her with my hand. But she doesn't notice me, and I keep holding on to the fence, ignoring the wounds the metal spikes make in my hands. Just look at me for a moment. Just lift your head.

Suddenly, the barrack's door opens once again, and someone stands at the door. I'm all coiled. The camp commander's two daughters drop the stones to the ground and run inside the barracks, leaving Rebecca alone. What will she do? She remains standing and looks around.

"Rebecca," I shout at her and wave my hand, but she doesn't hear me. Mathéo gets up and approaches her. What is he going to do to her? His gun rests on his shoulder. He doesn't point it at her. He says something and she nods, and they both walk side by side towards the gate. She comes back to me.

"I told you to stay away from the gate," the big policeman shouts at me. I don't listen to him. I'm focused on Rebecca coming closer to me, next to Mathéo. What right did he have to take her out and endanger her like that without my permission?

"Go inside," he smiles at her, opening the gate for her, and she slips in. I hold her, pick her up, and hug her tightly.

"So, what if I'm Jewish," I shout at Mathéo, no longer able to stop myself. I feel all my fears burst out in a flood of screams. "So what if I'm locked inside and have no rights? Why do you think you can take my daughter away from me?" I keep yelling at him while holding Rebecca, gasping, and crying.

At first, his smile disappears, and he takes half a step back. His hand comes up and grabs the weapon strap on his shoulder, but he doesn't take it down. An inner voice tells me to thank him and get up and leave, but I can't stop myself, and I keep yelling at him. Even though I'm not allowed to do it and even though I'm putting me and Rebecca at risk.

"Woman, be quiet, stay away," the other policeman yells at me and points his gun at me.

"It's okay, Fernando, I'll take care of it," Mathéo tells him, deflecting Fernando's rifle barrel away with his hand. He watches me through his glasses, his brown-green eyes studying me without moving. Will he discipline me? I can't apologize to him.

"I'm still human, even though I'm imprisoned here," I tell him and stop talking. I just keep watching him and breathing. I was so worried when the German soldier approached her, and he did nothing.

"It's not us who set the rules here; it's them, and they're also the camp commander's daughters," he tells me quietly, "and if they want to play with her, they'll play with her."

"We're locked up here like zoo animals," I tell him, even though I have to keep quiet. "For your amusement and theirs."

"Yes, sometimes they want to be amused, like their father, and that's what they do," he keeps watching me, "and maybe

ALEX AMIT

you should be happy that they like to play with your daughter, even if they do humiliate her."

"No one likes to be humiliated, even if they're a child," I reply while holding Rebecca in my arms.

"Your daughter won't be playing with them for much longer," the other guard, Fernando, interjects and laughs.

"What do you mean?" I turn to him.

"Soon you will know," he continues to smile, takes out a green cigarette case from his pocket, and puts a white cigarette in his mouth. His dark eyes look at me ominously. "Do you want it?" He hands me the box, "A gift from me. You don't have to pay the usual fee for it this time."

I want to turn around and walk away from him, but I need cigarettes. I need to purchase more straw for Rebecca's and my beds, and I have no other way to do so. I reach out to take the box, but he doesn't let go.

"What do you say?" he asks me, the white cigarette stuck in his mouth.

"Thanks," I whisper, feeling sick.

"You're welcome. Stinky Jewess, you should learn to be polite to the police," he releases his hand, and I hold the box tightly, feeling the lump of insult in my throat. I look at Mathéo, but he turns his back to me and walks away from the gate and us.

"What are you waiting for? Get away from here before I regret being so nice to you," Fernando yells at me, and I turn my back and walk while holding Rebecca in my arms. I slowly approach the group of men who are playing pétanque as if nothing happened.

"Mommy, you smell weird," Rebecca says.

130

"It's nothing, sweetie. I didn't feel well for a moment. Let's go stand in line for the water tap, and I'll wash my mouth." I continue to walk with her and watch the people peacefully pace around the yard. What did the other policeman mean by what he said?

"Why did you go play with those girls?" I ask Rebecca later in the evening while caressing her hair. We're lying on the straw bed I exchanged for the cigarettes, and our laundry is hanging on a rope strung across the room. The cigarettes were also enough to buy some soap.

"With Hilda and Liza?" She asks.

"These are their names?" I don't want to tell her what their father is doing. I mustn't scare her.

"Because Mr. Gaston wanted to hit me with the ruler, like he hits anyone who doesn't know the answer, so I ran out of class and waited for the bus with the other people and my suitcase, then the good hunter with the glasses came and told me that they wanted to play with me," she rambles on.

"The good hunter with the glasses?" I ask.

"Yes, and he took me from the gate and brought me to them, and we played with stones, and they told me that they'd tell me what to do, and I'd do it because the Jews have to serve the Germans, and I'd be their maid. They don't run fast at all. I'm faster."

"And you don't mind running and doing what they tell you to do?" I ask her, trying to think of how to convince her not to go near the barbed wire fence again.

"No, they're funny. They said I was the dog and should catch the stones and Mommy, they also know how to speak German, unlike all the other kids in Mr. Gaston's class, who only speak French, which is a funny language."

"But you should be at Mr. Gaston's class and listen, along with the other kids," I caress her hair.

"Mr. Gaston is always angry and spits when he talks and says I'm stupid and understand nothing. And the good hunter with the glasses said I should play with them. Can I keep playing with them? Why were you mad at him?"

"No, you must keep going to Mr. Gaston's class and learn French. And I wasn't mad at him. Now, close your eyes and dream sweet dreams about Sylvie, the girl bear," I reply and think that maybe Mathéo is right, and I should be happy they like to play with her. Perhaps the more they like her, the safer she'll be.

"And I'll also dream about Dad?"

"Yeah, about Dad too," I sigh, knowing he should've been here to discipline her. I haven't thought about him in a while.

"And the other hunter with the rifle also told you something. What did he say?" She adds, a moment later.

"He said you should listen to me and go to sleep," I kiss her forehead and remain sitting against the wall in the dark. What did the other policeman mean when he said it wouldn't last much longer?

"Everyone to the yard now." I hear the announcement through the window the next day, and I get up, go out, and run up the stairs. I have to find Rebecca.

"There's a place for everyone; they won't start without you," a man in a long coat says as I push myself between him and the wall and continue running down the stairs, but I don't answer him. I need to find her before the roll call starts or the police come inside the compound.

"Rebecca," I stand in the yard, shouting and looking around for her. My eyes scan the large yard that quickly fills up with people. "Rebecca..." More and more people emerge from the big building's entrances. "Rebecca..." She doesn't stand next to the fence. Policemen and German soldiers are already standing outside the gate at a respectful distance from Captain Becker, wearing his black uniform. Where can she be? I look around. Could she have gone outside the fence again? I look at the German commander's barrack, but the grass in front of it is empty. Where is she? "Rebecca...," I shout aloud.

"I found her. She's with me," Charlotte approaches me, holding her by the hand. "She was in the classroom with the other children for a change," she hands her over to me. "Let's go to the back," she paves our way through the crowd. The soldiers are entering the compound. We must not be in the first few rows, they're always the more dangerous ones.

One of the policemen is holding a megaphone, and when he raises his hand, the crowd falls silent. All I can hear is the sound of a plane in the sky. It looks like a big bird of prey that passes above us with its black wings, the German Iron Cross painted on its fuselage. I signal Rebecca to be quiet and carefully lower her to the ground. I want her to disappear among the standing crowd.

"The French Vichy government and the Third Reich have decided to expel you to this camp," the policeman begins to speak slowly through the megaphone, emphasizing each word. "You are expelled from society because you are a danger to it, with your ideas, your love of money, your greed…" he stops for a moment. I see the Nazi officer standing at a distance, watching us, his eyes almost hidden by the peaked cap he's wearing. Next to him are several other German soldiers, standing at attention while holding their weapons.

"But, as a gesture of goodwill," the policeman once again brings the megaphone to his mouth and continues to speak, "the Third Reich allows you to move to the East for resettlement. There, you will work in agriculture. You will work for the Third Reich in return for better food and, in the end, your freedom," he stops speaking again.

"This is our chance to get out of here," I hear a man whisper behind me, but I don't look back. Is this really our chance to leave this horrible place? I continue to hold Rebecca and look forward, staring at the Nazi officer. This is the father of the girls who are playing with my daughter as if she were their dog.

"Tomorrow morning," the announcer continues, "everyone who wants to volunteer to be the first to leave for resettlement, please show up in front of the registration office with all your belongings. Of course, those who choose to leave first will get better houses, better land, and a special allowance of butter, oil, flour, and chocolate." He stops talking again, and my mouth fills with saliva at the word 'chocolate.' I haven't eaten sweet chocolate in such a long time. Rebecca also shakes my hand upon hearing the word 'chocolate.' I think she didn't understand much of what he said, but I'm sure she understood 'chocolate.'

I keep watching the Nazi officer as he nods to the policeman, and the latter comes closer to him, listening to what he has to say before going back to stand before us.

"As I said, those of you who'll go to the East will get better conditions. For those who stay here, the food portions will be reduced. Remember, tomorrow at 7 AM, at the registration office, with all your belongings for the travel to the East. You are dismissed," he lowers the megaphone and turns around, but the people remain standing in silence until the Nazi officer leaves the camp, followed by the soldiers and policemen. Only then do people start talking to one another.

"Is this our chance?" I ask Charlotte.

"Do you think this terrible place is our chance?" She points to the big, gray building surrounding us and the barbed wire fences.

I look around at the people talking to each other while slowly dispersing. Is this a sign of a new beginning?

"Will we have chocolate?" Rebecca asks me as I pick her up in my arms.

"Yes, we'll get chocolate," I smile at her but look again at the camp commander's barrack on the other side of the fence. The commander goes inside and closes the door while the soldiers remain standing outside. My stomach churns, and not from hunger.

"Are you excited for tomorrow?" Charlotte asks me at night.

The building is quiet after the storm caused by the announcement. People were packing and arguing all evening,

ALEX AMIT

and there were also those who went to sleep in front of the registration office, looking to secure their place tomorrow morning on the train that would take us to the East. Rebecca's sleeping peacefully, and I caress her hair. She had a hard time falling asleep from the excitement.

"You know," I tell Charlotte, "I've made some big mistakes since we arrived in Paris - me and my husband, Erwin, who God knows where he is right now. My biggest one was going to the Paris Police with Rebecca back then," I recall that day and wince.

"They would've found you even if you hadn't gone to them," Charlotte says from the darkness.

"An inner voice whispered that I was doing the right thing by going to the police, but I was wrong," I say. I cannot tell her what happened with the smuggler, and about the chance Rebecca and I had to leave Paris.

"You did the right thing. We all got here in the end."

"Yes, I acted right," I gently stroke the wedding ring on my finger. I have to believe that I acted right at that time. And the smuggler probably would've taken his payment and then betrayed us and handed us over to the Nazis. I couldn't trust him. But my inner voice wouldn't stop bothering me, even now.

"We'll leave this place tomorrow. You'll see, we'll be better off in the East," Charlotte says.

"I know we'll be better there, and Rebecca is happy too, but I still have this inner voice."

"And what does it say?"

"That it's not true, that we shouldn't get on that train tomorrow."

Chapter Seven

Birthday

"Are you coming?" Charlotte asks me the following morning. I can hear the people in the other apartments going down the stairs.

"Charlotte, something doesn't feel right," I look out the window and see people walking down the yard with their suitcases in hand, standing outside the registration office. The line is getting longer, and some put their luggage on the ground, and sway from side to side to warm up.

"This place doesn't feel right; not the east," she grabs her suitcase and looks at me. "I won't miss this cardboard-straw bed," she points at the discarded pieces of cardboard that had been our mattresses for the past months. "Let's go, I can hear everyone going down the stairs."

"Charlotte, we mustn't go east," I turn around and look at her and Rebecca, who is standing nearby, looking at me.

"Why not?"

"I haven't slept all night; my stomach hurts, and not from hunger," I look at her. "Something is wrong."

"You're always afraid. You said that last night, and you also regretted being afraid then, in Paris," she lowers her voice so that Rebecca doesn't hear her, but Rebecca is right next to me; she can hear everything.

"Are we going to Paris?" She asks and smiles.

"No honey, we're staying," I walk over to my suitcase and pick it up. I put it down next to the piece of cardboard in a symbolic gesture. I'm tense. What if I'm wrong again? Why am I so afraid to go east? Why does it feel wrong? I try to explain this to myself so I can explain it to Charlotte, for her to understand why I'm so afraid. It doesn't feel like last time.

"Come on, don't worry," Charlotte says. "It's only a few days on a train, and we'll forget all about this terrible camp."

I struggle to find the right words and look around at the concrete walls. And then I understand.

"When have they ever asked us if we want to do something?" I whisper.

"What?"

"Aren't we going with Aunt Charlotte?" Rebecca asks me.

"When have the Nazis asked us if we wanted to do something?" I repeat and look into her eyes.

"I don't understand what you mean."

"You understand exactly what I mean. You're German, just like me. We Germans are organized. Everything has a reason; nothing is accidental."

"So? You don't see the reason for moving us east? I do. If I remember correctly, the Nazis don't like us that much."

"Come here, Rebecca, we're not going, we're staying," I tell her to stay by my side. "I know they don't like us. That's certainly a good reason to move us to the east," I reply. "But

139

what I can't understand is why are the Nazis so nice to us. Tell me, when have they become so nice?"

"What do you mean?" Charlotte asks, still holding her suitcase as if refusing to let it go. In the corridor, I can no longer hear people running down the stairs. They must have all lined up to register to go eastward.

"The Nazis hate us," I answer slowly, trying to organize my thoughts, which become clearer as I speak. "They call us rats and vermin, but more than that, they were never nice to us, they never asked whether we wanted to do something. They always ordered us, and reprimanded those who failed to obey. Has anyone asked you to wear a yellow badge? Has anyone asked you to leave your university? Or not to enter public parks? To stop practicing medicine, teach or research?"

"No," she replies after a moment.

"And has anyone asked you if you wanted to come here?"

"No."

"So why are they asking us now? Why are they voluntarily giving us extra food and chocolate?"

Charlotte remains motionless for a moment, considering what I had said. "You're wrong," she says after a while. "Your fears are preventing you from moving forward and doing the right thing. Just like you told me last night; you could have been in Spain right now with your husband," she takes a deep breath and continues. "I'm not like you, I always move forward."

"Please, Charlotte, don't go."

"Goodbye, Sarah," she puts the suitcase on the floor, approaches and hugs me. I can feel her warm hands almost crushing my body. "I'll try to save you a room in one of the houses they promised us. In the meantime, you can take the straw from my bed. The nights are getting cold," she whispers. I hug her back and my eyes well up.

"Don't go, please, don't believe them. Your place is here with us, on the straw on the floor," I whisper.

"Goodbye, Rebecca," she kneels and smiles at Rebecca. As she hugs her, I can tell her eyes are red with tears.

"Goodbye, Aunt Charlotte," Rebecca replies, hugging her back. Her small hands wrap around her neck and brown hair.

"Bye," she stands up, turns around and leaves with her suitcase. I hear her footsteps as she descends the stairs, until they slowly disappear.

"Why did Aunt Charlotte say we could have been with Dad now?" Rebecca asks after a moment.

"She didn't mean it," I sit next to her on the floor. "Dad isn't here."

"Is she going to meet him?"

"No, she isn't going to meet him," I wipe my tears away.

"Will she come back?"

"No, she won't come back. She's going to a place called 'the East.'"

"We won't get chocolate like all the people going there?"

"I promise you I'll find you chocolate," I stroke her hair. I've broken so many promises that I've made to her. What if I'm wrong, and Charlotte is right, and I'm afraid to move forward? I want to look at her from the window for the last time, but I can't. I can't join her either; something feels dangerous; although I can't put my finger on it. I'm going to miss her so much.

"Aunt Charlotte," I hear Rebecca call out. I look up. Charlotte walks back through the door and puts her suitcase down as Rebecca runs to hug her.

"I really hope you're right," she sighs and sits beside me.

"Me too," I wipe my tears away; unsure if they're tears of joy or sorrow.

"Let's take a quick look at the empty rooms. Maybe we can get some more straw for winter," she reaches her hand out.

I stand by the window and watch the convoy of people leaving the camp through the gate and on their way to the train station. They're surrounded by armed policemen and several German soldiers in gray-green uniforms. I gently caress the Star of Life and Death sewn to my dress. I very much hope that I've made the right decision.

Two weeks later, Rebecca and I stand next to the fence and watch the bus leaving the camp on its way back to Paris after dropping off more Jewish fugitives. They walk slowly towards the complex, looking around with fear, and I avert my gaze. I don't want to look them in the eyes.

"Maybe tomorrow," Rebecca says as the bus disappears behind the faraway houses.

"Maybe tomorrow," I answer and hold back the tears, like I do every day. She no longer asks about the suitcase, and waiting for the bus has become more of a ritual. "Let's go eat what Aunt Charlotte saved for us," I hold her hand as I walk past the policeman leading the new people to the registration office. Since they started sending people to the East, they have reduced the food rations as promised. We have to fend off the thieves. I also give some of my food to Rebecca to keep her strong.

"Today is May twenty-second," I hear one of the people waiting in line office say to another woman. I cringe.

"Time is meaningless in this place," I say later that night to Charlotte. Rebecca has been long asleep, and the voices in the neighboring apartments have also fallen silent.

"What do you mean?" She asks while drawing on the floor by candlelight. I look at her drawing of people waiting in line for food behind a barbed wire fence.

"It's Rebecca's sixth birthday in three days. I almost forgot about it," I answer. I'm too ashamed to tell her about the people in line who happened to mention the date.

"And what will you do for her birthday?"

"Do you think it matters to her? In this place?" I answer and make sure to look at the door. If we hear someone approaching, we immediately put out the candle. The women from the apartment across the corridor must not know about Charlotte's painting.

"If you were a child in here, would it matter to you?" Then, after a moment I add. "There's something I can do," I go to the corner, take a knife, and sit down. I start to unravel the hidden pocket in my dress. I have already used two gold coins to buy food. I have one more coin left, the birthday coin.

"I need you," I say to Mr. Charpak the following day as I walk past the man who guards the entrance to his apartment. This time, Mr. Charpak sits alone by the upside-down wooden box and plays solitaire. He places the cards in neat rows. The upside-down wooden buckets on which his friends would usually sit are currently unoccupied, as if waiting; but no one is there.

"What do you need?" He looks at me. His cigarette protrudes from between his lips, filling the small room with smoke.

"Your services." I show him the coin in my hand. "Where is everyone?" I gesture at the empty buckets.

"Some of them went to the East," he puts down a card and stands up. "Some of them are preparing for tomorrow, they're on the list. Let's go somewhere else and you can show me what you brought," he approaches and leads me to the side room where we always talk.

"What list?" I ask him.

"They ran out of volunteers to go east, so now they're making lists," he answers and throws the cigarette to the floor, crushing it with his shoe. "They probably have a lot of houses in the East." He says with a bitter smile. He approaches me and I can smell the cigarettes on his breath. "What did you bring me?"

"Why aren't you going east?"

"The Japanese attacked the Americans at Pearl Harbor. The whole world is at war. They send all the sick people to the East. No one has gotten word from the people who moved east, and yet they keep insisting that it's good for us. I don't believe them. You didn't go either. Do you believe them?"

I shake my head.

"Where are you from?" He asks. He has an unpleasant smell.

"From Germany, I lived in Berlin," I reply and take a step back.

"I wasn't born in France. I was born in Russia," he says. "We Jews were never liked there. When I was a child, my father would sit me on his lap and tell me stories." He says and stops talking for a moment, "He would tell me how he hid in a closet when the Cossacks came to kill Jews, how he would sit there as quiet as a mouse and tremble with fear. He taught me even then, as a child, to trust only two things."

"And what are they?"

"God," he says softly and raises his finger to the sky, "and Charpak," he points his finger at himself. "I don't believe in anything else, neither the French nor the Germans. And now, what did you bring me? You didn't come here to get to know me and hear my childhood stories."

"This," I open my fingers a bit and show him the gold coin, careful not to let him grab it. "This is my last coin."

"I thought last time was your last coin."

"I was born in Berlin to a wealthy family," I answer. "My father was a doctor, he attended Dr. Sigmund Freud's lectures at the University of Berlin. Later, they'd sit together in their suits, smoking cigars, drinking coffee and having Torte cakes in a café on the Unter den Linden Boulevard. When I was a child, no one told me stories about pogroms," I pause for a moment and look into his eyes. "But I'm a woman, and I'm here in this camp. I had to learn fast to trust no one but Him," I point to the sky, "and myself," I point to my chest.

"You definitely learned who to trust," Charpak laughs bitterly, "unlike all the Jews who followed the Nazi's promises. What do you want for your coin?"

"I want flour and oil and sugar, like last time, but there are a few more things."

"What?" He reaches for the coin, but I close my hand tightly and hold it behind my back.

"I want an old, old fabric. But you'll give me this one for free."

"Charpak doesn't give anything for free," he holds out his hand.

"A brown old fabric and gouache colors."

"Why do you need gouache colors?"

"It's none of your business, and I want chocolate."

"Chocolate is hard to find these days. It costs more."

"You want my coin. It's worth a lot more than that, you know it. You won't get more than that," I say to him. I'm tense. I have to make him agree.

"Why do you need chocolate?"

"Because it's my daughter's birthday, and she should be able to trust Him," I point to the sky.

"Come tomorrow," he holds out his hand, and I place my last coin in his palm. His thick fingers close around it, and the coin disappears forever.

On the way back to our room, as I walk through the large yard, I see the people lining up in front of the registration office. Charpak was right. They make lists every day, informing people that they must go to the East the next day. They also add the sick to the lists. This place became a transit station between the buses that continue to arrive from Paris and unload people, and the trains that take them to the East. Where are they taking them?

I notice a young woman and her daughter standing among the people. They're just like Rebecca and me. What are they thinking now? I stop for a moment, but then I look away and continue walking. They haven't sent us yet, and my daughter has a birthday. I have to think about that, not about the trains going east.

"Happy birthday," I whisper in Rebecca's ear and wake her up gently. "Happy birthday, my beloved girl, you are six years old," I smile at her, sitting by her side and hugging her tightly.

Rebecca smiles and sits up, looking around as if searching for something. What is she looking for? A cake or candies and gifts like we gave her two years ago in Berlin?

"Look what I brought you," I hand her three pieces of chocolate. She takes one piece and puts it in her mouth, savoring its sweet flavor.

"Mommy, can I eat another piece?" She asks after a moment.

"Yes, sweetie, they're all yours." I smile at her but want to burst into tears.

"I'll eat one now and save one for later," she takes both of them and puts one in her dress pocket and the other in her mouth.

"That's a good idea," I comb her hair with my fingers. The rest of the chocolate I had received from Mr. Charpak is hidden in the suitcase. I'll give her a piece every now and then if they cut our food rations again. Last night, my hands were shaking when I held the package of German army chocolate he had given me. The wrapping was stamped with an eagle holding a swastika in its claws.

"Happy birthday, Rebecca," Charlotte hugs her and hands her a drawing she drew of her.

"Aunt Charlotte, can I keep it?" Rebecca holds the plain brown paper and looks at the drawing.

"Of course, honey, it's yours," she replies.

"Charlotte, I also have something for you," I take out of the suitcase a small package. It's wrapped in brown paper and tied with a thin rope. I hand it to her.

"But it's not my birthday," she holds the package and looks at me awkwardly.

"I didn't know when your birthday was. Open it."

"I haven't gotten a birthday present in so many years," Charlotte softly says as she unties the string. "Thank you," she wipes the tears away.

"Mommy, what did Aunt Charlotte get for her birthday?"

"Ask her to show you."

"What is it?" Rebecca takes the metallic tubes from Charlotte's hands.

"These are gouache colors. Each tube is a different color. Do you see what it says on the package?"

"Blue," Rebecca manages to read.

"Exactly, I can use this blue to paint the sea."

"I've never been to the sea," Rebecca says.

"One day we'll go to the sea, and you can swim in it," I tell her and promise myself that I'll take her to the beach when all this is over.

"What's it like at the beach?" She asks.

"It's wet and salty," Charlotte laughs.

"Ugh…" Rebecca grimaces. "Mommy, can I eat the last piece of chocolate? And can I hang up Aunt Charlotte's painting?" Rebecca reaches into her pocket to grab the last piece of chocolate.

"Yes, you can eat it, and maybe we should keep Aunt Charlotte's painting under the cardboard you sleep on, so it won't crinkle up. What do you think?"

"Okay," Rebecca answers as she puts the piece of chocolate in her mouth, smiling again as she savors the sweetness.

"And I have one more present, especially for you," I tell her. "Last night, when you were sleeping, the bus came especially and brought you a birthday present," I take out a brown bear doll that I sewed all night, from the old fabric Mr. Charpak gave me, until my fingers hurt.

"Sylvie," Rebecca stretches out her arms and hugs the bear. "Sylvie, the bear."

"She came especially from Paris. She was bored there and came to be with you," I wipe my tears away as she hugs the ragged bear and kisses its tattered ears and nose.

"I knew you would come in the end," she whispers to the bear. "I knew you would come out of the book and manage to escape the hunters who were chasing you."

149

"And now, take your new friend, and we'll go to school." I stand her up and tie her hair with a ribbon.

"Do I have to? I don't feel well." She sticks her tongue out and shows it to me.

"You are perfectly healthy, and you can have Sylvie sit with you in class."

"But she doesn't have a ribbon in her hair."

"After school, we will sew a ribbon for her." How did I forget this is a female bear, not a male bear?

"Sylvie, did you hear that?" She whispers to her. "Our teacher, Mr. Gaston is always angry, so pretend like you don't understand what he's saying when he yells at you."

"Are you ready?" I tie her shoelaces and stand up. I hold her hand.

"We are ready." We both go down the stairs on our way to the improvised classroom.

"They tore my Sylvie," a teary Rebecca rushes into our small room at noon.

"What happened," I extend my arms to hug her.

"They took Sylvie from me and tore her," she stands in front of me sobbing. Her eyes are red, and her nose is runny. "They said she wasn't a bear girl, they said she was a boy, and she didn't come from Paris," she holds Sylvie's remains in front of me. The bear I had sown was now nothing more than a wrinkled lump of cloth. One of its ears was torn off, one button eye is missing, and its nose is also almost torn. Why did they do this to her?

"Who did it?"

"Alexadrin and her friends. They're older than me."

"Did you say anything to them?" I wipe her nose and clean her cheeks.

"They said I was a German like the Nazis and that I should be expelled, and that Sylvie is a French bear, and I shouldn't have her," she continues to sob. "And I pulled their hair after they snatched Sylvie away, and Mr. Gaston, the teacher, yelled at me and hit me with the ruler," she bursts into tears again.

"I'll tell you what we'll do," I hug her and sit her on my lap. "First, we'll send Sylvie to the clinic and fix her up, like in a hospital."

"And later?" She sniffles.

"Later, we'll figure out what to do," I retrieve the thread and needle from the suitcase and start repairing Sylvie, reattaching her nose. A few minutes later, I remove a button from the sleeve of Rebecca's coat, fashioning it into a new eye for the teddy bear, albeit slightly different in color and size than the original. "Here, she's all fixed," I finally hand her the bear after sewing it up as best as I can.

"But her eyes are different," Rebecca holds and examines her carefully.

"That's because she got hit in the eye, but the important thing is that she's still smiling," I touch the teddy bear's eyes, one black and the other burgundy. "Now listen to me, sweetie, and listen carefully," I tell her. I need to teach her to protect herself from the other children.

"Yes, Mommy," she continues to stroke Sylvie but looks up at me.

"Just as Sylvie watches over you, you must watch over her."

"Okay, Mommy," she nods, though I'm not entirely sure she understands.

"You have to. You have to protect her."

"Okay, Mommy," she sits down and plays with Sylvie, and I sigh and watch her. What will the girls in class do to her tomorrow?

"She'll be fine," Charlotte reassures me quietly at night after Rebecca falls asleep, "that's how kids are."

"She seems so vulnerable. The older girls in her class are bullying her."

"She needs to learn to defend herself."

"I hope so. She's still so young."

"You'll see, she'll find her way."

"Did you learn to defend yourself when you were little?"

"There was one boy, Franz, who wouldn't stop bullying me," Charlotte says after a pause, and I try to picture her as a child.

"And what did you do?"

"I survived. We all do, even those who are bullied by the toughest kids. I found my own way."

"And what about Franz? What did you do to him?"

"I escaped from the bullies into a world of imagination and paintings," she places her hand on mine, "Thank you for bringing me colors."

"It's for your birthday and for protecting us when we were new here, even though I didn't trust you."

"Thank you. Now I can paint this place in colors, not just with pencils."

"Aren't you afraid of them?"

"The Nazis?"

"Yes," I nod, "Afraid they'll find out."

"I can't stop. It's beyond me," she says after a moment.

"Why?"

"You know, I've been drawing people, families, thoughts for years," Charlotte says, pausing to gather her thoughts before continuing. "But since they arrived, I've changed and started drawing them."

"What do you mean by 'them'?" I ask, feeling a chill run down my spine.

"Them. Their parades, their swastika flags flying in the streets, the Jewish women they humiliated. All of it in colors, colors of freedom under the shadow of evil."

"In Nice?"

"Yes, until they banned and sent me here, with nothing but the dress on my back. And now you've brought me colors."

"Aren't you afraid they'll find out one day?" I ask again.

"I am afraid of them. Everyone here is afraid of them. That's why I want to paint so much," she pauses again to collect her thoughts, "I want my paintings to be a testament of me. No matter what happens in this detention camp, I want to leave behind paintings that capture the reality of life here: the orders, the hunger, the struggles. Not just smiling faces who pay me with cigarettes and pose for me on an upturned bucket. My legacy will be these paintings, because neither you nor I know what tomorrow will bring."

"Aunt Charlotte, can I have a pencil for school?" Rebecca asks her the following morning while I comb her hair. I look at her with apprehension. What will the other girls do to her today?

"Why do you need a pencil?" Charlotte hands her a pencil from her bag.

"I need it, and a sharpener too."

"Okay," Charlotte retrieves a small metal sharpener and passes it to Rebecca. Rebecca carefully sharpens the pencil, occasionally checking its tip before continuing.

"Let's go, you need to get to school," I finally tell her. I don't want her to be late and give Mr. Gaston a reason to punish her again. I fear what he might do to her.

Rebecca stands up, holding the pencil in one hand and the newly fixed Sylvie in the other.

"Are you sure you want to take her with you?" I ask.

"Yes," she nods. "I promise to take care of her."

"Remember not to fight with the older girls and to look after Sylvie. Do you promise?" I remind Rebecca outside the classroom door a few minutes later. From inside, I hear the voices of children who have already arrived, and Mr. Gaston yelling at them to be quiet.

"Yes, Mommy. Bye, Mommy," she says, entering the classroom and closing the door behind her.

I follow her with my gaze as she disappears behind the wooden door, but after a moment, I hear laughter inside. "Here comes the German girl with her ugly bear."

What should I do? How will she handle them? I turn around and open the classroom door, peering inside.

"Nobody touches my Sylvie," I hear Rebecca yell as she charges at a golden-haired girl at least two years older than her, brandishing the pencil she took from Charlotte that morning. "Sylvie belongs to Rebecca!" she shouts in German, raising the pencil and forcefully striking the golden-haired girl on the head with it. The girl starts screaming in pain as a red stain spreads across her head.

"Rebecca!" I shout, but she doesn't turn to me.

"Sylvie is mine, mine!" She continues to jab the screaming girl with the pencil, her brown hair flying in all directions as if she's a bird of prey, while the girl flees across the classroom in tears. All the other children stand up and shout until neither Mr. Gaston's nor my voice can be heard over the chaos in the room.

"She's crazy. Get her away from me!" The golden-haired girl continues to run between the tables as Rebecca pursues her, until she stops, one hand still clutching the pencil and the other holding Sylvie by the ear. Finally, Rebecca stops panting and looks around at the other children, who fall silent under her gaze. Then, she quietly returns to her seat.

"Rebecca Bloch, to the blackboard, now!" Mr. Gaston bellows at her in the now silent room. It seems he doesn't even notice my presence. I watch her get up quietly and approach him slowly. The children in the class are as silent as stones, saying nothing as she passes between the tables. She will be punished now. I can't bear to watch. I turn and leave the room, quietly closing the door behind me. Outside, in the yard, I wipe away my tears, but I also smile. I hope they won't seek revenge on her.

As evening approaches, I hear voices outside our room, either from the stairs or neighboring apartments. "Where are the Germans?" someone asks, and I tense up. More steps and murmurs echo in the stairwell.

"Rebecca, come here right away," I call her softly. "Charlotte," I signal her with a nod.

Charlotte is lying on the floor, painting on a brown piece of paper. With her brush in hand, she paints with swift motions a German officer standing in front of a group of people getting off a bus. She freezes and stares at me.

"They're right there. This is their room. Why are you looking for them?" Someone says.

"Charlotte," I whisper to her, and she hurries to hide the colors and the unfinished drawing under the cardboard she sleeps on.

"This is where you are?" A woman I don't recognize removes the sheet that serves as our door and enters the room. Her light hair is sloppily pulled up, and she has a simple brown belt around her gray dress. Several women stand behind her, as well as two men.

"Yes, we're here," I reply politely and stand up. "But you know the rules here. It's polite to ask before entering apartments. Nobody in this place has doors, including you."

"Polite?" She starts yelling at me. "Your daughter injured mine. Mr. Gaston said she chased her with a knife and wounded her," she advances threateningly. "You," she points at Rebecca, "you tried to kill my daughter."

"Don't speak to my daughter," I position myself between the woman and Rebecca to shield her. "Your daughter has been bullying mine day after day. She calls her a German." I try to keep my cool. I want them to get out of here and leave us alone.

"Because that's what you are, German," she shouts.

"Yes, they're German. They shouldn't be here," another woman joins in.

"We're Jewish, just like you," Charlotte responds, pushing the woman away while gripping her paintbrush. "Get out of here. Go back to your holes."

"That's exactly how Germans speak," someone shouts from behind.

"Why do you have a paintbrush? What are you doing with it?" One of the women tries to grab it from Charlotte's hand.

"It's none of your business," I retort, pushing her back. I don't have a choice. They keep closing in on me. More and more people from neighboring apartments join the commotion until the room is crowded. Charlotte and I step back, shielding Rebecca with our bodies. I see the loathing gazes of all the people surrounding us. I feel like an animal caught in a cage, unable to defend itself. We have to protect our belongings, so they don't steal them. The room is full of people, they're all shouting and watching us.

"Look what I found," a woman in a black dress raises a drawing above her head, one Charlotte had tried to hide. "She must be working for the Nazis," she declares, showing it to everyone, "documenting what they're doing here."

"It's none of your business," Charlotte tries to take it back, but it rips.

"That's everyone's business if you're collaborating with the Nazis," a man in a brown coat accuses. "She must have more paintings. Look for them."

"We are prisoners here, just like you," I answer. I must protect us, but it seems futile. All the people around us seem like one mass of voices and shouting. I feel Rebecca's hands clinging to my legs. Where is her pencil? I search the floor for the dinner knife near where I sleep.

"I found more paintings," someone shouts. I can't tell who it is anymore. I keep searching until I find the knife. I rise to my feet, holding it in my hand. I have to do something.

"No one touches the paintings!" I scream, holding the small knife in front of the man's face. "Leave them at once." Stepping forward, he throws them on the floor. "Everybody out of the room, now!" I wave the knife in front of the golden-haired woman who started the chaos.

"Stay away from her; she's crazy, like her daughter," she says, taking a step back.

"Leave them alone," someone else says, perhaps it's Mr. Charpak's voice, but I'm not sure anymore. Charlotte stands by my side, panting, and as soon as they retreat a few steps, she quickly starts collecting the paintings thrown on the floor, hugging them tightly.

"Get out of here now!" I continue to scream like a wild animal in a trap. "Get out of here."

"Let's go, but you, keep your daughter away from mine," the fair-haired woman takes a step back.

"And you, teach yourself to behave politely and ask for permission before breaking into someone's home," I answer angrily. "And teach your daughter not to bully younger girls." I continue to hold the knife in front of her face.

"It seems to me that the Germans have learned their lesson," says one of the men as they all slowly leave the room, leaving us alone.

Once they all leave, I look around. They've tossed the pieces of cardboard that we sleep on, and the straw is scattered all over the floor. Some of Charlotte's drawings, hidden underneath, are ripped and left on the floor. But where is our luggage? In the chaos, our luggage was stolen. What should we do?

"Mommy, did they go?" Rebecca continues to hug me, and I look at her. She holds her sharpened pencil in her small hand, the one that started the whole havoc.

For a moment, I want to slap her for everything she has done, but then I look at Charlotte, leaning on the floor, picking up her torn paintings and sitting beside her.

"Charlotte, are you okay?" I ask her, still gasping, my whole body tense. "They stole our luggage."

"I'm fine," she answers, trying to straighten a crumpled painting. "It could have been worse. I've had worse." But when I put my hand on her shoulder, she sheds a tear. What will we do without our luggage? Rebecca's coat is in there.

"Aunt Charlotte, take it," Rebecca hands her a crumpled drawing from the corner.

"Come, sit on my lap," I hug Rebecca. "It's not your fault," I kiss her.

"They hate us because we're Jewish? They also have the Star of Life and Death."

"They hate us because we're different. People don't like different people."

"That's why the hunters didn't like Sylvie the bear?"

"Yes, exactly, because she's different."

"But I love her," she hugs the ragged bear.

"Because you're special, and you protect her," I kiss her forehead. "Now help Aunt Charlotte put her paintings back in order." I get up and go to the door of the room, still holding the knife. In the other apartments, the conversations return to their normal tone, as if the quarrel never happened.

While I'm fixing the dividing sheet at the entrance door frame, I hear footsteps going up the stairs, and I tense again. My hand tightens around the knife handle, and I wait.

"It's yours. Someone took it from you," Mr. Charpak walks up the stairs and places the two suitcases at my feet. He wears a dirty white tank top and suspenders holding up his brown pants. He's lost weight in recent months.

"Why did you return them?" That's all I ask him, even though I have to thank him.

"Because I'm a dealer, not a thief," he stands close to me in the dark corridor. I can smell the pungent cigarette smoke on his breath. Few people have money left to buy cigarettes.

"I want a knife, a real knife," I whisper to him.

"You need a man to look after you," I can see his eyes fixed on me in the dark corridor.

"I'm done trusting men. The man I married isn't here to help me. I want a knife."

"Can you pay for the knife?"

"No, but I will."

"You can always pay me," he smiles, "after all, you have something that I want."

"I'll find a way."

"I know you will," he walks away and starts to go down the stairs, but after a moment, he turns around and goes up again. "You better keep your daughter out of the classroom. The other mothers don't like her."

"She has to go. She's a girl. She needs to learn French. Otherwise, how will she learn to get along with people who hate her?"

"She'll have to learn to get along, like you," he extends his hand as if debating whether to touch my body but regrets it. "Just keep an eye on your daughter," he says and returns his hand, turns, and goes down the stairs, disappearing into the darkness.

Chapter Eight

The Lists

End of May 1942

A few days after the altercation with the other women, I enter the room carrying a bowl of potato soup and half a loaf of bread.

"Rebecca, take a seat. I brought you some food."

"I'm not hungry," she replies, lying down.

"Sit down. You have to eat," I insist and force her to sit. Over the past few days, she's developed a cough and seems to be getting weaker. "Try it, you'll it." I spoon a bit of the watery potato soup into her mouth, my hand instinctively touching her forehead. She feels warm.

"That's enough for me. I'm full."

"Rebecca, you need to eat more to regain your strength so we can go out and see if the bus has arrived. Maybe the suitcase with Sylvie's book will be there today," I encouraged, supporting her back, and preventing her from lying down. She must eat.

"Maybe you could go in my place?"

"I can't. If the bus driver sees only me, he won't agree to give me the book. He'll only give it to you. Eat, and then we'll go wait for the bus."

"Okay," she relents, but after two spoons of soup, she stops. "I'm full."

"You need to eat the bread too. The bus driver won't give a book to girls who haven't eaten their bread," I insist, tearing off a small piece and putting it in her mouth. She chews slowly and swallows, coughing as she does so.

"That's it, Mommy. I'm not hungry anymore. I'll eat tomorrow."

"Just a little more, and then we'll go," I shove another piece of bread into her mouth. What's wrong with her? Why is she so weak? I glance towards the entrance door, feeling as if the other women in the building have cast some sort of curse on her.

"Enough, I'm not hungry," she spits out the bread.

"Let's go and wait for the bus," I say, lifting her to her feet. I need to know if she's okay.

"Okay," she agrees, taking Sylvie with her. She'll be fine. She has to be.

"You need to let her rest," Charlotte whispers to me.

"She just needs some air. It's nothing," I reply.

"She's sick. You know it."

"She's not sick," I retort in a whisper as I help Rebecca stand. I've seen what happens here to those who are sick. "Can you find her more food?" I take out two cigarettes from my dress pocket and hand them to Charlotte. I've been saving them in case of an emergency.

"Yes, of course," she takes them. The most important thing is that Rebecca gets stronger.

"Come on, honey, let's go wait for the bus," I say, picking her up and cradling her in my arms. I don't want the women in the other apartments to see that she can barely walk.

"Enjoy, tell me who came with him today," Charlotte strokes Rebecca's hair as we leave the room. The fresh air outside will make her feel better.

A cool breeze brushes against our faces as we stroll through the yard toward the fence, with me holding her tightly in my arms. Waiting for the bus with her will make her feel better, I'm sure of it.

For a moment, I entertain the thought of the bus driver arriving and handing us the suitcase, just like in the stories I tell Rebecca. But the barbed wire fence that contains us and the fair-haired policeman standing by the gate, scrutinizing my body, make it clear that nothing will change.

Even though holding her in my arms for so long weighs heavily on me, I don't put her down, not wanting him to see her weakness. No one can know that she is weak.

His eyes continue to stare at my breasts as he smiles at me, probably wondering if my proximity to him is an invitation for a nightly rendezvous in exchange for cigarettes or food. I avert my gaze and take a few steps further along the barbed wire fence.

Soon, the bus will arrive with more people, and I'll be able to divert my thoughts from Rebecca, who remains silent in my arms. Why is she so quiet? Soon, Charlotte will find more food for her, and she'll eat, regain her strength. I stroke her hair.

"Mommy, maybe the bus forgot the way, and we can go back to the room?"

"No, it will come soon. The driver promised me he would arrive today," I reply, continuing to cradle her in my weary arms.

Another policeman approaches the gate, replacing the one who had been making me uncomfortable. It's Mathéo, the policeman with the round glasses. Though I'm unsure if I can trust him, I lower Rebecca to the ground. I need to let my tired hands rest for a moment. There's no other choice. Rebecca grasps the barbed wire fence with her small hands, leaning against it.

"Can we go home? Sylvie is cold, she's shaking," Rebecca says, trembling.

"Yes, let's take her home so she won't get sick," I pick her up again. In what world does a six-year-old girl consider this place home?

"Is everything okay?" Mathéo calls from the other side of the fence. Can I trust him?

"Yes, everything is fine," I straighten up and force a smile, hoping he didn't notice my teary eyes. He is one of them. I can't trust him.

"There's a doctor at entrance four, maybe he'll agree to come and see Rebecca," Charlotte whispers to me the next day as I place a wet rag on Rebecca's forehead. She hasn't been able to stand up since the morning; she's been feverish all day. Yesterday, she still had a little to eat.

"He won't agree, they hate us."

"She won't recover without help. She's getting weaker."

"No, she'll get stronger. She looks better than she did yesterday," I reply, but I know she's right. Rebecca is getting weaker, and her fever doesn't seem to relent. She also threw up the food that Charlotte had managed to get her the previous day. "Can you look after her while I go?" I ask Charlotte after a few minutes and wipe my forehead. I'm sweating, too.

"Yes, go," she takes three cigarettes from her dress pocket and hands them to me. "Take these so you have something to pay with."

"Are you sure?" I look at her. She was going to trade the cigarettes for more food for herself. We all need more food in this camp.

"Yes, I'm sure. I haven't been hungry these last few days."

"Thank you," I take the cigarettes and put them in my dress pocket. I don't believe that she hasn't been hungry. We're all hungry. All the time.

"Who are you looking for?" A woman I don't recognize asks me at entrance number four. She appears to be around thirty, dressed in a light brown dress with a belt that was once fashionable. She is leaning against the exposed concrete wall by the stairs, smoking a cigarette. She seems to take pleasure in every drag from her cigarette.

"I'm looking for the doctor."

"He's gone. They took him in the transport a week ago. He was taking care of people, and they accused him of subversion," she says, casually flicking the finished butt onto the ground without bothering to extinguish it.

"What will I do?" I whisper to her, even though I don't know her, and she has no idea what I'm talking about.

"Do you think a doctor can help you here?" She laughs bitterly. "Even before they took him, he didn't have any medicine, just his notebook. He would write prescriptions without anyone being able to use them. Maybe it's good that they took him to the East. Maybe there they'll give him some medicine to prescribe."

"Thank you," I reply, turning away from her, starting to retreat. What will I do?

"There's the pharmacist. Maybe she will know what to do," I hear her voice again.

"Where is she?" I turn back to her.

"Do you have anything for me?" She asks, holding out her hand.

"One."

"That will do," she says, leaving her hand outstretched. "Anyway, she doesn't have any medicine either."

"So why am I paying you?"

"Because you're desperate for something, like everyone else here, and I'm desperate for a cigarette."

"Half a cigarette," I bargain.

"I'm not that desperate," she insists, keeping her hand out. "A cigarette, or you'll go back to your corner and never know if the pharmacist can help you or not."

"Take it," I hand her a cigarette.

"Floor three, apartment three-five-six," she says, bringing the cigarette to her nose, eyes closed. "You can go up there, but judging by your accent, she won't help you," she opens her eyes, looking at me.

"Why?" I ask, feeling my stomach tighten.

"That's how it is here. In the end, we all become animals, live in packs, and each pack hates the other."

"Thank you," I say and walk past her. We're human, not a pack of animals, and my daughter needs medicine.

"You're one of the foreign women, aren't you?" I hear her say, making me stop.

"Yes, so what?"

"I can hear your accent. You're one of the Germans," she says as if to herself. "Whose girl is it; yours or the other's?"

"That is none of your business."

"Is she the one that needs help? People here aren't really fond of Germans these days; you surely can understand them," she gestures to the gray building around us. "There are rumors that you have a connection with the Nazis outside. You know how it is with rumors; they are easy to spread, especially when your daughter beats the other girls. Was it your daughter? You look like a mother," she nonchalantly leans against the concrete wall, carefully holding the cigarette.

"I'm Jewish, just like you," I start shaking and show her my Star of Life and Death. She has one too.

"People here are like packs of wolves. When things get tough, they look for traitors to blame, and you're a stranger. I'll save the cigarette for later," she says to herself, tucking it into her dress pocket. "It's nice to know I have one in my pocket," she smiles at me.

"I'll pay them. Everyone here sells things for money or cigarettes, including you," I respond, though it's none of her business.

"She'll take the cigarettes from you as payment, but she won't help you. We French have our pride too, and you Germans aren't really popular here," she tells me, turning her back and disappearing into the stairwell. What should I do? Go after her and take a risk? I breathe slowly. I need help, and I need medicine. What if she's right and the pharmacist won't help me after she takes the cigarettes? I look at the dark opening of the stairwell as if it's a gaping mouth waiting to swallow me. I have to go or find someone else to help me.

"Who are you looking for?" An older man asks, leaning against the wall in the stairwell on the second floor. He's dressed in an old jacket, and his yellow badge is almost torn.

"I'm looking for Mr. Charpak," I reply, panting.

"What do you want from him?"

"He knows me," I answer, trying to hide my accent. I hope he hasn't heard the rumors about Charlotte and me.

"Let her in," I hear Mr. Charpak say. The man looks at me in silence, carefully scrutinizes my body, and only then does he move aside and let me walk under the sheet covering the front door. I enter the room and my eyes slowly adjust to the darkness. The table in the center of the room is deserted, and no one is sitting on the wooden buckets around it. There's a pack of cards on the table, and next to it are two half-empty glasses. Where is he? I hear a noise from the corner of the room and turn to look.

Mr. Charpak is sitting in the corner of the room on a straw bed. There's a woman sitting beside him. He stands up and

169

pulls his pants. Slowly, he tucks his tank top into his pants and hangs the suspenders on his shoulders. "I'll be right back," he softly says to the woman. She doesn't reply; all she does is look at me. She has black hair, and her purple dress is slightly unbuttoned. "Let's go," he says, leading me to the side room.

"My daughter," I say to him once we enter the small room, "she's sick. She has a fever. She's been vomiting, she has diarrhea, and she's breathing heavily. I need you to find out what medicine she needs and get it for me," I blurt as I put the two cigarettes in his hand.

"You don't need me. You need to go to the pharmacist, the woman from entrance number four, and I don't take that kind of payment," he hands me back the cigarettes. "Maybe she does."

"I can't go to her."

"Why not?"

"I can't tell you. I'm afraid she won't help me."

"Then why did you come to me? I'm busy," he leans in, almost clinging to me.

"Because I don't have anyone else who can help me," I gasp; I'm about to burst into tears. What will happen to my daughter if I fail to find her medicine?

"Shhh…" he whispers, "she might hear you," he puts his hand on my mouth. I'm disgusted by the touch of his fingers on my mouth, but I'm helpless. "You know you're going to pay for the medicine whatever price I demand? Do you have more gold coins?"

"No, I don't."

"I'm a merchant. I don't do things for free."

"I know," I whisper and nod. "Just go to the pharmacist and get me the medicine. I'll pay what needs to be paid," I tell him, knowing exactly what the price will be. It doesn't matter, I don't want to think about it now. The only thing that matters is that he'll get the medicine for Rebecca.

"Wait here. I'll be right back. The cigarettes?" He reaches out and touches my waist.

I place the cigarettes in his other hand, close my eyes, and ignore his hand on my waist. I have to get used to it. That will be the price. But after a moment, his hand seems to have disappeared, and when I open my eyes, he's no longer there. I hear whispers in the other room, followed by his steps descending the stairs.

"Please, help me, I'll pay any price, I'll pay it every day, I don't care. Just help me find medicine. That's all I ask," I whisper to myself as I lean against the wall and my fingers touch the Star of Life and Death on my dress. "Please," I raise my eyes to the sky and close them in prayer. "Please save her, she's only six."

I don't know how much time has passed, nor do I dare open my eyes as I mutter the same prayer over and over again. I occasionally hear noises coming from the other room; I'm afraid that the brunette woman will kick me out. Is she also paying him for something? But she doesn't approach me, and I'm left there, on my own, leaning against the wall and praying.

"They hate you and your girl," a voice jolts me awake, and I find Mr. Charpak standing before me.

"The medicine, do you have it?" I reach out my hand.

"There are those here who envy you, not the pharmacist. She's a good woman, but others."

"Do you have the medicine?" I grasp his hand and press it against my breasts. His touch sends shivers down my spine, but I don't care. I need medicine.

"I don't have the medicine. Nobody in this place has medicine," he withdraws his hand, "I'm a dealer, not a thief. I only take what I deserve. But I have managed to get something for you. I exchanged your cigarettes for it," he slips a note into my palm.

"What is it?"

"This is the medicine she needs."

"Then get it for me," I grasp his hand again, pressing it against my breast firmly. I made a deal with God, and I'm willing to pay the price.

"It's impossible," he says quietly, "it will take days. We're at war; obtaining medicine is difficult."

"She won't survive a few days," I tell him in a broken voice. "She's getting weaker, please." I start kissing his fingers, ignoring their bitter taste, "please."

"I'm sorry, I can't. I'm not God. I'm a Jew like you. Maybe everyone thinks I'm bad, but I'm just like you; I too have a yellow badge on my jacket. Maybe you should pray to God and trust in Him."

"Believe me, I haven't stopped praying."

"Or you could go to the Nazis. They can get anything. You just need to know who to ask and how. I think you already know how," he tells me before leaving the small room, joining the woman waiting for him on the straw bed in the corner.

I descend the stairs to the building's entrance, place my hand against the wall and lean forward. I feel nauseous. My other hand tightly grips the note with the name of the medicine. There's only one person in the world who can help me. Even if he isn't a Nazi, he still works for them. What will I do if he isn't on duty? I have no one but him.

I leave the building and walk past the people in the yard as they relish the last rays of the afternoon sun. Can't they see that I have a sick dying child? I want to stand in the middle of the yard and shout, 'Help me,' but I know no one will pay attention. It would just result in her and me being taken to the transport going east. They add to the list anyone who might seem sick or crazy, so they won't infect others. Too many have lost their minds in this place; too many have fallen sick and died.

The last rays of the sun blind me as I walk to the gate and the barbed wire fence. I squint, trying to distinguish whether he's at the gate today. But I can't see a thing; I have to get closer.

"What do you want?" A large policeman standing on the other side of the fence asks me.

"I'm just walking here," I reply. He examines me. I can ask him about Mathéo, but it's dangerous. He can also demand that I get away from the fence. The policeman continues to scan my body with his eyes while he carelessly touches his rifle. He doesn't say a thing when I approach the guard post. Mathéo isn't there.

I keep walking along the fence surrounding the building. I have to find him. The guards know exactly why women like me approach the fence. They'll get their reward later at night

173

at the dark entrances of the building. We women pay the price, wounded souls in exchange for slices of bread and cigarettes.

I see him standing in front of the policeman's barracks near watchtower three. He's speaking to another policeman. I approach the fence and pause, watching him, hoping he'll notice me.

The minutes go by, and he doesn't notice me or walk toward the fence. What should I do? What should I do if he goes inside?

My daughter is going to die. I have nothing to lose.

I look around to make sure there aren't any policemen nearby, bend down, pick up a stone, and throw it in his direction. He must notice me.

At first, he and the other policeman don't seem to notice the stone thrown right next to them. But a few seconds later, the other policeman turns and starts walking in my direction.

'Not you, I need Mathéo, not you,' I whisper, but he walks slowly and approaches me. He casually places his hand on the leather holster of his gun. He's large, has dark brown hair, and a well-kempt mustache.

"What do you want?" His dark eyes scan me from behind the fence. He smirks, as if he knows what I'm about to offer in exchange for his help.

"I want to talk to him," I gesture at Mathéo who's watching us. I don't know if I'm doing the right thing.

"You're not in a position to want anything," he gives me an evil smile. "You're only in a position to offer."

"I'm not offering anything," I quickly reply. He doesn't care about my daughter. Maybe I'm wrong, and Mathéo won't either, but I'm out of options.

174

"Then why do you want to talk to him?" The policeman continues to scrutinize me, his hand still on the holster.

Think, think quickly about an answer.

"He knows," I reply after a moment. I couldn't think of anything better.

"Then call him yourself, dirty Jewess," he spits in my direction. "I came all the way here for nothing," he turns and starts to walk back to the barracks.

What will he say to Mathéo? I look down at the spit on my dress and feel sick. But when I look up, I notice Mathéo walking towards me. I breathe slowly. I have to choose the right words.

"What do you want?" He asks from the other side of the fence.

"I want to see you later tonight."

"I don't do those things," he replies. His green-brown eyes look into mine.

"Please, I have to."

"Then you should have said yes to the other police officer."

"Please, meet me tonight at ten o'clock at entrance three," I quickly say and turn around. I start walking away without waiting for an answer. I feel his gaze fixed on my back as I hastily leave. I'm all out of breath. I need him to come. I need him to help my daughter stay alive.

It's nighttime, and I wait in our room for the guard's shift change, due at ten o'clock. Soon, I'll go out to meet him.

I gently stroke Rebecca's hair as she breathes heavily. Occasionally, she coughs. I'm exhausted and scared.

"You know," I say to Charlotte, "before we went to the police in Paris, there was another option."

"What?"

"There was another opportunity," I swallow, "going to the police wasn't my only mistake."

"What do you mean?" Charlotte asks, her hand find mine.

"Before everything that happened with the police, we could have attempted to escape from Paris, heading south to the Free Zone and from there to neutral Spain," I speak slowly, weighing my words, "with a smuggler. He had several Jews with him."

"And what happened?"

"He claimed that Rebecca was too small and put all of us at risk. He wanted me to pay a special fee for her."

"Money?"

"No," I answer, taking a deep breath, "all he wanted was the payment that men desire. I couldn't bring myself to pay it because I'm a married woman." My finger brushes against my wedding ring. It feels so heavy.

"You did the right thing," Charlotte reassures me, squeezing my hand. "You shouldn't blame yourself."

"If I had known where we would end up, I would have paid the price. Believe me, I would have paid it without hesitation." I whisper. Since arriving at this camp, I've been blaming myself.

"You couldn't have known."

"But now I can, and I'm going to pay him. I have a daughter to save," I gently kiss Rebecca's warm forehead and stand up in the darkness, turning toward the stairs and entrance number three. I'll wait for him there.

The building's entrance is dark at night. I crouch near the stairs and take a few steps inside to avoid the rain that has started falling. As I stand there, protected from the rain and embracing myself, all I can hear is the raindrops echoing through the large yard. I'm going to do it. I won't think about what he'll do to me. I'll give him what he wants as long as he gets here.

The watchtower's spotlight suddenly turns on and startles me. I peek out and see the beam of light scanning the barbed wire fence and the yard. The raindrops look like fireflies fluttering through the beam of light before crashing into the puddles on the muddy ground. For a second, the beam of light shines on a woman and a policeman who are pressed against each other in one of the entrances. They appear exposed, like an American bomber in the night sky caught in the glare of Nazi anti-aircraft searchlights. Yet, after a second, they rush inside, seeking refuge once more from the probing light that continues to sweep across the building and surrounding fences.

Mathéo will come. I need him to come. As the spotlight fades, I step outside the entrance, disregarding the rain and peering towards the dark gate. I shiver with cold as my wet dress clings to my skin. I clutch the note with the medicine's name tightly in my hand. How long have I been waiting here?

In the darkness, I hear footsteps in the mud. I become tense, hopeful yet afraid. Then, I see a silhouette standing before me. Is it him? I struggle to recognize him in the dark. His body is completely covered by a military cape made of tarpaulin fabric.

177

The raindrops loudly tap on its thick surface. Is it him? Or did he send his friend? He stands at a distance and says nothing.

I nervously approach him without saying a word. The cold water seeps through my shoes. I notice the frame of his glasses.

"Come with me," I whisper, even though I can speak aloud. No one will hear us in this rain.

Wordlessly, he follows me to the building's entrance. All I can hear is his heavy breathing. He must have run in the rain. Why isn't he undressing and touching me?

I reach out, grab his hand, and place it on my wet dress, forcefully pressing his fingers against my breasts. I've done it with Mr. Charpak. I can do it now. "Take me," I say.

"I told you, I don't do those things," he pulls his hand away.

"I need this medicine," I grab his hand again and force it open, placing the note in it. "My daughter is going to die," my voice trembles; I sound like a wounded animal. "Please," I open the top buttons of my dress, grab his other hand, and place it on my belly. "Just take me, I want you to do it," I try to push his hand down. His fingers feel warm against my cold skin. "Please, I need to save my daughter. Just tell me what to do, and I'll do it."

"Sorry, I can't," he repeats and pulls his hand away. He turns around and walks into the rain.

"Please," I follow him and try to grab his cape, but in vain. He continues walking, disappearing into the darkness. What shall I do? I need medicine. My whole face is wet; I can't tell if it's covered in tears or rain.

"Please," I shout to the darkness as I drop to my knees and frantically search for the note in the puddles. Did he take it or throw it away when we spoke? I dig through the mud while the rain continues to hit my back like sharp pins. My tears mix with the raindrops falling on my face. But as much as I look for it, I can't find the piece of paper in the dark.

"Sarah," Charlotte calls me the next day at noon, after having looked out the window.

"What?" I respond. I'm sitting next to Rebecca, wiping her face with a wet cloth, trying to break the fever. She's breathing heavily.

"Your policeman is standing by the fence and looking inside."

"Where?" I stand up, go to the window, and look outside. My heart starts to pound in my chest.

He stands by the fence and watches the people walking in the yard among the puddles after the rain has stopped.

"Go to him," I think she says, but I can barely hear her. I'm already running down the stairs, panting. Did he change his mind? Will he agree to meet me at night?

In the yard, I stop running and start walking as fast as possible to avoid attracting attention. My gaze is focused on him. I long to believe he has changed his mind.

He stands upright behind the fence and looks inside. His arm is behind his back, and he scans the yard left and right until he notices me.

He has good news. He didn't just come to talk to me. He'll agree to meet me. I tell myself as I quickly approach him yet refrain from running.

179

"Good afternoon," I say, trying to catch my breath.

"Good afternoon," he examines me with his green-brown eyes. The golden frame of his glasses glint in the sun.

"Will you meet me in the evening?"

"Take this," he reaches into his pocket and pulls out a small cardboard box.

"What is it?" I reach over the wire fence and take the box, feel his warm fingers for a split second, and hastily pull my hand away. I don't want to draw any attention.

"Give her one pill at a time, three times a day, for at least a week," he continues to look at me and takes a step back. The touch of the cardboard box in my hand feels like the flame of a campfire in the darkest forest. He got me the medicine. How can I thank him?

I try to say something, but I'm choked, and can't utter a single word. I look down at the small cardboard box with German words, and a swastika stamp under the red cross. I have to say something. He waits.

"Why did you do this?" I finally ask, though I should thank him. But the thoughts spin through my mind. I look into his eyes, and all I can think about is Rebecca. "Why did you help me?" I try to catch my breath.

"Because I also believe in God," he replies, turns around, and walks back to the barracks.

"Thanks," I whisper, but I don't think he can hear me. "Thank you," I repeat and bring the cardboard box to my mouth, kiss the Nazi eagle clutching the swastika and the red cross, and tuck it into my pocket. I would hug him and place my head on his shoulder if I could. I tremble with excitement and am overwhelmed to the point that I have to hold onto the barbed wire fence, before I collect myself and walk quickly back to our room. I might be able to save my daughter.

Chapter Nine

The Summer of 1942

July 1942

"Mommy, look, another bus is coming," Rebecca stands by the fence and calls out excitedly, "and another bus, and another one," she points, reaching over the barbed wire fence, "Mommy, look how many buses."

"Try to count them. Let's see if you succeed," I tell her and watch the never-ending convoy of buses arriving at the road leading up to the camp. The buses' convoy is led by many black police cars, their fronts, with headlights on both sides, remind me of a bird of prey with wicked eyes and pointy beak. What's going on? Why do they bring so many buses here?

I put my hand on the barbed wire fence and look at the policemen coming out of their barracks, but I can't notice him.

I've been looking for him since that day, two weeks ago, when he brought me the medicine. I wanted to thank him, but each time I saw him, he stood at a distance and didn't come near the fence, even though I had stood and waited until the guards banished me.

"Seven, eight, nine, ten," Rebecca counts aloud, "Mommy, they keep coming."

What's going on here? Did they come to take us away from here and deport us to the Free Zone? I breathe anxiously. Could it be that the Red Cross came to free us? I'm searching for cars with a red cross symbol on them or a flag of the Red Cross. But no, the black police cars surround the buses outside the camp like a pack of wolves surrounding a herd of frightened sheep, and I see that the buses are full of people through their windows. They're not getting ready to send us from here to the Free Zone. They're filling this camp with more prisoners. Where do they get all these people from?

I look back. More people in the yard are approaching the fence and looking at the buses stopped outside the complex, and the policemen are now getting out of the police cars and standing around them.

"Everybody, move back," the large-bodied policeman with the thin mustache shouts to the people approaching the fence. "You too," he scolds Rebecca, and I hasten to pick her up and move a few steps back.

"Mommy, look, they're getting off the buses," Rebecca points. The newcomers get off the buses and gather, like a huge flock, directed by the policemen inside the registration office.

"Mommy, where will all these people live?" Rebecca asks and I think what to answer her. Where will they all stay? Other than the trains to the East, the camp is full.

"Each of them has a place waiting for them in the building, just like we do," I assure her, "the good policemen took care of everyone, and look, they're holding suitcases in their hands, unlike ours, which we forgot in Paris."

"Right, they have suitcases with pretty dresses and books and toys and chocolate," she says thoughtfully.

"And look," I point to two girls getting off one of the buses, holding on to their mother, "new girls are also coming, so you can play with them."

"Do you think they speak German and not just funny French?"

"I'm sure they'll speak German with you."

"Then maybe we should go and say hello to them? I'll tell Liza and Hilda to open the gate."

"Let's wait a bit. Let's let them come and settle in. They must be excited to come to a new place."

"Okay," Rebecca nods.

"Try to count the children who come in, but in French."

"Do I have to count in French?"

"Yes, those are the rules of the camp. Counting children is only allowed in French."

"Un, deux, trois, quatre..." Rebecca counts while I watch the people entering the camp holding on to their luggage, looking around in fear and shock.

"Water, do you have water?" A woman about my age with disheveled hair approaches us and points to a girl that a man is holding in his arms, "We haven't had any water for three days." She looks tired.

"Right away, I'll get you some," I put Rebecca down. "Rebecca, go to Charlotte and tell her to bring the bucket with the water to the yard."

"May I stop counting in French?"

"Yes, now go as fast as you can." I send her on her way and watch the deshelled woman. She has her Star of Life and Death on her dress. "Where are you from?" I ask her.

"From all around Paris," she replies. "Three days ago, we were gathered from all around Paris to the Winter Stadium, south of the Eiffel," she speaks quietly, "and we've been there since, without any water and food."

"Take it," I take the slice of bread I saved to give Rebecca later out of my dress pocket. I'll give her my dinner instead.

"Thank you," she holds the slice of bread and approaches the girl cradled in the man's arms, strokes her hair, and gives her the bread.

I look at the man holding the young girl and want to cry. I wish I had such a family.

"Sarah," Charlotte comes over, panting and holding the bucket of water. "Rebecca told me there are a lot of thirsty people here and that she couldn't count the children," she puts the bucket on the ground and hands the woman an enamel cup full of water. The woman first gives the young girl to drink, then the man, and finally drinks some herself.

More people gather around us and some other people from the camp bring buckets of water and hand them out. Some take food out and share it with them. What happened in Paris? I look at the new people's faces. They're all wearing a yellow badge, and most are healthier than us, but their faces express confusion and a lack of understanding.

"They knocked on our door at 6 a.m. and gave us ten minutes to get organized," a man of fifty or more tells another man standing next to him. He's wearing a business suit and tie with a hat, and his wife is standing next to him wearing a fur coat. "I bravely fought in the French Army in the previous war. All my life, I was a respectable banker, and now they imprisoned me like a criminal," he adds and reaches for the plain enamel cup.

"The big stadium was full. There was no room to move," adds a woman wearing a blue summer dress. "And this morning, they started moving us here. They're going to bring everyone here, to this camp. There are no Jews left in Paris. They've arrested all of us."

I also hand her a cup of water and look at Charlotte. Is she thinking what I'm thinking? Are they preparing to move us all to the East? Where will they accommodate us all? What did the Germans decide regarding us?

"Rebecca, come on," I take her hand in mine and grab the empty water bucket, "we need to go back to our room."

"Can I say hello to the new girl?" She walks in her direction and starts talking to her in German. But the little girl remains in the man's arms and watches her without answering.

"Mommy, I think she doesn't know how to speak neither French nor German. Maybe she's still afraid of the hunters. I'll tell her there are good hunters too," Rebecca tells me as we walk hand in hand back to the big building with Charlotte. She gets stronger and talks more with every day that passes.

I see the first families, who've already registered, moving toward the building. They'll look for a place to sleep just like we did on our first night here.

"May I?" A man wearing a long, brown coat and carrying a suitcase enters our room later that day. He moves the sheet hanging on the door, which gives us a little privacy, and stands in the doorway.

"Yes, please," Charlotte and I rise to see him. Behind him stand two women with black, curly hair tied up in a ribbon. "I'm Sarah," I get up and reach out my hand, "come in." The women are about my age.

"I'm Charlotte," Charlotte also holds out her hand.

"Laurent Levy," he shakes our hands, "and this is my wife, Naomi, and her sister, Pauline," he introduces them as they smile awkwardly. "We're from the Paris' 3rd arrondissement."

"Come in, welcome."

"So, this is where you live?" He carefully steps in, looking around the small room and the straw scattered on the floor.

"Yes, we have for a year now," Charlotte answers.

"Don't go into their room. They're German," I hear the voice of Alexandrine, our neighbor from the other side of the corridor, behind them.

"It's okay, we're Jewish, like you," I place my hand on my yellow badge. But they remain standing hesitantly at the door.

"Just so you know, there are some people among the residents who report to the Nazis. We don't trust them." Alexandrine keeps talking to them from the corridor.

For a moment, Mr. Levy stands and holds his suitcase, debating whether to put it on the floor, but then, his wife whispers something to him.

"I'm sorry," he says with an embarrassed smile and leaves the room after his wife and her sister, who disappeared down the corridor.

"She's dangerous to us," Charlotte whispers to me.

"At least they didn't move in with us," I answer.

"Do I have to give the man with the suitcase my bed? Where will I sleep?" Rebecca asks.

"No honey, you won't have to give up your bed," I caress her hair, knowing that Charlotte is right. Everyone here is afraid of what is going to happen, and when people are afraid, they search for traitors to blame.

"They're taking the teacher," someone says as we stand in the long line for water a few days later.

I look up and see two policemen walking behind Mr. Gaston, their hands resting on the leather holsters.

"What will happen to the children?" Some woman whispers.

I should look away, but I can't; I stare at him. Mr. Gaston walks in front of them slowly, wearing a beret hat and brown coat, holding a simple suitcase. For a split second, our eyes meet before he turns his gaze away and keeps walking towards the gate, to the collection point, where the people are going before heading towards the train. For a moment, he stops, takes his glasses off, and cleans them with a handkerchief he took out of his coat pocket. I watch his fingers slide gently over the glass before he examines it against the sun, and places them back on his nose. One of the policemen approaches and pushes him, and he keeps walking. Even though I hate him, I feel nauseated.

"Is that Mr. Gaston, the teacher?" Charlotte asks me.

"Yes," I nod, still following him with my eyes, watching his hunched back as he walks slowly to the gate.

"No one will return from the East," I hear one of the men say. "My neighbor, when I was in Paris, worked for the railway company. He said that the Nazis are sending all the Jews to one place by trains from all over Europe."

"Maybe they're settling them there," someone else replies.

"All the Jews? In one place?" The man answers.

"In his book, Mein Kampf, Hitler said he wanted to exterminate us, the Jews," a woman standing in line joins the conversation.

"He doesn't really mean it," someone replies.

"Doesn't he?" She turns to him, "What do you think this place is?" She points at the building surrounding us, "A holiday resort?"

"It's just a transit camp, it's temporary," he replies.

"If it's better in the East, then how is it that no one here received news from anyone who went there?" She asks him.

"They're not sending the ones of German origin to the East," I hear a woman say behind me. Is that Alexandrine, who hates us? I turn to look, but it's not her. It's some other woman that I don't know.

"They must have contacts with the Nazis," someone else tells her, also standing behind us.

Do they know us? Maybe these are mothers of girls who study with Rebecca?

"They'll send us all to the East, eventually, and the German Jews will be left in this French camp," a third woman says.

"Don't answer them," Charlotte whispers to me, "they're looking to fight. That's all they want." And I turn my back to them and keep standing in line.

"I heard that they know who's being taken in advance and manage to get them removed from the lists," says another woman. I cannot recognize who she is.

"Come on, the line is moving," Charlotte whispers and takes my hand. I walk with her and clutch my hand around the heavy wooden bucket's handle until my fingers turn white. I can try and hit them with the bucket should a fight start.

"Some of the families who have children were taken, but not German woman's daughter, her mother must've taken care of that," says one of them, and I feel her words hit my back as if they were red-hot iron nails. *Breathe, breathe, don't answer her. They're looking for a fight.*

"Everyone in the camp is talking about it." the other woman says, "Maybe they pass information to the Nazis. How did they even get here? They should've been in the camp in Germany," She keeps talking. Charlotte's hand grips my arm.

"Maybe we should report them so the Nazis, have them take them first."

"I'm Jewish, just like you!" I turn around and shout at the women, showing them the yellow badge embroidered on my dress, almost tearing it off with my fingers, "and no one will touch my girl."

"We don't believe you," one of them says. She wears a black dress, and her dark eyes stare at me, "You get preferential treatment."

"Do you really think we get preferential treatment?" I show her the empty bucket and point to the line, waiting for the water faucet, "Does this seem like preferential treatment to you?" I fight the tears, a lump in my throat.

"So why have you been here for a year and still haven't been taken to the trains?" Her friend asks me.

"How do you know how long we've been here? How long have you been here?" Charlotte responds.

"It's none of your business how long I've been here. I'm French. This is my country," she replies.

"Believe me that when the war is over, I'd love to leave France and never return, but I'm here now, and you'll have to get used to it," Charlotte shouts at her.

"We heard what women like you do at night with the German soldiers," another woman joins the conversation and yells at Charlotte. I look around at the women, their eyes watching us with hatred, like a pack of wolves surrounding its pray, waiting for it to make a mistake and stumble.

"Enough, enough, it's hard enough here without looking reasons to fight," a large man, wearing a blue shirt, steps in and stand between us. "Do you want the police to come here and see what's going on?"

"Never mind them," Charlotte grabs my arm again, and I return to the queue. But I'm still breathing heavily. Everyone here is looking for culprits.

"I don't believe them," I can still hear one of the women whispering to her friend.

I rub my forehead. I'm tired of being so different, hated by the Germans, hated by the French. The lump in my throat

ALEX AMIT

doesn't fade, like there's an invisible rope tightening around it.

"What's the name of this camp, the one all the Jews are being sent to?" Someone asks the man who started the conversation and led to the quarrel.

"Auschwitz," he answers. "Here, in the camp, you don't know what's going on outside. My neighbor, the one who works for the railway company, said that the Germans are killing the Russians as if they were mice, including all the Jews they find there."

❧

"Mommy, I don't want to die," Rebecca bursts into our small room a few days later, her face drenched in tears.

"Of course, you won't die," I hug her, "I'm protecting you."

"But they said I'd die, that they'd take us all to the East, and we'll die there," she whines and refuses to relax.

"Who said that? Liza and Hilda, the German commander's daughters?" I wipe her tears with a handkerchief that I take out of my dress pocket. Charlotte stops drawing and watches us both. Do the daughters of the German commander know something they're not telling us? They'd taken Rebecca outside the fence on two more occasions since the first time she'd played with them. Even though I'm afraid of them and watch her from afar, I try to convince myself that Mathéo is right and it's better for her that they like her. Anyway, I can't tell her not to go. They're Captain Becker's daughters.

192

"No, not Liza and Hilda, they make me laugh. They say I'm a German Shepherd that needs to pick up Sylvie in the field when she runs away and throw her to me so I can catch her, or they tell me to crawl on the ground like all the Jews."

"So, who told you that awful thing?" I ask her, holding myself from explaining the meaning of their behavior to her. It's better that she won't understand.

"One of the new French girls," she resumes crying, "we were playing catch, and I caught her by the hair, and she cried and said I was a stinky German and that her father said that soon they'd take me on a train to the East and kill me like they took Mr. Gaston, the teacher. Did they take Mr. Gaston, the teacher, on a train to the East?"

"Yes, they took Mr. Gaston to the East, but just because he wanted to go there. No one will take you to the East, I promise," I keep hugging her.

"So, I no longer need to go to his class and have him beat me with the ruler?" She wipes her tears.

"No, you don't have to go to his class anymore. Now, he'll teach children in the East," I turn my gaze to Charlotte. She's drawing a group of Jews leaving the camp toward the train. Has anything changed? Have the Germans decided to deport us all from here?

"So, what will I do during school time?"

"Let's go out into the sun," I stand up and hold Rebecca's hand. "Let's see if Liza and Hilda are there, and you can play with them. Would you like that?"

"Yes," she nods and takes my hand, and we head for the stairs. How low have I sunk that I suggest she plays with the camp commander's daughters? I feel sick to my stomach, fearing I had made an unwise decision. I hope they're not out there today.

"They're not here," Rebecca says as we stand by the fence and look out. The grass in front of the German commander's barracks is empty. Only two German soldiers are standing on the road leading up to the camp. Their rifles are on their shoulders, and they're looking toward the houses surrounding the camp as if waiting for something to happen. The buses' parking lot is also empty.

"Maybe they'll arrive soon," I tell her. It's nice being outside in the sun and not inside a crowded building full of voices and smells of people all around.

"Mommy, there's a car coming. Maybe they're coming," Rebecca says and reaches her hand beyond the barbed wire fence.

"Maybe it's them," I say and look at the car, but I realize I'm wrong, a moment later. This isn't the usual military vehicle of the camp commander, Captain Becker. It's a larger and more luxurious, teal-colored military vehicle with an open top and small red swastika flag flying on both sides of its hood. While the car is approaching the camp, the two soldiers stand still and salute. I see the uniforms and the black caps of the Nazi officers' sitting in the car. Why did they come here?

"Let's go back to Charlotte and our room," I say to Rebecca.

"But you told me we'd wait to see when Hilda and Liza will arrive. Maybe they're in this car."

"We should go back. I forgot Charlotte told me she wanted to draw you. Would you like Charlotte to draw you?" I pick her up and start walking away from the fence, not waiting for her to reply.

194

"And what about Liza and the Hilda?"

"They're sick today. They'll come tomorrow," I'm ashamed of all the lies I tell her, but I have no other choice.

Far from the fence, among the people, I stop and turn around to look at the Nazi vehicle. Who are these commanders?

While the car approaches Captain Becker's barracks, I see him coming outside with several soldiers and standing in attention, waiting for the car to stop while he salutes.

Several German officers get out of the vehicle. One of them salutes back at Captain Becker and then shakes his hand. They all approach the camp barbed wire fence while talking, and Captain Becker explains something to him while pointing at us. What are they planning for us? Again, I feel that uneasy feeling in my stomach. Could the rumors be true?

"Mommy, you said Aunt Charlotte wanted to draw me, but now you just stand and look at the long German car with the little red flags."

"You're right, I forgot. Let's go back to Aunt Charlotte and she'll draw you," I tell her and turn around. On the way to our room, I pass other people in the yard, who are strolling as if enjoying the sun but are actually looking at the group of Nazi officers in black uniforms standing outside the fence and talking about us.

"I'm scared for Rebecca. I'm scared for us," I tell Charlotte later that night. We both stand and lean on the windowsill of our small room, feeling the warm summer breeze on my face while Rebecca sleeps quietly. "Today, I saw a group of Nazi officers in black SS uniforms outside the camp. They are planning something for us."

"Sometimes I think they sealed our fate," she says. "No one will succeed in defeating the Nazis, not even the Americans who joined the war. They're too far away. The British won't succeed either."

"I always believed that good will prevail over evil and light will defeat darkness," I caress the Star of Life and Death on my dress, "but I'm not sure about that anymore."

"Do you think they'll send us to the East?"

"Yes. I think you believe that too. We both know we're here on borrowed time."

"I really want to smoke a cigarette right now," she says quietly, "I earned two today, and I don't know whether to exchange one for two potatoes or a few moments of silent pleasure."

"What will happen to Rebecca?" I turn to her. I can see her silhouette in the dark as she sleeps on the straw. "I want to get her out of here so badly, hide her in a safe place, wrap her so nothing bad happens to her."

"For how long?"

"Until there's a miracle and the Nazis lose, until she grows up, I don't know how long; she's so small. A little girl like her shouldn't be in a place like this."

"Yes, little girls shouldn't be in a place like this, not even big girls. I'm afraid of the East. I believe the stories," Charlotte says.

"I want her to be saved should anything happen to me." I hold myself back from going over and hugging her. She'll wake up. "After the way she got sick, I'm afraid she won't survive the winter in the East."

"When I was in the south of France," Charlotte speaks slowly, "when the Nazis arrived and started banishing Jews, there was a family I knew there, the Hirschs. They smuggled their two children to a monastery to look after them until the war will end."

"And what happened to them? To the parents?"

"I don't know. One day they disappeared, the police probably caught them. I hadn't heard from them since."

"And if the war doesn't end? Will she grow up as a Christian girl?" I caress my Star of Life and Death again. What is Rebecca's Star of Life and Death?

"At least she'll grow up," Charlotte bends down and lights herself a cigarette, sitting on the room's floor so the flicker of the cigarette won't be seen outside; only the acrid smell of smoke wafts through the space and out of the open window, into the dark night. I look out the window at the stars in the sky. What's more important to me? To stay together or to try and get her out of here and maybe save her? What's riskier?

"Do you think getting a girl out of here is possible? Without them noticing?" I ask her. I can hardly get those words out of my mouth. I feel like I'm breaking down just thinking about it. What would I do without her?

"I don't know," she inhales from the cigarette again, and the light flickers for a moment, "maybe the police can; maybe that one you went to back then."

"Mathéo? He works for them. Even if he helped me, would you entrust your daughter's life in his hands?" I ask her and regret it. I shouldn't have said that to her. "I'm sorry," I add, "I know Rebecca is important to you, and you treat her as if she is your own daughter."

"You know, when I was a rebellious girl and would run away from the outside world into painting, I thought I wouldn't be a good mother, that something was wrong with me."

"Nothing's wrong with you," I tell her.

"And I convinced myself that I didn't need a family and that I'd manage with my paintings, which are my family," she keeps speaking, "Until you came along."

"At first, I didn't trust you. I was wrong."

"I know," she inhales from her cigarette, "but there was that time Rebecca called me Aunt Charlotte. That was the moment I realized you're not afraid of me anymore. I love that she calls me Aunt Charlotte."

"You're her aunt," I move away from the window and sit beside her on the floor, placing my hands on hers.

"Sarah, I've wanted to have a daughter like Rebecca ever since I've met you, but I now know it's too late," she says quietly.

"It'll happen, I promise."

"No, you can't promise me that. I'm not a six-year-old like Rebecca," she smiles at me, "and that's okay. I've accepted that I'll never have a child of my own," she inhales from her cigarette again. "But you must protect your daughter, you need to get her out of here, ask your policeman, your dealer, whoever will get her out of here; that's what I'd do if she were my daughter. That's what you need to do."

"Angelina," I whisper.

"What?"

"Angelina is the owner of the hotel we stayed at in Paris for a year. She's the only one who might take care of her," I spit the words out, looking to get them out so I won't be able to regret having said them. "I have no other place to take her to. I'm Jewish, and I'm a foreigner. I don't know a priest, or anyone connected to the church or the monastery. I have no idea where her father is. Only God knows where her father is, whether in Madrid or elsewhere. He didn't come to help us, that's for sure. I'm a stranger here, in this country, just like you. Angelina's the only one I know outside of this camp who I can somewhat trust." I stop talking, feeling both relief and fear after having said those words, as if they took on a meaning and a life of their own.

"And will she accept her?"

"She won't accept her for free. She may be nice, but no one will risk their lives to hide Jews for free, especially after everything that those who arrived here in the last few days have told us about." I get up and go back to look out the window at the dark night outside.

"So, what will you do?"

"I'll pay her with the last thing I have left to pay with," I caress my wedding ring.

"And how do you know she'll accept Rebecca?"

"I don't know. I have no way of checking. I don't even know if I can get her out of here," I say quickly, before regretting my thoughts. Is it right to get her out of here? Why don't I have the right answer? What if I'm wrong?

"The policeman or the dealer?" Charlotte puts out her cigarette and stands up, joining me by the window.

"I don't trust either one of them, but I have to choose between the one who'll sell anything for money and the one who works with the Nazis and might throw her on the train without me knowing."

"You're doing the right thing," she places her hand on mine.

"Thanks," I say. I'm not sure that I'm doing the right thing at all. "Can you watch her for a few minutes?" I ask her after a while.

"Yes," she replies, and I leave for the stairwell before I regret it. I have to take the risk and get her out of here. Deep down, I know she won't be able to survive if they take us to the East. And I must choose who I trust more.

"What do you want now?" Charpak raises his gaze from the deck of cards he's holding and asks me as he notices me standing in the doorway. He and several other men I'd never seen here before sit around the improvised table. The crowded room is stifled with cigarette smoke and the smell of sweat. I look at the table full of coins, bills, and cigarettes. Where does all this money come from?

"Who's she?" A man in a blue jacket turns and examines me, his hair carefully styled with gel and his blue pin-striped tie matches his tailored jacket. Only the yellow badge stands out against his fancy outfit. The other men, who had stopped playing and are looking at me, are also well-dressed. I feel embarrassed in my simple dress. It's the only one I've had since we got here.

"Leave her alone," Charpak says to the man who asked, crushing his cigarette, and placing his cards on the table, "Continue without me. I'm done. I've got bad ones anyway," he gets up and approaches me. Of all the men around the table, he's the only one wearing a plain, dirty, white tank top.

"Let's go," he holds my arm and leads me over to the wall, "They're still new here," he says. "They arrived in the last batch from Paris with all the Jews the Nazis had banned," he points at the men behind the wall, "they don't yet understand that they'll need this money and cigarettes to buy food. And that a nice jacket and tie are worth as much as an old tank top here," he smiles at me. "Why did you come here now? Is your daughter okay? Have you made up with the other women who're angry at you?"

"Yes, she's fine," I answer, ignoring his second question. I didn't come here to talk about myself. "Have you ever gotten anyone out of this camp?" I look into his eyes in the weak light.

"I won't answer that question," he looks back at me, his brown eyes studying me while his bald head sweats from the summer heat.

"Can you do it?"

"Depends on the price. Getting someone out of here isn't a small thing. It's not like getting a few slices of bread, oil, or potatoes. It's also not like smuggling shoes or a coat inside the camp. It's getting someone out under the watchful eyes of the Nazis as well as passing the checkpoints on the roads."

"I want you to get my girl out of here."

"The one who was sick?"

"I almost lost her. I'm afraid she won't survive the journey to the East and whatever they have prepared for us there."

Charpak says nothing. But keeps watching me.

"Can you do it?" I ask him after a moment. I'm afraid to go to Mathéo, he's on the Nazis' side.

"You're a smart woman, unlike them," Charpak signals at the men playing cards. I can hear their laughter beyond the wall.

"I'm a woman alone. I have to be smart," I keep looking into his eyes, even though he's standing too close. His body smells unpleasantly sour.

"Will you pay me what I want?" He reaches out and takes my hand, stroking the wedding ring I'm wearing on my finger, "I want that."

"You won't get it," I breathe deeply. The touch of his hand makes me feel uncomfortable, but I don't move his fingers away. I'm going to offer him much more than a touch, "You'll get this. I already know how things work in this place," I hold his hand and place it on my chest, breathing deeply. He's already touched them the previous time, and Mathéo also touched them as well. I'm a woman, and this is the only currency I have to pay for my daughter's life. I hear his breaths and see his smile, fighting my urge not to flinch or run away from the small room.

"What happened?" His hand forcefully squeezes my breasts through my dress, "You keep the ring because you still believe in marriage, but you don't believe in fidelity?" He keeps holding on to my breasts, crushing them as if they were dough.

"I don't believe in anything anymore," I take a deep breath and take his hand off my breasts, "You get my daughter out, and I'll pay you. And now you know exactly what payment you'll receive." I get the words out of my mouth, knowing I won't be able to take them back. I won't take them back. I need him to get my daughter out of here.

"And where shall I take her?" He continues to hold my hand, "You know the Nazis are still looking for Jews all over Paris. Even if I get her out, she'll be like an abandoned, stray cat to them, an easy target to collect."

"I'll give you an address in Paris. You'll make sure she gets there," I answer.

"Give me an advance."

"This is your downpayment," I unbutton the top three buttons of my dress and pull the camisole aside, showing him my breasts. Despite the warm evening air, I tremble before him. I hate myself for what I do, feeling small, low, like an object. I'm an object to him, an object to Mathéo when I stood before him in the rain, begging for medicine for Rebecca, and an object to my husband who had to watch over us. My body is a currency that passes to whoever's willing to give me something I desperately need. I forcefully hold his hands with mine, so that he won't try to touch my bare breasts.

"In four days, on Tuesday, bring her to me at noon. I'll wait for you," he says after a moment.

"How will you get her out?" I cover my breasts and button up my dress, breathing slowly.

"It's none of your business. I have my ways."

"Have you done this before?"

"That's also none of your business."

"She's my daughter, so it is my business." I insist. I must be sure that I can trust him.

"You bring her to me. There's a bread and potatoes truck that comes over every day. I'll take care of her. I'll put her in an empty potato sack, and they'll get her out. They'll bribe whoever needs to be bribed."

"She'll have a note in her dress pocket with the address."

"They'll take her there."

"In four days, I'll bring her to you," I repeat his words, starting to realize their meaning. "You can go back to your friends," I gesture at the men who continue to play cards in the main room. Standing in front of him makes me nervous.

"They're not my friends, they think they'll make money here, and they don't realize they'll lose their lives."

"Four more days," I turn to leave the room; I want to return to my daughter.

"Wait," he puts his hand on my arm.

"What?" I once again turn to him. Did he change his mind?

"You never told me your name," he looks at me.

"Does it matter to you?" I want to get out of this stifling room.

"I'm asking."

"Sarah. My name is Sarah."

"Sarah, you're a good mother. You're doing the right thing," he looks into my eyes, serious.

"In four days, she'll be here at noon," I say to him quickly and leave the room, heading for the stairwell. Did he tell me these things so I'd trust him and not regret it? Was I right to choose him and not Mathéo?

"Deal the cards," I can still hear Charpak saying to the other men before I go down the stairs. I feel nauseous, and as I go down the stairs, the nausea increases.

What if I'm wrong? What if Angelina is no longer at the hotel? What if she doesn't accept Rebecca or throws her out on the street? A year has passed since we left her hotel. What if he's cheating me? What choice do I have in choosing someone else? What mother sends her daughter away like that? I stop at the bottom of the stairwell and throw up.

"Are you okay? Are you sick?" A strange man entering the stairwell asks me.

"Yes, I'm fine, I'm not sick," I wipe my mouth with my hand, ignoring the sour taste in my mouth. I'm not telling him that I'm a mother who has to say goodbye to her daughter.

"Rebecca, sit down. I need to talk to you," I tell her the following day.

"Mommy, look what I drew," she shows me a sheet of paper with three women painted on it, two big ones with hands like broomsticks, and a small girl standing between them, with wild hair, and smiling.

"It's a lovely painting. Can I keep it?" I look at the smiling girl.

"Yes, but wait, I still need to add Sylvie and also chocolate, because Sylvie loves chocolate very much and Aunt Charlotte hasn't given me brown color yet, because she said she uses it, but she will soon."

"I'll give it to you right away," Charlotte tells her as she bends down on the floor and draws the building and the people standing in line for the water.

"Rebecca, come on, sit next to me. I need you to listen to me and do everything I tell you to." I hold her hand, trying to concentrate on the words I'm about to say to her.

"Mr. Gaston is back from the train to the East, and I have to go back to school?" She remains standing and watches me.

"No, Mr. Gaston didn't come back from the train to the East," I take a deep breath. How will I tell her that no one is returning from the train to the East and that I have to leave her? "Rebecca, do you like to play?"

"Yes," she nods.

"And do you like to play hide and seek?"

"Yes," she nods again.

"And do you love Angelina?"

"Aunt Angelina, who smells like flowers?"

"Yes," I smile at her.

"She gave me chocolate, Mommy. Does she still have the suitcase with the book? Didn't she send it on the bus?" She asks excitedly.

"Yes, she has the suitcase," I smile at her, "and in three days, we'll have a surprise."

"What kind of surprise?"

"I'll take you to a nice man, named Mr. Charpak, who likes to play hide and seek, and he'll hide you in a big canvas sack," I say, trying to choose my words so as not to scare her off, "Do you agree?"

"Can I hide Sylvie in there with me? She also wants to play."

"Of course, she loves to play hide-and-seek. It'll be fun for you both inside the sack. But you must be quiet and not move until they open the sack."

"And what if they find us in the sack?"

"You'll be quiet, and no one will find you. They'll put you on a truck, and no one will discover you, and then, they'll take you to Angelina."

"Who, Mr. Chambu?"

"Mr. Charpak or someone else who will take you, but the most important thing is that you have to do whatever he tells you until they bring you to Angelina. You won't be allowed to leave the sack until they open it."

"And the bad hunters will look for me like they searched for Sylvie in the forest?"

"No, the bad hunters won't be looking for you. They'll be taking their noon nap. And the good hunters will be watching over you."

"Like the good hunter with the glasses?" She keeps asking.

"Yes, like the good hunter with the glasses, but not him. There'll be another good hunter watching over you. Even if you can't see him."

"Where will he be?"

"He'll hide in the bushes or a tree, like hunters do, but you mustn't look for him. Just know that he's watching over you and that they'll take you to Angelina."

"And where will you be?" She asks me, and I gasp. What should I tell her?

"I'll look after Aunt Charlotte, and in a few days, I'll join you at Angelina's, and we'll be there until the war is over."

"And will Aunt Charlotte come with you to Angelina?"

"Sure. Do you want her to come too?"

"Yes," Rebecca nods, "and Dad will also come?"

"Yes, Dad will come too," I promise her, knowing that nothing I promise her will ever come true.

"And we'll all be at Angelina's until the bad hunters leave?"

"Yes, exactly like that," I caress her hair, scared of what will happen.

"Dear Angelina," I write on a piece of paper later at night, watching my tears get the thin paper wet.

"...I am sending you Rebecca, my dearest daughter. I had no other choice.

I'll come to get her when I can.

Check her dress, there's a hidden payment for you there.

Thanks,

Sarah"

I then take the wedding ring off. It easily slips off my thin finger.

"Three more days," Charlotte whispers to me.

"Yes, three more days," I watch Rebecca as she's sleeping. I carefully sew a hidden pocket in her dress and hide the ring there. I'll miss her so much.

✦

"Two more days," I whisper to myself as I look out the window in the morning - two more days of tension. I watch two policemen walking in the yard and pointing a gun at a man who's walking in front of them. He walks towards the gate and the train gathering area carrying a suitcase. I won't have to worry so much for my daughter in two more days.

Beyond the barbed wire fences, I see the camp commander's military vehicle arriving. The driver gets out and opens the back door for the camp commander's daughters. Maybe it's not a good idea for Rebecca to play with them? What if she tells them something regarding what I talked to her about yesterday?

I turn back and see her feeding Sylvie, the girl bear, a breakfast made of straws.

"Today we only have two slices of straw, but tomorrow you might get a potato, and for your birthday a piece of chocolate," she explains to the rag doll sitting next to her on an old blanket, "and if you behave, you can go play with Hilda and Liza in the yard in front of the barracks of the eagle with the sharp claws. We'll play hide and seek with them."

I want to ask her why she calls him the eagle with the sharp claws and why she mentions a game of hide and seek. Could it be that I was wrong and spoke to her too soon? I had to prepare her. I'm breathing slowly. There are only two more days to go, and I'll be able to get her out of this scary place. Charlotte sits in the corner of the room and draws one of her paintings: a woman raises her hands before a policeman pointing a gun at her. She focuses on painting while holding an extinguished cigarette in her mouth. Only once every few days does she allow herself to light a cigarette.

"Mommy, have they arrived yet?" Rebecca asks me.

"Who?" I ask back, knowing who she's waiting for. I hoped she'd forgotten about them.

"Hilda and Liza," Rebecca leaves breakfast with Sylvie and gets up, runs to the window, and looks outside. "They're here, let's go," she goes over and picks up the rag doll and holds my hand, "Bye Aunt Charlotte," she says to her.

"Bye, Rebecca, behave." Charlotte tells her without raising her eyes from the painting on the floor, her hands holding the brush and dipping it in the gouache colors.

A pleasant sun lights the yard as we walk toward the fence. Before we approach the gate, I stop and bend over to Rebecca, placing my hand on her shoulder.

"Rebecca, sweety, listen to me. It's very important," I look into her eyes.

"Yes, Mummy," she looks back at me, but after a moment, grabs Sylvie and takes out a piece of straw left over from breakfast out of her mouth.

"It's important that Sylvie also listens. Do you think she knows how to keep a secret?"

"Yes," Rebecca nods.

"And do you promise me she that won't tell the secret?"

"Secrets must not be told," Rebecca looks at me seriously.

"Exactly, no telling secrets," I smile at her. "So, do you remember what I talked to you about last night?"

"About Angelina, and the hide and seek and the man with the note?"

"Yes, exactly, so it's a secret you mustn't tell anyone, absolutely nobody, only you and Sylvie know about it. You mustn't tell anyone, not even Liza and Hilda," I keep holding on to her shoulder, making sure she listens to me. What will happen to her if she tells them?

"Even if they give me chocolate?"

"Even if they give you chocolate."

"Okay," she nods and looks towards the barbed wire fence and their direction. "Can we go?"

"Do you promise? And Sylvie mustn't tell them either."

"Okay," she nods, "even if they offer her chocolate; she won't tell."

"Okay," I hug her tightly, desperately hoping that she understands that she has to keep the secret.

"Mommy, you're hurting me."

"Sorry, let's go to them," I stand up and take her hand, and we walk to the barbed wire fence so she can wave to them. On the side of the gate, the people on the way to the train and the policemen watching them are already gathered. I turn my eyes from them and look at Rebecca waving to Hilda and Liza, reaching her hand through the fence.

Two more policemen enter the yard. One of them examines Rebecca and me with his gaze. His eyes scan my face and body and move on to Rebecca. I feel that I'm all tense. But after a moment, they walk inside, and I breathe in relief. Just two more days.

"Bye, Mommy," Rebecca waves goodbye at me as another policeman approaches the gate and orders her to go out and to the camp commander's daughters. I examine him with my eyes. I don't know him. Will she be okay when she's out of the fence?

Slowly, I walk back toward our room, stopping now and then and looking back. Everything's fine. I'm just nervous about this place. Outside the fence, the camp commander's daughters throw Sylvie on the ground, and Rebecca crawls to their feet. The fact that they like to play with her guarantees she stays alive here for at least two more days.

The stairwell is quieter than usual as I climb up to our room, ignoring the woman peeking at me from one of the other apartments. But only as I move the sheet aside and go inside do I feel the cold wave down my back. Charlotte is standing against the wall with her hands above her head, the extinguished cigarette still stuck in her mouth, and a policeman standing in front of her pointing his gun at her, while the other policeman – the one who surveyed Rebecca and me earlier, at the gate – scatters her paintings all over the floor.

Chapter Ten

The train

"Start moving, get out now," the policeman points his rifle at Charlotte. "Both of you," he points his rifle at me next.

"What about our belongings?" Charlotte asks. She is still standing against the wall with her hands up in the air.

"You won't need them," the second policeman says. He stands up over her scattered drawings, lights a cigarette for himself, and smiles. "You won't need your drawings either," he throws the burning match on one of the drawings. I watch as the small flame trying to spread and eat away at a drawing of people in the yard standing in line in front of a Nazi officer, their heads hanging low. But the match goes out and fails to ignite the paper, leaving only a black ash stain, and the policeman steps on it with his boots.

Think, think, what can I do? What about Rebecca? I just need a few more days.

"Just two more days, then I'll go wherever you want," I quickly tell him and gasp. What will they do with us? Will they put us against the wall? I must save her.

213

"You know exactly where those who break the rules go," he blows the smelly cigarette smoke at my face. "The train is waiting for you. Start moving, get out," he also points his gun's barrel at me, "now."

"Two more days, please. I'll do whatever you want," I look at him with teary eyes. I think I can hear the women from the neighboring apartments whisper outside, but I'm not sure with all the screaming in my head. What will happen to Rebecca? I must find her and take her with me. I look at the foreigner's suitcase. It's closed in the corner of the room, next to the straw bed on which we sleep. It contains all the clothes I've collected over the past few months. Shall I take it or leave it behind?

"Move, now, without taking anything. What you're wearing is good enough for your trip," he shouts at me, taking my hand forcefully and pushing me toward the stairs.

Go down the stairs, ignore the people watching us from the corridors, ignore his rifle's barrel, which he occasionally sticks into my back, urging me to go faster. I'll see Rebecca, and I'll call her, she should come with me, this is the right thing. I go down the stairs and out to the yard. Next to me, I hear Charlotte's breaths. I think she's trying to tell me something, but I don't understand what it is. Where is my daughter? I'm all out of breath. I'm looking for her outside the camp's barbed wire fence.

"Where are you going?" The policeman hits my arm with his rifle and directs me toward the group huddled next to the gate. I'm not part of them. I have a girl here. I only have to take care of her for two more days and get her out of this terrible place. "Go ahead, join them," he grabs my hand again, pushes me into the crowd, and walks among the other policemen surrounding us. What about Rebecca? I can't see her outside the fence. There is talking and murmurs all around me. More people join the group and push me toward the barbed wire fence and the closed gate. Their body odor makes me sick.

"Sarah, are you okay?" Charlotte holds my hand, pushes through the people, and manages to get close to me.

"I have to find Rebecca," I yell at her. I don't think about the road and the journey to the East. All I can think about now is her. She's my daughter. She must come with me. I push through the people and approach the fence, leaving the group.

"You, go back," one policeman raises his voice and points his weapon at me.

"I have to find my daughter," I ignore his threat. "Rebecca," I shout, panting, "Rebecca," I look toward the commander's barracks. She's playing with the commander's daughters. "Rebecca," I shout and wave my hand at her.

"Mrs., I'm warning you," the policeman yells at me, but I ignore him.

"My daughter is there. I need to get her," I shout to him.

"You can't leave the group. Go back in," he shouts back at me. "You're on the list."

"I have to," I wave my hand at her. The policeman at the gate opens it, and the people start walking out slowly. "Rebecca," I shout, and I move toward the gate. A few people stand in the yard and watch us in silence. Where is Charlotte? I lost her among the crowd. Where's Mathéo? He'll help me, he must; he'll take us off the list. I'm looking for him among all the policemen, but he's nowhere to be found.

ALEX AMIT

"Please, help me," I run and fall at the feet of the large policeman with the thin mustache. "Please, my daughter," I whimper as I clutch his legs.

"Get back to the group," he yells at me and kicks my face, trying to free his legs, and I'm thrown backward onto the ground. For a moment, I fold at his feet, wipe the tears from my eyes, and try to get up, ignoring the metallic taste of blood in my mouth.

"I must get her. Where is Mathéo? The policemen," I whisper and get up, walk away a few steps from him, then start running toward the gate and the people passing through it. "Rebecca," I shout to her as I pass through the open gate along with all the people leaving the camp and keep running in her direction. But then I feel a terrible blow to my head, and there's darkness all around me.

"Sarah, are you okay? Sarah, get up, keep walking," someone caresses and holds on to my arm, and I try to get up. My head hurts so bad. "Sarah, are you okay?" The voice continues.

I'm out of the gate. My mouth is full of dirt and the taste of blood. Where is Rebecca? I look around.

The people keep walking around me; they overtake me.

"Sarah, you must get up. Put your hand on my shoulder, like this," I feel Charlotte's hands trying to pull me up so I can stand. A man I don't know in a bright button-up shirt, who smells of cigarettes, approaches us and helps her get me up. I put my hands on Charlotte's and his shoulders.

"You have to walk," he tells me. "They're looking at you," he turns his gaze to the two policemen slowly walking toward me.

"Rebecca," I say quietly, looking at her direction. As if in slow motion, I see her running with the camp commander's daughters, not noticing me. They throw Sylvie the bear in the air as she runs and tries to catch her. "My Rebecca," I whisper. My head hurts so much.

"Walk, keep walking," the man in the button-up shirt supports me as I lean on Charlotte's shoulder, and we walk among the people on the road leading to the houses around the camp. Once again, I turn my head and look for her, but the people around me hide her from me, and I can no longer see her. "My Rebecca," I whisper.

"I'm so sorry," Charlotte repeatedly says to me as she helps me walk slowly among the people on the main street, but I don't know why she's saying that. My head hurts so much, and I feel dizzy. The people walking around me seem to have nothing to do with me. They carry suitcases or bundles of clothes tied in a blanket on their backs. I watch a woman holding her daughter's hand. Her child walks quietly beside her and occasionally starts to run, trying to keep up the pace. She hasn't forgotten her Rebecca. Why does my head hurt so much? I touch my scalp, feeling a big, painful bump. What happened in the last few minutes? Everything is so unclear to me.

"Sarah, I'm so sorry," Charlotte continues to whisper to me while panting. My legs seem to continue on their own. I feel Charlotte's hand around my waist, supporting me all this time. Sometimes, the man in the button-down shirt helps her. Some people from the town are standing by the side of the road and looking at us. Only now, do I notice that German soldiers have replaced the French policemen, and they're walking beside us, holding on to their guns. I should try to escape, like that young man who tried to escape the day we arrived. I'll run away and get back to Rebecca. But I'm dizzy and nauseous, and I can barely walk. If Charlotte or the stranger will stop supporting me, I'll probably fall on the road, and the German soldiers will come to me. I feel like vomiting.

"I'm so sorry, it's my fault," Charlotte says again, as we enter the small train station with all the people and stand on the platform. The word 'Drancy' is written in large black letters on the wall of the two-storied small station building. Only one long freight train is waiting at the station. The doors of the brown, wooden carriages are wide open.

"What do you mean?" I finally turn to her and ask, speaking for the first time since what had happened at the gate.

"It's because of me, they took us because of my paintings. I'm so sorry," she looks at me, all teary-eyed.

I feel I'm getting even more nauseated. I can't answer her. I'm being taken away from my daughter because of her. Because of her paintings.

"Please, Sarah, say something," she looks at me pleadingly. But I have nothing to say to her. Not now. Her hand touches me, it feels like a branding iron searing my flesh. I want to expel all the pain from my heart, but I can't say a single word. I can't have her beside me. I let go of her hand supporting my body and slowly walk away from her, along the platform, making my way through the crowd.

"Everyone, get onto the carriages," someone holding a megaphone announces in German, his metal voice blows like a chilly wind through the platform.

We've been huddling in the crowded train car for several days now. I have no idea how long. I lost count. I stand inside the car and raise my head, trying to look above the people's heads at the light penetrating through the small window at the end of the car, during the day, or the few stars at night. The small window is covered with barbed wire, so no one tries to escape. Sometimes, I can see the tops of the trees when we pass through forests. Sometimes, I sleep standing up. Sometimes, I hallucinate and imagine Rebecca's voice calling or talking to me. I'm so thirsty. My throat is dry.

A day or two ago, we got water from people when the train stopped at one of the stations. I have no idea who they were. I didn't even see them. One of the men standing near the window said they spoke Polish. We carefully passed the enamel cup from one hand to another, over the people's heads, so that everyone could drink before the train continued on its way. My legs are so sore from standing for so long. Sometimes, I try to move a little, but it's impossible with all the people around me. I'm huddled between several women, but I have no idea where Charlotte is. I hadn't seen her since I walked away from her at the train station in Drancy, and we got into the carriages. And all this time, I hear the locomotive blowing like a dog that won't stop running. And all this time, I'm thinking about the fact that I lost my daughter.

"Auschwitz," a tall man standing next to the small window shouts in the car. "On the sign, it says that we're arriving at

Auschwitz," he shouts again and keeps looking out. "There are some village houses and a large camp here."

The people murmur louder as the train slows down. I'm so thirsty. Maybe we've arrived at our destination, at the resettlement camp.

The train suddenly stops, and the people in the car become quiet. Outside, I hear voices talking and dogs barking. Have we arrived?

Suddenly, the car door opens, and bright daylight breaks in. I blink, adjusting to it.

"Everyone, get off, leave all your belongings on the train," someone from outside shouts at us in German. "Schnell, schnell," and we hurry to get out and huddle on the platform. My legs almost refuse to walk after the prolonged standing. I look around at the large camp, the platform full of people, and German soldiers standing and guarding it, holding on to German Shepherds that are barking at us.

"Everyone, line up in two rows, men and women separately," someone shouts. I can make out Charlotte at the end of the platform. She seems to be watching me but doesn't walk in my direction. I don't approach her either.

What is this place?

The people begin to walk toward an S.S. officer standing at the end of the platform. He keeps his leather glove-clad hand indifferently in the air and signals the people in what direction to go - left or right. He sends most of the people to the left. What does it mean? I carefully touch the Star of Life and Death sewn to my dress. Who will take care of my daughter should something happen to me?

Chapter Eleven

Drancy, August 1942

"Mathéo, how much are you betting?" Sergeant Pascal turns to me as I exit the police barracks' door and stand on the balcony overlooking the camp.

"On what?" I ask him and look down, checking that my gun belt is properly secured and that I'm ready for duty.

"On her. We started a bet," he laughs and points toward the barbed wire fence and the yard full of people. I slide my fingers over my gun's leather holster, make sure it's secured, and the pistol is in place, then look up in the direction Sergeant Pascal is pointing.

Among all the people strolling the yard, one girl stands by the barbed wire fence and looks out. I know her, it's the wild-haired German girl.

"The girl standing by the fence?" I ask him and go inside the barracks for a moment, taking the rifle for my shift. No one should notice that I know her. This is against our orders.

"Yeah, the girl with the shaggy teddy bear," Sergeant Pascal says as I walk back out, putting the bullet belt over my shoulder. "She's been hanging around the fence for three days now," he says and sits on the bench on the wooden porch, lighting himself a cigarette. "We think they put her parents on the train to the East, and she was accidentally left behind. Do you know her?"

"No," I lie to him. I remember her and her mother.

Since I've arrived here, eighteen months ago, I've managed not to think about the people inside the fences. I've made sure to treat them as nameless people without an identity until the day her mother tried to get out and talk to the camp commander, and I stopped her. I have no idea why I did it; maybe her act surprised me. Her desire to go outside the fences, her confidence that she won't be harmed. A few days later, I saw her again in the roll call in the yard; this time, she was holding on to a wild-haired girl. Later, I was once again surprised when the girl approached me - the same girl who's now standing alone by the fence.

"What are you betting on?" I ask him and look at Sergent Pascal's big fingers holding his cigarette. He sits on the wooden bench and leans back, his belly protruding above his leather belt. The reduction of food in Paris in the last two years didn't seem to have affected him.

"We started betting on how long it would take her to collapse and go *kaput*," he says and laughs. "I don't believe it will take long. So, how much do you bet?"

"How do you know they took her parents?" I ask him while I keep looking at her. Was her mother sent to the East? Does she even have a father? "Are you sure they took her parents?" I ask him again.

"Trust me, I've been here long enough to know," he laughs and inhales from his cigarette. "A new policeman arrived here today. His name is Fernard," he gestures at a man standing on the grass in front of the barrack and waiting. "I want you to take him and show him the camp, show him the ropes."

I give the girl another quick look. She rests one hand on the barbed wire fence, and her other hand is holding on to something, some vague stuffed animal. Maybe it's the raggedy bear that Sergeant Pascal mentioned. "She looks like an abandoned stray cat to me," I say.

"Someone suggested that we just throw her on the train, but then we wouldn't have a bet. I informed everyone that no one is to touch her, so that the bet would be fair," he looks at me. "The minimum is five Francs. Cigarettes are also allowed."

"Thanks, but I'm not betting," I reply and put the rifle on my shoulder.

"Do you like Jews? I didn't think you were one of those Jew supporters," he says as he remains seated on the wooden bench.

"No, I don't like Jews. I like my money," I turn my back to him and go down the porch stairs. I have work to do.

"Good morning. Are you Fernard?" I ask the new policeman standing beside the police pick-up truck parked near the barracks. He's about twenty-one or twenty-two years old, his hair is fair, and he looks excited in his newly ironed uniform.

"Yes, sir, good morning, sir," he replies as I approach him.

"Don't call me sir. I'm not your commander. I'm a policeman, like you, and I'm only older than you. Mathéo," I shake his hand, "let's go inside, and I'll show you how things work here. Is today your first day?"

"Yes, I finished training, and I was assigned here," he answers as we approach the camp gate. "How long have you been a policeman?"

"Ten years," I reply. "Long before they arrived," I point at the Nazi barracks and their flag waving above it. "Let's go inside," I signal to the policeman at the guard post to open the gate.

"It's crowded here," Fernard looks around and says as we walk among the people strolling in the yard. The people anxiously watch us. I hate seeing the fear in their eyes; it makes me ashamed of myself.

"Yes, it's crowded here. There are a few thousand prisoners in the camp," I tell him.

"Is everyone here Jewish?"

"Most of them, but not all."

"Where are they from?"

"From all over France," I watch the long line of people waiting for water. "It seems that they send here anyone they don't want in France: Jews, communists, intellectuals, gay people. Anyone that doesn't fit their race policy."

"They're definitely cleaning up France."

"Yes..." I stand momentarily in front of one of the entrances to the large concrete building. This is the entrance where she waited for me in the rain, begging for medicine for her sick daughter. I feel the weapon strap with my fingers. I can still feel her warm skin on my fingertips, where she begged me to touch her that rainy night, holding my hand forcefully, making me feel her body. Where is she now? I look up at the windows full of people standing and looking down at the yard and us, but I can't see her.

"And how long will they be here?" Fernard asks me as we keep walking.

"Until the Germans decide; they make the rules here," I answer, thinking we're just their servants, even though they treat us well.

"Are they making any trouble?"

"The Jews inside? No, they're usually quiet and polite."

"They know who's in charge here," he smiles at me.

"Yes... although, sometimes there are quarrels and shouting..." I say and think about how she yelled at me when I took her girl to play with the camp commander's daughters. She was a proud woman in this place, struggling to keep her dignity. "Let's start heading back. My shift at the watchtower is about to start," I turn toward the entrance gate.

"Who's that girl standing by the fence and looking out? Are they allowed to touch the fence?" He points to the wild-haired girl.

"Yes, they're allowed to approach the fence. It's just one girl," I signal to the guard at the gate to open it. I stand in front of him as we get out of the camp, "Listen, Fernard, this place isn't a nice place. It's an internment camp. There are many people here who were free, proud French citizens and then were one day arrested. They don't get a lot of food or supplies here, and sometimes male or female prisoners try to contact us, the policemen. You must remember one thing."

"What?" He looks at me.

"Don't get attached to them, the prisoners," I watch him.

"What do you mean?"

"You'll understand after some time here," I pause for a moment. "Always remember, they're here temporarily, and we didn't bring them here. They're not our problem."

"I'll remember. Thanks for the patrol."

"Now return to Sergeant Pascal. Good luck to you," I say goodbye to him and walk toward the watchtower. My shift is about to start.

Time passes slowly as I stand on the tall watchtower and look around. The tower's wooden floors creak under my boots each time I move from one side to the other in the small space. Every now and then, I look at her. She remains standing by the fence, holding on to the barbed wire with her hands. What is she waiting for? For the German commander's daughters? Doesn't she know they went on a summer vacation in Bavaria with their mother?

She leaves the fence for a few minutes and approaches some children, trying to play with them, but they chase her away, and she goes back to stand by the fence, clinging on to it as if it was her safe place.

"Mathéo, you can get off. Sergeant Pascal is waiting for you in the pick-up truck," the policeman who replaces me at the tower arrives and climbs the ladder. "Is everything quiet around?" He stands beside me on the tower and places his rifle on the wooden floor, leaning it against the wall.

"Yes, everything's quiet. See you tomorrow," I take my rifle and put it on my shoulder. The little girl keeps standing by the fence. I must remember not to get attached to anyone here, just like I told the new policeman, Fernard.

Back in the barracks, I return the rifle to its stand and go outside, walk over to the black Peugeot police pick-up truck parked on the grass. Sergeant Pascal is already sitting in the passenger seat, waiting for me to drive him to town. I look at the big camp's ugly concrete building. The afternoon sun paints it a pleasant cream color.

"How was the shift?" Pascal asks as I sit in the driver's seat, slam the metal door, and start the engine. The engine comes to life with a monotonous rumble, and the car slightly shakes as I press the accelerator and move the vehicle from the grass onto the road leading to the village and Paris.

"It was quiet," I answer. With him, I'm always careful with what I say. He's the sergeant in charge of us at the camp. He's also in daily contact with the Nazis.

"Yes, we've had a few quiet days. It'll end tomorrow. Captain Becker is coming back from Berlin," he says, lighting himself a cigarette as the rambling car passes the village's small train station.

I look at the station's building, with its triangular roof and large black letters spelling 'Drancy' on its stone wall. The platform is now empty. There was no transport to the East today.

"I thought he went with the family on vacation to Bavaria," I look away from the empty platform onto the road passing between the small buildings. There are only a few people walking or riding bicycles in the streets. There are many abandoned wooden carts in the houses' yards. Since the German invasion to Russia, which began last summer, the Germans confiscated most of the horses and sent them to the Eastern front. Fuel also hardly reaches Paris anymore, only for the needs of the German army and the police.

"He went to Berlin for a commands' meeting, and his family went to Bavaria," Pascal replies as I slow down the car and overtake two men pulling a wooden cart. I smile at them, but they look at the police car and don't smile back. "His wife will also come back with the girls," Pascal keeps talking and laughing. "She doesn't trust her husband to be here alone with all the beautiful French women of Paris," he keeps laughing as I speed up the bumpy road again.

"I thought he was busy commanding the camp and not the women of Paris," I politely say to him. Sergeant Pascal often goes to the German and Captain Becker's barracks. The German soldiers usually ignore us, the ordinary policemen. Maybe it's better this way.

"Everyone should do their job," Pascal says while looking at a young woman riding her bicycle on the narrow road. "Captain Becker is doing his job with the Jews. We're doing our job by serving the Germans, and his wife is doing her job by watching him. This way, everyone's happy, and order is maintained."

"Yes, that's how everyone's happy," I say. I shouldn't think about the Jews imprisoned inside the camp. We, policemen, are just doing our job.

Two German transport planes pass overhead, approaching the landing at the nearby Le Bourget airport, their engines roaring and are heard above the car's rumble. I look at their light, blue-painted bellies. They seem like big whales to me. Only the big, black German crosses on their wings remind me that they're our conquerors, and that we're being conquered. Another moment passes, and they disappear behind the village's low buildings, and only the rumble of our car's engine remains.

"Have you ever flown on a plane?" Sergeant Pascal asks me.

"No," I shake my head, "Humans aren't birds. I think humans should stay on the ground."

"They, the Germans, do not lack planes."

"They don't lack anything," I reply. I don't want to add that they take everything from us and rob us of everything they can. Even though I've been working with Pascal for over a year, and he treats me well, I don't know how much I can trust him. The Gestapo is searching for informants all around Paris. Once they receive a name, they take them for an inquiry in their terrifying basements.

"These days, you have to know how to get along," he sighs and throws the cigarette out of the car window as we slow down and approach the German roadblock before entering Paris. "If there's a need to talk, I talk," he says.

A thick wooden post is laid out on the road, a checkpoint with barbed wire fences on both sides. Behind it is a wooden shack and the guard post, painted in white, black, and red stripes. A large red Nazi flag leisurely waves above in the afternoon sun, as two Germans soldiers start walking toward, signaling us to stop.

One of the soldiers approaches the vehicle, holding a gun with a long bayonet attached to its barrel. He's wearing a field teal uniform and a helmet, ready to fight in case something goes wrong. The second soldier, a sergeant, also walks slowly and approaches the vehicle from the other side, holding a submachine gun in his hand. They're the ones who decide who gets in and who doesn't in my country, at the entrance to Paris.

"Where are you from, and where are you going?" The first one asks, in broken French.

"To Paris, we're from the Drancy camp," Pascal sticks his head out of the open window and replies.

"Turn off the engine," he instructs me, and I obey. "Papers, please," he reaches out his hand. Pascal takes his policeman's ID from his uniform pocket and hands it to him.

"They look fine," the soldier tells the sergeant after looking at Pascal's ID.

"What do you have in the trunk?" the sergeant asks, his fingers resting carelessly on his submachine gun.

"Nothing," Sergeant Pascal replies.

"Look in the trunk," the sergeant orders the soldier, and the latter walks over and picks up the tarp covering the trunk. Two more German transport planes are approaching to land at the nearby airport. The noise of their engines is deafening for a moment.

"Commander, there's a sack of potatoes here," the soldier tells the sergeant, and I look at Sergeant Pascal surprised; the trunk should be empty.

"What's this sack of potatoes?" The sergeant asks me. What should I answer?

"It's from the village, intended for the police headquarters in the city," Pascal replies. "You know how it is in the city; we want to help."

"Commander, shall I stab the sack and see if they're not hiding anything inside?" The German soldier asks the sergeant.

"Can I offer you a cigarette?" Pascal smiles at the German sergeant and pulls a cigarette box out of his uniform pocket, holding it out to him.

"No need, they're fine," the sergeant reaches out, takes a few cigarettes, and puts one in his mouth. He bends down and lights one for himself. "Let them go," he gestures, and the soldier quickly returns and opens the wood post blocking the road.

I start the car again, and we slowly cross the checkpoint, and go on driving in silence. What's in that bag he brought with him?

"There're so many Jews in the camp," he says after a while. "They won't notice one missing sack of potatoes."

"Yes," I say, thinking about the long line of people in the camp waiting for their meager daily meal every day.

"And our police officers' salary is never enough. A little extra always helps."

I nod and don't say a thing. It's none of my business. I just have to do my job. I turn the steering wheel, and the vehicle goes on the main road leading into the city. In the distance, on the hill, I can already see the Basilica du Sacré-Cœur, which for me symbolizes the entrance to the city.

Inside the city, there are hardly any cars on the main avenue. Only German army vehicles drive on the roads, and here and there you see a car with a special fuel permit, a supply truck, or someone connected to the German authorities.

We overtake two German army trucks and pass several cafés full of German soldiers sitting around the small tables and enjoying the afternoon sun. A few French women sit next to them, but most people ignore them, and some move to the other side of the street.

"They're our friends. They're not going anywhere," Pascal says as he notices me watching a group of German officers sitting outside a café, laughing while raising their glasses of wine.

"No one will beat them, certainly not us," I say. I don't like sitting in cafés anyway.

"And we have to decide which side we're on," he looks at me.

"We're on the side of the law. That's why we're on the police force. We've already decided," I look back at him before looking back onto the road and turning to his street.

"Exactly," he says to me as I slow the car down and stop in the quiet street in front of his building's entrance.

"See you tomorrow. Are you going home from here?" Pascal gets out of the car.

"Yes," I reply.

"How's your mother doing?"

"She's fine, thanks."

"Say hello to her," he slams the car door, then goes to the back of the car and takes out the sack of potatoes.

"Thanks, see you tomorrow."

"Mathéo, one more thing," he calls me through the open window, the sack of potatoes on his shoulder.

"Yes?"

"Place a bet on the Jewish girl. Everyone placed a bet. It doesn't look good that you're the only one who doesn't. The other policeman might think you love Jews," he looks at me with his dark eyes, then turns away and enters the building. I watch the building's big, brown, wooden door close behind him and drive slowly down the street, leaving behind me a whiff of gasoline.

I stop the vehicle on a small street next to Mrs. Sophie's hair salon, pull on the handbrake, and turn off the engine. The street's almost deserted and quiet in the afternoon. The hair salon is closed, and heavy beige curtains cover the display window facing the street. Since they've occupied Paris, people prefer to hide behind curtains and closed doors. The grocery store is also closed by now, and only a few empty wooden carts stand outside, one full of empty glass bottles. Only Luc, the boy who will become a teenager in a few years, plays football with himself in the street. He kicks the ball at the wall, and the wall faithfully returns it. I get out of the car, take out my small leather bag, and walk to the house entrance, next to Mrs. Sophie's salon. On the large, wooden bulletin board is a series of government posters showing a French worker shaking the hand of a German worker and calling for cooperation.

"Good evening, Mr. Allard," Luc stops kicking the rag ball he's playing with, stands in front of me, and salutes. He's about ten years old, and his simple, button-down shirt peeks out of his shorts.

"Good evening, soldier," I salute him back.

"Shall we play?" He kicks the ball at me.

"Two passes," I reply and kick the ball back at him, "How's your mother?"

"Mom's fine, Mr. Allard. She says she heard on the radio that the Germans have reached Stalingrad and will soon take it over," he kicks the ball to me.

"Luc, the Germans are strong, but we'll still beat them in football," I kick the ball back. "Did she hear anything?"

"No, nothing, but she won't stop listening to the radio. One more pass?"

"Last one," I kick the ball to him. "Goodbye," I approach him and caress his brown hair. "Take care of your mom; you're the man of the house now."

"Yes, Mr. Allard," he holds the ball in his hand and salutes me again. I smile at him and enter the building, climbing up to the third floor.

"You're late. I was getting worried," Mom calls me from the kitchen as I close the door behind me and lock the bolt.

"How are you?" I go into the kitchen and bend down a little to hug her. She isn't young anymore. She's already a little stooped and slower than she used to be, but she still dresses in the same clean, black dress she always wears, and her gray hair is neatly pulled back.

"Stay away from the pot. Your glasses will steam up," she tries to push me back.

"I managed to get some cheese, some vegetables, and oil," I take the ingredients out of my small leather bag and place them in the pantry. "Did you use the coupons I gave you?"

"No, he ran out of groceries at the grocery store. I'll try again tomorrow."

"I'll try to get some more coupons next week."

"Wait in the guest room. The food will be ready soon, don't disturb me," she kicks me out of the small kitchen, and I walk around the house and close the blinds and curtains. Night will soon fall, and lights shouldn't be seen from outside.

After moving through all the small apartment rooms, I sit in the green armchair and close my eyes for a few minutes. I used to like to listen to songs on the radio while I waited for the food to be ready, but since they've occupied Paris, they've been broadcasting German propaganda non-stop, and I prefer

235

leaving the big device turned off. They arrest anyone they find listening to the BBC.

Beside the radio on the dresser, inside a dark wooden frame, stands a yellowed picture of Dad. He stands proud in his uniform. I hardly remember him. I was a child back then, and I vaguely remember the touch of his uniform's rough fabric when he came on vacation from the war and picked me up in his arms, hugging me tightly.

"Mathéo, come to the table. The food is ready," Mom touches my shoulder and walks to the table, taking off the apron she wore while cooking.

We both sit down and eat the soup, which mainly contains water and some potatoes and vegetables. I'll also try to get more food in the next few days.

"Thank you, Mom, the food's delicious," I say after a while.

"How was work?" She asks.

"It was fine."

"It's always fine. You don't tell me anything about your work."

"Because not everything can be told," I say to her and think about the people between the fences and the little girl with the wild hair.

"Will you come with me to church on Sunday? You haven't been there in a long time?"

"I had work."

"God wants to listen to his followers," she sips her soup and watches me.

"I know. I'll try to come," I say, and once again, we go back to that same silence.

"I met Fleur today, the pharmacist," Mom says after a few minutes.

"What did you need at the pharmacy? Is everything okay?"

"Just a bit of a sore throat, nothing to worry about," she sips from her soup. "She told me you were at her place a while ago because you needed some medicine."

"Yes," I reply. Fleur shouldn't have told her that.

"Why did you need medicine? Are you sick?"

"No, I'm not sick, I'm perfectly fine."

"Then why did you need the medicine?"

"A friend asked for my help," I keep on sipping the soup. I don't want to tell her about that woman; she won't understand.

"And did you eventually manage to get the medicine? She told me you can't get this medicine anywhere in Paris."

"Yes, I finally succeeded," I reply, sipping from my soup. Pharmacist Fleur has a big mouth. What happened to the girl's mother?

"I'm glad you helped someone with their medicine at least."

"Thanks, Mom."

"Fleur is very nice. She's a good woman and still single."

"Yes, she's very nice."

"Then why don't you ask her out?"

"Where? To a café full of German soldiers on Champs Elysees?"

"You don't have to be angry. I'm just trying to help, you're already thirty-one, and she's really nice. She also asked me about you."

"Thanks, but no need," I say, even though I know she's right. But I can't.

"It's not good to live alone," Mom continues.

"You've lived alone for many years."

"Because I had no choice, and I had to raise you," she tells me after a moment.

"Sorry, Mom, I didn't mean that," I get up from my seat and hug her. I shouldn't have said that to her.

"It's okay. I'm used to being alone, and I have you," she wipes away a tear.

"I'll try to talk to Fleur," I return to my seat, knowing I won't talk to her. Mom won't understand.

"What about Colette, Luc's mother?"

"They haven't heard anything. They're still looking for information," I finish the soup. "She keeps listening to the German radio, praying it would turn out that he's a prisoner in Germany. Thanks, Mom, for the food."

"She has to raise their child alone in wartime. It's hard."

"You did it too," I look at the picture of Dad in uniform. He stands proudly in his French army uniform, on his last vacation before the great Somme battle in the previous war. Did he know he wouldn't come back from battle? Did he know the Germans would return after twenty-four years and conquer France and Paris?

"Yes, I did it too," she says quietly, and I get up and hug her again.

After dinner, I sit in the guest room and read a book until I feel my eyelids getting heavy. Mother sits beside me, in her armchair, knitting a blue sweater, her fingers holding the knitting needles that are constantly moving.

"Good night, Mom," I finally get up from the armchair, go over to her, bend down, and kiss her cheek.

"Good night, Mathéo," she smiles at me. "I'll stay here a little longer."

Before I fall asleep, I recall the little girl, but I try to banish her from my thoughts. I don't have to think about her. I just have to do my job.

"Has anyone seen the girl with the shaggy teddy bear today?" Sergeant Pascal asks us two days later. He walks into the barracks in the morning, after the briefing with the German commanders.

"I saw her yesterday," one of the policemen answers while Pascal hands him a piece of paper. He takes it and starts writing the shifts for the next few days in chalk on the wooden board.

"And today?" Pascal looks around at all the policemen, who are standing inside the barracks.

"I didn't see her today," the policeman replies.

"Me neither," adds another.

"Has anyone seen her?" Pascal asks.

I look at the faces around me. They all shake their heads. What happened to her?

"Does that mean whoever bet on today wins?" One of them asks.

"It doesn't mean anything," Pascal answers. "Nobody wins until there's confirmation. Fernard," he calls the new policeman and hands him another piece of paper. "This is for you, get her. You're new. That's a task for the new ones."

"Who is she?" Fernard reads the name on the paper and looks up at Sergeant Pascal, embarrassed.

"Ms. Suzette, she's in charge of subversion. I got her name."

"What did she do?" Fernard asks.

"It shouldn't concern you. You ask too many questions. That's what they decided," Pascal replies. "Do your job and bring her here. But if you really want to know, she's a pharmacist who gave out prescriptions without permission."

"And what should I do with her?" Fernard keeps holding on to the note.

"Find her among all the Jews here in camp and send her to the train. There's a train leaving today. She'll be happy to travel to the East and perform her subversive acts there."

"Am I going to look for her out there alone?"

"You're a police officer, aren't you? Are you afraid of them?" Pascal laughs.

"Give it to me, I'll do it," I say to Sergeant Pascal, taking the note from Fernard's hand. "You'll do my shift in guard tower number three."

"Thank you," Fernard smiles at me and takes a rifle from the stand, attached to the shack's wall.

"You're too good to the newbies. They need to learn," Pascal tells me.

"I want to place a bet on the girl," I take a bill out of my wallet, attempting to change the subject.

"But you can't bet on today. We have to be fair," Pascal takes the money from my hand and puts it in his pocket.

"Then place the bet on the day after tomorrow." I check that my uniform is tidy and make sure my gun is in its holster, then

240

I go to the gun stand and take a rifle and a bullet belt, placing them on my shoulder.

"I'm putting you down for the day after tomorrow. I knew you were one of us," Pascal lights himself a cigarette. "Let's go, everyone to their positions," he says to all of us. "And Mathéo," he grabs my hand, "be careful not to catch anything from them; I'm sending the new ones inside for a reason."

"I know," I nod. "I'll be careful," I put on my policeman's cap and leave the barracks. In the sun, I check the rifle and adjust the bullet belt on my chest. Only then do I walk to the camp entrance gate while holding on to the note with the pharmacist's name. What happened to the girl with the shaggy bear?

"Going for a walk among the Jews?" The policeman at the guard post near the gate asks me.

"Yes," I answer. "Someone has to do the dirty work."

"There's a lot of dirty work to be done here. They keep finding them hiding in Paris."

"Yeah..., they're trying to save themselves from this place," I say as he opens the gate for me. Is this what he thought about the Jews before the war broke out, or did he change his mind to please the victorious Nazis?

The yard's full of people strolling, and I walk among them and look around. I need to find her. In the corner of the large building, near the registration office, people start to gather for the journey to the East. Soon, the policemen will go inside and escort them to the train station. I think of the pharmacist who still doesn't know that she'll be boarding the train to the East today. She shouldn't have done what she did. She shouldn't have stood out.

The people in the yard pull away from me or stop walking and look down, hoping I'll pass them by and not engage them. They make me recall how I acted when I was young and would cover my eyes, believing no one could see me.

"Where's Mrs. Suzette, the pharmacist?" I stand in front of a woman about thirty-five years old. She's wearing a simple, dirty, mud-stained, dark purple dress, and her black hair is pulled up.

"Please, sir, I don't know; don't hurt me," she looks at me with fearful eyes. "Please."

"Go," I say to her, nauseated from having caused people so much fear. But I must find her. I keep walking in the yard and call out to a man in his forties wearing a brown suit and tie, I ask him about the pharmacist.

"I don't know, sir," he replies. "But some say she's at entrance four," he whispers as he takes off his beret, holds it tightly in his hand and bows.

"Thanks." I dismiss him and start walking towards entrance four.

"I'm looking for Mrs. Suzette, the pharmacist," I stand in front of a woman at entrance number four. She's about thirty and wearing a light brown dress and matching belt. She's listlessly standing by the stairs, leaning against the bare concrete wall, slowly smoking a cigarette butt.

"I don't think you need her," she takes the cigarette out of her mouth and looks at me. "You have a policeman's uniform; I don't see a yellow badge."

"You shouldn't talk to policemen like that, not if you have anything to lose," I place my hand on my holster, feeling the smooth leather under my fingers.

"I'm locked up here. Do you think I have anything to lose?" She keeps looking at me and shows me the cigarette butt she's holding. "I'm picking up cigarette butts from the ground. There's hardly anywhere left to go from here."

"Ms. Suzette has something to lose, and so do you. I can take you to today's train instead of her. Nobody cares who I take. It's all about quotas and numbers."

"What do you want from her?" She tucks the cigarette butt into her dress pocket, "I'll keep smoking that later," she says more to herself than to me.

"Tell Ms. Suzette that people are talking about her," I say to her after a moment.

"What are they saying?"

"It doesn't matter what people say about her; she should stop handing out prescriptions, disappear, and change her name. She should be on the train to the East today. Now go, find her." I keep my hand on my holster. The lump in my throat is somewhat relieved for the first time since I entered the barbed wire fence gate of the camp this morning. I must go up the stairs and find her. I already know how to do that. I've done it before. I'm familiar with their initial look of surprise, and the look of resignation that follows, with the humiliated look in their eyes. I'm familiar with the quick collection of their few belongings in the crowded, stuffy room, and the slow walk towards the gate. But today, for some reason, I can't do it. For once, I'll let her off the hook. I'll tell Sergeant Pascal that I found her sister and that she said she was sent by train a few days ago and that the Germans no longer have to worry about her. I'll tell him I checked and made sure it was true. I've been here enough time for him to believe me. For once, I won't scare anyone.

I remain standing at entrance number four and look at the yard. Some people approach the entrance but move away when they notice me. They'll wait until I've gone.

A few minutes later, I hear footsteps down the stairs, and the woman I was talking to earlier comes down.

"She says that she doesn't know who you are but that you're kindhearted," she says.

"Believe me, I'm not kindhearted," I reply. I don't want to think about all the people I'd sent to the trains.

"You're a good man, I know. I see people," she looks at me.

"Make sure she disappears," I tell her, turn my back, and start walking away, but after a moment, I change my mind and walk back to her. She's still standing there, leaning against the concrete wall, watching me.

"One more thing. Do you know a girl who hangs around alone with a shaggy bear?"

"The German girl?"

"Yes, the German girl. Where are her parents?"

"People here don't like her," she says after a moment. "All the kids beat her."

"Why is that?"

"She cries in German; it gives them satisfaction. You can probably understand them. There are very few things here that give children satisfaction," she points to the fenced yard and the ugly concrete building, "And adults, too."

"Where are her parents?" I once again ask her.

"You took them. You took her mother."

"And her father?"

"You must've taken care of him before."

"And where is the girl? Do you know?"

"I don't know if she's even alive."

"And if she is alive?"

"A few cigarettes might help me," she puts her hand in her dress pocket and takes out the cigarette butt, showing it to me.

"The list for the train is still open. The pharmacist's place is available," I look into her eyes and put my hand on my holster again.

"Try the abandoned places, maybe in the former classroom; you also took the teacher, remember? You accused him of subversion."

"Where's the classroom?"

"Over there," she points toward one of the other entrances.

"Thank you," I tell her, taking a bill out of my pocket and placing it in the palm of her hand. I don't have any cigarettes, "Make sure the pharmacist changes her name."

She nods and disappears up the stairs.

I move towards the entrance the woman had pointed to. I just want to see if she's still alive. I bet on her for two days from now.

Outside one of the rooms, on the first floor, it says 'Classroom' on the wall in large letters.

I press my ears to the closed door. At first, I don't hear anything, but after a while, I hear rustling. I put my hand on my holster and open the door.

The classroom looks empty. I can make out the green wooden board hanging on the wall in the weak light coming from the lamp, there are several words still written on it. A few dusty tables are arranged in straight rows in the center of the room, and the wooden chairs are vacant, as if waiting for pupils. The room looks empty, but a noise from the corner makes me go there. Two upside-down tables are placed on the floor, as if they were built as a hiding place or a fortress set up by a child who wants to play. I move towards the room's corner, and then I see her.

She crouches behind the tables in her simple, brown dress and wild hair. When she notices me looking at her, she slowly gets up. In her hand, she is firmly holding on to a pencil.

"Do you have a sharpener? Mine got lost," she asks me in broken French with a German accent.

"No, I don't have a sharpener," I reply in German. Only policemen who know German can work for the Nazis.

"Will you beat me if I speak German?"

"No, I won't hit you." I take another step closer, noticing that she flinched a little and slightly raises her hand holding the pencil, although she realizes she has no chance.

"Is your name Mr. Chambu?"

"Who is Mr. Chambu?" I ask her.

"He needs to take me to Angelina."

"I'm not Mr. Chambu," I reply. How did she end up staying here without her mother? What happened?

"Are you a good hunter?"

"I'm not a hunter. I'm a policeman."

"But you have a gun," she looks at the rifle on my shoulder, as if checking to see if she can trust me.

"Right, I have a rifle," I gently touch its wooden stock.

"Will you take me to Angelina?" She asks me and I don't understand what she's talking about. How many days has she been here without her mother?

"Who is Angelina?"

"She has a big house with many rooms and stairs to climb, and in our room, there are small purple flowers on the wall and the burgundy bedspread. Do you know her?"

"Where is your mother?" I ask her.

"I don't know."

"Did they take her?"

"Yes," she nods.

"On the train?"

"I don't know."

"And when was the last time you ate?"

"I don't know."

"Are you sleeping here?"

"Do you have a piece of chocolate to give me?" She asks, looking at my uniform pocket.

"No, sorry," I put my hand in my uniform pocket. I only have an apple I brought with me to eat soon when I thought I'd be in a watchtower. "Do you want it?" I hand her the apple; she grabs it from my hand and bites it ravenously.

"Where do you sleep?" I ask her a moment later.

She doesn't answer but looks around at the empty classroom.

"Are you sleeping here?"

"Yes," she nods. "They kicked me out of my, Mom's and Aunt Charlotte's room," she tells me.

"And where is Aunt Charlotte?"

"Disappeared," she answers and keeps eating the apple. I keep watching her. I have to leave her here. I can't help her anymore.

"Are you going to be okay?" I ask her, but she doesn't answer, she just keeps eating the apple.

"Goodbye," I finally tell her, turn around and leave the classroom. She'll have to fend for herself. I'm not responsible for her.

But as I walk across the yard toward the gate and turn back, I see her following me. She keeps a safe distance from me, like a stray cat looking for an owner to adopt him.

"Where are you going?" I ask her.

"I'll wait for the bus. Maybe my suitcase will arrive," she replies. I want to ask her what she means, but I don't think I'll understand. I'm not sure she understands either, and I must return to my shift. She's just another girl among many. She'll be fine. I must also report to Sergeant Pascal that the pharmacist was sent to the East a few days ago.

I exit the compound and resume my shift in the tower. And every now and then, I look at her. She keeps standing by the barbed wire fence, holding the shaggy bear in one hand and the pencil in the other.

"Are you coming to eat?" One of the policemen calls me when my shift is over.

"Yes, I'm coming," I answer and give her one last look before I enter the barracks. I wonder how long she'll last like this.

"Did you see that the girl is still alive?" Sergeant Pascal enters the barracks and announces. "Mathéo, you have a chance to win the bet," he smiles and pats me on my shoulder.

"Yes, I have a chance," I reply, knowing it won't be long before someone wins. Maybe I should've put her on the train to the East, where she'd meet her mother.

Chapter Twelve

Auschwitz, Concentration Labor Camp

I'm not Sarah Bloch, twenty-nine years old, wife of Erwin Bloch and mother of six-year-old Rebecca. I'm number 132698. My whole identity has been imprinted into these ugly blue digits they tattooed on my arm. If the woman in charge of the block wants to complain about me to the SS, she'll write down this number. If the foreman wants to punish me, he'll use this number. All of us, all the women on the block, are faceless numbers. We're nothing more than thin women with shaved heads, dressed in ragged prison uniforms. We walk slowly in the chilly morning to work at the Weichsel Metall-Union factory that produces explosives and detonators for the German army.

"Faster, lazy pigs," the guard shouts at us in German if she thinks we've slowed down. It's best to walk at the head of the column and in the center, following the foreman leading us along the road to the factory whose chimneys become visible in the light of dawn. Those who walk at the head of the column don't have to run and close in the gaps, and are usually at a safe distance from the sadistic Polish guard's whip.

We walk past the train platform on our way to the camp gate. At the train platform, on the ramp called the Jewish Ramp, there are two long queues, one of men and one of women and children. Every morning, when we pass near the ramp, I try to look for Rebecca among the children standing on the platform. There's little chance that I'll be able to spot her among the crowds. I don't know whether I'd rather notice her or not. There's an SS officer facing the lines in his black uniform, pointing left and then right, splitting the people into groups. Some go right, but most of them go left. I know by now what being on the left means.

"Faster, lazy pigs," the Polish guard menacingly raises her whip, and we try to pick up the pace. My feet ache in the torn and uncomfortable shoes, worn without socks, but I push aside the pain with every step. I focus solely on moving forward.

The sun is already rising over the horizon as we enter the gate of the factory complex outside Auschwitz, passing the synthetic rubber factory and approaching our destination—the explosives factory.

"When they ask you in a few minutes, tell them you used to work in an optics factory, they're looking for skilled women with delicate hands," a prisoner whispered to me the day we arrived, right after the first selection. She ordered us to undress before they shaved our heads and gave us the prisoners' uniforms. She was happy to hear a German speaker among the women and gave me that advice. I decided to trust her and said it when asked. Charlotte was also at the other end of the spacious room. She survived the first selection and was assigned to my work group at the explosives factory. She sleeps on the other side of the block. We haven't spoken since that day in Drancy. Even during the marches to the factory and back, we didn't walk side by side. I miss our nightly conversations.

"Let's move, useless pigs, start working," the foreman whistles shrilly, and we rush to our workstations, replacing the night shift workers. The factory works nonstop in two shifts, twenty-four hours a day, producing ammunition and shells for the German army fighting in Russia. I operate the machine engraving the detonators.

The machines' noise never ceases. I pull the lever and direct the metal blade, etching thin stripes onto the steel block—one after another, and another, and another. I work without thinking about the constant hunger, without thinking about my aching feet, without thinking about my wavy hair being shorn, and without thinking about my daughter. I work like the machine that spits out blocks of metal, carving them repeatedly, ensuring a good job so that the foreman doesn't report me to the SS sergeant. If that happened, my fate would be sealed. At least we get better food rations than the other prisoners, and we're not forced to work outside like most of the men in the labor camps around the Auschwitz main camp.

We have a brief break during the workday for a meal of bread and soup. If the prisoner in charge of pouring the soup likes me, she'll dip the ladle deeper into the pot, and that way, I'll get more peas and maybe even a potato. Then, we resume working until the evening when the night shift arrives, and march back to our block in the women's camp.

"Ugly slow pigs, walk faster," I hear the sadistic Polish guard shouting, then the whip's crack, followed by painful sobs. My body tenses up even though I'm not the one delaying the convoy and feeling the pain. All the women at the head of the column huddle together while walking.

"Sorry," whispers someone who bumped into me.

"It's okay," I whisper back, noticing it's Charlotte. She has lost so much weight since our time in Drancy. I must have lost weight too.

She doesn't say anything other than 'Sorry' and keeps walking, faintly coughing so as not to attract the attention of the sadistic guard.

"Are you okay?" I whisper to her.

"Yes," she replies, but after a moment, she coughs again and nearly stumbles. I reach out my arm to support her so she doesn't fall. If she stumbles, the whole column will be delayed and the guard will punish her.

"Thank you," she says as we enter the camp and walk along the train platform.

The last rays of the sun illuminate the platform. No one is there. The long freight train is also gone. Only a group of prisoners in striped uniforms collect the belongings of those who had arrived, their possessions scattered on the platform. Several SS soldiers guard them as they work. All around, the lanterns on the electrified wire fences flicker to life, and we enter the women's camp and march to our block.

Without saying a word, Charlotte slowly walks to the wooden bunk she shares with other women at the other end of the block. Is she okay?

I eat dinner, slowly chewing on the slice of bread, and then slip the other slice into my pocket. I'll eat it later if I get really hungry. The women climb into the dense triple wooden bunks. I hear coughing and sighing. What about Charlotte?

I walk across the block, looking for her. In the dim light of the lamp we all look the same, all of us thin, pale, and hairless.

This is not a place for anger and resentment; it's a place and time for compassion.

"Are you all right?" I ask her when I finally find her. I miss talking to her.

"I'm still alive," she replies and tries to smile.

"Maybe you can sleep with me in my bunk?"

"Are you sure?"

"Yes," I nod. She is so weak.

She tries to smile again and gets up from the wooden bunk, follows me to my corner, and we lie down together on the wood. She shivers even though it isn't winter yet.

"I'm sorry we came here," she says after a while.

"I'm glad she didn't come here with us," I reply, even though deep down I know that everyone in Drancy has arrived or will arrive here. It's only a matter of time.

"I'm sure she isn't here," Charlotte whispers. She knows the fate of the children who arrive at this place.

"There must be someone watching over her there in Drancy. There are good people there," I tell her, knowing it isn't true.

"I'm sure of it. I'm sure there's at least one person out there taking care of her."

"Lights off," the woman in charge of the block announces, and the dim light goes out. Darkness settles in the block, and only the sounds of the women's breathing, coughs, and sighs linger for a few minutes.

I'm not Sarah Bloch, twenty-nine years old, wife of Erwin Bloch and mother of six-year-old Rebecca. I'm number 132698. But in a minute, I'll close my eyes and escape this horrible place to the world of dreams. I'll dream about my Rebecca, about hugging and talking to her. And even though it's unlikely, I wish to believe that she stayed in Drancy and that someone there is watching over her.

Chapter Thirteen

Shoes

"Soldier, soldier," the daughters of the camp commander get out of the military vehicle that pulled over in front of Captain Becker's barracks, and they start running toward me. They don't bother closing the car door, and the German soldier who brought them here slams the door behind them. He remains standing next to the gray-green military car.

"I'm not a soldier; I'm a policeman," I say as I put on my blue police cap and step away from our barracks' balcony. Their floral dresses flutter as they run through the grass, wearing brown shoes and white socks. They look as though they belong in a poster on a billboard, in a world before the war broke, a world that is so far away from Nazi officers, French policemen, and Jewish prisoners.

"Policeman, we want to play with the dirty Jewess," the older of the two says as they stop running. She is about eight or ten years old. Her curly hair is tied up with a pink ribbon.

"Are you allowed to play with her?" I ask and look at the German soldier who brought them here. He's leaning against the car with indifference, takes a pack of cigarettes from his pocket, and lights one.

"You know we are. You already brought her to us last time, and my father says we can do whatever we want here," she says and stands up, putting her hands on her hips.

"She belongs to us. We can do anything to her. We throw her things away, and she keeps bringing them back," the younger one says. She's only slightly younger than her sister, but older than the girl with the wild hair.

"The dirty Jewess also speaks German. Father says it's the language of the superior race, not like the French who can't fight," the older sister says, her hands are still on her hips.

"I'll see what I can do," I reply in French and turn to the gate.

"Tell her to bring her raggy bear," the little sister says.

"And hurry up, we're waiting," the older sister adds as I start walking toward the gate. "Dad says all the French are lazy," I can hear her saying, but don't turn around.

I walk to the gate slowly on purpose. My entire body is tense, and I place my hand on the leather holster strapped to my waist. It's been two years since they occupied us, and I still feel shamed every time I face a German soldier who speaks disdainfully to me or a German girl who patronizes me. I need to be careful and tread lightly. Her father is the camp's commander. He can punish the French policemen however he chooses to. I continue walking slowly so they'll keep thinking that the French are idle.

"Are you going to take more instigators to the East?" one of the policemen at the gate asks me and laughs.

"No, not today, maybe tomorrow," I reply, wondering what's so funny about the Jewish prisoners suffering in this camp.

I cross the yard taking big strides, ignoring the people clearing my path. I know where to find her.

"Girl," I slowly open the abandoned classroom door and call her. The tables have been pushed to the corner. But I can't hear a sound.

"Girl," I call her again and enter the empty classroom. Did something happen to her?

"Girl," I say and walk to the corner, look at the makeshift fortress that she had built and find her curled up, looking at me.

"The good hunter with the glasses," she says with a small smile.

"Why didn't you answer?"

"Because you spoke French, and I thought you wanted to catch me."

"Come with me. The commander's daughters want to play with you."

"Hilda and Liza?"

"Is that their names?"

"Yes," she nods.

"And what's your name?"

"Rebecca."

"Rebecca, come with me to play with Hilda and Liza."

"Do you have a piece of chocolate for me?"

"No, but I have some bread and cheese," I reach into my pocket and pull out two slices of bread and a small block of cheese wrapped in parchment paper. It was supposed to be my breakfast, but I put it aside.

"Will you watch over me?" She glares at me while hungrily munching the food.

"Yes, I'm a policeman," I place my hand on my rifle's strap.

"Good," she says after she finishes eating. She comes out of her hiding place, holding the ragged teddy bear, then takes my hand.

Her little hand feels strange in my big palm. I've never held a little girl's hand. I feel her fingers against mine. As we start walking, I look down and notice she's barefoot.

"You forgot to put your shoes on."

"I don't have any," she looks up.

"You don't have shoes?"

"No," she replies. I remember she had shoes the last time I saw her.

"What happened?"

But she doesn't respond. She just keeps looking at me.

"Did they take your shoes?"

"Yes," she nods.

"Let's go," I start walking, and she runs while holding my hand. But I let go of it. We can't form a connection. I'm a policeman, and she's a Jewish prisoner who I mustn't care for. I'm only here to bring her to the German girls to play with her.

When we go out into the yard, I deliberately walk faster so she won't be able to keep up. She runs behind me until we reach the gate. I'll just do my job, nothing more.

"It's okay," I say to the policeman at the gate. "I'm taking her outside to play with the commander's daughters." The other policeman opens the gate for us. I wonder how she feels about being free for a few moments.

"There she is," says the commander's younger daughter, as she claps and jumps, her golden curls bouncing merrily. "Let's play," she runs to Rebecca and snatches her teddy bear from her hand.

"You'll be the dog," the older sister says to her as they run to the German barracks, and Rebecca runs after them.

"Catch," they shout to her and throw the bear to each other.

I stand on the porch and watch them play. Rebecca runs between the two girls and tries to catch her teddy bear, her wild brown hair blows in the wind.

On the other side of the fence, the German soldier who brought them earlier is leaning against the military vehicle while smoking his cigarette and watching them. His black holster is almost invisible over his black ironed uniform. I can go back into our barracks, it's my break time, but I stay on the porch, watching Rebecca. She runs around and only occasionally stops to rest while the girls toss her the bear. I leave my lunch untouched.

The barracks door opens, and I turn around to see Sergeant Pascal come out and stand next to me.

"Mathéo, I think you've lost the bet. The girl is still alive, and you bet on today," he patted me on the shoulder.

"Maybe one of the Jews in the camp takes pity on her and gives her food," I reply.

"At least she's barefoot. Even if someone gives her food, she'll struggle to survive. The nights are getting colder," Sergeant Pascal says, lighting a cigarette. "How did she even get here?"

"The German commander's girls like playing with her. They asked me to bring her over. So, I found her," I reply, watching as she runs between them like a brown puppy trying to catch a ball of rags.

"Yes, the Nazis like to have fun with the Jews. They are allowed to have fun," he takes a drag from his cigarette.

"She lives by the water faucet outside," I tell him, not wanting to reveal her hiding place.

"I think the German commander's daughters will soon have to find another Jewish girl to play with."

"Can I bet on her again?" Another policeman joins us.

"Of course," Pascal replies. "We're open for another bet. How about you?" He turns to me. "Want to place another bet?"

"Yes, I do," I say and continue watching Rebecca running in the yard. I must behave like a French policeman under the German regime and do what is expected of me.

"I'll take your bet later," Pascal says when he returns inside with the other policeman.

The German soldier in the black uniform finishes smoking his cigarette, throws it on the ground, and disappears into the German barracks.

"Hilda, Liza," he comes out a few minutes later and calls them. He says something to them, and then approaches the military vehicle and opens the door.

The girls run to him and enter the vehicle. One of them throws the ragged bear on the ground near the car while the driver slams the door behind her and sits behind the wheel.

I see Rebecca approaching the bear when the driver starts the car. The car runs over the bear, almost hitting Rebecca.

Instinctively, I put my hand on my gun, even though it doesn't make sense. Anyway, I won't pull it out and protect her against the German driver.

Confused, Rebecca remains standing next to her bear, even when the vehicle passes close to her and drives away on the road leading to Paris. I can still see the commander's daughters looking out the window and laughing at Rebecca standing alone in the yard.

After they disappear, she sits down on the ground. At first, I assume she was hit by the vehicle, and I didn't notice. But a few seconds later, she slowly gets up, walks over to her runover bear, and picks it up. She looks right and left, as if searching for something. Sergeant Pascal is right. She won't survive much longer. Even the commander's daughters won't give her extra time because she speaks German and plays with them.

I go into the barracks for a moment and then come out and call her. It's time to take her back to her hiding place.

"Rebecca, will you be okay?" I ask her as we enter the abandoned classroom.

"Yes," she nods.

"Take it," I give her my lunch. "Eat it now, don't save the food for later, so someone won't take it from you."

"Okay," she nods, "will you bring me more food tomorrow?"

"Rebecca, you have to learn to get by," I tell her, deliberating how to explain to her what she needs to do. "You have to get food for yourself like other people who trade their cigarettes for food," I try to explain.

"Do you have any cigarettes?" She looks up and asks me, her dark-brown eyes watching me.

"No, I don't have cigarettes, but you must learn to get by. Do you understand what I'm telling you?"

"Yes," she nods.

"Good, bye," I say to her and walk out of the deserted class-room, leaving her on her own. I can't be responsible for her. It's not my job.

"See you tomorrow," I say goodbye to Fernard and step out of the Peugeot pickup truck, slamming the door behind me.

"Bye, Mathéo," he waves goodbye and slowly drives away down the street. He waits patiently for a young cyclist pedaling down the road, the fabric of her blue dress rubs against her hips with every move she makes. It's Fernard's turn to take the police car today. Tomorrow, he has to bring supplies from the police headquarters.

"Good evening, Mr. Allard," Luc stops kicking the ball of rags he's been playing with on the street. He stands at atten-tion, salutes, and then asks: "Want to play ball?"

"Good evening, soldier," I salute back and stand at a distance from him. "Go ahead, pass the ball."

"Does the police have guns?" He asks and kicks the ball at me.

"We have everything, including guns," I show him the gun in my holster as I kick the ball back.

"Will we ever beat the Germans?" He asks.

"We will," I reply confidently, still kicking the ball. But deep down I know we don't stand a chance, not after what I've seen in this war. We'll live under occupation for many years to come.

"Because we, the French people, are brave," he says and kicks the ball as hard as he can.

"Say, Luc, where does your mother buy shoes for you these days?"

"I don't know. She takes me to a shoemaker," he answers awkwardly.

"But how about now, when no one can get leather?"

"I don't know, she just gave me a pair. Do you want me to ask her?"

"No, it's fine, don't worry about it," I continue playing. I shouldn't have asked him. He's too young to know.

"She always takes care of everything. She says I should go to school and be a good student."

"She's a good mother," I tell him, thinking of my own mother who raised me alone during the previous war and after. "Luc," I stop kicking for a moment and pull out a stack of food coupons from my leather bag. "Give these to your mother, it'll help her," I hand him the stack. As a policeman, I get extra coupons. Mother and I can manage with less. They need it more than we do.

"But what will I tell her?" He holds the coupons.

"Don't tell her it's from me," I reply and think for a moment. "Tell her it's from Reverend Nicholas. You met him on the street, and he gave them to you."

"She won't believe me."

"Make sure she does," I smile at him. "Now that your father is gone, you must help her. You're the man of the house now."

"Say, Mathéo, will my father come back one day?" He stops playing and looks at me.

"Yes, he will. The war will end, and your father will come back," I gaze at him.

"My mom will be really happy when he comes back."

"I know. He'll be back, I'm sure of it," I approach him and stroke his hair. "Give her my warmest regard." I say goodbye to him and turn to the entrance of the house.

"Goodbye, Mathéo," he calls after me, "will we play tomorrow too?"

"Of course, Luc, see you then," I walk past Mrs. Sophie's barbershop and the large bulletin board. They've hung new posters depicting the Americans and the English as evil venomous snakes. Behind me, I hear Luc kicking the ball against the wall. The wall consistently bounces the ball back, instead of his father who disappeared in the war. The Germans won't say what happened to him. His mother doesn't know if he fell in battle, was taken prisoner, or maybe lying wounded in a POW camp.

At least I knew what happened to my father in that war, but I was too young to understand. I played football against the wall for years and waited for my father to return.

"Mom, was it difficult raising me?" I ask her later that evening as we both eat simple onion soup in the kitchen.

"It isn't difficult for any mother to raise her child," she replies. "That's why we're mothers."

I turn my gaze to Dad's picture next to the radio. In the dim lamplight, I can only make his figure. Night has already fallen, and the curtains are shut so that no one can see the light in our house, violating the blackout regulations.

"Mom, where can you get shoes in town these days?"

"It's hard to get shoes now. They use all the leather for army boots. It's hard to get anything," she continues sipping the soup.

"And if I want to get shoes for a girl?"

"Why do you need shoes for a girl?" She stops eating and looks at me.

"I don't need to. I just asked where I could get a pair."

"Did you get involved with a woman who has children and want to be her knight in shining armor?"

"No, I didn't get involved with a woman," I continue sipping the soup. I shouldn't have asked her. I can't explain it to her.

"How old is the girl?" She resumes eating her soup.

"Five or six or seven, I don't know."

"So how are you going to get her shoes if you don't know what size she is?"

"I don't want to get her shoes. I just asked."

"Is it Colette? Luc's mom? Did you get involved with her? She's married," she stops eating again and looks at me angrily.

"No, Mom, I'm not involved with Colette, and Luc is a boy not a girl. Soon he'll be as tall as me. And I know she's married," I don't tell her about the coupons I gave her son.

"You always want to help others," she stands up from and takes the empty bowls. "When you were a child, you would lie in bed and read books about knights who defeated evil dragons and saved the world. But you're older now. You know that the knights lost, and the Nazi monster won."

"Yes, Mother, I know. Thanks for the food," I stand up and hug her. "I know the Germans won. I work for them. Forget that I asked about the shoes. It's not important."

But the next day, when I return from work, there's a pair of brown leather shoes for a five- or six- or seven- year-old girl on the small chair by the entrance hall. They're polished and shiny, and there's a pair of small cream-colored socks next to them.

"I'm going to patrol the camp and inspect the Jews," I say the next day to Sergeant Pascal. I've hidden the shoes in the small leather bag on my shoulder.

"If you're going, take Fernard with you. Show him how we handle Jews who don't follow the rules," he takes a piece of paper out of his pocket. There's a name written on it. "This man would be happy to get on the train east today," he hands me the note.

"Excellent," I take the note and tuck it into my shirt pocket. I can't refuse his request. He mustn't suspect anything is wrong. "Fernard, take a rifle. We're going on patrol," I head to the gun stand and take out a rifle and a bullet belt.

Fernard rushes after me and takes a weapon, loads it, and ties the bullet belt around his waist. "I'm ready," he says.

"Let's do our job," I turn my back to him and leave the barracks. I can hear his boots pacing on the porch behind me.

"Don't you feel sorry for them?" Fernard asks me as we walk through the yard. The people walking outside clear our path.

"There's no reason to pity them at all. They brought it on themselves by failing to follow the rules," I reply and hate myself for having said those words. "For example, look at Mr. Arsenault," I read from the note in my hand, "he's accused of spreading false rumors."

"What did he say?" Fernard places his hand on his rifle's stock.

"I don't know, but it doesn't matter. It's treason. The people here are traitors," I continue walking quickly through the yard and look at the people with the yellow badges. I know I'm lying to him. I'm also lying to myself.

"Hey, soldier, do you need help again?" The woman who always stands at entrance number four calls out to me. Her light brown dress looks too big for her size. "I'll be happy for a cigarette," she says, putting her hand in her dress pocket while leaning against the concrete wall at the building's entrance.

"Who is she?" Fernard asks me.

"Never mind, ignore her," I reply and keep walking. She has a big mouth. I'm afraid she'll start talking about the girl I was looking for last time. Even policemen have to be careful here. I have to be careful. I'm holding the note with his name and his apartment number. Mr. Arsenault wasn't careful enough, and the Germans have all the information they needed about him.

We enter entrance number five and climb the stairs to the second floor. Despite the autumn breeze, there's a foul smell in the stairwell. I look away from the people peering at us from the apartments. They pull into the shadows and fall silent as if we were wolves coming to collect our prey. We're just doing our job.

"It's here," I whisper to Fernard. We move the sheet hanging over the door frame and enter the room, my hand resting on my gun and Fernard holding his rifle.

It takes me a second to adjust to the dim light inside. A man about thirty-five years old leans on an upturned wooden crate. He is wearing blue workers' pants and a dirty white workers' tank top. When he notices us, he turns around and raises his hands. I can see that his fingertips are stained with black ink.

"Quentin Arsenault?" I ask.

"I knew you'd come eventually," he says with his hands up. "I was wondering what took you so long." He tries to speak calmly, but I can sense the excitement in his voice.

"You are accused of subversion and of spreading false news," I read from the note. "Come with us, please."

"Where are you taking me?" He remains standing upright. There are some papers and a large print stamp on the up-side-down crate. I pick up one of the papers, reading it in the weak light, 'The Germans fail to capture Stalingrad. The Americans have invaded North Africa.'

"You're going east," I reply. He doesn't deserve to be punished. Nor does he deserve to be sent east.

"I am a French citizen. This is my country."

"This is the law, and we don't decide, they do. And they decided that you are spreading propaganda and false news inside the camp." I say and present him the note. I speak to him in a clear voice while standing up straight, but I feel ashamed.

"Since I was fifteen, I have been working in a printing house, preparing newspapers daily and ensuring people read the news. I've devoted my entire life to telling the truth. People in the camp should know what's happening in the world."

"It's subversion," I repeat, trying to sound indifferent.

"I'm a proud Frenchman. I'm not ashamed of what I did. It's the truth, and you know it. The Germans will lose in the end, and all those who collaborated with them will be punished too. You should be ashamed of what you're doing," he says, still holding his hands in the air.

"Is he allowed to talk to us like that? We're policemen," Fernard asks me, and aims his rifle at Mr. Arsenault.

"Don't hurt him," I say, "they'll take care of him in the East. Come with us," I turn to him.

"Can I take my things with me?" He asks, lowering his hands.

"Yes, but hurry up."

He slowly puts on his shirt. The yellow badge stands out in the dim light. Then he turns to the corner, bends down, and picks up a simple brown leather suitcase. He leaves behind the sheets of paper on the cart, as well as the inkwell and stamp.

"Vive la France," he stands up straight while holding the suitcase, "let's go." He looks into my eyes with pride rather than hate. I look back but want to lower my gaze. I'm ashamed of myself.

"After you," I move a little and make room for him. He walks past me to the stairs. People peek at us from the apartments as we follow him down the stairs, and Fernard approaches me.

"Sergeant Pascal said that a while ago we found someone here who painted subversive paintings, so we transferred her east," he whispers.

"The Nazis don't like free-spirited people," I reply, feeling bad for the free-spirited people we've imprisoned here. But I mustn't tell him my thoughts. He's still new here. What if he said something to Sergeant Pascal?

"Faster, Jew, go," I say to Mr. Arsenault, even though he doesn't need to be prompted. He walks proudly in the yard with big steps, walking past other people.

The people stop and look at him. An older man in a suit tips his hat at him. More people stop and fall silent as we walk past them. I look at Mr. Arsenault and avoid their eyes. We'll soon reach the group of Jews gathered by the gate on their way to the train.

"Keep an eye on him until they leave the camp for the train," I say to Fernard and turn around once we reach the group.

"Will things be better for us in the East?" I hear a woman in a scarf ask a man standing beside her. He must be her husband.

"Are you going to bring another Jewboy?" Fernard asks.

"Yes," I reply and walk away, ashamed that he chose that word to impress me. I hope things will be better for them in the East. I need to find the girl, that's why I entered the camp.

"Rebecca," I quietly say as I enter the empty classroom, but she doesn't answer me.

"Rebecca, it's me, the good hunter with the glasses," I say in German, but no one answers.

I approach her hiding place behind the tables, but she isn't there. All I find is her ragged bear on the floor. Did someone take her?

She isn't in the yard. I look around and can't find her. Nor is she by the gate where she usually waits for the bus or for the commander's daughters. Where can she be?

I look at the dark group of people waiting by the gate. The guards will open it in a few minutes, and the group will head to the train station. Could she be among them? Did someone take her to the train going east?

I start walking to the people; I want to find and protect her. But then I stop. Isn't that what I wanted? Isn't it best if someone put her on the train and sent east, where she can find her mother? It's not my job to try to help her.

Even though it's not my job, I continue to move slowly toward the group of people, scanning them with my eyes and searching for her. There are very few children left in the camp, so I'll be able to see if she's among them. But then I notice her, not among the people, but at the edge of the camp, close to the barbed wire fence under the guard tower. She bends down and picks something up.

What is she doing there? I approach her. She's holding a tray while collecting something from the ground. Suddenly, she notices me and stands up.

"Do you want to buy cigarettes?" She shows me a cardboard tray with cigarette butts and snipes. I raise my eyes to the watchtower towering over us. The guards usually throw their cigarette butts from there.

"How much for a cigarette?" I ask her.

"One potato," she looks at me, serious. "Do you want one?"

"But I don't have a potato."

"How about half a potato? Or some chocolate? I'll give you these," she points to two cigarette butts with a bit of tobacco.

"I'll take them. Is this enough?" I take out a bill and give it to her.

"What will I do with the money?" She holds the bill and looks at me. "Can I buy a potato with it?"

"I'll tell you what we'll do," I look up at the watchtower. They mustn't see that I'm giving her food. "Take me to your hiding place, and I'll exchange your money for food."

"With a potato?"

"No, something better than a potato."

"Chocolate?" Her eyes light up. "I really like chocolate. One time you gave me chocolate."

"No, not chocolate, but something delicious."

"Okay," she tells me and reaches her hand out. But I move away from her. They mustn't see that we formed a bond.

"Let's see who can run faster to the classroom."

"Okay," she says, throwing the cardboard tray on the ground and starting to run. I follow, seeing her brown dress fluttering as her bare feet hit the ground. I'll do without food until I get home tonight.

"This is for you, in exchange for the cigarettes," I pull out of my side bag buttered bread wrapped in parchment paper and a small block of cheese.

"Will you bring me some food tomorrow?" She chews the bread greedily.

"Yes, I will."

"And I'll give you cigarettes in exchange for the food?"

"No. I'll get you food tomorrow even without the cigarettes."

"Well, I'll sell cigarettes to other people," she continues to chew, biting hungrily into the block of cheese.

"And I brought you something else," I take the small shoes out of the bag.

"Did Mommy send me this?" Her eyes light up, and she smiles.

"Yes, this is what Mommy sent you," I reply.

"Have you seen her?" Her dark-brown eyes look at me. What do I tell her?

"No, I didn't see her, but someone brought the shoes and said it was from your mommy and that she loves you."

"Angelina?"

"Who is Angelina?" I try to remember.

"The woman from Paris, with the room with the flowers on the wall, I told you."

"No, it wasn't Angelina. It was someone else you don't know. Do you want to put the shoes on?" I take the socks out of my leather bag.

"Yes," she sits on the floor, stretches her legs forward and starts to put on the socks and then her shoes. She stands up and looks at me, as if waiting for something.

"Is everything okay? Are they comfortable?" I ask her.

"Yes," she nods, "you have to tie my shoelaces."

"Don't you know how to tie your shoelaces?"

"No," she shakes her head. "Mommy ties them for me. She makes bunny ears, then the bunny runs away and hops into its burrow."

"What?"

"That's how she does it," Rebecca explains, "that's how she ties my shoes."

"Well," I say and kneel to tie her shoelaces, "you need to learn to tie shoelaces by yourself. You need to learn," I add.

"Will you teach me?"

"Tomorrow," I reply. I've been here for too long. Sergeant Pascal must be looking for me.

"And bring me food? Like you promised in exchange for cigarettes? Mommy says you have to keep promises."

"Yes," I reply, "tomorrow I'll bring you food as promised, but you also have to promise me something."

"What?"

"That you only sell cigarettes to me. Not to anyone else."

"Okay," she nods, "I'll go look for more cigarettes."

"See you tomorrow," I stand up and leave. I have work to do. I'll bring her food tomorrow as well.

As I leave through the gate, I see Rebecca approaching the barbed wire fence and standing behind it, her small hands holding the wire fence.

"What are you doing?" I approach her from the other side of the fence.

"I'm waiting for Mommy to see what she'll bring me besides shoes."

"Mommy won't be here today," I tell her, seeing her expression turn sad. "She probably won't come tomorrow either. But if you stay away from the fence, I'll bring you some food tomorrow as I promised.

"Mommy will send me food?" She looks at me and smiles again.

"Yes, Mommy will send you food," I say. I have nothing better to tell her. "Now go back to the classroom and hide, okay?"

"Yes," she replies but remains standing by the fence.

"Why are you still here?" I ask her.

"Because you're protecting me," she continues to look at me.

"I'm leaving," I tell her, walking to the guards' barracks, but she stays there. I try not to think about her, but occasionally, I glance back and see her still standing by the fence with her new shoes, waiting for her mother.

"See you tomorrow," I say later to Sergeant Pascal as I pull over the Peugeot pickup truck next to his house.

"Bye, Mathéo, see you tomorrow," he takes a sack of potatoes from the trunk and walks toward the building's entrance.

I accelerate and drive slowly down the narrow street. The sun has almost set, and Mom is probably waiting for me to have dinner. But I drive past the house and continue a couple of minutes later I pull over by the church.

The small church's heavy wooden door is only partially open. I walk in, and my eyes adjust to the darkness. There are several lit candles in front of the altar, and several dim lightbulbs illuminate the hall. I walk down the aisle between the empty wooden pews. In front of the altar, before Jesus and the Virgin Mary, I cross myself and sit on the first pew, put my head in my hands, and pray.

I pray that no one steals her shoes or beats her because she's German and for her mother to come back from the East and take her.

"Mathéo, I haven't seen you here in a long time. Is everything all right?" Priest Nicholas sits beside me.

I look down and notice Priest Nicholas's palm in his lap. He's about sixty years old, and his wrinkly fingers tell the story of all the souls he has touched and encouraged. He has known me since I was a child.

"These are troubling times, Father," I say softly.

"I've heard that I gave out food coupons to boys whose fathers disappeared," he says, and as I turn to face him, I can see that he's smiling. His once brown hair has turned white over the years.

"It's hard for mothers to survive alone in times of war, Father," I reply.

"Yes, the war is long. No one knows when it will end, and you, Mathéo, are a good man."

"Thank you, Father," I gaze at the statues of the Virgin Mary and Jesus behind the altar. He wouldn't think I was a good man if he knew what I was doing in this camp.

"But that's not why you came here to pray, to let me know that you are a man of faith," he says to me quietly, his voice reassuring and comforting. "I know that thanks to your mother who comes in every Sunday and Mrs. Colette who tells me that you devotedly play with her son."

"Father," I turn my gaze to him again, "I am a policeman, a man of law. I'm responsible for keeping it and following orders. But what if those who created the laws are monsters?"

"These are difficult times," Father Nicholas sighs. "There's a war between evil and good. Evil has conquered us, and good has been diminished. Who knows, maybe good will never be able to free us, not in this lifetime," he turns his gaze to the crucifix.

"And what should we do?" I ask him. "Keep the law? Look the other way? Be the servant of the devil? I'm a policeman. If my commander gives me an order, I have to carry it out," I tell him, thinking of Mr. Arsenault, whom I had sent to the train today. And what about all the other Jews I took to the train whose names I don't even know? And what about Rebecca?

"I've known you since you were a little boy," Father Nicholas says, looking at me. "I remember how you would come to church every Sunday, sit upright on the wooden pew with a serious expression even before your feet touched the ground," he smiles at me again. "You didn't run wild like the other children, even though you didn't have a father to punish you if needed. Even when you were a child, you understood what was required of you. I'm sure that now you'll do the right thing."

"Father, I'm no longer sure what I should do," I think about the camp's barbed wire fences.

"Deep down, you know. Mrs. Colette thinks you're an angel watching over her son, even if all you've been doing as far as you can see it, is play football with him for a few minutes after work. Maybe there are others who think you're an angel."

"The good hunter with the glasses," I whisper to myself.

"What did you say?"

"Thank you, Father," I reply, knowing that I won't be able to tell him about the Jewish girl who was left there alone.

"You're welcome, Mathéo. You're welcome to come to me anytime," he stands up. "Say hello to your mom for me."

I park the vehicle in the quiet street and step out. The people rush to their homes before night falls as the last rays of sun paint the streets violet. Luc isn't playing ball against the wall, either. The silence without the sounds of the ball seems strange. He must be helping his mother, or he's tired of playing alone. I take my leather bag from the pickup truck and rush home. Mother must be waiting for me. She doesn't know that I was delayed at the church.

"Mom, what kind of child was I?" I ask her later as we sit at the table. The smell of the meat she cooked fills the house. I managed to buy meat yesterday with my additional food coupons.

"What do you mean, what kind of boy were you?" She looks up from her plate.

"Was I like all the other children? Was I a happy child? Sad? A coward? Grumpy?"

"You were a child, and you grew up. What does it matter what kind of child you were?"

"It didn't bother me that Dad wasn't here?"

"A lot of children didn't have a father after that war," she puts the fork on the table and sighs. "I raised you," she picks up the fork. "I didn't have time to think about what kind of child you are, I had to work and raise you, so you just grew up." She stops eating and looks at Dad's picture beside the big radio.

I want to ask her if she remembers me sitting on the steps at the building's entrance and waiting for him. But I know it will make her sad. I don't want to hurt her.

"Mom, do you remember teaching me to tie my shoelaces?"

"Of course, I remember teaching you to tie your shoelaces. Every mother remembers how she taught her child to tie their shoelaces. Why do you want to know?"

"Is it something with a story about bunny ears?"

"Why do you want to know? Is it because of the girl's shoes?"

"No, Mom."

"I know it is," she says while eating. "Did you get involved with a married woman?"

"No, Mom, it's not because of the shoes."

"I was so proud of you when you became a policeman, and now you're involved with a married woman? What would your father say?"

"No, Mom, it's not because of a married woman," I reply and glance at Dad's picture. What would he suggest that I do? I mustn't tell her about the girl in the camp, it's dangerous.

"What will happen when her husband returns from the war?"

"Mom, I don't want to talk about it," I say and put my fork down.

"I'm just saying that you should think carefully about what you're doing. A single woman with a child is no joke."

"I know," I reply and think of Rebecca's mother. I remember her, even though I only saw her for a short while. What happened to her in the East? Is she even married?

I turn my gaze again to Dad's picture, standing proudly in his uniform. *Why did you die and fail to see me grow up?*

"I'll show you later how to teach a child to tie their shoelaces," Mom says after a few minutes as we continue to eat in silence.

"Thanks, Mom," I say, wanting to get up and hug her. But I know it will embarrass her.

"You just have to tell the girl a story about a bunny, who hops and hides in a burrow," she adds and looks at me.

"Holding the bunny's ear..." Rebecca speaks to herself while sitting on the cardboard in her corner, "...and then the bunny runs around the tree, hops and hides from the bad hunters," her little fingers grip the brown laces. She struggles to create a loop. "I did it," she looks at me and stands up, stomping happily.

"Great, now I have to go," I say, rising to my feet. I should hurry so they don't start looking for me.

"Do you want to buy cigarettes?" She turns and approaches the cardboard tray behind her.

"No, I don't want you to sell me cigarettes."

"But you told me that I need to learn to manage on my own and that I should only sell to you," she holds the cardboard tray in front of me.

"But I brought you food today, didn't I?" I look at the package wrapped in parchment paper in her hiding place. There is also meat in today's meal.

"Where's the food from? Did Mommy send it to me?" She looks at me. I can see the hope in her eyes.

"Yes, Mommy sent it," I reply. "She said she can't come to visit you, but she loves you very much and misses you."

"Then I'll wait for her to come back," Rebecca sits down and opens the parchment paper with the food I brought her.

"But don't wait by the fence and don't sell cigarettes, promise?"

"Yes," she nods, chewing the food and smiling.

"Bye, Rebecca, I'll bring you food from Mommy tomorrow too," I walk away and leave the classroom, not before making sure the hallway is empty, and no one notices me. No one can find her hiding place, but I know it's only a matter of time before someone does.

"Where have you been? Three buses full of Jews from Paris are about to arrive," Sergeant Pascal asks me when I enter the guards' barracks.

"I walked around the yard. I searched for the girl we're betting on. Today's my day."

"Did you see her?"

"No, I couldn't find her. Maybe I'll win today," I go to the gun stand and take a rifle.

"Only when we find her lying dead on the ground do we pay the winner. Disappearing doesn't count," he also goes to the weapons stand and takes a rifle. "Let's go. We have work to do," he tells me and two other policemen on duty. We head to the parking lot to wait for the buses arriving from Paris.

A cool autumn breeze blows while we wait outside. I turn my gaze to the Germans' barracks. Captain Becker is standing on the balcony, watching us. He has his black visor hat with the SS skull. His hooked nose reminds me of the German eagle that sank its claws into our nation.

"Your girl," Sergeant Pascal touches my arm, and I turn to him. What did he mean?

"What about her?" I try to sound indifferent.

"She's alive. You lost the bet," he laughs and points at her. Even though I had asked her to stay away from the fence, she's standing next to the barbed wire fence, waiting for the buses like us.

"She doesn't want to die," I say what he expects to hear.

"No one asked her. We're betting on her," he lights a cigarette. "Someone must be giving her food. She also managed to get shoes. It's taking too long, and I've already lost money on this bet."

"Maybe some family adopted her," I suggest.

"I don't believe that. All the Jews care about is their money. They won't share their food, but it doesn't matter. We'll have to help her fulfill the purpose for which she was left here rather than thrown into a train," he takes a drag from his cigarette as we observe her. I hear the buses approaching and turn my gaze. Three green buses accompanied by a black police car drive to the camp. "Let's leave her alone for now. The Germans keep sending us new Jews," he pats me on the shoulder, and we line up in the parking lot to welcome the newcomers. They'll soon get off the buses.

I look at them as they slowly get off the buses. I can see on their faces the fatigue after long months of escaping the Nazi's clutches. It's been several months since that summer day when the Nazis hunted down all the Jews in Paris and France. Ever since, they've been searching for the ones who got away.

I can infer where they were caught from their clothes. The young man wearing a beret, dirty work clothes, and a torn tank top must have been hiding in a basement. He's holding a bag containing all of his belongings on his shoulder. He glances at us loathingly. Walking before him is a couple, a man wearing a fancy suit, and a woman in an elegant dress. They're looking in horror at the rifle in my hands. They must have been carrying fake documents and were caught in a surprise inspection by the Gestapo. I notice a young woman getting off the bus. She's wearing a wrinkled dress and looks humiliated. What happened to her? Did she hide in an attic? Did someone tip off the Nazis?

"Traitor," I hear Sergeant Pascal whisper and turn my gaze. A man about my age steps off the bus. He's wearing a police uniform.

He walks slowly, slightly limping, his uniform is torn, and his police cap is missing. His ranks and police insignia were also torn. I notice the bruises on his face. He doesn't have a suitcase or a bag with him. He walks past me with indifference, avoiding eye contact, pacing among the Jews who arrived with him as if he had decided that he was one of them.

"Who is he? Do you know him?" I approach Pascal and ask.

"No, I have no idea who he is," he replies, while aiming his rifle at the people gathered near the gate.

"Why is he here?"

"He must have tried to help the Jews or opposed the Germans, and he was wrong."

"He's French, he's one of us."

"We all choose a side," Pascal looks at me. "Strong or weak, and he chose the wrong side."

"Yes, you're right," I touch my rifle and point it to the ground, "he shouldn't have resisted them. We're the law."

"Those who want to survive need to make the right choice," Pascal says and turns to two elderly women walking past us.

"Go to the entrance gate, to Drancy's vacation camp," he says to them.

"Yes, he deserves to be punished," I respond. "He should be here until they release him."

"He won't be released anywhere," Pascal says mockingly. "He'll be on the first train out. Traitors like him have no place on French soil."

"They'll transfer him to resettle in the East?"

"Do you really think they're being resettled?" Pascal looks away from the people and turns his gaze to me. "Hitler promised he'd cleanse the world of Jews and rats, and he's definitely cleansing the world of Jews. About rats, I'm not so sure. They still roam the streets of Paris at night," he laughs, takes a pack of cigarettes from his pocket and lights one.

"What do you mean?" I glare at him; I feel nauseated. The other policemen push the last people in the camp through the open gate.

"No one should know about this. It's an SS secret." Sergeant Pascal approaches me. "The Germans send trains full of Jews to a camp in the east. No one leaves the camp. And surprisingly enough, the camp doesn't get overcrowded. The Nazis 'handle' the Jews, and they disappear forever," he exhales, and the smoke rises for a moment like a bluish cloud in the air until it evaporates.

"What is this place?" I watch the policemen close the camp gate behind the people.

"It's called Auschwitz. It's in Poland, far from France," he smiles at me. "I never liked Jews. No one escapes Auschwitz, and no one survives."

Chapter Fourteen

Charlotte

Auschwitz, Prisoners Hospital Block 20

"Number 132689, you are not allowed to enter. You are not sick. You know the rules," the hospital block's supervisor stands before me at the door and doesn't let me in. She speaks to me in Polish.

"Take it," I tell her in Polish and put in her hand a slightly rotten potato I hid in my ragged prisoner's uniform. It's amazing how quickly I learned to say basic sentences in all the languages spoken here in camp. Everyone here speaks a mixture of German, Russian, French, Polish, Yiddish, and Ukrainian.

"I give you five minutes. If one of the Germans in charge comes in here, you'll be punished," she says while examining the potato and tucking it into her prisoner uniform.

"I know," I reply and enter the smelly block.

"Wait, what is this?" She reaches out to the enamel cup I hold and blocks my way again. She's stronger than me. She's not skinny like us, the other prisoners. She receives double food rations from the Germans for her job as well as bribes from anyone who wants anything from her.

"It's none of your business. You got your potato," I push her hand away with my skinny arm and move inside. It's amazing how quickly I learned to be tough in this place. Those who aren't tough don't survive.

"Five minutes," she says and lets me through. But I don't even answer; my eyes are already scanning the beds, looking for her.

The sick female prisoners lie in this part of the block, crowded on wooden beds. At least they have thin mattresses stuffed with a bit of straw or sawdust and crumbling blankets to cover themselves with.

People cough from all sides as I walk between the beds, looking for her. Some follow me with their eyes, but most of them just lie there and stare at the ceiling.

"Charlotte," I bend down next to her.

"Sarah, you shouldn't have come," she rises a little and whispers. She's almost the only one in this place who knows me by name and not by number.

"I brought you some soup," I take a plain metal spoon out of my uniform pocket.

"You shouldn't have. We get food here."

"You get less. Try to eat," I dip the spoon in the watery soup and bring it to her mouth. Here, in the labor camp, those who are sick and can't work are worthless and receive only half the food ration.

Charlotte takes several sips of the soup I pour into her mouth, but then she stops and leans back. She's become so thin.

"Enough, no more for me," she says and looks at me. Her brown eyes look cloudy.

"You have to eat and get out of here. You have two days to rest here and go back to work. Otherwise, your fate is sealed."

"I won't return to work. You know that."

"Charlotte, please, you can get better," I try to give her another spoonful of soup.

"I have some cigarettes in my pocket, take them, my shoes also, they're better than yours. Yours are torn," she tries to speak.

"I won't take your shoes."

"You know that if you don't take them, someone else will. Please, help me take them off," she tries to sit up but can't.

"Charlotte, no..."

"Please, Sarah, you'd do it for me," she puts her arm on mine.

I look back at the hospital block's supervisor, she sits with her back to me, and I turn to Charlotte. My fingers untie the laces of her shoes, and I gently remove them, trying not to hurt her. We all have calluses on our feet from walking in shoes without socks.

"Are you in pain?" I ask her as I put my shoes on her.

"It doesn't hurt. I'm okay," she whispers. "Sarah, the cigarettes in my pocket," she reaches for her prison uniform pocket under the thin blanket. I help her and take out two cigarettes.

"Thank you, Charlotte," I hold her hand, knowing this is the last time we meet.

"Sarah..." She makes another effort and slightly raises her head from the mattress.

"Yes, Charlotte?"

"Give Rebecca a hug from me," she says slowly, resting her head on the mattress again.

"I will," I reply, knowing she's already hallucinating. I don't want to tell her that I lost my daughter, and I have no idea where she is.

"Thank you," she says and takes a deep breath, closing her eyes.

"Tell Rebecca that I love her," I whisper to her, teary-eyed.

"No..." she keeps speaking and opens her eyes. "Sarah, promise me that you'll live and that you'll find her, and tell her that I love her," she raises her skinny hand and touches the yellow Star of Life and Death on my prisoner uniform. I can hardly feel her fingers touching it.

"I promise," I say to her, tears rolling down my cheeks.

"And now, get out of here," she puts her hand on the thin mattress. "Remember, you promised me."

Chapter Fifteen

The Decision

Mathéo

I sit down on the wooden pew in the small church and place my hands on my knees. My blue uniform's fabric feels rough on my skin even though I've been wearing it for many years. I look up at the Virgin's statue. I think she's looking back at me. Behind her, on the mural-decorated wall, stands out a yellow star of the morning. The artist who painted it shimmering, so many years ago, probably wanted to give hope to those who'd come and pray here. But I don't know if there's any hope left. I know there's no hope left for the people I guard in the camp. And what about the girl? What do I do with what Sergeant Pascal told me about sending the Jews to Auschwitz?

The church is empty. The curfew will soon begin, and everyone hurries back to their homes. I put my hands together, kneel, and silently pray, stopping only as I hear footsteps and look back.

Father Nicholas slowly approaches and smiles at me, his black cloak moves with his every movement.

"Good evening, Mathéo," he sits down next to me.

"Good evening, Father."

"Is everything okay?"

"Everything is fine. I just came to pray," I answer. I don't know if I can trust him or tell him anything.

"You know Mathéo," he says. "I've gotten used to you no longer coming to my sermons. It's okay," he smiles at me. "I have an agreement with God that your mother comes every Sunday to pray for both of you."

"She's a good woman. She raised me all by herself," I say back.

"Yes, your mother is a good woman," he sighed. "And it's hard for women in times of war. But I have a feeling that's not why you came here to pray," he places his hand on my shoulder.

"No, it isn't," I whisper.

"Would you like to tell me the reason, or would you like to keep it in your prayer only?"

"They're sending them to a horrible place," I tell him, quietly.

"The Jews from the camp?"

"Yes," I nod.

"The Nazis have been here for over two years, and the rumors are only getting worse."

"These are not rumors, Father."

"If only we could help them, but the Nazis are our occupiers, and they're cruel. You and I both know that the black cars of the Gestapo are roaming the city searching for Jews and traitors."

"There's one girl there," I tell him after a moment, "without her mother, the mother was sent away."

"And what about that girl?"

"It doesn't matter, Father. What about all those other people in the camp?"

"You know, Mathéo, there's a saying in Judaism: 'whoever saves a life, it is as if he saved the whole world'," I feel his warm hand on my shoulder.

"And how can I help one girl?" I look up at the Virgin and the yellow star painted on the wall behind her.

"Sometimes God has power, and not just prayer," Father Nicholas says. "I've known you since you were born, and I know I can trust you," he pauses for a moment before he keeps speaking. "Sometimes God's messengers have powers, too. There are those among us who don't care, but there are the ones who're trying to help. I told you last time you came to me, I'm here to help, and I've known you long enough to know you need help."

"I need help saving one girl," I tell him and turn to look at him, into his blue eyes.

A few days later, I look at the blue sky. They're too beautiful for this small train station full of people.

Along the track stands a freight train. The black locomotive carries ten brown-painted wooden cars, usually used to transport cattle. The car's big doors are opened to the platform full of prisoners from the camp waiting to board them. Today is my day to escort the transport from the camp to the station.

Despite the pleasant autumn day, the people are sweating from walking all the way from the camp to the train station, some carry suitcases containing all their possessions or supporting a family member. I feel a lump in my throat as I see an older man hobbling with a cane onto the platform.

"Achtung. Everyone, get into the cars," a Nazi soldier shouts into a megaphone he's holding. "Schnell, fast," he keeps shouting. Recently, more soldiers in black uniforms arrived at the Germans' barracks. Shipments to the East are also increasing. Father Nicholas told me to come back next week. He'll find out what can be done.

The men and women begin to enter the carriages at a slow pace.

"Schnell, fast," the Nazi soldier continues to shout through the megaphone. The cars fill up, and the platform empties. Another soldier passes from one car to another and closes the large wooden doors. His hand turns and closes the large metal bolt that locks the door from the outside. The people standing inside the freight cars look at the blue sky one last time before the door slams in their faces, and they disappear behind the heavy wooden doors.

Only a few French policemen and Nazi soldiers remain standing on the empty platform. In the distance, at the end of the platform, I can make out Captain Becker, standing in his black uniform, watching us. Are they planning to send everyone to the East soon?

"I think we're done here for the day," Sergeant Pascal tells me as the Nazi soldier closes the bolt of the last car and locks it with a bang. "Let's go. We can start heading back to the camp," he calls to the other policemen standing along the platform. A different German soldier whistles and signals with his hand, and the locomotive fills the sky with black smoke, and starts pulling the cars forward.

"Will it last much longer?" I ask him as I watch the train slowly pull away from the station. How much time do I have left to try and get that girl out of here?

"Do you think they'll let this go on much longer? He's now personally coming to watch the trains," Sergent Pascal points at Captain Becker. "Their only problem now is getting more train cars. After all, transporting so many Jews to the East is damaging their war effort," he grins.

"And what will they do after they send them all?" I ask him as we walk down the empty platform. I bend down and pick up a woman's beret that fell off one of the prisoners and remains lying on the concrete.

"Are you worried? They'll make sure to fill it with prisoners of war from the East, with American pilots who were shot down and captured. You don't need to worry about them. They'll find someone to bring here after they cleanse France of Jews. We'll always have work."

"Excellent," I say, feeling the lump in my throat. The train had already disappeared from the station, and the black cloud had also gone, leaving the sky blue once again.

"Mathéo," Sergeant Pascal says as we walk to the police pick-up truck waiting to take us back to the camp. "Do you remember that motherless girl, the one we bet on?"

ALEX AMIT

"Yes, I remember," I answer, all tense. Did he find out about me? I keep matching his pace. "I lost the bet," I tell him, trying to hide the tension in my voice.

"Yes, we all lost a lot of money on her. The little Jewess refuses to die. She somehow manages to get food," he tells me, taking out a pack of cigarettes from his uniform shirt pocket. "Do you want one?" He offers it to me.

"No, thanks," I reply. Does he suspect me? "Surely someone feels sorry for her and helps her," I add.

"Yes, of course someone's watching over her," he says, thoughtfully, "but that's not the point. I don't care if someone's helping her."

"So, what's the matter with her?" I ask. I have to choose my words carefully.

"I want you to take care of her."

"What does that mean?" I place my hand on my holster, feeling the warm leather in the heat of the afternoon sun.

"I bet on her for two more days. I put a lot of money on her," he blows the cigarette smoke in the air. "I want to win. I want her to be *kaput* in exactly two days. Until then, I want her to stay alive."

"What do you want me to do?" I ask him and look back. The other policemen are at a distance from us. They walk and talk to each other.

"I want you to take care of that," he puffs on his cigarette. "You owe me. I got you the medicine from the Germans, back then, when your mother was sick. You owe me." He stops and looks at me seriously, his dark eyes examining me.

"I'll take care of it," I look back at him. I can't lower my eyes, "I'll make sure she's *kaput* in two days."

296

Chapter Sixteen

Saving Rebecca

I park the police pick-up car on the street and turn off the engine, but I remain sitting in the car. I have to decide whether I should do it or not. Luc is playing with a ball in the middle of the street, kicking it against the building wall at a safe distance from Ms. Sophie's barber shop glass storefront. Years ago, he accidentally broke it, and there were many shouts and anger. But I think she's since forgiven him, especially now that he's so alone. What will I do with the girl? Should I risk my life? I can still regret it. I'm not responsible for her.

"Hey, Luc," I get out of the car and slam the door behind me.

"Hey, Mr. Allard," he smiles at me. "Shall we play?"

"Pass the ball," I stand on the other side of the street and wait.

"Here it comes," he kicks the ball to me.

"Say, Luc," I kick the ball back, "can you stay still for a long time?"

"How do you mean? Mr. Allard."

"If I tell you to be still and not move, how long can you do it?" I ask him as we play.

"I can do it for a while," he answers. "Sometimes I sit quietly in the street and wait, without moving even a bit."

"Without moving at all?"

"Can I tell you something, Mr. Allard? But promise you won't tell anyone," Luc stops the ball with his foot.

"I promise," I come closer to him.

"Sometimes I make a deal with God," he looks at me with an embarrassed look. "For example, if I manage to hold my breath and not move for a really long time, then my father will come back. Or there was that time, a long time ago, when Mom was able to bring me two pieces of chocolate, and I decided that if I won't eat them for a week, then my father would come back. And I wanted the chocolate so badly, but I managed to hold back," he smiles at me.

"I promise, your dad will be back," I caress his hair. "Goodbye, Luc, say hello to your mom for me," I walk to the building's entrance. My mom must already be waiting for me with dinner.

"Shall we play tomorrow too?"

"We'll play tomorrow," I reply, knowing that tomorrow may be different.

"You're different," Mom says to me later, when we're sitting together and eating dinner. "You're quiet today."

"I'm always quiet," I answer.

"But today, you're a different kind of quiet," she watches me while eating.

"The news about the war bothers me," I say the first thing that comes to mind. I need to think of a plan and don't know what to do. Am I even capable of doing such a thing?

"I gave birth to you. I'm your mother. I know you. You're not bothered by the German army's war in Russia," she stops eating and looks at me.

"I have to go to somewhere after dinner," I say. She mustn't know anything of what I might do.

"Where are you going in the dark? It's late, and there's a curfew."

"I'm going; I'm a policeman, I can go."

"You shouldn't talk to me like that. I'm your mother."

"I'm sorry, Mom. It's better that you don't know where I'm going."

"Is it to that woman?"

"No, Mother, it's not to that woman. I'm not going to any woman," I answer and recall that woman, even though there was nothing between us.

"So, where are you going?"

"I have to sort something out," I don't want to tell her I'm going to the priest. It's better she doesn't know.

"Can't it wait for tomorrow? You didn't use to hide things from me."

"Trust me, it's okay. You don't have to worry."

"I just don't want you walking in the dark. It's not safe out there with the Germans."

"I'll be fine," I reply, trying to sound reassuring.

"I hope this woman's worth it," she quietly says as she resumes eating.

"It's not a woman," I say and bite my food. I still remember the touch of her wet skin that night she asked me to help her. I still remember her warmth at the tip of my fingers when she took my hand and placed it on her breasts. Why did she choose me?

"Bye, Mom," I say to her later, as I stand by the door and put on my coat.

"Beware of the Nazis," she hugs me.

"I won't be back late, don't worry," I hug her.

"You're a good man, Mathéo. I know Dad would've been proud of you."

"Thanks, Mom," I say, wondering if, in some secret motherly way, she knows where I'm going and why.

On the way to the priest's house, I stop at the building entrance of Mrs. Colette, Luc's mother, and put half a German army chocolate bar into their mailbox. Sometimes, the Germans give us some of the army rations they receive. I need the other half of the chocolate bar.

Then, when on the street, I stop for a few minutes, take out a box of cigarettes, and light a cigarette for myself. The taste of smoke chokes my breath and burns my throat. I cough, and I feel dizzy, but I don't stop.

After I finish it, I light another one. I need to get used to it. I need to be ready. I couldn't think of a better plan. It has to be tomorrow. There won't be another chance.

"Mathéo, come in, don't stand outside," Father Nicholas opens the door of his house and leads me inside. I follow him and look around. I've never been here; I've only seen him in church. His apartment is simple, similar to ours. The cloak he wears during sermons is hanging on a hanger by the door, and there's a large bookcase in the guest room, it's full of black and brown religious manuscripts.

"Good evening, Father," I say. "I apologize for bothering you with this."

"Is everything okay? We agreed that you would come to the sermon on Sunday," he stares at me. It's strange for me to see him without the cloak he wears at church. Now he wears simple, black pants and a plain button-down shirt, and only a chain with a silver cross hanging around his neck, as if to remind himself that even at home, he's still a man of God.

"I apologize, Father, but it has to be tomorrow."

"What has to be tomorrow?"

"The girl."

"Is she in danger?"

"Yes, it has to be tomorrow. Can you help me?" I can't explain to him what Sergeant Pascal said, but it doesn't matter.

"I don't know if they're ready. I don't have answers yet," he sighed. "But God will help you," he looks at me, "and I'm God's messenger. We'll do everything we can and pray."

"Thank you, Father," I say, realizing that I've decided what I should do at this moment. I feel my entire body tensing up, yet his presence relaxes me.

"Do you have a plan?"

"Partly, Father, I'll get her out of the camp hidden in a burlap sack. I have to pass the German checkpoint on the way to Paris. I think I can do it, and I'll bring her to you, Father."

"Don't bring her here. It's more dangerous here. Bring her to the church," he tells me. "I'll wait for her in the church, there are places to hide her there, and there's a chance they won't dare enter."

"And what will happen to her after that?"

"I'll hand her over to someone who'll take her out of Paris, to a monastery, where they won't look for her; but she'll have to have a new identity - as a Christian girl. You'll have to prepare her for that," he looks at me. "She doesn't know me, and she'll have to trust me. Otherwise, she'll put us all in danger; you, me, and herself."

"I'll take care of it," I reply. I'll have to think about it through the night. I have so many more details to figure out.

"Do you know her from before? Will she trust you?"

"No, Father, I met her in the camp," I answer, recalling the moment she asked me if I was a good hunter. Am I a good hunter?

"I trust you," he keeps scanning me with his blue eyes.

"Thank you, Father. I should go home, it's already late. Mother is worried about me," I say goodbye to him and head for the door.

"Mathéo," he calls out to me as I'm standing outside the open door.

"Yes, Father?" I turn to him.

"Are you sure you want to do this?" He looks at me. "It's dangerous. You're putting yourself at risk in order to save a Jewish girl you don't know. Are you sure you want to do this?"

"I know, Father," I say. "It's true, I don't really know her. But I'm not risking myself for a Jewish girl I don't know. I know the look in her eyes, and I remember the look in her mother's eyes. I'm doing it to help someone in this horrible war. I'm risking myself so I know that I did something, as small as it may be. I'm doing it for myself, so I know that I choose to be on the right side. I'm risking myself so that I can sleep at night without their looks haunting me for the rest of my life, knowing I could've done something."

"Your father would be proud of you, Mathéo, I know that. He would have been proud to meet the man you've become. Godspeed tomorrow," he places his hand on my shoulder.

"Thank you, Father," I turn my face away from him, I don't want him to see the anticipation and tension on my face. "I'll see you tomorrow evening at church. I'll bring the girl with me."

"Mathéo, do you have the pick-up truck today? Fernard told me you switched with him," Sergeant Pascal asks me at the end of the day, as I prepare to leave the barracks. The time has come. Clouds are covering the sky, and it's getting dark outside.

"Yes, Fernard will take the car tomorrow," I reply and try to speak calmly. I'm very tense.

"Take me with you to the city. I have something to deliver there," he smiles at me.

"No problem," I answer. "Me too," I smile back at him and try to hide my nervousness. I knew it could happen, that he'd want to join, but I have no choice. I have to take the risk. There's no other solution.

"I knew you were one of ours, that you know how to take care of yourself and not just work as a guard here," he pats my shoulder. "Have you finished your shift for today?"

"In a little while, I'll call you before I leave for town," I open the barracks door.

"Don't forget," he sits on the wooden bench inside the barracks and lights himself a cigarette.

I rush out and into the compound. I need to find her and take her with me. Fortunately, it's starting to rain. This increases the chance that I'll be able to pass the Nazi checkpoint on the way to Paris.

"Patrol," I say to the guard at the gate and go inside. The empty burlap sack is tucked under my shirt; I feel the rough fabric against my skin. The guard watches me for a moment then silently opens the gate. He's one of the new ones, which is also good; he won't ask any questions.

"Rebecca," I walk into the empty classroom and call her name, seeing her peering out of her hiding place.

"The good hunter with the glasses," she smiles at me. "What did you bring me?"

"Rebecca," I approach her and try to say the right words, so as not to scare her. "Do you trust me?"

"Yes," she nods. "You're a good hunter."

"True," I say. "But there's a problem."

"What's the problem?"

"A lot of bad new hunters have arrived at the camp," I see how she coils a little. Her hand tightly grips the pencil she's holding. "We need to escape from the camp, so they don't catch you," I continue as I take out the burlap sack that I've hidden under my shirt. "We'll hide you in the sack, and that's how we'll escape the bad hunters."

"Like Mommy wanted me to do with Mr. Chambu?" She asks and nods.

"Yes," I reply, even though I don't understand what she's talking about.

"And you'll hide me and take me to Mrs. Angelina, even though I lost the note?"

"No, I won't take you to Mrs. Angelina. I'll take you somewhere else."

"And Mommy will be there?"

"Mommy will come and visit in a while, but only if you wait for her silently and hide without moving. Will you be able to hide without moving?"

"Yes," she answers. "I won't move at all."

"And if you hide and don't move, and be really quiet, I'll give you a surprise," I take the half package of chocolate out of my uniform pocket and show it to her.

"I promise."

"Great, but one more thing, you can't go by Rebecca from now on."

"Why?"

"Because the bad hunters are looking for Rebecca, and we want to confuse them."

"So, what's my name?" She looks at me with sad eyes.

"What's your name?"

"Yes," she looks at me, and it seems as if she's about to start crying. What women's name do I know? I'm trying to think.

"Your name is Sophie. From now on, your name is Sophie," I tell her the first name I can think of.

"That's an ugly name."

"That's your name from now on. What's your name?" I ask her. I have to hurry. This is taking too long.

"Sophie."

"Good, and if you hear the name Rebecca, you mustn't answer."

"Okay."

"Rebecca," I call her. I have to check on her.

"What?"

"You mustn't answer me, only if I call you Sophie," I raise my hand and slap her.

The look of interest in her eyes turns to shock, and she pulls back in panic, trying to steady herself and struggling not to cry. I feel a terrible lump in my throat, but I had to do it.

"What's your name?" I once again ask her.

"Sophie."

"Is your name Rebecca?"

"No," she shakes her head and looks fearfully at my hand.

"Rebecca, take it," I take out half the chocolate bar, break off a piece and hand it to her.

"My name is Sophie," she says in a shaky voice and doesn't extend her hand.

"Sophie, are you Jewish?"

"No," she shakes her head.

"What's your mother's name?"

"Mommy."

"Sophie, take it."

"Thanks," she reaches out and shoves the piece into her mouth, but she doesn't smile at me. How will I explain to her that I did it for her sake?

"Now you need to get into the sack, and I'll take you," I tell her. "But first, we need to take the yellow badge off your dress," I pull a penknife out of my pants pocket and kneel down in front of her.

"It's forbidden," she says to me, her eyes looking at the knife I'm holding in my hand in fear. Does she still trust me?

"Sophie, you have to trust me. I won't hurt you. I'll just cut the yellow badge off."

"It's forbidden. It's the Star of Life and Death. It mustn't be taken off. Mommy doesn't allow it," she keeps looking at me.

"You must, or the bad hunters will find you." Does she still think I'm a good hunter?

"Will you hit me if I take it off?"

"No, I won't beat you if you take it off. No one will beat you anymore." I tell her and am ashamed of what I did.

"And if you take it off, can I keep it in my pocket?"

"Yes," I reply.

"Okay," she says, and I carefully unravel the yellow badge from her dress. When I finish, I place the yellow badge in her hand and stand up. Without it, she looks like an ordinary, thin, wild, and dirty girl.

"Now, get into the sack," I open the burlap sack. "We have to hurry. Soon, the bad hunters will come looking for you."

"Hang on," she tells me. She runs behind her hiding place, brings her shaggy teddy bear, and stands before me.

"Remember, don't move, don't talk, and don't try to get out of the sack until I open it," I tell her as she sits inside the big sack, and I close over her. Then, I tie it, lift her on my shoulders, and start walking toward the gate. I can't take it back from now on. None of us can afford to make a mistake - neither I nor her.

"What's in the sack?" The guard at the camp gate asks me as I leave with the sack on my shoulders. The rain continues to fall, and it's already dark outside. Everything will be fine as long as he doesn't shine his flashlight on the sack.

"Jewish goods they don't need," I answer.

"They keep robbing the world, even from here." he opens the gate for me and hurries back to the guard post that shelters him from the rain.

I walk with her on my shoulders, in the mud, surprised at how light she is. I've passed the first barrier. Now, we need to successfully pass the trip to Paris with Sergeant Pascal and the German checkpoint.

"Sophie, I'm putting you in a car, don't move," I whisper to her as I place her in the trunk, next to the sack of potatoes Sergeant Pascal has already placed there.

"Good," she whispers back to me.

In the dark, I make sure the sack rests firmly on the metal floor. I have nothing to put under it that would make her comfortable. She'll have to survive the trip. I close the trunk tarp cover and go to the barracks to call Sergeant Pascal.

"Why did you take so long?" He asks me.

"I picked only the best Jewish items," I answer and smile, but inside I feel the tension rise. "Let's go. Our warm homes are waiting for us in Paris."

We step into the car and start driving, passing the houses in Drancy, and getting on the road leading to Paris. Fortunately, the rain doesn't stop falling, although it's making me drive slower. Shortly before the German checkpoint I light myself a cigarette. I need to have a pack of cigarettes ready in my uniform pocket for the German soldier at the checkpoint.

"What happened that made you start smoking?" Sergeant Pascal asks me and lights himself one.

"If the Germans give us gifts, we should enjoy them," I reply.

"We should definitely enjoy what this war has to offer us, especially the Jewish women who are willing to give themselves to us in exchange for the Nazis' cigarettes," I hear him laugh. His cigarette looks like a firefly in the dark, momentarily lighting up as he inhales. I look away from his cigarette and concentrate on the dark road. The car's wartime headlights mask only allow for two narrow light strips to illuminate the road. The cigarette I smoke makes me nauseous, as well as his statement about the Jewish women. I mustn't think about what he said. I have to focus. We'll arrive at the German checkpoint at the next turn.

"Let me do the talking, if we have to," Pascal says, exhaling smoke as the road curves. I can barely make out the German barrier in the dark and rain. I slow down the vehicle and stop in front of it. A soldier holding a flashlight runs out of the guard post, approaches us, and shines it on us, blinding us for a moment. He then immediately moves away and lifts the barrier, signaling us to pass without asking us as to the purpose of our drive. Either he already knows us, or he doesn't want to get wet in the pouring rain, like all soldiers around the world.

"That was easy," Sergeant Pascal says, and I remain silent. I've also passed the second barrier. So far, everything is going to plan. But I can't smile yet. I'm too tense, so I open the car window momentarily and throw out the cigarette I'm holding. I don't need it anymore. Now, all I have to do is bring Sergeant Pascal home.

The city is dark, and I move slowly through the deserted streets. A few more minutes, and it'll all be over.

I park the car next to his house and hurry out to open the trunk in the rain. He mustn't accidentally touch the bag Rebecca is hiding in and find out.

"All is well?" he asks me as I pull the sack of potatoes from the back and hand it to him. What should I answer? I need to think of an answer fast.

"I chose the heavier sack for you. After all, you're the Sergeant, and I'm not," I reply.

"You should know that I'm very pleased with you. I recommended you for a promotion," he says. "We'll talk about it in the next few days."

"Thank you. Good night. Don't stay out in the rain," I tell him as he turns.

"Good night. See you tomorrow," I still hear him as he walks to the building with the sack on his shoulder. I rush to the car and start it. Now, all I have to do is get to the church without encountering any sudden German patrol on the street. It's not curfew yet.

I drive slowly on the wet streets, to avoid slipping, staying away from the main avenue, and prefer the side streets. Just a few more minutes and all this will be behind me.

In the distance, I notice a German patrol, but I turn into one of the alleys, and they don't signal me to stop. Shortly before the church, I stop and turn off the engine. I remain seated in the quiet car for a few minutes and look at the street in front of the church. The street is quiet, and I can only hear the rain hitting the tin roof and the trunk's tarp. There's no one waiting for me there.

I try to start the engine again, but it won't start. Is it possible that it got wet from the rain? I curse silently and repeatedly flick the starter. The engine screeches and wails but finally starts. I sigh in relief, drive the short distance, and park next to the church door.

"Rebecca," I open the tarp cover and whisper in the dark.

"My name is Sophie," she answers from the sack, and I smile. Carefully, I untie the rope tying the sack.

"Let's go, Sophie, get out. We've arrived," I whisper, and she gets out of the bag and stands in front of me.

I help her out of the trunk and give her a hand as we rush to the church, my other hand holding the empty burlap sack so as not to leave any traces. The heavy church door is closed, and I forcefully pull it open.

The hall inside is dark. Only a few candles are lit in front of the altar. I walk with Sophie in the aisle between the dark pews and hold her hand. Only the sound of our steps is heard.

"You have arrived," Father Nicholas emerges from a side room.

"Sophie, this is Father Nicholas. Go to him and do what he tells you," I bend down on my knees and tell her.

But she stands there, looking at me, holding on to her rag bear.

"It's okay. You can go with him. He's a good hunter," I say and smile at her, although I'm not sure if she can see my smile in the dark.

"You promised," she tells me.

"What did I promise?"

"The chocolate. I was quiet the whole time."

"Right, I forgot," I take the half bar of chocolate out of my uniform pocket and give it to her.

She holds it and turns, walks over to Father Nicholas. He puts his hand on her shoulder, and they disappear into the side room, leaving me standing on my knees in the passage. She didn't say goodbye to me.

"Goodbye, Sophie," I whisper and cross myself, looking up at the Virgin statue above me. I managed to get her out of the camp. She'll be fine.

The following day at the camp, I hand over the car to Fernard. He needs to get goods from Le Bourget airport and later from the police headquarters in Paris.

Towards noon, I go up to guard in tower number two. My eyes examine the people inside the camp, and I try not to think about Sophie.

But when I finish my shift and approach the barracks, I see all the policemen standing in attention, in a straight line, before Captain Becker.

The Nazi officer watches Fernard, who's standing one step ahead of all the others. German soldiers holding submachine

313

guns are standing on both sides of the captain, and on the ground, at his black boots, lies a yellow badge.

Chapter Seventeen

One Step

"Are you the traitor who drove the pickup truck?" Captain Becker says slowly to Fernard, scanning him like a bird of prey eyeing a small field mouse. He glances at me when I join the line of policemen standing in order. But immediately returns his look to Fernard who's standing in front of him. Only Sergeant Pascal stands on the side of the line next to the SS soldiers and watches us.

"Yes, Commander," Fernard replies in German.

"Don't speak to me German," the Captain holds up the small leather whip and strikes Fernard's face. The whip's cracking echoes through the air, followed by Fernard's groan as he nearly stumbles.

"Yes, Commander," Fernard replies in French. He has a red streak of blood on his cheek.

"What happened?" I whisper to the policeman standing next to me.

ALEX AMIT

"They found a yellow badge in the trunk of the pickup truck, and the Nazis accuse him of smuggling Jews out." He whispers back.

"Did you smuggle Jewish rats out of my camp?" Captain Becker asks him.

"No, Commander," Fernard says. He's whipped again and falls to the ground at Captain Becker's feet.

"We Germans," Captain Becker addresses all the policemen, "are people of honor. Even though we conquered you and could have locked you up in cages just like the Jewish rats, we chose to treat you fairly," he walks paces back and forth, his blue eyes are like flashlights examining us one after the other. The silver SS skull on his black visor glistens in the sun. "But we will not tolerate traitors, and traitors must be punished," he returns to face Fernard who's lying on the ground.

I look at Fernard who's flat on the ground next to the yellow badge in the mud. Is that Rebecca's badge that she wanted to keep? Did it fall out of her pocket? What if it's my fault?

"We're trying to clean the world of Jews, and you send them back to Paris. Do you know what's the punishment for that?" Captain Becker asks Fernard, who is lying at his feet.

What should I do? Confess? I can keep quiet. No one knows it was me. I'm not a suspect. He's new here. No one knows him. No one will care if they punish him. I feel a lump lodged in my throat as I stand up straight. I mustn't confess. I have to stay put for a few more minutes. Pretend that yesterday never happened.

"No, Commander," Fernard mutters in French, his mouth full of blood.

"We make those who help Jews feel what it's like to be one of them," Captain Becker says slowly. "Take the traitor to the corral," he turns to Sergeant Pascal. "But first, tear off all his badges," he adds and turns around, starting to walk back to the Germans' barracks. The two SS soldiers stay in attention and continue looking at us as Sergeant Pascal approaches Fernard, lifts him to his feet, and reaches out to pull his badge off his uniform.

"It was me," I say in German and take one step forward. Everyone turns to look at me. Captain Becker also stops and turns around.

"You?" Sergeant Pascal barks and starts to approach me, but as Captain Becker heads in my direction, the former stops and steps back.

The Nazi officer approaches me, and I look into his blue eyes. Out the corner of my eye, I notice his black-gloved hand holding the small leather whip. My whole body tenses up, and I await the whipping that will soon commence. I can't take back those three fatal words.

"Bend down and take the badge of those Jews whom you love so much," Captain Becker says almost in a whisper.

I bend down and reach out to the yellow badge in the mud. It doesn't matter anymore if Rebecca lost it when she got out of the trunk last night or if it belongs to some other Jew.

Like a flash of pain, I feel Captain Becker's hobnailed leather boot kick me in the face, and I flinch and groan. I taste blood in my mouth, and my cheek burns. But I still reach out and pick up the yellow badge from the mud.

"Sergeant Pascal," I hear Captain Becker say, "I'm not going to take care of all your traitors. It's your job. You know what you have to do."

I look up and see Captain Becker turning and walking away from me. The two SS soldiers follow him. My mouth is full of blood.

"Stand up, traitor," Sergeant Pascal shouts at me, and I struggle to rise to my feet.

"You? It was you? The man I trusted?" He approaches me and rips my ranks from my shoulders. The sound of the fabric ripping sounds like a growl of a wild boar. "You love them now? Who was it?" He spits in anger, his face close to mine.

"Just a boy who managed to escape," I barely whisper.

"Was it that girl we bet on?" He punches me in the gut.

I collapse to the ground and feel the urge to throw up, but I manage to stand up.

"It was just a boy. I don't know him," I reply slowly. I struggle to breathe. I mustn't put her or Priest Nicholas at risk. My fate was sealed, but I must protect them.

"Where is the girl?" He hits me again, and I groan. "I thought you were my friend."

"It's not her. It was just a boy who managed to escape and climbed into the trunk, begging me to take him," I whisper. I fight the impulse to hurl. A sour feeling of nausea fills my throat. I won't break.

"So where is he?" Sergeant Pascal grips my hair and whispers in my ear. "You're not a policeman anymore," he swipes away my police hat, throws it on the muddy ground, and takes my pistol from its holster.

"He ran away. When I reached Paris, he just ran away," I whisper. What would my mother think of me?

"One Jew escaped, and one traitor will replace him," Sergeant Pascal spits in my face. "Good luck in the camp in the East," he whispers to me. "Go ahead, take him inside. He loves Jews, he wants to be with them," he punches me one last time and walks away.

Two policemen approach and hold me, helping me to my feet.

"I'm sorry," one of them whispers to me.

"It's not your fault," I reply and wipe my mouth, "with your permission, I'll go by myself," I manage to say.

I slowly walk to the gate. My whole body aches and I feel dizzy. I do my best not to fall to the ground, but when the policemen try to help me, I refuse.

"Open the gate for me, please," I say to the policeman guarding it. He silently does as I say, only his gaze following me. I knew what I did was dangerous. I hear the wooden gate close behind me. I feel lightheaded. I take a few steps into the yard and collapse on the ground. I need to rest for a short while. My whole body hurts. The other prisoners look at me with fear and keep their distance from me. I have to get used to the fact that from now on, I'm a prisoner just like them. I hope someone tells my Mom what happened. I hope she'll be proud of me.

I need to lie down; I close my eyes for just a few minutes.

"Are you okay?" I hear someone ask and I open my eyes. There's a bald man standing over me. He's about fifty years old, and he's dressed in a dirty white tank top and brown pants held up with suspenders. "You can't lie in the mud like that," he says. "You'll get sick and die. Let me help you up," he reaches out. "Do you have a place to sleep?"

"No, I don't."

"Come with me. I'll help you find a room," he says, supporting me as I try to stay on my feet. "Do you have any cigarettes? You must know that cigarettes equal food here, and food is life."

"I have some," I tell him, knowing it doesn't really matter. They're going to send me on the next train to where Rebecca's mother was sent to die.

Chapter Eighteen

Auschwitz, a Glimpse of Hope

Early 1943

"Pigs, we've got new ones. You're all dispensable," the block's Polish supervisor opens the door and announces in Polish. "Go in, come on. They won't bite you," she turns and talks to the women outside, as they fearfully walk into the block. They're shaved and dressed as prisoners, but they're much healthier than us. Every few days, they replace the women who didn't survive. The Nazis have no shortage of women who arrive in transports from all over Europe. A frosty winter wind blows through the open door. I raise my head from the wooden bunk and look at them.

They stand at the entrance, observing us women as we lie on the wooden bunks in the stuffy block. They seem to be in shock. Their bodies still haven't adjusted to the tattered, thin prisoners' uniforms and the sensation of their shaved heads. They must have arrived in the morning transport and still haven't realized that these are the gates to hell. The only thing they can be thankful for is that, for now, they're alive. Soon, they'll adopt the same indifferent look that we have, the more experienced prisoners; a look that has been keeping us alive in this place for months.

"Does anyone here speak French?" One of them asks, and I look at her. Even though her hair is shaved off, she seems familiar. I examine her.

"Did you come from Drancy?" I finally ask her. Do I know her?

"Yes," she replies, turns her gaze, and looks at me. She seems to be trying to recall who I am but fails. I have changed, too.

"I'm Sarah," I tell her after a while.

"The German woman?" She asks, and for the first time, this question doesn't sound derogatory but rather as a sigh in relief.

"Josephine?" I ask and sit up. She was one of the women who yelled at us after Rebecca stabbed another girl with a pencil.

"Is that you, Sarah?" She asks and takes a step closer, as if wanting to hug someone familiar, but is startled by the other women's and my appearance.

"Yes, it's me. Where's my daughter? Did you see her in the camp after they took me?" I get off the bunk and stand in front of her. Maybe she knows what happened to her? My stomach churns with excitement. For the first time in months, I don't feel famished or exhausted.

"I'm so sorry that they took you. They're taking everyone, train after train. They're emptying the camp," she replies and looks around in horror. "Where are all the women who arrived on the train with me? Why aren't they here, too?"

"What about my daughter? What about Rebecca? The girl you called 'the German girl'? Do you perhaps know what happened to her?" I ask her again. I can't tell her where they took all the other people who were transported here with her.

"The girl with the teddy bear and the pencil?" She looks at me again.

"Yes," I reply. I'm shaking.

"I saw her once or twice walking around with her teddy bear, but she disappeared. I didn't see her after that," Josephine feels the torn fabric of her uniform, as if trying to get used to them.

"What do you mean 'she disappeared'?" I ask her, but deep down I know the answer. Has anyone put her on one of the transports? I feel weak and grab one of the wooden bunks to stabilize myself.

"What is this place?" She asks.

"You lucked out. We work in an explosives and detonators factory and get some food."

"And the rest?"

"They ran out of luck," I respond and climb back into my bunk. I have to believe that Rebecca is still alive and survived the transport. I heard there are children in one of the labor camps. She's there, I'm sure. I touch the Star of Life and Death on my uniform. It's the star that keeps us connected.

"Let's go, dirty pigs, out now," the block supervisor shouts, and we rush outside.

"Come on, Josephine, hurry, don't be last in line," I pull her after me into the line, even though she hated me in Drancy.

Later, when we march to the explosives factory and walk past the platform, I search for Rebecca among the crowds who step off the train. I notice a man in a torn blue uniform and round glasses among the people. Could it be Mathéo, the policeman? It looks like him. I look at him for another moment, but the supervisor shouts at me to walk faster and catch up. Was it him? I'm not sure anymore. Perhaps I only imagined him among the crowd. When I look back again, the man in the torn blue uniform is gone. I'm not sure I didn't just imagine him.

All I know is one thing. I have to work every day and stay alive. This is the only thing I know. On challenging days, I talk to Rebecca in my thoughts and comb her hair. I know she's alive. I have to believe it. Otherwise, there's no point in my staying alive.

Two years later, in January 1945, four months before Nazi Germany surrendered, the Eastern German front collapsed under the Red Army attacks.

"Listen, anyone who can stand on their feet, go outside now," the Polish supervisor enters the block and shouts. She eats better than us. She has the strength to shout.

Slowly, the women get off the wooden bunks and face the door. I can hear her footsteps on the wooden floor, but I stay in my bunk. I'm too frail. What's the point?

"Come on, 132689, get up and step outside," she approaches me. "Don't stay here," she tells me softly, "if you don't get up you won't survive. Come on, it's almost the end of the war, get up," she takes a step back and resumed shouting at the rest. "Everyone, get out."

She loves me and treats me better than the previous supervisor. Sometimes, she also gives me half a slice of bread.

I force myself to get off the bunk, put on my shoes, and go outside to the snow. My feet are injured and sore. I have to be strong.

It's still dark outside, and the lanterns illuminating the electrified fences around us look like distant stars in the snow. We huddle together to keep warm. Not far away, dogs bark, disrupting the early morning silence. Occasionally, thunder rumbles in the distance.

"It's the Russian army. They're coming," someone whispers.

"Come on, everyone, start walking," the supervisor yells out, and we start walking slowly, dragging our feet through the snow. I try to push forward to the head of the column, where the supervisor is, so I won't be whipped like those who lag behind.

Our torn shoes squeak as we walk on the frozen road. I mustn't think about my frozen feet. I mustn't think about anything. On our way, we walk past the train platform. To my surprise, it's deserted in the morning twilight. There's no train at the station. In the distance, I can see the chimneys of the synthetic rubber factory spewing black smoke into the sky. Our explosives factory is behind it, but instead of turning right on the road leading to the factory complex, the foreman continues walking down road toward the forest surrounding the camp. The SS guards who guide us every morning on our

ALEX AMIT

way to the factory, continue to march in silence, their cocked rifles aimed at us. Where are they taking us?

I look ahead and see a large group of male prisoners walking slowly in front of us. Are the Nazis evacuating the camp because of the approaching Red Army?

"Keep walking," the supervisor shouts at us, dropping the usual derogatory 'pigs.'

I look back at the camp. Another group of female prisoners is walking behind us. In the gray morning light, I see the chimneys that work ceaselessly and the brown watchtowers surrounding the camp. Another moment passes, and we walk along a paved road into the forest. When I look back again, I can no longer see the camp.

I feel nothing; joy, sorrow, sadness, nothing at all. I'm hollow. I can only think about one thing – moving forward. I concentrate on nothing but my next step. I don't care where they take us. We are a long line of prisoners walking west on the frozen road. I can only hear our footsteps on the road and the clatter of the small enamel food bowls tied with rope to our uniforms.

We've been marching west for days. I have no idea how many days have passed since we left Auschwitz. The supervisor and the SS soldiers no longer bother to call us by our number. The guards take out those who can no longer walk. That's what their rifles are for. They don't let anyone linger. *Walk, walk, walk.* Only in the evening do we stop for the night in a barn or an open field in the snow, and then we get some soup and half a loaf of bread per prisoner. *Walk, walk, walk.* Sometimes, we walk past other groups of prisoners. Once, we passed a group of POWs who were standing on the side of the road. They were

American pilots in khaki uniforms. Most of them had good military coats and boots. They weren't as skinny as we were. They ignored the German guards and took army biscuits and milk cans out of their pockets and threw them to us. I managed to catch two biscuits and a milk can. I drank the milk, slowly ate one biscuit, and left one in my pocket for a day when I'd be really hungry. *Walk, walk, walk, don't stop for a second.*

One day, a Polish farmer gave me two potatoes, and the next day, a Czech farmer ran from the field and placed a small block of cheese and some bread in my weak hands. He quickly walked away before the Nazi guards could hurt him, and I couldn't thank him. I think I'm too feeble to speak; I can only whisper.

One evening, I hear two guards speaking in German and saying that we're about to walk to a camp in southern Germany, but I don't care anymore. I just walk, mindlessly, step after step, after step. I need to keep walking. Only when I think I'm about to collapse do I talk to Rebecca. I can't tell whether it's real or imaginary. I ask her how she is and if she had soup and chocolate today. I promised Charlotte that I'd believe she was alive. And as long as she's alive and I can talk to her, then I'm alive, too.

Chapter Nineteen

Liberation

Four months later, on April 24, 1945, two weeks before Nazi Germany surrendered. South Germany, Kaufering Concentration Camp.

"They ran away. They abandoned the camp," the prisoner standing at the barracks says. I barely raise my head and look at her. I don't know her. We arrived at this camp two weeks ago. We were the few women who survived the long march. We have been here ever since, waiting. No one knows what we're waiting for.

"No more SS guards?" I ask her quietly, but I don't think she heard my whisper. My head falls on the hard wooden bunk that has been padded with some straw. I no longer have the strength to get up from the bunk I've been lying on for two days. I'll rest here for a while, then I'll try to get up. I promised

Charlotte and Rebecca that I'd survive. I can't think clearly anymore. I'm so tired.

I manage to turn on my side. Two female prisoners who had walked with me all the way from the East, hobble to the door and disappear into the daylight outside. I close my eyes. Is that how you feel at the end? Infinitely calm?

Yesterday I thought I heard thundering cannons, but perhaps I imagined it; I don't know anymore. We haven't eaten in three days.

I struggle to rise from the bunk and support my thin body, then make my way down to the wooden floor of the barracks. Finally, I managed to reach the door and go through it. The spring morning sun blinds me. I blink and try to adjust to the light. Everything is quiet.

Several prisoners walk toward the gate, but I can no longer stand or walk, so I sit at the shack door, leaning against the wooden frame. The camp gate is wide open. The SS soldiers who were standing at the entrance have disappeared. The watchtower is also abandoned.

Two prisoners walk through the open gate and start walking on the road outside the camp. But a few steps later, they turn around and come back inside.

Everything is quiet, there are no sounds of gunfire or roars of battle. I can't even hear the birds chirping; maybe I imagined it all. I close my eyes, exhausted, and open them after some time. Then I notice three soldiers.

They're standing by the breached gate. They have helmets on their heads and weapons in their hands. Did they come to kill us? It doesn't matter anymore. I lean back and watch them indifferently. I can no longer walk or even go back into the hut and try to hide.

They remain standing by the gate, looking in without entering. More soldiers join them. I hear a noise and a military jeep drives in. But it's khaki, not blue green like the Germans' vehicles. Their uniforms are also khaki.

They start walking slowly into the camp, their weapons drawn, and they look around. But they don't shoot. Several prisoners advance toward them, and one of them starts talking to one of the soldiers. Who are these soldiers? One of the prisoners hugs the soldier standing in front of him.

More and more soldiers arrive and enter the camp, and a large military truck full of soldiers pulls over in front of the gate. They jump off the jeep and enter the camp. Some have white ribbons with a red cross on their arm. They examine us but don't shoot.

One of the soldiers walks toward me and stares. He holds his weapon but doesn't point it at me. I slowly look up at him. He's leaning over me.

"Are you alive?" I think he asks me in English. I'm not sure anymore. I can't respond. I'm exhausted.

He bends down, takes a metallic water bottle from his army belt, takes the cap off, and puts it in my mouth. I sip the water slowly and choke. I didn't drink in two days.

More soldiers enter the camp. Another soldier approaches me and leans against the wall next to me. There's something sewn to his shoulder.

"Are you hungry?" He asks me in broken German and takes out a packet of food from his pocket. "Take it, eat, but a little, you shouldn't eat a lot, a few bites and that's it," he breaks off a piece and brings it to my mouth. I close my eyes and savor the sweetness of the chocolate. Is he German? How does he speak German?

"My daughter," I whisper to him in German and open my eyes. I look into his brown eyes. Slowly, I raise my hand and touch the Star-Spangled Flag embroidered to his uniform. There are so many white stars on the flag's blue background sewn to his shoulder.

"What's your name? Where's your daughter?" He looks around. "Can we save your daughter?"

"I lost her," is all I manage to say to him before I close my eyes again.

"Medic, I need a Medic here. She's still alive," I think one of the soldiers is shouting in English.

Chapter Twenty

Drancy, September 1945

Five months later.

"Drancy," the bus driver announces and stops at the small square in the town center.

I run my hand through my short hair. It's already started to grow, but it'll take a long time to return to what it used to be, or maybe it doesn't matter. Nothing will ever be the same again. The touch of the soft fabric of my simple, light-green summer dress also feels strange to me.

I look around, trying to recall, but I can't remember the square and the houses around it. Could it be that I've never been here before?

The driver pulls the metal handle that opens the door, and the people around me stand up and get off the bus, their noise overcomes the engine's rumble. There's no policeman in a blue uniform holding a drawn weapon who shouts at us to get in line.

I get off the bus and feel the square's pavement under my feet. Most of the shops around the square are closed, only one grocery store is open, and there's a sign at its entrance announcing, 'There is butter, there are eggs.' There is no line of people waiting to enter the store.

The bus continues on its way with a slow rumble, disappearing from the square, leaving behind only silence and the smell of burnt gasoline. The people who got off the bus also scatter around. A second later, they'll disappear into the nearby streets, leaving the square deserted again.

Where's the huge internment camp building? I try to find, maybe it's peaking over the roofs of the houses surrounding the square, but I can't. Could it have been destroyed? I have to get there. To find some clue as to what happened to her.

"Excuse me," I call tp one of the women who arrived with me on the bus and hurry after her. "Do you happen to know where the internment camp is?"

"Where the German camp was?" She stops and asks me. "Why do you want to know?" Her brown eyes study me. She's wearing a simple, light blue country dress. Is she from here?

"Not a German army camp, a camp where they kept prisoners, Jews," I look back at her. Does she notice my German accent? Does she suspect I'm one of them? One of the Germans?

"It's over there," she points toward one of the streets and walks away before I can ask her another question. I watch her back as she enters one of the houses and disappears. Did she know about that camp when I was there? Did she know what they did to us there?

After a few minutes of walking down the street, I come out of the row of houses at the edge of town and suddenly see it. I stand and start shaking. The big, gray concrete monster stands before me, its open windows watching me as if threatening to take me back inside.

"Breathe, breathe," I whisper to myself, "They're not here. The war is over. They lost."

I keep standing in my place, watching it. I know it doesn't make any sense, but all the way here from Paris, I imagine that as soon as I get close to the building, Rebecca would run toward me in her brown dress, and I'd hug and whisper to her that she had grown and changed so much. It's been three years already. *Breathe, breathe. You knew it was just a fantasy and that she isn't here.*

I'm waiting for the tears to come, but there's nothing. I just feel the dryness in my throat in the warm wind, like a big hole that has gaped and refuses to be filled. I have to go to the camp and the building inside it, I have to know.

From a distance, it seems empty, the wire fences surrounding it are still there, but the gate is open, and the two policemen who always stood guard next to it are gone. The main yard, where I walked for so many hours among all the other prisoners, is also deserted.

I hear footsteps behind me and turn around. A woman walking on the road, pulling a goat by a rope, is approaching me. Was she here three years ago and saw me from the other side of the fence?

"Excuse me, do you know what happened to the people who were here?" I asked her. Maybe she knows what happened to my Rebecca. Perhaps she'll give me some clue?

"They took them," she says after a moment, and I feel the hole inside me get bigger.

"Do you know where?"

"To the trains, to the station. The Nazis who were here took them," she spits on the ground. "And then they brought captured American pilots here. We tried to bring them food," she looks at me, "for the Jews, who were here, but they didn't let us. It was forbidden. They didn't let us get close to the fences. There's no one here now."

"Is there anyone here who knows if there were any survivors?" I ask her and look at the houses around.

"I'm sorry, we tried," she says, moving away from me, pulling the goat behind her by the rope. "This is a cursed place. I can't enter it even after they've gone."

I watch her until she disappears between the houses, turns around, and walk towards the camp. Maybe I'll find a clue there.

The three wooden steps leading up to the German commander's barracks creak under my feet as I slowly go up them. "Breathe, there's no one here," I whisper to myself, but the tension doesn't let go. "You have to go on. You have to find her." I stand in front of the closed wooden door. The metal sign 'Captain Carl Becker' is still attached to the wooden door by two screws. I take a deep breath, reach my trembling hand to the door, and open it, flinching back at the creaking of the metal hinges.

Meow, A skinny, dirty, stray cat runs out of the barracks and makes me take a step back. But after a moment, I take a deep breath and go inside, and look around.

The inside of the barracks is empty. There's nothing left in it. Everything inside was taken, either by the Americans or the French. Only a large picture of the Führer is thrown in the corner, full of bullet holes. Everything else is gone. How do things disappear this way during war?

I leave the barracks and enter the camp, pass the barbed wire fence, cross the deserted square, and walk to the building, to our entrance. My legs seem to know the way to the room where Charlotte, Rebecca, and I lived for such a long time on their own. I look around at the bare concrete walls. They look unfamiliar to me. Everything that was ours is gone: the straw we slept on, her paintings, the stranger's suitcase – as if there was no trace of us, as if we were never there.

I get down on my knees and search the ground, looking around. Maybe Rebecca wrote something down, but there was nothing written by her, not even on the walls. What happened to my daughter?

I leave the room, exit the building and the gate, I spit on the gate's wooden beam and the barbed wire fence wrapped around it. I need to go back to Poland and look for clues in that place I can't even name without trembling, although I know I can't go back there. I know what happened to all the children who arrived there. I try to cry, but I can't. Maybe I should go back home, to Berlin, although I no longer know where my home is without her. I take one last look at the gray concrete monster and turn my back to it, start walking between the houses, back to the square and the bus stop. I have one more place I need to go to before leaving Paris.

'The New Republic Hotel' is written in black letters on the sign above the building door in the third arrondissement. I stop in front of the five wide stairs leading to the hotel's entrance and look around. Nothing in the street has changed. There are no destroyed buildings around and no bullet holes that have left their mark on the walls from the war. I look up at the windows decorated with wrought iron railings. The hotel remains as it was.

"Un, deux, trois, quatre, cinq," I whisper to myself as I walk up the stairs and stand before the closed door. I take a deep breath, open the front door, and enter the lobby. I want to say goodbye to her before I leave this city forever.

"Good afternoon. Can I help you?" A man standing behind the reception looks up at me. Where is Angelina?

I look around. The green armchair with floral upholstery still stands in the corner of the small lobby. She used to sit on it in the evenings and read. Next to it is the reading lamp that was turned off while she was reading by candlelight. Nothing in the lobby has changed except the stranger standing at reception.

"Mrs.?" He turns to me again. He's about my age, maybe a bit older than me, thirty or so. He's wearing a light-blue, button-up shirt and a dark tie, and his black hair is a little disheveled.

"I was here once," I awkwardly smile at him, looking at the dark mahogany mailbox and key cabinet behind it, on the wall. My eyes examine the cabinet cube where our key used to be, recalling all those times I looked at it and searched for another letter from my husband.

"And would you like to return and rent a room again?" He politely smiles at me.

"No, thanks," I answer and turn to leave. I should ask him what happened to Angelina, but I can't. I've lost too many people in the last few years, I'm not sure I can hear another lost name.

"Have a good day, Madam," I still hear him as I place my hand on the door's copper handle.

"Every guest in my hotel leaves something behind, but leaving your lover's earrings in the laundry is a bit excessive..." I hear someone say from the back room as I stop and start to shake. "Sarah?" I hear her say after a second and turn around. It's her.

"Sarah?" Angelina says again, running toward me behind the counter and hugging me tightly. "You're back," she whispers while we hug, and I feel her warm hands holding me. "René, this is Sarah. I told you that I was keeping all her things and that she'd come back," she tells him and takes my hand, pulling me behind the counter with her. "Sarah, this is René, my husband. He came back from Germany five months ago," she smiles, and I notice her tearful eyes. "You're back too; I knew you'd come back, your suitcase is waiting for you," she doesn't hold back and hugs me again, and I feel embarrassed.

"Yes, I'm back," I keep holding her hand and look at her. Her black hair is still neatly tied in a ponytail, but something about her has changed. Her face is glowing. I step back and look down, noticing a slight bump through her dress.

"Are you...?" I look at her belly.

"Yes..." she smiles at me and caresses her belly. "Where's...?" She looks toward the door.

"No..." I tell her and shake my head. That's all I can say.

"Oh... Sarah," I see the tears in her eyes, and she hugs me again. "I've been thinking about you all this time."

"At least he came back, and you're expecting," I change the subject. I can't talk about her.

"There's something else," she tells me.

"What do you mean?" I watch her and her husband.

"Someone is waiting for you upstairs, in the room that was once yours."

"Who?"

"He's been here for two weeks, hoping you'd come, and you did."

"Who is he?" I ask her. Who can be waiting for me here, at this hotel? Could it be someone who has a clue about Rebecca?

"I'm not telling you. Go up and see for yourself," she smiles at me. "You'll be glad to see him."

"Thank you," I hug her and rush up the stairs. Who could it be? Heavily breathing, I stop in front of the door on the fourth floor, arrange my dress and hair, wait a moment, then knock on the door.

I hear footsteps from inside, the door opens, and I see him.

"Sarah," Erwin, my husband, stands and looks at me. He hasn't changed. He looks exactly the way he did when he left us on the train platform five years ago.

"Sarah," he walks up to me and hugs me tightly. I feel his big hands are crushing and hurting me. Although several months

339

have passed since I was freed, and I've gained some weight, my body is still weak, and I'm groaning in pain.

"Sarah, I've missed you so much," he says and kisses my cheeks and lips non-stop. "You don't know how much I've tried to bring you to the Free Zone and from there to Spain," he caresses my short hair. "I've tried every possible way. I've waited for you in Madrid the entire war. What happened to your hair? Why did you cut it?" He keeps on speaking, more and more. His voice sounds like a muffled noise far away from me, as if he's behind a large glass window. I'm unable to reach out and hug him back. He suddenly seems like a stranger I once knew and belongs to another life, a life that no longer exists. It seems like he keeps talking to me, but I cannot understand what he's saying. "Sarah, where is Rebecca?" I think he's asking me in his flow speech.

"Sarah, where is Rebecca?" He asks me again, holding onto my shoulders and shaking me.

I don't reply. I release myself from his embrace and go to the window from which I used to look at the city's rooftops in order to relax, but I can't. He keeps talking behind my back non-stop. I need a cigarette.

With a trembling hand, I open my bag and take out a pack of US Army cigarettes. My fingers tear the white paper, and I place the cigarette in my mouth, light it with a Zippo, and deeply inhale. I have to calm down. I need him to stop talking to me, just for a few minutes, so that I can lean quietly on the windowsill and look outside.

"Sarah, turn around, I'm talking to you. Where's Rebecca?"

"There's no Rebecca," I turn around and answer, exhaling the smoke into the room.

"Where is she? What happened to her?"

"I lost her," I inhale once again. I need him to shut up. Please shut up. Stop talking to me. I need silence.

"Did you lose our daughter?" It seems to me that he's shouting at me, but his lips as if voicelessly move in front of me. "What mother loses her daughter? And what happened to your hair? And why do you smoke?" He approaches me and grabs the cigarette from my hand, holds it in disgust, and extinguishes it in the metal ashtray on the small table in the corner of the room. "And where's your wedding ring?" He returns to me and grabs my hand. "Aren't you a married woman? Where's your devotion to our marriage while I've been waiting for you all this time?" The touch of his fingers hurts me as if ice picks are trying to peel my skin off.

I'm unable to answer, and I look at the cigarette crushed in the ashtray.

"Why don't you answer me?" He approaches and keeps talking to me. "Don't you have any answers for me?" He grabs my shoulders once again and shakes me. Who is this foreign man?

"You know," I grab his hands and push them off my shoulders, annunciating every word. "When the Americans came to the camp and freed us," I once again take out the cigarette box from my bag, pull out a cigarette and light it, blowing the smoke in his face. "We were so hungry, all we had to eat in our last month there were a few slices of bread per day, and not even that in the last few days," I inhale from the cigarette again. "And when they arrived, with their trucks and their weapons and their food, we wanted to eat so much, but those who did died, simply because were no longer used to eating," I turn

341

my back to him and walk to the window, my fingers holding the lit cigarette and shaking. "And then, the American soldiers gave us cigarettes, they told us to smoke, smoke and eat a little, because otherwise, we'll die," I keep talking and look outside at the houses of the peaceful city. "So, I smoke. And yes, I lost my wedding ring, and I lost Rebecca, our daughter," I turn to him. "And I don't know who you are anymore."

"Sarah, I'm your husband," he tries to come closer and hug me, but I push him away.

"No, you're not my husband anymore. You're a stranger," I say to him. "You're a stranger who wasn't by my side and didn't help me in any of the horrible places I've been to. You're a stranger who lived in a world without Nazis, hunger, death all around, and things that I'd never be able to talk about, and all you can do is complain about who I've become. You might not have changed, but I have. I'm not the same Sarah you left on the train platform five years ago, promising to meet a month later. I'm Sarah, who's died a thousand times and lost her daughter," I say to him and can't stop myself.

"Sarah, I'm your husband, Erwin, the one you've married," he says, and I look at him and just want him to leave. I can't be in the same room as him.

"You're not my husband anymore. I have no idea who you are," I tell him. "I'm going to freshen up in the bathroom at the end of the corridor now. I had a long drive," I inhale once more, feel the hot air in my throat, go over to the ashtray, and forcefully crush the cigarette. "And when I come back," I look into his eyes and speak slowly, "I don't want to see you here. If you're still here by the time I back, I'll call the hotel's owner, and she'll kick you out. Trust me, she'll do it for me."

"Come sit by my side," Angelina tells me later at night as I step into the lobby. "René has already gone to sleep, and I can't fall asleep," she puts aside the book she's been reading and moves a little in her armchair, making room for me.

"Thank you," I smile and huddle beside her on the arm-chair, feeling her warmth. Erwin had left the hotel earlier, leaving me to the silence I so badly needed, in front of the window and the city's rooftops. But later, as night fell, I felt lonely, and I went down the creaking wooden stairs to the lobby, finding her sitting on the armchair in the corner of the room, reading a book by the lamp light. There are no longer blackouts and we're allowed to turn on lights at night. The war is over.

"Are you okay?" She asks after a while.

"I lost her," I say softly. "At some point, they sent me to a camp in the East, and she stayed here, in Drancy, and she's disappeared ever since," I'm unable to say the camp's name.

"And is there any chance she survived?" She puts her arm on mine.

"I dream that she did, but I know that It's impossible," I quietly say. "I keep dreaming of her."

"Do you want me to go with you to Drancy and search? Ask people around?"

"I was there this morning, before I got here. I tried and asked around. The place is deserted."

"And don't you know anyone who was in the camp after they sent you?"

"Everyone I know ended up in this camp in the East."

"Don't lose hope," she keeps holding my hand.

"It's no longer a matter of hope. I just want to know. I'll keep dreaming of her," I breathe slowly.

"Maybe one of the Germans that was there? Maybe you can go to Germany and try to find out?"

"There was a Nazi officer there. He had two girls. They treated her like a puppy. I hope the Americans settled the score with him for what he did. I can't go back to Germany."

"Weren't there any good Germans? Sometimes, even in hell, among monsters, there are people who spread some light."

"I was in hell, and I didn't meet anyone among them who spread any light," I answer, trying not to think about that place. "But there was one policeman there, at Drancy, a Frenchman," I tell her after a few seconds. I feel comfortable sitting next to her like this.

"What do you know about him?"

"His name was Mathéo, and he had good eyes. That's all I know about him."

"Mathéo is a name of a good man. Maybe you can search for him."

"Yes, maybe," I look at the streetlamp outside the hotel that illuminates the street with its weak light. It looks like a star that twinkles in the dark and lights my way.

I reach out and caress the Star of Life and Death in my dress pocket. I couldn't bring myself to throw it away.

Chapter Twenty-One

Paris, September 1945

Paris Police Headquarters, Place Louis Lépine

"How can I help you, Madame?" The police inspector looks up from the document before him, puts down the fountain pen he's holding, looks at me, intertwines his fingers, and leisurely leans back.

"I'd like to locate a policeman who works for the Paris police," I sit upright before him on the hard wooden chair.

"And why do you want to locate him, if I may ask?" He examines me from the other side of the dark mahogany desk, his black eyes look like tiny beads that stand out against his light skin.

"It's personal, sir." I look at his blue ironed uniform. Although there's no officer insignia on his shoulders, gold-colored buttons adorn them as if they were valuable coins that emphasize his high status. His black mustache is also neatly trimmed, as if it were part of his uniform.

"Can I see your certificates, please?" His beady eyes continue to scan me while he hides under a blue peaked cap that proudly presents the de Gaulle administration.

"My certificate," I take the yellow badge out of my dress pocket and place it on the table. I wonder if he remembers me. I can put the refugee certificate produced for me by the American military authorities in front of him, a certificate that confirms that I'm a Jew who stayed in a concentration camp, its name I'm still unable to say, and that every authority should help her in any formal request.

"What is this?" He looks at the Star of Life and Death as if he doesn't know its meaning. I don't think he recognizes me either. How many people did he bring here under false pretenses and send to the camps?

"It's mine," I quietly reply. "And now I'm asking for the list of all the policemen who were in the Drancy camp in 1941."

"I'm sorry, this is classified information. I can't provide you with it. It needs special authorization," he looks into my eyes and smiles. His eyes are evil.

"I'm asking for the list of all the policemen who were in the Drancy camp in 1941," I repeat my words.

"Madam," he leans back and keeps smiling. "This is a police station. We don't help refugees, not even if they happen to be Jewish. Do I notice from your accent that you're of German origin?"

"I'm Jewish, and it doesn't matter where I'm from, and I have a special permit," I feel the rage rising in me. He doesn't even remember me.

"Can I see it?"

"Yes," I take a bayonet out of my handbag and hold it in my hand in front of him. "This is my special permit," I tell him quietly, unable to stop myself any longer. "Inspector Plessis, do you know what this is?"

"Yes, Madam; no, Madam," he shifted in his chair uncomfortably.

"Well," I tell him. "It's a Nazi bayonet collected from a dead Nazi soldier. I got it from an American soldier who killed a lot of Nazis and their collaborators. If you look closely, you'll see that there's still clotted blood on its blade. I haven't used it yet, but I've seen enough death, and I know how to use it. I've come a long way to get here. Maybe it's time I used it for the first time against a French traitor."

"Yes, Madam," he nervously replies, and I notice his fingers slowly moving toward his leather holster.

"I know you have a gun," I quietly say. "And I'm not afraid of it anymore. I've seen more death than you can imagine. Some of them were people you've sent to their deaths. You can use your gun, but if you use it, everyone around the station will ask why you shot a Jewish refugee instead of protecting her. They'll also start asking whether you're a traitor or not, and how is it that you worked under the Vichy administration and you're still not in prison."

"Yes, Madam," he nervously smiles and moves his hand away from the gun. I can see beads of sweat on his forehead.

"So, as I said, I request the list of all the policemen who were in the Drancy camp in 1941."

"Madam, I'll see what I can do," he stands up and walks away as I follow him with my gaze. I'm no longer afraid if he calls for help. I'm no longer afraid of death. I've already been in hell.

I look around at the great space, put the bayonet back in my bag, still holding on to it. An American soldier gave it to me the day I left the camp and went on the road, still weak. 'Take it,' he said to me, 'it'll protect you. I've carried it with me since D-Day. This bayonet and God will keep you safe on your way.'

I silently took it from him, stuffed it into my handbag. I didn't want to tell him that God didn't protect me and probably didn't protect my daughter either.

The noise of typewriters and quiet conversation fills the hall. Several police officers are sitting next to wooden desks like, the one I'm sitting in front of writing reports or talking to their friends. They're busy, and none of them look at me. Even the secretaries, who are typing on the typewriters nonstop, are focused on their work. It seems to me that nothing's changed since that day I was here, four years ago, pleading, except for the flags. Above the windows, at the end of the hall, hang two flags side by side, the liberated France flag, with the Lorraine cross in the center, beside the American flag. Between them is a large picture of General de Gaulle overlooking the hall. My hand, which used to caress Rebecca, tightly grips the bayonet in my handbag, until my fingers turn white. Nothing's changed, yet everything's changed.

"The lists, Madam," Inspector Plessis places a thick binder covered in greenish-gray canvas before me. I slide my hand over the rough fabric and look at the name 'Drancy' written on it.

"Madam, are you looking for someone in particular?" He asks me as he sits down. But I don't reply. I open the binder and start looking at the names and faces, scanning the photos attached to the personal cards.

I need to get up and go. There's no point in all this searching. But something stops me. Maybe it's the disdainful look of Inspector Plessis drumming his finger on the mahogany desk. As I turn page after page, I feel this place suffocating me. The ticking noises of the secretaries typing on the typewriters make me nauseous.

But then I see him.

"The good hunter with the glasses," I whisper.

"Sorry, I didn't hear you. What did you say?" He asks me.

"Never mind," I reply and look at the personal details card in the binder. 'Mathéo Allard' is written at the top of the card, and a picture of him is attached, looking serious look, wearing his round glasses. He was born in 1914. He's thirty-one years old.

"Are you looking for this man?"

"What's this red stamp, 'Judged,' on the card?" I look up at Inspector Plessis and show him Mathéo's card. Below it, there's a Nazi stamp of an eagle holding a swastika in its claws and a handwritten date: September 22nd, 1942, and an indistinct signature.

"It means the Nazis accused and judged him of something," Inspector Plessis politely answers.

"What did they accuse him of?" I was no longer there on September 22nd, 1942.

"Do you think it made any difference what they accuse him of?"

"And what did they do to him?" I run my finger over his picture, wanting him to come out of it and tell me that he knows what happened to my Rebecca.

"What they did to all those they'd suspected, they either imprisoned, executed, or sent them to the camps. They had very few punishments, even for policemen," he replies, and my stomach churns. What did he do? Was I not imagining and actually saw him back then, in the camp, among the people who arrived on the transport? I'm trying to recover the times and dates but can't.

"Write down his address for me on a piece of paper," I tell the Inspector, even though I don't believe it can help me find out anything about my daughter. But maybe I'm wrong, maybe they just imprisoned him, and he was released. Maybe I was imagining it back then.

"Do you think they didn't wait for an opportunity to accuse me, too? Do you think it was easy to be a policeman under the Nazi regime here in Paris?" Inspector Plessis says as he writes down the address on piece of paper, his hand holding the fountain pen and slightly shaking.

"You both served under it, and you both made a choice," I stand up and snatch the note from his outstretched hand, can't wait to get out of this place. "The only difference is that he chose to do something, I don't know what yet, and you chose to send Jews to their deaths."

I step out of the metro, walk through the streets, holding the sheet of paper with Mathéo's address, and turn onto quiet street.

'Sophie's Salon' is written in purple above a shop window. Inside, I notice a woman my age standing behind an older woman and giving her a haircut. Near the grocery store, a skinny, stray cat lay in the sun, on a wooden crate, and on the adjacent bulletin board hung posters with the American and French flags detailing the procedures of the Provisional Authorities.

I stand before the address written on the note and look around. This is the place. Next to me, a boy is playing football with some man. One of the man's shirt sleeves is folded, and he's missing an arm. Did he lose it during the war?

"Do you need help, Madam? Are you looking for anyone?" The man turns to me. He's about my age.

"I'm looking for Mr. Allard, Mathéo Allard. He's a police-man," I awkwardly reply.

"Do you know him?" He asks.

"A little. I want to ask him something, see if he can help me. Does he live here?"

"I'm sorry," he looks at me, sad, and stops playing. "He's not here."

"When will he be back?"

"You misunderstand," he kicks the ball back to the boy and approaches me. "The Germans took him in the war, probably to the East. He never came back."

"I'm sorry," I say to him, turn around and start walking away, back to the metro station. I lost the only chance to find out what happened to my daughter. My hand grips the note tightly, crumpling it and fighting the urge to tear it apart.

"Maybe he'll eventually come back. You never know," the man calls to me. "People come back all the time. I came back, too."

"Thank you," I stop and say, knowing that if they sent Mathéo to where I was, he'd probably never return.

"Maybe his mom can help you. Maybe she knows something," the boy also says.

"Where does she live? Do you have her address?" I ask them. I mustn't lose hope.

"She lives here. He used to live with her. He was never married," the man says, pointing to the brown, wooden door at the entrance to the cream-colored building on the other side of the street. "Margot Allard, that's her name. Third floor, dark-brown door," he adds. "She's a good woman."

"Thanks," I say and walk to the front door of the building, my hand still tightly gripping the crumpled sheet of paper. Maybe she can tell me something.

As I climb to the third floor, the curving wooden stairs creak under my shoes. I still haven't gotten used to the comfort of wearing shoes my size that don't hurt my feet, with soft and cozy socks. It's hard for me to get used to all those simple things that were so obvious to me.

I stand in front of the dark-brown door on the third floor, take a deep breath before ringing the brass bell, and wait.

I don't hear footsteps on the other side of the heavy door, but suddenly, the door opens to a crack, and an older woman looks at me.

She's about sixty or so, her white hair is neatly pulled back, and she's wearing round glasses. Her green-brown eyes are studying me.

"Hello, I..." and I stop for a second. "I'm Sara Bloch," it's so strange for me to pronounce my name and not call myself number 132698. It is as if my name belongs in another life that no longer exists. The woman continues to watch me through the crack in the door and says nothing.

"Are you French?" She finally asks. Did she notice my accent?

"No," I take a breath, and quickly say, "I'm not French, but I've lived here for two years. I'm looking for the policeman, Mathéo Allard."

She keeps examining me through the slightly open door and finally steps back, "Come in," she opens the door, and I follow her inside.

The small living room is painted dark green, and soft, diffused light filters through heavy velvet curtains. Against one wall stands an antique armoire, and against the other, a dark mahogany cabinet with a big radio on it. I watch the photo next to the radio of a man in military uniform from the previous war. He looks like Mathéo.

"Have a seat," she motions to the armchair decorated with delicate flowers upholstery. "Meet Father Nicholas," she looks at a priest sitting in an armchair by the fireplace holding a cup of tea in his hand. The priest places the cup on the coffee table and stands up.

"Nice to meet you," he shakes my hand and looks at me, his blue eyes watching me peacefully. He's about Mrs. Allard's age. He has good eyes.

"Sarah Bloch," I introduce myself. "I apologize. I didn't mean to interrupt. I can go and come back another time."

"You're not interrupting," he says. "I'm on a courtesy visit. I'll finish drinking the tea in a moment and go, you know how it is," he smiles at me. "I have many community members to visit."

"Yes," I smile at him politely and sit down, embarrassed, placing my palms on my knees. Sitting like this in front of a priest is strange for me.

"Mrs. Bloch has come to ask about Mathéo," Mrs. Allard enters the room from the small kitchen carrying a teacup and saucer. In a gentle movement, she pours from the kettle and hands me the cup of tea, "Please."

"Thank you, Mrs. Allard," I hold the saucer and the teacup and look at her and the priest. They look at me silently and wait for me to explain what I came for. I'm searching for the right words to ask her where her son is and what happened to him.

"Did you know Mathéo?" The priest finally asks me.

"Not really," I reply, feeling embarrassed. "I was in the camp," I go on explaining. "In Drancy. I was a prisoner there," I lower my gaze.

"A lot of people were arrested for no good reason and sent to this place," he says.

"I am a Jew," I awkwardly smile. "I met him there. He was a good man. He was nice to me even though he was a policeman and was guarding us," I look at Mrs. Allard. "And I'm looking for him. Maybe he can help me," I stop talking. It's hard for me to tell them what happened to Rebecca and me. They weren't there, they wouldn't understand. They're unable to understand.

"I apologize," the priest says. "He is not here. They caught him, the Germans, they accused him of something."

"What did they accuse him of?"

"They didn't tell us," the priest replies.

"And what did they do to him?" I ask, looking at Mrs. Allard. But she stays silent and looks back at me, surveying me.

"We only know that he was caught and imprisoned and that he was sent to a camp in the East, to Auschwitz. Have you heard of this place?" The priest asks me.

"I was there," I tell him after a moment, slowly getting the words out of my mouth.

"Did you see him there?" Mrs. Allard asks me for the first time, her voice shaking.

"No, I didn't see him there," I tell her. "The men and women were separated. There were several labor camps. I was in the women's camp," I try to explain. I don't tell her what happened to most of those who came there. I also don't tell her that I thought I saw him once when he got off the train and stood on the platform in his blue uniform. I no longer remember what I saw there and what I had imagined out of hunger and fatigue in that horrible place. "But I came back from there. I stayed alive," I'm looking for something to say to encourage her.

"He didn't come back," Mrs. Allard says, and silence falls again.

"Every day, people come back from the war. One must not lose hope," the priest tells her. "When did you get to Paris?" he asks me.

"Yesterday," I answer. I know that if he doesn't return, my hope of knowing what happened to Rebecca is lost.

"And you came to look for Mathéo?" The priest asks me as Mrs. Allard returns to her silence.

"I had a daughter, in Drancy," I struggle to say the words and steady my breath. "And I was sent to Auschwitz, and she stayed behind, in Drancy. I'm trying to find out, maybe someone knows..." I lower my gaze to the teacup and saucer I'm holding.

"... what happened to her there?" The priest asks.

"Yes," I nod. "I have no idea what happened to her."

"You're the woman with the shoes," Mrs. Allard suddenly says.

"What do you mean?" I look up at her. I do not understand.

"You're the woman with the shoes," she says again, examining me, not with malice or anger, but with compassion.

"He didn't bring me any shoes."

"You're the woman whose girl he gave shoes," she places her teacup on the table. "He was looking for shoes for a girl, five, six or seven years old, and I thought he was meeting up with a married woman. I was angry at him," she sighs.

"My girl had shoes. When was that?" I feel dizzy for a moment.

"I no longer remember, my dear, just before he was captured and sent away. In the fall of 1942, three years ago."

"He didn't bring me shoes. I wasn't there in the fall of 1942," I whisper, feeling the room spin around me.

Then I hear Priest Nicholas say, "He brought me a girl."

"I'm sorry," I say, looking at the smashed saucer pieces scattered on the floor. "I'm so sorry. I don't know what happened to me," I try to take a few deep breaths and place the delicate teacup still in my hand on the table. Then, I bend down and start collecting the pieces of porcelain from the hardwood floor. More than anything, I'm afraid to ask him one thing, what her name was.

"It's okay, my dear, I'll handle it," Mrs. Allard rises from her chair and walks over to me, placing her warm hand on my shoulder. "We're all filled with emotions of hope and despair these days."

"What was her name?" I take a deep breath and rise to my knees, watching the priest. I want to touch my Star of Life and Death that has been with me for so long, but it's no longer with me. I left it on the desk at the police station.

"Her name is Sophie," he answers, and my face falls.

"It's not her," I whisper. "My girl's name was Rebecca."

"I'm so sorry," he says, looking sad. I can feel Mrs. Allard's hand on my shoulder. "I remember she was stubborn," he keeps talking.

"Why was she stubborn?" I'm asking. Maybe this is my Rebecca after all? Perhaps he remembers the name wrong?

"She insisted on things, she had a doll, and she refused to part with it."

"Doll or a teddy bear?"

357

"I think doll, she spoke to it as if she were a girl doll, explained to it that they'd be fine; that's all I remember, it was three years ago, and it was nighttime, I don't remember so well anymore," he looks at me with his kind eyes, as if wanting to comfort me. Could he be wrong? She sounds so much like my Rebecca.

"And are you sure her name was Sophie?"

"Yes, I asked her several times. With all the dread of that night, I wanted to be sure that I remember her name, that if someone came looking for her one day, I'd at least remember that."

"And what did she look like?" I refuse to give up. I can't give up. Hope kept me alive in the camp. I won't give up hope now.

"Like a girl, brown hair, messy, I don't know how old she was exactly."

"And what happened to her, to Sophie?" I must keep believing.

"I don't know, I wasn't supposed to know. I passed her on to a trustworthy man who took her to a monastery."

"And do you know which monastery?" I ask him and hold my breath.

"Yes, although I've never been there."

"Can you take me there?"

"Are you sure you want to go? It's outside of Paris. And what if your girl isn't there?"

"Yes, I'm sure. When can we go?" I quickly reply. I must know.

"Today is already late, but we can go tomorrow. Are you staying in Paris? Do you have a place to sleep?"

"Yes, I'm in the hotel in the third arrondissement," I give him the address, bend to the floor again, and continue picking up the pieces of the porcelain from the hardwood floor.

I must know. I must keep looking for her. Maybe someone else sent my girl to this monastery as well, like they took Sophie, who was holding a doll in her hand. I mustn't lose hope.

A summer morning sun paints the street in cream colors while I stand outside the hotel and wait for him to arrive. I couldn't sleep all night. I stood at the window and smoked, looking at the street lanterns and wondering if she was there. Is she alive? Does she remember me?

I know the odds are slim, but maybe she's survived? She should be nine by now. How does she look? How much has she changed? I need to believe she's still alive.

I light another cigarette and look down the street. What's taking him so long?

A few minutes later, a blue car approaches from the back alley and stops, its engine stuttering and rattling.

"Good morning," Father Nicholas gets out of the car and hurries to open the passenger door for me.

"Thanks," I say to him as I sit down, and he closes the door. It's strange for me to travel in the company of a Christian Priest.

We leave the city behind us and drive in silence. I have so many questions to ask him, but I don't know where to start.

I also don't want to get my hopes up. I'm so afraid of being disappointed.

"Did she have anything else besides the doll she took with her?" I finally ask.

"No," he answers as we overtake a convoy of US Army trucks driving down the road, white stars painted on the truck's side.

"Is it okay if I smoke?" I ask him after a while. I don't know what a Priest thinks about a woman smoking.

"Yes, of course," he looks at me for a moment and looks back at the road. "The war was tough on all of us, relaxing with a cigarette is allowed."

"Thank you," I light another cigarette and look out the window. We drive slowly through a small village. Several buildings have been destroyed, and bullet holes can be seen on the walls of some other ones. In the center of the village, near the square, stands a destroyed German tank, and some children are playing on it, waving sticks and shouting, but I can't hear what they're saying. I miss her so much. What if I don't find her?

"There was something," Father Nicholas suddenly says. "She had half a pack of German chocolate that she kept. She said she'll eat one piece of it every day."

"I didn't give Rebecca any chocolate. I didn't have any," I inhale from the cigarette and look out the window at a horse pulling a hay cart.

"And she was wearing a normal, brown dress," he continues. "Like a normal girl. It didn't even have a yellow badge on it."

Rebecca had a yellow badge on her dress, I think to myself, but keep quiet and don't tell him. I'm afraid he'll suggest that we turn around and go back. I'm afraid I'll agree.

"It should be here," he says after a while, when the road passes through a forest, and a small wooden sign indicates a dirt road leading to the place.

I hear the gravel under the car's wheels as we approach an old, gray stone building with a triangular roof. In the yard in front of the building, there are straight beds of vegetables, and a large wooden cart stands on the corner of the yard.

"This is the place," Father Nicholas stops the car and watches me. I light another cigarette with trembling hands. We've arrived.

Chapter Twenty-Two

The Monastery

"Many girls came here during the war," the Mother Superior sits across from us in her small office. She's about sixty or older, wearing a black dress, habit, and black-rimmed glasses. I look at the large, simple, silver cross pendant around her neck. It's hard for me to concentrate. I'm so tense.

"We're looking for a girl named Rebecca, about nine years old," Father Nicholas tells her. I look around at the small office. A simple wooden table, a large wooden cupboard by the window that's facing the yard, and a simple wooden cross hanging above her head. Everything is so quiet here. I can't hear the children.

"I don't think a girl named Rebecca came here, but that shouldn't worry you," she smiles at me. "Many girls came here with pseudo names and fake identity cards, you see, the Germans..."

"So, could my Rebecca be here?" I ask her.

"We will do what we always do when parents come looking for lost children," she looks at me. "In a few minutes, they will finish class and go to lunch. Before that, we will line them up, and you will walk among them and try to recognize her, or she will recognize you."

"I hope so," I whisper.

"Me too," she smiles at me. "And if not, there are other monasteries that hid children during the war. You mustn't despair."

"Thank you," I tell her, feeling my stomach churn with tension.

I hear the scutter of feet in the corridor outside the door, "Here, they have finished studying. We will go soon," she says. I'm so afraid to stand up and see the girls. What if she's not here?

"What's with this teddy bear? It's a little girl's toy," I hear shouting in the corridor.

"It's not a bear. It's a girl bear," someone replies, and I hold my breath, feeling dizzy.

"It's a teddy bear, and now it's mine," the first girl shouts outside the door.

"I apologize," I think I hear Mother Superior say. "They can sometimes be a bit wild," and then I hear shouts and crying voices and someone wailing outside, "She stabbed me with a pencil. She wounded me."

"It's okay, I'm sorry," I say to the Mother Superior, get up, walk to the door, and open it. My heart is pounding, and I think I'm going to faint. I go out into the corridor and look at the two girls fighting. The bigger one with golden hair is standing there, crying, and the other is slightly shorter than her with wild brown hair. She holds on to a torn raggedy bear with button eyes – one eye small and the other one big – in one hand, and a pencil in the other. Rebecca, my Rebecca.

Chapter Twenty-Three

To America

Paris, Madame Angelina's hotel. Two weeks later

"Are you ready? Is everything packed?" I ask Rebecca.

"Yes, Mom," she smiles at me. I'm not used to having her with me again, and I occasionally ask her questions, just to hear her answer. It's also hard for me to get used to the fact that she's already nine. She's grown so much.

"Did you also pack the book with you?"

"Mom, I'm too old for this book. It's for girls who believe in hunters in the forest," she replies, smiling. Sometimes, I think she calls me 'Mom' just to hear me reply.

I walk over to the window, lean on the windowsill, and light my last cigarette in this room. I went through so many lifetimes of hope and despair, and hope again, in this small room. I don't regret leaving it, but I will miss Angelina.

"Mom, are things going to be better for us in America?" Rebecca asks me.

"The Americans are good people. They set us free. I'm sure we'll have a good life in America," I answer and continue to look out the window at the city's rooftops. "We also have two weeks on a ship. We've never sailed before. We'll have a new beginning," I need a fresh start from everything we've both been through here.

"And what about Dad? Will he be joining us in America?"

"What about Dad? Dad might join us in America after a while, maybe not. Rebecca, I don't know. So many things have changed."

He moved to a different hotel, and Rebecca met him twice. He wanted us to talk and get back together, but I'm not sure anymore. Maybe he'll go back to Madrid, to conduct his business there.

I look outside the window for the last time, at the rooftops that have accompanied my thoughts and fears for so long. We must go downstairs and say goodbye to Angelina. Then we'll take a bus to Cherbourg, and board a ship to America, to the port of New York City.

"Mom, are you coming?" Rebecca grabs her suitcase and opens the door.

"Yes, I'm coming," I put out the cigarette, grab my suitcase, look at the room for the last time, and close the door behind me. "Let's go down."

Our steps are noisy against the wooden stairs as we both go down them, holding on to our suitcases. Rebecca hurries ahead of me, and when I'm about to get to the bottom of the stairs, I hear her yelling, "The good hunter with the glasses," and the sounds of her feet running on the hardwood floor, and I stop and hold onto the railing. I feel dizzy.

I stand up and take a breath, trying to calm myself. I fix my short hair with my fingers and try to get it in line. I'm ashamed it's still so short. I haven't been to a hairdresser since I arrived in Paris either. I didn't think it was necessary. I then take a deep breath, and step by step, go down the stairs, afraid that I'll stumble from the excitement, until I reach the lobby and watch the man Rebecca's hugging.

He is no longer wearing the blue uniform of the Paris police but is now wearing a brown suit. And he's thinner than I remembered him. His brown hair hardly had time to grow either. But he has Windsor Glasses with a delicate gold frame. He looks up at me and smiles, and I tremble with excitement.

Chapter Twenty-Four

Rebecca

Paris, Paris City Hall, May 1948, three years later

"Mom, I don't want to comb my hair, that's how I like it, and I hate this dress; it's ugly. I look like a little girl with a ribbon in my hair. I'm not a child anymore." I say to her and throw the pink ribbon on the dresser. "I'm already twelve years old," I announce and angrily leave the side room in City Hall before she can answer. I don't care that she's getting married in a few minutes, and I don't care that it's important to her that I be beautiful. That's how I want it, and that's that. I want to have wild hair. That's how I like it.

To my surprise, the small city hall is already full of people, some are standing and talking to each other, and others are sitting on the wooden benches arranged in front of the judge's stand. He'll soon conduct the wedding ceremony. Earlier, when Mom and I arrived, the hall was still empty. I didn't think so many people would show up. Mom and I hardly know anyone there.

"Rebecca, is Mom ready yet?" Margot, Mathéo's mother, approached me.

"Yes, she's so beautiful," I tell her and smile. She's treated me as if I were her granddaughter ever since she met me three years ago, after the war ended.

"And don't you want to fix your hair?" She asks.

"No, I like it wild, and Mom argued with me and said that I should be tidier. She doesn't understand anything," I shake my hair to the sides.

"She'll understand. You are already grown up," Margot smiles at me.

"Has Mathéo arrived yet?" I ask.

"Yes, he has already arrived and is waiting for Sarah to come out," she points at him. "Can I go in and help her get organized?"

"I think she'd like that," I proudly reply. She treats me like I'm an adult and consults me.

Margot enters the side room, to help Mom, and I stand in the hall and look around. Mrs. Angelina stands by the entrance with her husband and tries to calm down two-year-old Jolie, who's screaming. And there are a few other people I don't know there, could be Mathéo's friends from the police.

Mathéo's already standing next to the judge's stand, wearing a suit. He's no longer as thin as the day we met him when we were on our way to America yet ended up staying here. Mom was also thinner back then. He's talking to Father Nicholas, who rescued me that night. From time to time, Mom and I come to visit Father Nicholas in his church, even though we're Jewish. He says God opens His heart for everyone. He also keeps calling me Sophie, even though he knows it's not my name. Every time he calls me that, I smile and recall the chocolate bar and the teddy bear that I had with me in those days. The girl bear is no longer with me. She's thrown under my bed. I'm all grown up.

Next to Mathéo and Father Nicholas stands a man with an amputated arm, probably from the war, and next to him is a woman and a boy who's a few years older than me. He must be fourteen or fifteen, and he's so handsome. He has black, greasy hair. His mustache has already started to grow. He's so handsome, and he's looking at me. I feel myself blushing, and I escape to the side room.

"Margot, I need you to help me fix my hair," I reluctantly tell Mathéo's mother.

"What happened? What changed in the last five minutes?" Mom asks me.

"Nothing," I reply. "That's what I've decided," I don't want to tell her about the handsome boy who's looking at me.

Mom is wearing a white dress and looks so beautiful, and Margot is helping her fix the dress' hem.

"I'll take care of you in a second," she smiles at me, leaves the room, and returns after a moment accompanied by a young woman of twenty or thirty. "Rebecca, this is Mrs. Sophie. Mrs. Sophie is a hairdresser and our neighbor," she introduces her to me.

"Sit here," Mrs. Sophie points to an empty chair in the small room. "And we'll see what can be done with your messy hair," she looks at me with a scrutinizing look.

"Mom, can I put on lipstick?" I ask Mom a minute later as Sophie combs my hair and turns it wavy and beautiful. I want to tell her that I also went by the name Sophie for a few years, but I'm ashamed.

"No, you can't put on lipstick. You're not old enough," Mom tells me, and I feel like crying. He won't look at me anymore. He won't like me.

"Are you ready?" Mrs. Angelina opens the door. "You're so beautiful," she walks over to Mom and hugs her as little Jolie smiles at me.

"We're ready," Mom stands up and looks in the mirror. I can see she's excited.

"Let's go, Rebecca," she reaches out her hand.

"I'll be there in a second. Thank you, Mrs. Sophie," I tell Mom and thank the hairdresser, who combed my hair and tied it beautifully.

Once they close the door behind them, I look in the mirror, slap my cheeks hard, and pinch them, giving them some natural blush. I want the boy to think I'm wearing make-up. I then rummage through Mom's make-up bag, take some pink lipstick, and apply it to my lips. I'm ready.

When I go out into the hall, everyone's already seated and Mom and Mathéo are already standing in front of the judge.

"Where were you?" Margot asks me as I sit down next to her.

"I finished getting ready," I answer and search for the boy among the people in the hall. He's sitting in the second row to my right, not far from me. He also looks to the sides as if searching for someone. Is he looking for me?

"His name is Luc," Margot whispers to me after a few minutes as the judge speaks and reads the marriage agreement.

"Who?" I ask her, whispering.

"The boy you keep looking at."

"I'm not looking at him," I reply and blush. "And why is there a male judge and not a female judge anyway?"

"Because it's a man's job," she whispers to me.

"Then I'll be a judge," I whisper back to her.

"First, you must study law. Now be quiet and look at your mother; look how beautiful she is."

I look at my beautiful mother and Mathéo, who are getting married. When I grow up, I'll be a lawyer, and then a judge, and I will marry Luc.

The End

Chapter Twenty-Five

Author Notes, Pieces of History

Six million Jews were murdered in the Holocaust. I wanted to tell the story of a mother who struggled to save her daughter.

With the rise of Nazism in Germany, in 1933, the Nazis began to enact racist laws against the Jews. Jews were fired from public positions, universities, theaters, and the press. Later, racial laws were passed and declared the Jews as second-class citizens. As of 1938, the Nazis also began to nationalize Jewish property.

As a result, many Jew families tried to leave Germany and find refuge in Western European countries. The Bloch family is one of those families.

As World War II broke out, in 1939, there were thousands of Jewish refugees in Paris. They believed that they had managed to escape the jaws of the Nazi machine, but all of that changed in May 1940, when Germany stormed France and conquered it in just a few weeks.

Overnight, those thousands of Jews became not only persecuted by the Nazis, but also devoid of status in France, since they did not have a French citizenship. This is where the book begins.

At the beginning of the German occupation, France was divided into two zones: northern and western France, including Paris, which was under complete German control, and southern France, which was under the control of the pro-German Vichy government. This area was also called 'Free France,' since the conditions of the occupation there were less severe.

At the beginning of the story, Sarah tries to leave Paris and go south, to the Free France Zone and, from there, cross the border to Spain, which was neutral throughout the entire World War II. Crossing the border between France and Spain required a passage through the high Pyrenees mountain-range, which was possible only with the help of smugglers who knew the mountain paths and how to stay away from the border patrols of the Vichy regime. Such a smuggler appears at the beginning of the story.

In August 1941, the Paris police arrested 4,000 Jews. Most of the Jews arrested were refugees who did not have French citizenship. Sarah and Rebecca were also among them. The French police sent all those Jews to the Drancy camp.

The Drancy camp, located north of Paris, was different from the concentration camps that the Germans build throughout Europe and are familiar from the pictures in the history books.

The camp was in an existing, huge, four-floor concrete **n**-shaped building. The building was built before the war as a residential building, but it was never completed, and no windows or doors were installed in the apartments. The Nazis took over the building, set barbed wire fences around it, and began imprisoning Jews, intellectuals, and opponents of the regime from occupied Paris and the rest of France there.

The conditions in the camp were harsh, and the calorie allowance per person was 600-800 calories a day. Despite the difficult conditions, the prisoners establish social activities and a school for the children. I mention them in the story through Mr. Gaston, the teacher, and the printer, Quentin Arsenault, who printed an underground newspaper.

Out of all the Jews that were imprisoned in the camp, I mentioned one woman by her real name: Charlotte Salomon, who is Sarah's friend. Charlotte was born in Berlin in 1917 to a wealthy Jewish family. She studied art at the university for two years, but in 1936, she was expelled from the university simply for being Jewish. In 1938, she fled with her family from Germany to Nice in southern France, where she continued to paint. In her expressive gouache color paintings, Charlotte combined the reality of her life with imagination, integrated by text. Charlotte used to paint everyday life under the Nazi rule: demonstrations, marches, and humiliations – combined with her dreams. In 1943, she was captured by the Germans, sent to Drancy, and from there to Auschwitz, where she died. In the story, I placed her in Drancy earlier than she did in real life.

In June of 1942, the Germans launched 'Operation Spring Breeze,' in which they arrested all Jews in Paris, including the ones who had French citizenship. 13,000 Jews were captured and concentrated in the winter stadium, south of the Eiffel Tower, in tough conditions (the stadium no longer exists today), and after five days, they were sent to Drancy. This event is mentioned in the book when buses full of thirsty Jews arrive.

During its years as an internment camp, more than 67,000 Jews passed through Drancy, but the Germans' goal was not to imprison the Jews there. The camp was used by the Germans only as a transit station before the 'Final Solution' – the extermination of all Jews in Europe. From June 1942 to July 1944, the camp's Jews were sent by trains to the extermination camps, and most of them arrived at Auschwitz.

The camp was liberated in August 1944 by the American army. However, the building where the prisoners stayed remains standing to this day and is used for residence after having been renovated.

Most of the French Jews who arrived in Auschwitz were sent to extermination, but a minority remained to work as forced labor prisoners in one of the forty labor camps around Auschwitz. The average lifespan in these camps was three months. Some of the jobs that female prisoners held were in the German 'Weichsel Metall-Union Werk' factory, which established a branch in the industrial complex a few kilometers east of Auschwitz. In the factory, women prisoners worked to create explosives and detonators for the German war machine. Sarah and Charlotte were among them, until Charlotte got sick.

There was a prisoners' hospital block in Auschwitz that is mentioned in the book. It was for forced labor prisoners, but the conditions there were terrible, and only a few recovered and returned to the hard work.

By the end of 1944, beginning of 1945, the German Eastern front collapsed against the advancing Red Army. The Nazis began evacuating the concentration camps, sending the prisoners west, toward the German Reich and trying to hide the crimes against humanity they have committed. The exhausted prisoners were forced to walk for miles in the infamous 'death marches.' They were weak, sick, and had to walk for days without a break, often without a clear destination. The roads of Poland and South Germany were filled with convoys of prisoners from various camps, including convoys of prisoners of war. The SS guards shot anyone who lingered. Sarah's death march is described in the book, during it she is in poor physical condition and is no longer sure whether she is hallucinating or not.

In March 1945, the Allies crossed the Rhine and broke into Germany from the west, and advancing forces started liberating concentration camps. On April 27th, 1945, American troops of the 101st Airborne Division arrived at the Kaufering concentration camp in southern Germany and liberated it. The 101st Airborne Division fought from the day of the invasion, when it was dropped in Normandy, until the surrender of Nazi Germany. The liberation of the camp is described through Sarah's eyes.

Other than the brutality of World War II, there were also acts of heroism by many people who hid Jews and risked their lives. During the war, thousands of Jewish children were sent to monasteries to save their lives. Rebecca's life was saved this way. After the war, parents who survived the inferno wandered between monasteries, looking for their children in the hope of discovering that they had survived.

This book is about a woman who faces hard choices in an uncertain future, as she stands before the Nazi monsters. One woman who is trying to do one thing – save her daughter.

Thank you for reading,
Alex Amit

Made in the USA
Las Vegas, NV
22 June 2024

91344525R00225